BYE BYE, BABY

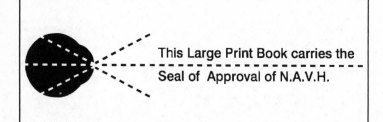

This Large Print Book carries the Seal of Approval of N.A.V.H.

Bye Bye, Baby

Max Allan Collins

THORNDIKE PRESS
A part of Gale, Cengage Learning

GALE
CENGAGE Learning

Detroit • New York • San Francisco • New Haven, Conn • Waterville, Maine • London

GALE
CENGAGE Learning™

LIBRARY OF CONGRESS CATALOGING-IN-PUBLICATION DATA

Collins, Max Allan.
    Bye bye, baby / by Max Allan Collins. — Large print ed.
       p. cm. — (Thorndike Press large print mystery)
    ISBN-13: 978-1-4104-4312-0 (hardcover)
    ISBN-10: 1-4104-4312-4 (hardcover)
    1. Heller, Nathan (Fictitious character)—Fiction. 2. Monroe, Marilyn,
1926–1962—Fiction. 3. Private investigators—California—Los
Angeles—Fiction. 4. Large type books. I. Title.
PS3553.O4753B94 2011
813'.54—dc23   2011032429

Published in 2011 by arrangement with Tom Doherty Associates, LLC

Printed in the United States of America
1 2 3 4 5 6 7 15 14 13 12 11

For my favorite Marilyn look-alike . . .
. . . the one I married

Everybody is always tugging at you. They'd all like sort of a chunk of you. They kind of like to take pieces out of you.

— **Marilyn Monroe**

Marilyn never liked good-byes.

— **Lee Strasberg,
from his funeral eulogy**

ONE:
SOMETHING'S GOT TO GIVE!
MAY 23–JULY 29, 1962

CHAPTER 1

The naked actress was laughing, splashing, her flesh incandescent against the shimmer of blue, now on her back, then bottoms up, her happy sounds echoing, as if she were the only woman in the world — and wasn't she?

She was, after all, Marilyn Monroe, and this was Fox's Soundstage 14, where she was shooting the film *Something's Got to Give,* under the supervision of legendary Hollywood director George Cukor.

Nude scenes were common overseas — Bardot had become famous flashing her fanny in *And God Created Woman* — but a major star like Monroe shedding for the CinemaScope camera? Just not done, even if she did have those notorious calendar shots in her past.

This was the closed set of all closed sets. A small army of security guards had been summoned by producer Henry Weinstein to cover the five entrances to the soundstage, after word of the nude scene wildfired across the lot. This was the toughest ticket in town, unless you had an in.

I had an in. Last night I'd heard from Marilyn's personal publicist, Pat Newcomb (calling at the star's request), that tomorrow would be the "day of days" on the *Something's Got to Give* set.

"Marilyn says you wanted to visit," Pat said, in her pleasantly professional way, "sometime during filming. And this is it."

"Mind my asking what's special about tomorrow?"

"She has a swimming scene and, knowing Marilyn, might just slip out of her suit. . . ."

I reminded Miss Newcomb that I needed two passes, and was assured they'd be waiting at the studio gate.

So how did *I* rate? Big-shot agent? Top Hollywood columnist? Producer sizing up MM for his next picture, maybe?

No. I was just a private detective, or anyway I used to be. Since my agency grew to three locations (LA, Manhattan, and the original Chicago office), I'd become mostly a figurehead, bouncing between them, handling publicity and sucking up to big-money clients. I couldn't remember when I last knocked on a strange door or parked outside some motel with a camera, much less carried a gun.

But Nathan Heller, president of the A-1 Detective Agency, me, had indeed done a number of private eye jobs for Miss Monroe, starting with bodyguard duty in Chicago on her *Gentlemen Prefer Blondes* junket, and more recently tracking down a guy named C. Stanley Gifford, who she thought was her father, in the sense that he was the likeliest candidate for having knocked up Mom, who currently resided in the latest of many nuthouses.

Old C. Stanley missed the boat, or maybe his gravy train, when my client used the info I gathered to call her potential pop and say, "This is Norma Jeane — I'm Gladys Baker's daughter." Apparently thinking this was a touch, the idiot — unaware that Norma Jeane Baker had transformed herself, through no little effort, into Marilyn Monroe — hung up. On her second try, she got C. Stanley's wife, who told the caller to contact her husband's lawyer if she "had a complaint."

Anyway, we were friendly, Marilyn and I, and for a while had been very friendly. In the interim I had transformed myself, through no little effort, into "the private eye to the stars." This was a nice trick since I lived in Chicago, though the A-1's ongoing security job with the Beverly Hills Hotel meant I had a bungalow whenever and for however long I might need one.

I also had an ex-wife out here, a former actress now married to a once successful producer, neither of whom I gave a shit about. I gave much more than a shit about my teenage son, Sam, who was actually Nathan Samuel Heller, Jr., only we had called him "Sam" when he was little, to avoid having two Nates around. Before long, my wife was happy not to have *any* Nate around.

So Sam it was, now a happy fourteen-year-old. Why happy? Wouldn't you be, if you were a fourteen-year-old male whose father had got him onto the set of Marilyn Monroe's nude swimming scene?

When you are divorced and your wife has custody of your only child, and the other "dad" is a film producer (once successful or otherwise), you have to work to stay on your kid's good side. Sam was not impressed with celebrities, generally, having seen plenty, but this was different. I was fairly certain his first sexual experience had been with the signed-to-him nude Monroe calendar I'd given him on his thirteenth birthday (his mother still didn't know about that).

14

This was his fifteenth-birthday present, even though this was May and the real date wasn't till September. Some gifts you grab when they present themselves.

I'd kept the nature of what we'd be witnessing to myself, just promising Sam a "treat," and he put up with that. We cut each other plenty of slack, since we often had half a continent between us, and anyway, in my mid-fifties, I was pretty old for a teen's dad.

Sam looked a lot like me, identical except for his mother's brown hair and not my reddish variety, and was already within two inches of my six feet. He was slender and so was I — I'd lost my paunch in an effort to regain my youth.

So I looked goddamn good in my lightweight gray glen plaid Clipper Craft suit with lighter gray shirt (Van Heusen tab collar) and thin black silk tie. Sam was in a tan striped Catalina pullover and brown beltless Jaymar slacks. We were a sporty pair.

Keep in mind that I was already in solid with the kid for getting him out of school for the day. This was a Wednesday, and he had something like a week and a half left before summer vacation. So I was cool, for a dad.

He did complain that I didn't have a

convertible, which in California was a criminal offense. My wheels, technically part of the A-1's fleet, were merely a white 1960 Jaguar 3.8, leather seats, walnut interior, disk brakes, automatic transmission.

"Convertibles blow my business papers around," I said at the wheel, tooling around the Fox lot. "And muss my hair."

"Get it cut," he said, rubbing his hand over the bristle of his crew cut.

"I don't like the smell of butch wax."

"Come on, Dad. Grow up."

I didn't share with Sam my opinion of crew cuts, which was that they were for servicemen, bodybuilders, and homosexuals, not necessarily mutually exclusive groups. Kids his age didn't need having their sexuality undermined. In fact, my mission today was just the opposite.

Of course, in trying to impress my kid — whose "other" father was a producer (did I mention the fat prick used to be successful?) — I should have picked a lot other than Fox's. The grand old studio was scrambling to stay afloat. Clouds of dust crowded the blue out of the sky over bulldozers making way for apartment buildings and office towers. The out-of-control Liz Taylor picture *Cleopatra,* currently filming in Rome, had required the selling off of such fabled back-lot locations as Tyrone Power's *Zorro* hacienda, Betty Grable's *Down Argentine Way* ranch, and Lana Turner's *Peyton Place* town square.

Marilyn's new picture, which Hedda Hopper and Louella Parsons called "troubled," was in fact the only going project on the lot.

"Jeez," Sam said, elbow out the rolled-down window. "It's a lousy ghost town."

The streets of this soundstage city had once been hopping with cowboys and Indians, pirates and dancing girls. Even the trees and lawns were brown and dying — palms and ferns, too. Had they cut off the water? Or had the water company cut off Fox?

As per Pat Newcomb's instructions, I drove directly to Marilyn's recently constructed bungalow, which had the look of a small prefab suburban house. I left Sam in the Jag and went up to the door, where a security guard was on watch; I showed my special pass, and he knocked for me.

I was greeted by Pat Newcomb — slim in a yellow blouse and tan slacks, thirty or so, her light brown hair cut chin-length. We knew each other only slightly. She was attractive, but not *too* attractive — that wouldn't do for the woman assigned by the

Arthur Jacobs PR agency to be Marilyn's right hand.

The interior was mostly one big bustling room, as buzzing as the lot was otherwise dead. A battalion of technicians was at work on creating the fabled Marilyn Monroe "look." Each seemed to operate off caffeine, as one hand would bear a coffee cup, the other whatever tool of the trade was required: comb, brush, makeup jar.

Wearing only a flesh-colored bikini, the object of their artistry reclined on a slant board like the bride of Frankenstein waiting to be awakened. She was more slender than I'd ever seen her, but her prominent rib cage made her handful breasts jut nicely, and her narrow waist and flaring hips suggested a voluptuousness that wasn't really earned.

I shouldered my way in. "Afraid I'm gonna have to take you in for public nudity."

Marilyn beamed at me but didn't turn her head — her makeup man of many years, Whitey Snyder, a pleasant sharp-featured guy, was using a watercolor brush to highlight her cheekbones.

"Are you going to make me laugh, Nate?" she asked, with only a hint of her trademark halting screen delivery. "Because if you are, I am going to have to throw you out on your you-know-what."

An almost naked broad using a euphemism like "you-know-what" was pretty funny.

"I wouldn't want to ruin your face," I said.

"Takes more and more work to *make* it a face," she said, rueful but good-humored. Her mouth was on, but not as full as before, if just as lushly red. Her whole look had been adjusted to make the switch from the fifties to the sixties, more fashion model than pinup.

At a counter facing the slant board, a heavyset woman in a pale blue smock was mixing body makeup. Then she began applying the goop with a rubber-gloved hand.

"I'm going to be in that chlorinated water a long time," Marilyn said by way of explanation, batting her mascaraed lashes at me. "This is the mixture Esther Williams used to use. Where's your son?"

"Out in the car."

"Leave him there. We'll let him see the magic. But *not* how the trick is done. . . . *Ooh,* this is nasty stuff. Again, you know, it's because of the water. . . ."

A skinny effeminate man also in a pale blue smock had begun spraying hairspray that turned her platinum locks, already put to the test by God knew how many and what chemicals, into something brittle and stiff.

"Everybody! This is my friend Nate Heller — you know that private eye on TV? Peter Gunn? He's based on Nate. . . ."

Everybody gave me a fraction-of-a-second glance, and a few even pretended to be impressed. They'd have been more impressed if *Peter Gunn* hadn't been canceled recently.

Having tossed me my cookie, she said, "You run along, Nate."

I ran along.

(By the way, *Peter Gunn* was *not* based on me, though I was a paid consultant the first season.)

When I climbed into the Jag, Sam gave me a wide-eyed welcome. It was like looking into the mirror and seeing my fourteen-year-old self look back at me. Horny fourteen-year-old self.

"Was she in there?"

"Yup."

"Jeez, Pop. What was she wearing!"

"Quit talking like an old Charlie Chan picture."

"*All* Charlie Chan pictures are old. *What* was she *wearing?*"

"Not much."

He leaned against the leather seat and

smiled to himself. He was gazing straight ahead — into that calendar he kept hidden under his gym socks. So I started up the Jag and headed through the lot to Soundstage 14.

Funny to think that Marilyn Monroe was the last hope of this dying beast. She'd been at odds with Twentieth Century–Fox almost from the start. Back in the middle 1940s, she'd struggled to get picked out of cattle calls, just another pretty blonde looking for extra work or bit parts. Then she'd tried to get noticed in small roles. Finally she worked her way up to being the worst-paid star on this or any other lot. *Something's Got to Give* signaled her exit from Fox bondage — that one last picture she owed them.

From what I'd read, it wasn't much of a picture, and of course getting stuck with lousy scripts had been why Marilyn had walked from Fox back in the fifties and gone east to form her own company. She'd wound up in the prestigious Actors Studio, a fairly unlikely berth for a bombshell.

Not that Marilyn was your average bombshell. She'd married Joe DiMaggio and Arthur Miller, hadn't she? She even turned her bubbleheaded shtick into something more with her *Bus Stop* and *Some Like It Hot* performances. Who but Marilyn could have found nuances in dumb-blonde roles?

She was special, and I liked her, on-screen and off. She had a reputation for driving directors and costars and studio execs crazy, but I knew that came from a kind of cock-eyed perfectionism born out of insecurity. The hard-drinking, drug-abusing Marilyn of rumor was a stranger to me. I'd always found her sweet and sexy and funny, if needy, and if she had a bad side, I'd been privileged not to see it.

Anyway, this *Something's Got to Give* should have been an easy payday for her. She had a copasetic costar in Dean Martin — she hung around with the Rat Pack boys, having been Sinatra's sweetheart off and on — and the director was on her very short approved list with the likes of Billy Wilder and Alfred Hitchcock.

Trifle though it might be, the picture was a remake of a comedy classic, *My Favorite Wife,* where remarried hubby Cary Grant is confronted by his suddenly-not-dead first wife, Irene Dunne, who's been on a desert island with hunk Randolph Scott. Similar shenanigans should ensue second time around, with the current loosening of the Production Code meaning the sex stuff could be sexier stuff.

So the gig should have been painless for

Marilyn, but the papers said she'd been out sick for half the production days. On the phone last night, I'd asked Pat Newcomb about it.

"So what's up? Is Marilyn really sick?"

"She has been, yes. Sinusitis, flu, running a high temperature. The studio's own physician has found her unfit for work."

"So the columns saying she's being a prima donna, that's crap?"

A pause. "Mr. Heller, Marilyn is a *star* and has certain . . . eccentricities, and expectations. But no, she's really sick."

"Not so sick that she didn't show up to sing 'Happy Birthday' to the president at Madison Square Garden the other night."

It had been a big, gaudy televised event. Marilyn had done her dumb-blonde bit, not this new sixties model, and Jack Kennedy had damn near drooled over the attention. No wonder Jackie Kennedy had stayed away.

"That had been agreed to months ago," the publicist said, defensively. "The studio tried to renege at the last moment, but how does a star like Marilyn turn down a command performance for the president?"

"She doesn't," I said. "But what kind of studio doesn't see the PR value in that?"

"*This* one," the publicist said bitterly. "They let Elizabeth Taylor run wild and stick adultery in their faces and rack up cost overruns that would bankrupt a European nation, and then punish Marilyn for it."

"Is this a happy set I'm visiting tomorrow?"

Her tone lightened. "Oh, yes. And you have to *love* it — Marilyn knows just how to play these kind of people."

These kind of people were mostly men, of course. And Marilyn had known all she had to do to get them eating out of her hand was take off her clothes.

When Sam and I stepped onto Soundstage 14, the world turned a bilious shade of pink. The elaborate, expansive set would have filled Soldier Field: spread out before us was the ass end of a stone-and-stucco Mediterranean mansion with a vast, angular pool surrounded by rococo lawn furniture and bushes and trees, one bearing a tree house.

Catwalks and lighting platforms made a spiderweb sky. A dapper little old gnome of a man was strutting around up there barking commands, and spotlights took various angles, as if searching for an escaped prisoner. This, I later learned, was Cukor, who — other than issuing very general orders, including the obligatory "Action!" and "Cut!" — gave Marilyn scant direction that afternoon.

On the fringes of the brightly lit set, an inky darkness prevailed. In one such pocket Sam and I positioned ourselves.

When a blue-robed Marilyn arrived with Pat Newcomb, a phalanx of attendees formed around her like Secret Service agents guarding the president. This group included Snyder and other hair and makeup techs, as well as Marilyn's acting coach, Paula Strasberg, a fat witchy-looking figure in a black muumuu. Another slant board was waiting for Marilyn between takes, but the truth is — except for a lunch break, which for her was coffee — she never got completely out of the pool, once she got in.

She just swam happily, the center of attention in the elaborate set in the cavernous soundstage, queen of her domain. At first — when she slipped out of the blue terrycloth robe, and into the pool — she wore a flesh-colored swimsuit. But after only a few minutes, a voice called down from a catwalk.

Not Cukor's, rather that of one of the two cinematographers (one camera was going poolside, this other up top) yelling down, echoingly, "I'm sorry, darling — but the lines in the swimsuit are showing up!"

This was a stilted reading, obviously planned, but Marilyn quickly, and deftly, slipped off the suit. That left only the very sheer bra and panties beneath, and those soon followed, deposited at the edge of the pool as if put out to dry.

Sam's mouth was hanging open. I started to laugh, then realized mine was yawning, too.

She was a vision, a nymph, if a nymph was as womanly as that, a pink ghost flickering beneath the turquoise glimmer, occasionally exposing more than just a limb, a delicious rump, a pert breast — even the amber pubic triangle made its presence known, if fleetingly.

Pat Newcomb, at my side, said softly, "Having fun?"

"I guess she's showing the Fox boys she isn't over the hill."

The publicist grunted a little laugh. "She had to get Black Bart's blessing, you know."

"Who?"

She nodded toward the stout woman in the black muumuu, just beyond the big camera. "Had to have Paula's blessing. Had to be approved 'Method' technique for Marilyn to swim in the nude."

"Yeah? What's the scene about?"

"Tempting her husband out of Cyd Charisse's bed."

"This is the method that would do that."

Cukor would occasionally call "Cut," mostly for a camera reload, and during one such break, Pat called an assistant director over and said, "Now."

Soon a couple of photographers came in, and the publicist walked them to their respective spots and said, "You have half an hour, fellas. Don't waste it."

They didn't. They had those new motor-driven Nikons that could snap half a dozen frames per second.

They caught her bobbing in the turquoise water. Got her pool-side getting in and out of the nappy blue robe, even providing a few glimpses of dimpled behind. Captured incredible shots of her gripping the pool's rim while a shapely leg slid up onto the Spanish tiles. All that, and one dazzling, knowing smile after another. . . .

Then when she sat on the steps and let the robe disappear and showed the fantastic sweep of her back into her narrow waist and out into the full hips, water beading, sparkling on that gorgeous flesh, audible gasps (including from Heller Father and Son) could be heard.

She just looked over her shoulder at everybody, with that old Betty Boop innocence, as if to say, "Whatever are you boys so excited about?"

And my son said, "Best birthday ever, Dad. Hell. Best *dad* ever."

And father and son just stood there in the dark, bonding, ignoring each other's erection.

CHAPTER 2

Two weeks ago, more or less, I had left Marilyn Monroe on top of the world, or anyway the part of it that included a soundstage swimming pool at Twentieth Century–Fox, whose executives were at her feet. Now, having breakfast at Nate 'n Al's in Beverly Hills, I was reading in the *LA Times* about a very different Marilyn from the one Sam and I had watched doing a sexy water ballet.

According to Hedda Hopper, Marilyn had been "half mad" on the set of *Something's Got to Give,* unable to remember her lines, sleepwalking through her performance, and — on the day of her nude swim — stripping off her Jean Louis bikini, so high on drugs "she didn't even know where she was."

Around me in the showbiz-heavy deli, Marilyn arguments pro and con raged, and when I went around picking up various other papers, including the trades, I found amazing quotes: director Cukor saying, "This is the end of the poor girl's career," Fox studio head Peter Levathes claiming, "Miss Monroe is not temperamental, she is mentally ill," producer Walter Bernstein insisting, "By her willful irresponsibility, Marilyn Monroe has taken the bread right out of the mouths of men who depend on this film to feed their families."

"This film" had officially been shut down by Fox for recasting or outright scrapping, and Marilyn fired.

I pushed aside half a plate of scrambled eggs and lox, quickly paid the check, and tooled the Jag back to my bungalow at the Beverly Hills Hotel. My digs were just the basics — living room, marble fireplace, two bedrooms, two baths, private patio. The spare bedroom had a desk that I used for work, and from there I tried to phone Marilyn at her North Doheny Drive apartment, but a dozen rings got me nowhere.

Trying Pat Newcomb at the Arthur Jacobs agency got me a little somewhere — a receptionist put me through to the publicist's male assistant, who took my name and number and said he would pass it right on to Miss Newcomb, who was out.

I went on about my business, spending the day at the A-1 office in the Bradbury

Building in downtown Los Angeles — we were hiring, and my partner, Fred Rubinski, and I interviewed half a dozen ex–LA cops. Despite what Jack Webb might have you believe, not every LA cop is intelligent, reliable, and honest, and it was a chore.

Anyway, the following Monday I was reaching for the phone to make a TWA booking back to Chicago when the damn thing rang, making me jump a little. Maybe I wasn't as tough as I used to be.

"Sorry I didn't get back to you sooner," Pat Newcomb said. She sounded tired.

"I guess you've had your hands full."

"I have. I'm at Marilyn's now, as it happens."

"The Doheny pad?"

Marilyn's actual residence was an apartment on East Fifty-seventh in New York, but since she and Arthur Miller divorced, her Hollywood address had been at a triplex in West Hollywood, owned by Frank Sinatra. Frank's Negro valet, George Jacobs, lived there, and usually one or two of the singer's squeezes, or sometimes a pal needing a temporary roof. Which category Marilyn fell into, I wasn't sure.

"No, she's not there anymore," Newcomb said. "She has a house in Brentwood."

"How's she doing? This shit in the papers,

it just doesn't let up."

And it hadn't.

"It's a smear campaign by the studio."

"You're not asking me to believe Hedda Hopper is untrustworthy, are you? She has such a nice smile."

"She's a bitch," Pat snapped, maybe not reading my sarcasm. "As for Marilyn, she's had a rough couple days and nights, but . . . Well, come see for yourself."

"Yeah?"

"Yes. She wants to see you. She likes you."

"Don't sound surprised. Haven't you noticed how lovable I am?"

She wasn't in the mood for banter, and just gave me the address and the directions.

On the way over, I wondered if I would at last encounter the Marilyn of Hollywood rumor — the notorious drug-addicted dumb-blonde diva. Would I finally see that dark, self-pitying side of her that had caused, supposedly, half a dozen or more suicide attempts? Would she be a slurry wreck, or perhaps a paranoid harridan blaming the Fox executives for all her woes?

The closest I'd come to knowing the troubled Marilyn was the occasional very-late-night phone call from her — I was one of her long-distance buddies who she might reach out to when she was having trouble sleeping. Insomnia was her real archenemy, worse than Fox or Hedda Hopper.

That phone-friend list must have been fairly long, because I'd had only five or six of these calls over the years, coming at two or three in morning, and always starting the same way: "This is Marilyn Monroe. You know, the actress?"

That was silly, of course, but usually enough time had passed since I'd heard from her to make it credible, coming from that oddly shy, modest part of this girl who must have been in some manner an egotist to have made it so far.

But I'd never got a drugged-up or drunk Marilyn on the line — just that familiar, breathy female voice. The kind no healthy heterosexual male would respond to with, "Do you have any idea what time it is?"

What you say is, "Yeah, I remember you. I think maybe I saw one of your pictures," or maybe, "I know you. I'm a detective, remember?"

And she would laugh and you'd talk till finally she started getting sleepy enough to sign off.

Brentwood had recovered from its disastrous fire of the previous November, once again a sleepy upper-middle-class community whose main drag was San Vicente

Boulevard, its wide median home to sculpted coral trees. I wheeled the Jag onto Carmelina Avenue, a winding affair off of which were various greenery-swarmed cul-de-sacs. I was looking for Fifth Helena Drive, only Pat Newcomb warned me that it wasn't marked — I had to count the cul-de-sacs, plus she described the houses on either corner.

Somehow I got it on the first try, though calling this short narrow strip a cul-de-sac was rather grand — I knew an alley when I saw one. At the mouth, on either side, were the homes the publicist had described for me, and at the end of the alley were two more homes, a two-story to the right, and Marilyn's to the left.

You couldn't see much of Marilyn's place, though — a whitewashed seven-foot brick wall smothered in blooming bougainvillea vines blocked everything but a glimpse of red barrel-tiled roof of what would prove to be the garage.

The Jag I left half on the grass in case some other vehicle needed the space, and stepped from air-conditioning into a pleasantly warm sunny Cal afternoon, kissed with a nice coastal ocean breeze from the west.

Hollywood royalty lived here, but I was

informal — black-collared gray Ban-Lon sport shirt; beltless, cuffless H.I.S. gray slacks; black suede loafers — and I'd taken to going hatless. Our young president's fault.

I knocked at the double scalloped-topped wooden gate, and then knocked some more, and at last a middle-range female voice (definitely not Marilyn's) responded drowsily from a distance, making three sluggish syllables out of "Yes."

"Nathan Heller," I said to the gate, loud but not yelling. "Miss Monroe is expecting me."

The breeze ruffled pond fronds as footsteps minced on hard surface.

The gate wasn't locked, although swinging it open seemed to take a lot out of the small dowdy middle-aged woman. She had short-cut wispy dark hair and unflattering dark-rimmed cat's-eye glasses, and her shapeless floral housedress covered a stumpy asexual figure.

She gazed at me as if we were both underwater and I was a rare fish she'd come across, only she wasn't interested in rare fish.

"You are . . . ?"

"Nathan Heller? Miss Monroe's expecting me?"

Was there a fucking echo in here?

"Oh. Yes. Well, all right."

She turned her back to me and trundled across the tile courtyard toward the house, a quietly handsome L-shaped Spanish colonial with stuccoed adobe walls. But this absentminded troll belonged guarding a ramshackle middle-of-nowhere mansion, the kind where you ask to use the phone because your car broke down, and wind up a mad doctor's next experiment.

She was reaching for the front door, but I said, "Let me get that," ever the gentleman. Glancing down at the four tiles on the doorstep, depicting a coat of arms, I noted an inscription in blue on gray: *Cursum Perficio.*

"What's that mean?" I said, more to myself than my hostess.

"Latin," she whispered, as if this were a secret. "For 'I have completed my journey.' Marilyn finds comfort in that."

She gave me a sick smile and went in. I closed the door after us, moving through the entryway into a wide living room dominated by a fireplace and glass doors onto the swimming pool. Thick white carpeting and textured white walls made a sharp contrast with bright colors courtesy of Mexican art and dark, rustic furnishings

36

that matched the open beams.

In a white cotton short-sleeve blouse and dark capri pants, Marilyn — sitting Indian-style on the carpet near the unlighted fireplace — wore only a touch of lipstick, her platinum hair tousled, though her toes did reveal red nails. She had a fresh, freckled, youthful look, more Norma Jeane than MM.

She just smiled and waved, like a beauty queen on a float who'd spotted a homely gal friend in the crowd, and returned to her dictation.

Because that's what she was doing, giving dictation to Pat Newcomb, who was seated on a Mexican-style wooden chair with insufficient cushions, taking down Marilyn's crisp words on a steno pad. Some kind of list was in her lap. The publicist was looking haggard, though still attractive in her eternal sorority-girl way; she was in a blue blouse and darker blue slacks.

" 'Shutting the film down was none of my doing,' " Marilyn was saying. " 'I hope you know that. I am working to get us all back working again. Say hi to your lovely girls. Love, Marilyn.' . . . How many does that make?"

Newcomb's smile was strained. "That's one hundred and four."

I had taken a seat at a low-slung black-leather-covered coffee table nearby. Newcomb glanced at me, and I must have raised an eyebrow or something, because she explained: "Marilyn has dictated telegrams to every crew member on *Something's Got to Give.* Each one personalized."

Marilyn was nodding. "I always know everyone on the crew. . . . Hi, Nate. Thanks for coming."

"Hi, Marilyn. Pleasure's mine."

She little-girl frowned at me. "You saw that ad, didn't you? The one signed by all the crew members?"

I nodded. In *Variety,* an ad supposedly signed by all the propmen, carpenters, electricians, and so on had said: *"Thank you, Marilyn Monroe, for the loss of our livelihoods."*

Newcomb said, "It was a fraud. We called around. Nobody on the crew knew anything about that ad. Everybody knows Marilyn is a friend to the workingman."

Marilyn giggled. "That sounds dirty." She had a glass of champagne going, resting where the carpet gave way and the fireplace began; no bottle was in sight, though.

The publicist shut the steno pad. "That's it, then?"

"No! Send this to Arlington, Virginia. You

know where."

"Marilyn . . . honey . . . what —"

Comically commanding, Marilyn pointed at the publicist. "Write! I have to decline a formal invitation, don't I? It wouldn't be polite otherwise, would it? . . . 'Dear Attorney General and Mrs. Robert Kennedy. I would have been delighted to have accepted your invitation honoring Pat and Peter Lawford.' "

Newcomb was hunkered over her pad like a slave at an oar, pencil tip scratching paper.

" 'Unfortunately, I am involved in a freedom ride protesting the loss of minority rights belonging to the few remaining . . .' " She looked toward the open beams for guidance. " '. . . *earthbound* stars.' "

"Signed, respectfully . . . ?"

"Keep writing. 'After all, all we demanded was our right to twinkle.' " She blurted a "Ha!" and rocked on her bottom, then had a sip of champagne.

Then she remembered me. "Nate, would you like something? There's plenty of Dom Pérignon."

"I bet there is. No."

"I can get you some other drink, what is it you like? Rum and Coke?"

"I switched to vodka gimlets."

"Ooh, how sixties of you. I can have Mrs.

Murray fetch you —"

"Is that your housekeeper or —"

"She's more a companion. Social secretary."

She'd have made a better companion or social secretary for Vincent Price than Marilyn Monroe. But whatever she was, I hadn't even seen her go. Mrs. Murray had vanished without even a puff of smoke.

"No, thanks," I said. "You girls finish up your work."

Marilyn shrugged exaggeratedly, then extended both hands. "That's all! We're done!" She clapped once, got to her bare feet. "Come on, Pat — don't be so glum. We're making strides."

Newcomb smiled, nodded wearily. "We are. I'm really happy to see you in such good spirits."

"You have to be in good spirits to fight back. And that's what we're doing. And after *this* good news —"

I interrupted: "What good news?"

She turned her big blue eyes on me, very wide. "I guess it hasn't hit the papers yet. Might be on the radio and TV."

"What might be on the radio and TV?"

"Dean. Dean Martin? My costar?"

"Yeah, guy who used to work with Jerry Lewis. What about him?"

Her smile was fetchingly smug. "Those smart-asses at Fox didn't think to look at *his* contract — he has costar approval! When Kim and Shirley turned them down, they talked Lee Remick into taking my part. . . . Lee *Remick?* I mean, she's cute, but. . . . Anyway, Dean quit the picture."

Newcomb was smiling. "That's right. He said, 'No Marilyn, no Martin.' "

"He's a sweetie," Marilyn said, and her eyes got misty. "I mean, it's touching, isn't it? That kind of loyalty? In *this* town?"

She swallowed, and Newcomb went over and gave her a hug, then moved away, saying, "I better get out of here. I have a hundred and five telegrams to post."

Marilyn's smile was a beacon in the little room. "Yes, you do! Now scoot!"

Newcomb scooted, though she did take time to cast me a glance and a smile. I did her the same.

As the door closed, Marilyn came over to me and said, "Your turn," and gave me a big hug. She smelled great — Chanel No. 5, as usual, but probably not directly applied; she always dumped a bottle in her bath.

"I have to say you look great," I said.

She spread her hands in a presentational manner. "Not bad for thirty-six, huh? You

41

think I've lost too much weight?"

"I like you any way I can get you. But this, this I think is your ideal fighting weight."

"Fighting weight is right," she said, and made two fists and held them up muscleman style. "You have no idea what these bastards are trying to do to me."

"What can I do to help?"

She gave me another hug, then a sweet, short kiss that hovered somewhere between brother and lover. "First let me give you the dime tour. Don't you just *love* this place? It's my safe haven, it really is."

So she took me by the hand like Mommy leading her favorite little boy, chattering on about how it was the first home she'd ever owned and how she cried when she signed the papers, pausing when we reached a point of interest.

To the left of the living room was a small dining room that led to a bright, cheery, wicker-filled sunroom at right and a modern kitchen at left, the latter a real point of pride to her.

"Have I ever cooked for you? You would *love* my pasta. And my guacamole? To die for. Remember when I was Jewish for a while?"

"Sure," I said. When she was married to Miller.

"Well, I can still whip up a mean borscht, and my matzoh ball soup is incredible. You just won't believe it. You *are* Jewish, aren't you?"

We'd never talked about it.

"Yes and no," I said. "My mom was Irish Catholic and died when I was a brat."

"How sad. . . ."

"My pop was a nonpracticing Jew, and the only part of it I have any interest in is that food you were talking about."

"Well, it doesn't hurt to be Jewish out here."

"Done wonders for Sammy Davis, Jr."

She laughed a little too hard at that. She seemed a tad high, but I'd been around enough pill-poppers to recognize the signs, and these weren't those. This was a combo of champagne and renewed self-confidence, and nice to see. Fun to see.

Back through the living room, she led me to the master bedroom, which had a witch's hat fireplace (maybe this was where Mrs. Murray disappeared to) and blackout curtains, with a portable phonograph on the floor, Sinatra albums scattered nearby. The double bed with its white satin comforter took up much of the space in the modest-sized room.

"Everything looks a little naked," she said.

"There's a lot of stuff I bought in Mexico that hasn't come yet."

Then she caught me looking at the pills on her small round-topped nightstand — dozens of little bottles crowding a tiny lamp with a couple of red-covered spiral pads stuffed between.

"Those are all empty, Nate, except for one bottle of sleeping pills — go ahead, look."

"No, I believe you. It's your business, anyway."

She put her arms around my waist from behind, pulling me near her with a nice familiarity. "I'm clean. I'm not taking anything except a little chloral hydrate, if I'm having sleep trouble."

"Well, that's great."

"I have a fantastic shrink right now, and he's done wonders. And, anyway, I never have any trouble kicking."

"Really?"

"Yeah, I'm a freak of nature. All I have to do is decide I don't need to take anything anymore. Cold turkey is just a deli sandwich, far as I know."

I didn't know whether to buy this or not, but didn't say anything. I turned to face her, still close enough to whiff the Chanel.

She said, "My biggest problem right now is sinusitis, and all I'm taking, cross my heart, is liver extract. You know, every day I called in sick, Fox's own doctor came and looked at me, and said I wasn't fit for duty. I've been fighting cold and fever and ten kinds of God knows what since last spring."

"Maybe you shouldn't stand so close to me, then. Why don't you stop in an hour or so."

She laughed at that, gave me another quick kiss, and took my hand again, back in tour-guide mode.

"None of the rooms are big," she was saying, "but they're nice. Wait till you see it fully decorated."

Another bathroom joined the other two bedrooms, across the hall. One she described as the guest bedroom, outfitted with walnut cabinets and a twin bed, but the other was designated her "fitting room," with a large wardrobe cabinet ("Not much closet space — Depression-era home, y'know") and three floor-length mirrors hinged together into one big viewing space.

The fitting room had another function — two telephones, one pink, one white, perched on a walnut table near the door. They had endless spiral cords, which enabled her to walk around the house talking and even take a phone to bed.

"The pink phone's a number for . . . usual

callers. The white phone has a number only for special, select people . . . like you, Nate."

She gave me that number and, feeling special and select, I jotted it in my little notepad.

"Actually," she said, and bit her lip, shyly, "those phones are kind of why I wanted you to come see me."

"Really."

She nodded, frowned, glanced toward the hall. "Why don't we go out and sit by the pool."

"Sure."

We did that, settling into black wrought-iron chairs. This was a more modest pool than the Fox soundstage one, and she quickly said she rarely used it, but encouraged guests to do so. We had a view of the narrow sloping backyard with eucalyptus and other trees.

Some hammering and other construction sounds came from her guesthouse, and I had the feeling that was partly why we were seated here, where our conversation would be concealed.

"I have to be careful," she said softly. Then she smiled past me at Mrs. Murray, framed in the glass doors. She gave her housekeeper/companion/social secretary a little wave and the woman smiled and nodded and faded back into the living room, like a ghost.

"*She's* a ray of sunshine," I said.

"I don't really like her," Marilyn said, matter of fact. "But she's a friend of Dr. Greenson's and needs the job."

"Dr. Greenson is . . . the shrink you mentioned?"

She nodded. "The remodeling I'm doing?" She flicked a red-nailed finger toward the guest house and the hammering. "Mrs. Murray's son-in-law Norman is doing that. He's harmless. Maf likes him."

"Maf?"

"My little poodle. Short for Mafia. Guess who gave him to me?"

"Sinatra."

"Ha! You're good. Anyway, Maf tags around after Norman, and that's fine. When I have company, Maf can be a pesky little bother, the sweetie."

I shifted, and the wrought-iron squeaked. "So what do you need, Marilyn?"

She gave me an impish look, reached over and squeezed my hand. "What if I said I needed a man?"

"I'd say you came to the right place."

"Could I trust you not to fall in love with me?"

"No. But you can trust me not to marry

you. I've married one actress and that's my limit."

She laughed soundlessly, flicked her head, and the platinum stuff bounced. "Maybe one of these days or nights, we can have a little fun. Would you like that, Nate?"

"I don't hate the thought."

Her eyes widened and her smile broadened. "Did your *son* have fun? At the set?"

"You bet."

"I'm sorry they shooed you off with the photographers." She shivered. "I was in that water for *four* hours!"

"Sam would've liked to meet you."

"We'll correct that one of these days." She shifted; more squeaking. "Now . . . about my phones."

"What about your phones?"

"I want you to tap them for me. You know — record my calls?"

"I know what phone-tapping is, Marilyn. Why?"

Her eyes went to the pool, where sunlight glittered like her best friends. "It's this studio fight. I'm trying to get reinstated, and I'm having to talk to some . . . *unlikely* bedfellows."

"What kind?"

"For instance — if you can believe it — Darryl Zanuck. He never liked me, you

know. Thought I was just another bimbo —
didn't 'get' it. But he gets it now. He and
Spyros Skouras are trying to get reinstated,
too — trying to sell the Fox board that these
Wall Street lawyers who took over don't
know rule one about movies. Rule one being, don't fuck with Marilyn unless she's in
the mood."

"And for this you need your phone
tapped?"

"Yes. I want to keep track. What do they
call it, a paper trail? I want a *tape* trail. Do
you know how to do that?"

"Not personally, no, but there's a guy we
use."

Roger Pryor, an ex–FBI man, did all the
A-1's work out here. He was a whiz at this
spy stuff.

"When can you . . . Sorry." She had raised
a finger to her lips, and was looking past
me.

A guy who might have been Tony Perkins'
homelier, taller brother ambled over, a tool
kit clanking in his grasp. He was wearing
coveralls and a blank expression. "Excuse
me, Miz Monroe. I need to get some things
from the house."

"That's fine, Norman. You really don't
have to ask."

"Well, I saw you got company and figured

maybe I should."

"That's thoughtful, Norman. Thanks."

He ambled off.

"That was Norman," she said.

No kidding.

"If this is about something else," I said, "something more than just this movie studio nonsense, you should tell me. Like you'd tell your shrink."

"What makes you think that?"

"The way you couldn't meet my eyes when you were going on about it. If you're in trouble, if somebody's bothering you, I *am* that man you said you needed."

"No, really, Nate — just do this job."

"Okay. I'll find out when my guy is available, and call you on your private line. You'll need to make sure both Mrs. Murray and Norman are out of the house."

"That shouldn't be a problem. There's always shopping to be done. Will a thousand-dollar retainer do?"

"Sure."

She'd anticipated this and drew a checkbook out of her capris. She was handing me the check with her famous signature still glistening when Mrs. Murray stuck her head out of the house, like a cuckoo from a clock, and informed Marilyn that Mr. Zanuck was on the line.

I wasn't an actor, but I knew my cue. We both stood, then I got one more quick kiss from Marilyn, and took my leave.

Pulling the Jag away from the peaceful little hacienda, I couldn't shake the feeling that there was more to this than Marilyn was sharing. But for right now I'd have to settle for the thousand she'd given me.

CHAPTER 3

When I exited the unmarked cul-de-sac onto quietly residential Carmelina Avenue, I noticed a nondescript vehicle parked just around the corner. On my right as the Jag turned left, the white panel truck may or may not have been there before. On my way here, I hadn't been in any kind of investigative mode, and was trying to find the unmarked street half of a strange address.

Maybe it was this phone-bugging job of Marilyn's that made me notice now.

But I would like to think I hadn't been so distracted that seeing the enclosed Hollywood TV Repair van, parked near the mouth of Fifth Helena, wouldn't have jumped out at me, anyway.

And now we had the disturbing coincidence of this vehicle belonging to Roger Pryor, the guy who did A-1's electronic surveillance work. The same Roger Pryor whose name had popped into my head when Marilyn asked me to tap her phone.

Of course another question also came immediately to mind: *Did Roger's job in Brentwood have anything to do with Marilyn?*

She was not the only actor or actress living around here; probably not even the only famous one. And you didn't have to be in show business to get spied on — one of the doctors or lawyers living in these nice, mostly mission-style homes might be checking up on their better halves. Not all tennis coaches coached on the court, you know.

Still, that surveillance van was parked within spitting distance of Marilyn Monroe. *Marilyn Monroe.* Who had just hired me, for stated reasons that I didn't feel covered all her actual concerns, to tap her phone.

I pulled over and parked in front of an English Tudor mini-mansion where palms had been banished from the lush landscaping. This neighborhood was money — modest money compared to Beverly Hills or Bel Air, but enough so that a truck like that couldn't park forever without annoying somebody.

And when people in a neighborhood like this got annoyed, they let somebody know about it.

Sitting in the parked Jag, watching the white van in my rearview mirror, I wondered if there was any chance Pryor himself was on this job. He had only a handful of employees, and was fussy about his equipment, which he created himself; he was an inventor and tinkerer whose skill in the bugging department dated back to his decade-long stint with the FBI after the war.

Pryor, or one of his boys, might be sitting in that van listening to a tapped phone or bugged room, but I doubted it. First, though this was a pleasant enough June afternoon with ocean breeze making the trip inland, the inside of that van would be an oven.

Second, Roger was more advanced than that. His favorite toy, whether he was bugging a phone or a room or a whole damn house, was a line transmitter, to send eavesdropped conversions by radio waves via FM bands to voice-activated tape recorders as far away as a quarter of a mile.

If he was tapping a phone, Roger would simply gain access to the house, posing as a telephone company repairman, and replace Ma Bell's phone transmitter with his own gimmick, a bug that looked exactly like what he'd removed. Or he would switch phones entirely, with an identical pre-bugged model.

If he was bugging rooms, Roger would use

carbon button mikes, tiny things that could be hidden most anywhere, hooked up to a radio frequency transmitter tied in to (again) a voice-activated tape recorder.

That, beyond the ability to recognize some of the hardware, was about all I knew on the subject. And I wouldn't have known that much, caring only that jobs got done (not how they got done), but I'd spent enough time with Roger to have some of it creep in by osmosis. He was proud of his work and liked to brag and chatter about his latest gizmos.

That truck was probably empty right now. The voice-activated four-track tape recorders didn't have to be checked or reloaded for hours. More important to the program was moving the truck now and then, so as not to attract undue notice in these well-off surroundings.

Toward that end, sometimes Roger would bring in one of at least two other vehicles and alternate — Ace Roofing Company, Acme Carpet Cleaners, Southland 24-Hour Plumbing & Heating.

All it required was occasional new paint jobs, a few magnetic business-logo signs, and, presto, the surveillance fleet was ready to snoop (no truck bore Pryor's own logo, though).

I got out and stretched. In my sport shirt and slacks, I looked not at all suspicious, and of course the Jag was right at home. I crossed the street, which had very light traffic, and walked up to the van and circled it.

Nobody in front, of course.

I knocked at the back door. If someone was in there, my knocking might be ignored, so I had to keep it up a while — long enough for any occupant to get worried that my metallic banging would attract more attention than just dealing with whoever was out there.

No response.

Nothing to do but head back to the Jag, where I sat on the passenger side so that it looked like I was waiting for the driver. I angled the rearview mirror to keep the white van in sight, and about fifteen minutes in, I laughed, thinking that this was the first time I'd felt like a private eye in years.

Not that it felt good or bad — butt-in-the-seat surveillance is always boring as hell — but it did seem right. I took my paperback of *The Carpetbaggers* from the backseat. I picked up where I'd left off, flicking my eyes to the rearview about three times a page. It was a stupid goddamn book but I couldn't stop reading it, except when a red Mustang convertible with some giddy girls in their late teens pulled into the mouth of the Tudor's drive and two got out and two others stayed in the car and all four were in bikinis, their hair wet, towels over arms. They were probably legal age but I wasn't proud of the thoughts I was having. Wasn't ashamed, either.

That teenage tail almost made me miss the guy in the gray repairman's coveralls who was approaching the rear of the van. He parked another vehicle somewhere down the street, no doubt.

As I was climbing out of the Jag, the girls giggled and pointed at me — at my age, I never knew whether it was a compliment or not — and the guy (who might have been Roger, but his back was to me and it was half a block down) was working a key in a rear lock.

He climbed in, shut the double door.

I crossed the street and jogged over.

I could hear him moving around in there as I raised my knuckles to the metal and knocked. After only two raps, the doors parted and presented a sliver of a pleasant-faced Roger — in the mode of dealing with a curious neighbor. He seemed about to say "Yes" when he frowned, then a half smile formed though his shaggy eyebrows kept frowning.

"Nate?" he asked.

"It's not my stunt double."

He froze while trying to process my presence. His hair a golden, thinning blond, his face a broad, bland oval with a well-creased boyishness, he was about forty and five ten or so, with a modest paunch. He looked convincing in the repairman uniform, which even had a sewn-on Hollywood TV Repair insignia. Actually he had a long-ago legal degree he never used, which had gotten him into the FBI.

"What the hell are you . . . ? Get up in here."

He shut me in.

It was predictably warm, though a good-size floor fan was going, up near the divider closing off the front from the back, the path of the blades cooling both us and a three-tiered metal rack with eight reel-to-reel upright recorders churning, amidst various electronic gadgets and gauges, a few lineman headsets tossed casually here and there. This was at my left as I crouched inside the windowless rear doors. At my right was a small, well-worn yellow-and-gold nubby upholstered couch, which my host plopped down on, leaving plenty of room for me.

"Want a cold one?" he asked, digging in a

cooler just beyond the couch. He demonstrated what he was offering by holding up a sweating can of Schlitz.

"Why not?"

He church-keyed it open and I took that one while he fished for another.

"What's the occasion?" he asked. Very good-naturedly, and if I hadn't been in the business myself, and hadn't known Roger, I'd have missed the suspicion. "You never bother dropping by my little penthouse on wheels when I'm doing a job for you. And I'm not doing a job for you."

I sipped the Schlitz. With the beer, and the floor fan, it was like sitting on a back porch somewhere in the dead of summer.

"That's the funny thing," I said. "I just told a client, oh . . . not an hour ago . . . that I'd be getting back to her with details on how my man would be around tomorrow to put a bug on her phone."

He laughed. "Do tell. And I'm that man? And you spotted the truck, and decided to save yourself a phone call?" He sipped the beer.

"Here's the thing," I said, and wiped foam off my upper lip. "My client? It's Marilyn Monroe."

I'll give him this much — he didn't cough beer out of his nose or anything, and the eyes flickered only a little, not even enough to make the shaggy eyebrows wiggle.

"I thought she lived over on North Doheny," he said casually.

"No you didn't." I gestured with a hitch-hiker's thumb. "You *know* she lives down this highfalutin alley. Are you bugging her phone, or her bedroom, or her whole damn house?"

He gave me another half a smile, then shook his head and gave me a hooded-eyed look. He brushed a little spilled foam off his gray coveralls. "What if I said this was a divorce case?"

"I'd say you're full of shit. Who hired you, the studio?"

He shook his head, and the smile widened into a give-me-a-break-buddy grin. "Look, Nate — I have a client. And it's not you. There's such a thing as ethics and profes-sional courtesy and conflict of interest and, you know, all kinds of factors at play."

"This afternoon," I said, "or tomorrow, I would have given you a call, telling you Marilyn wants her phones tapped. Wants tapes of all her calls. And you'd have said, 'Sure.' Or would you have told me no, because you already were doing a job involv-ing her? That kind of ethics and professional courtesy and conflict of interest, Roger?"

His face went expressionless; then one caterpillar eyebrow jerked. "I could claim that . . . but you wouldn't believe me."

"Right."

"So . . . are you going to screw it up for me, and tell Marilyn she needs somebody to come in to sweep for bugs? Least you could do is give *me* the job."

"Answer my question, Roger. You already have her phone tapped?"

"No."

"The house . . . ?"

"No. Just the bedroom. Master bedroom. I can pick up some stuff from other rooms from there. Small house for a big star."

"Who's your client?"

He shook his head, drank his beer, then leaned back with folded arms and a defensive posture. "No. I can't do that."

"Let me give you your options. First, I can tell Marilyn her house is bugged and help her get rid of the pests . . . and no you don't get the gig. After which the A-1 can, in future, find some firm other than Pryor Investigative Services, Inc., to use for its surveillance work. How much do you bill us on the average year, do you suppose?"

". . . And the other option?"

"You can tell me who your clients are, and I will give Marilyn a bullshit story about how she needs to be discreet in her pillow talk, because once she has her own phone tapped, it's easy for somebody else to listen in."

"Well, that's true, actually."

"And I *will* send you in to do the phone-tap job for me, as promised."

He twitched something that was neither a smile nor a frown. "The thing is, Nate . . . I already got more than one client, here. It's one of those situations where the commodity in question has a lot of interested buyers, and why not keep them all happy, and me prosperous?"

"You wanna give me the ethics speech again, Roger, the conflict of interest thing? I think maybe I missed part of it."

He moved a palm against the air as if he were polishing it. "Anyway, Nate, these are not the kind of clients you pull anything on."

"What, are you worried? Is this van bugged? Are your clients listening in on us?"

"Really, Nate. These aren't pleasant people."

I let an edge into my voice. "Who wants to hear Marilyn's bedroom talk, Roger?"

"Well, you wouldn't know the intermediary's name, probably. But it's . . . Christ on a crutch, Nate, it's for Hoffa." He whispered as if afraid his own machines might pick it up: "Jimmy fucking *Hoffa.*"

I frowned. "Jimmy Hoffa wants to know who Marilyn is diddling? The head of the Teamsters cares who a Hollywood sex symbol takes to bed?"

He made a palms-up gesture with his free hand. "I'm in the surveillance business, Nate. Mine is not to reason why. Mine is but to make the recordings and gather same and ship 'em the hell off."

Hoffa wasn't just a name in the headlines to me. Everybody knew him as a controversial labor leader with obvious ties to organized crime. But I knew him personally. In 1957 Hoffa had hired me to infiltrate the so-called Rackets Committee run by Senator John L. McClellan. I had done this, but with the full knowledge of Robert Kennedy, chief counsel of the Rackets Committee.

As a double agent, I'd done Hoffa a good share of harm, but the president of the Teamsters Union didn't know as much. Jimmy still thought I was a dirty ex-cop from Chicago. And maybe I was. But I'd never really been *his* dirty ex-cop from Chicago.

Nonetheless, I knew better than most the dangers of tangling asses with the affable, ruthless Teamster boss.

As reel-to-reel tape hummed on the rack nearby, Roger was saying, "And I'm pretty sure Hoffa is in this with another guy nobody oughta try to fuck with. Old friend of yours, Nate — Chicago friend?"

"I have a lot of Chicago friends."

"So I hear. And one of 'em is Sam Giancana, right?"

Warm though it was in the enclosed space, I felt a chill, and it wasn't the beer and it wasn't the floor fan.

From Hoffa we'd gone in an instant to the current operating head of the Chicago mob. Called "Mooney" by friends and foes alike (it signified his craziness), Giancana had started out a street punk on the Near North Side's Patch, worked his way up to the Capone Outfit, where he became Tony Accardo's bodyguard. Once the top chair was his, Giancana wrested the numbers racket from the colored gangsters and expanded every other criminal enterprise in the Windy City.

Now he was a well-dressed psychopathic moneymaking machine with all kinds of show business pals, including Frank Sinatra — it was enough to make me wish I hadn't introduced the two of them.

"*Is* he a friend of yours, Nate — Giancana?"

"We get along. Never really had any trouble with him."

"That friendship you had with Frank Nitti, back when you were starting out, it's held you in good stead."

"Yeah." I didn't want to talk about it. "So Hoffa's your client, and you think Giancana is, too. Why do they care who Marilyn is entertaining?"

He blinked at me, then grinned — amused, amazed. "You're kidding, right? Marilyn's your client, and you don't know?"

"Don't know what?"

He had the goofy grin of a high schooler telling a pal about a girl who put out. "Her and the prez — that poon hound Jack Kennedy. You know the Kennedy boys, don't you, Nate? *More* famous pals of yours. You bragged about your Rackets Committee days in the press enough."

"I don't brag. My press agent does." I shrugged. "I'm aware Jack has a wandering eye."

"Also a wandering dick."

I grunted a laugh. Pawed the air. "But this is silly, Rodge. I mean, ridiculous. Marilyn and Jack Kennedy . . . the president . . . of the United States? They're, what — having an affair?"

"You *are* a detective, Heller. Trust me on

this one — I heard it with my own ears. Those aren't tough voices to ID — unless maybe it was Vaughn Meader and Edie Adams havin' fun with me."

He was referring to a couple of well-known impressionists, the former a Kennedy mimic, the latter Ernie Kovacs' sexy widow, who did a mean Marilyn.

I motioned with my half-empty beer can, the tapes whispering at me. Grinned at him. "Come on, Rodge. You're saying the president of the United States himself just stops by Marilyn's place, and partakes of a piece of ass, while the Secret Service waits on the front stoop? Don't the neighbors mind?"

Pryor shrugged. "He doesn't stop by her house."

"Then how the hell do you know —"

"Tapes I heard are from . . . another place."

"What other place?"

"Another place Hoffa's guy asked me to cover."

"Do I have to ask again?"

"Heller, honest to Christ, you don't wanna know this."

"Whose place, Rodge?"

". . . Lawford's place. That big beach mansion out Santa Monica way."

"*Peter* Lawford's place."

66

"What other Lawford is there?"

"Peter Lawford, the actor, who's married to Pat Kennedy, the president's sister. . . . *That* Peter Lawford's place."

"I told you. A detective. There's four bedrooms in that joint. All covered. Funny thing is, even with famous people? Listening to people screw? Bores the fuckin' tears out of me, at this point in my jaded career."

I finished the beer, then said, "Gimme another."

He selected another Schlitz, like I gave a damn what brand, opened it with the church key. It foamed nicely. I drank.

And thought.

Roger and I didn't have to discuss why Jimmy Hoffa and Sam Giancana might want incriminating tapes on JFK, although their real mutual enemy was brother Bobby, who had made a hobby out of targeting organized crime, and was an old, hated adversary of both men.

Finally, with a glance at the wall of recorders, I asked, "Why so many tapes rolling, Roger? One little blonde woman, one little bed, one little microphone?"

He looked mildly surprised that I'd figured out the significance of that. "Well, you know, with these electronics, you need a backup."

"Right. What, six, eight backups? What's this about, anyway?"

"Like I said, I . . . got a couple other clients."

"Wanting the same . . . commodity?"

"Same sort of stuff, yeah."

"Are they really *good* clients? The kind of clients who give you maybe half the work your agency does, that type client?"

"Nobody gives me more business than the A-1, Nate, you know that. You and Fred are good to me. You're great." He shook his head, his expression ominous. "But this is *not* shit that you need to know."

Interesting — he'd already told me Hoffa and Giancana were involved. This was something or somebody *more* dangerous?

"Roger, I'll just find out myself, other ways — you mentioned I was a detective, remember? But that will waste time and piss me off and, by the way, cost you your favorite meal ticket. Like we used to say downstairs at the PD in Chicago, when we got the goldfish out . . . the rubber hose? Spill."

He spilled. One set of tapes, he said, was for the LAPD's notorious Intelligence Division.

That was a surprise. "Don't they have their own surveillance experts?"

"Yeah, but this they don't want traced back to them. Frankly, I think it's a job they're doing for Fox. The movie studio?"

"I know what Fox is. Why wouldn't Fox go directly to you?"

"Everybody's got layers of protection, these days, Nate. Nobody wants anything coming back on them."

"I'll remember that. Who else?"

"Who else what?"

"Who else are you making goddamn tapes for?"

"You really don't want —"

I grabbed him by the front of his coveralls, fists full of cloth. "You shouldn't give a girl a beer, Roger. We lose all sense of propriety. Now, when I toss you into those fucking tape recorders, you won't get hurt that bad, probably. But your toys might get broken. Wouldn't that be sad?"

"Nate! Stop it!" He pulled away from my grasp and flopped back on the couch. "Come on. We're friends. Business associates."

"Is that rack of shit screwed in? Or will it tip over?"

"I do certain sub-rosa jobs."

"All your jobs are sub-rosa."

"Not *this* sub-rosa."

"What are we talking about, Roger?"

". . . Spooks."

I blinked. I admit it — I blinked.

"Roger, you're not talking about ghosts."

"No."

The Company. CIA. *Christ, why would*
they *care who Marilyn was fucking?* The FBI
I could understand — everybody knew
J. Edgar Hoover and the Kennedy brothers
were not each other's biggest fans. That
Hoover kept a legendary cache of dirt on
the rich, famous, and powerful.

"And . . . that's it? That's the client list?"

The shaggy eyebrows climbed his forehead. "Jesus, Nate, isn't it enough?"

"That's a lot of tapes you got spooling."

"Well, of course, one set's for me. For the
safe-deposit vault. You never know when
you, uh, you know . . . you *need* to know?"

I wasn't sure what that meant, and wasn't
sure I wanted to.

"Sorry about getting rough," I said.

"It was the beer."

"No. It's Marilyn. I like her. And I don't
like seeing all these dark clouds gathering
around her. So this conversation, Roger, it
never happened. I will call you tomorrow at
your office — you'll be in? Good. And we'll
set up you going over to her place, and putting the tap on for her."

"Okay. You mind if I check on my other

stuff, while I'm there, if she isn't looking?"

I belched. The beer.

"Let your conscience be your guide, Roger," I said, and climbed out of the van.

CHAPTER 4

At first blush, Roger Pryor's assertion that the president of the USA and the reigning sex goddess of Hollywood were having a torrid affair sounded crazy to me.

But Pryor's seemingly outrageous claim did have a certain credibility. The beach mansion of Mr. and Mrs. Peter Lawford (or was that Mr. and Mrs. Patricia Kennedy?) *would* make the ideal love nest — after all, Marilyn was friendly with the Lawfords and lived maybe fifteen minutes away. You had to accept that the president's own sister would look the other way, but the men in that family did whatever they wanted, so that didn't necessarily ring false. Nor did Roger's apt if indelicate description of John Fitzgerald Kennedy as a "poon hound."

Not that I was a close pal of Jack Kennedy's. I knew his brother Robert pretty well, and my dealings with the family went back to Chicago in the mid-1940s, around when old Joe Kennedy bought the mammoth Merchandise Mart. Either an incorrigible rascal or a flaming asshole (depending on who you asked), the Kennedy patriarch was still in the liquor business at the time.

That Joe Kennedy had been a bootlegger starting in the mid-twenties, with a fleet of trucks and an armada of boats, was no secret in my circles; his specialty had been shipping liquor into the U.S. from abroad. Such connections allowed him to make legal distribution agreements immediately after Prohibition for Gordon's gin and other brand-name liquor and spirits. Even as ambassador to Britain, before the war, he'd used his position to further his booze-importing interests, when he wasn't busy pitching isolationism.

His cronies in the booze game included such underworld luminaries as Owney Madden and Frank Costello, and his Prohibition-era mistress had been the widow of late gangster Larry Fay, the guy F. Scott Fitzgerald based Gatsby on. When money-magnet Joe finally sold his liquor business in '46, the major buyer was New Jersey gangster Abner "Longie" Zwillman.

It was said that Old Joe only got out of the liquor business because of the pending congressional race of his son Jack, who had become the clan's golden boy after Joe Jr. bought it in the war. Others said the decision grew out of a Chicago mobster with Kennedy ties getting shot in the head in January of '46 in front of the Tradewinds on Rush Street.

That Joe's middle son Bobby had made a name as a racket buster on the McClellan Committee was a source of amusement to cops and disgust to crooks. In fact, Zwillman's 1959 suicide (or was it a mob rubout?) happened in the shadow of a Bobby Kennedy subpoena — ironic coincidence, or cause and effect?

Anyway, I knew Jack only slightly, although a job I did had made me popular with him — I was the guy Old Joe chose to "take care of" the president's first marriage.

In '47, the first-term congressman wed a Palm Beach socialite named Dulcie Something, a quickie justice-of-the-peace deal that was probably one part impulse and two parts gin, Gordon's or otherwise. Within days, the marriage disintegrated, and Old Joe hired me to handle it. I found a local Palm Beach attorney with the right (wrong) reputation, and together — with money and matches — we gave Dulcie amnesia and made the wedding documents in the local courthouse disappear.

Shortly after, I got a nice phone call from Jack, thanking me, and he expressed his gratitude in person a few times, once in Chicago at a Palmer House event, again in Vegas when we were both guests of Sinatra at a show at the Sands. Later, Jack was on the Rackets Committee, too, but not involved to the extent Bobby was, and in that capacity never mentioned or even vaguely referred to what I'd done for him. And for two grand.

We'd most recently socialized not long before he won the presidency — September of 1960, when he was campaigning hard to win Illinois, which of course he did, thanks to Sam Giancana, Mayor Daley, and a bunch of people in graveyards around the greater Chicago area whose civic duty had them voting above and (from) beyond.

One of JFK's biggest supporters in Chicago was Hugh Hefner, perhaps America's most unlikely Horatio Alger story, a shy would-be cartoonist who became the sophisticated king of a twenty-million-dollar empire. Hef, only in his early thirties, was the scourge of moralists and the envy of thirteen-year-old boys of all ages.

He had basically taken the format of the slick men's magazine *Esquire*, where he'd once held a lowly sixty-buck-a-month position, and to its big-name fiction and fashion tips and automotive write-ups and sexy cartoons added a younger, more rebellious touch . . .

. . . and a monthly nude pinup — the centerfold spread of supposed "girls next door," the likes of whom would have kept most healthy men at home and not seeking fame and fortune in the big city like Hef.

The first "Playmate" had been Marilyn Monroe, but Hef had merely bought magazine publication rights to one of her infamous calendar photos. Nonetheless, Marilyn's image on the cover — and in the sideways pinup — made the first issue a smash back in '53. Now, less than ten years later, *Playboy* was outselling *Time* and *Newsweek*.

I take the liberty of calling Hugh M. Hefner "Hef" because we were friendly, if not friends. For five years now, the A-1 Agency had been on a fifteen-hundred-dollar-a-year retainer for *Playboy,* which got hit with threats, scams, and various lawsuits that required immediate access to the kind of investigative services we offered. Not a year had gone by that we hadn't eaten up that retainer and more.

The Playboy Mansion, as Hef called it,

was on North State Parkway, two blocks from Lake Michigan on the Chicago Gold Coast. The iron-fenced turn-of-the-century four-story brick-and-limestone structure, once a showplace of the rich and famous, had by the Depression become a shabby apartment house. Just a year before, Hef had shown me around the huge, unoccupied and quite dingy structure.

"Has possibilities, don't you think?" Hefner — lanky, dark-haired, almost handsome, with a Lincoln-esque, awkward air — seemed always to be puffing a pipe. Otherwise he looked like a kid in an overcoat over lounging pajamas and slippers that were dangerous in this place. We'd jumped in a cab from his office, where he worked odd hours and had a bachelor apartment. It was a Sunday in December and cold as hell.

"It won't be cheap to renovate," I said. "It's like a small hotel."

"I *love* Rodgers and Hart," Hef said with a grin. Pipe in his teeth, he looked like a skinny and very lost Mark Trail. "Let me show you the crowning touch."

That turned out to be a second-floor ballroom with decoratively carved woodwork, a marble fireplace, massive French doors, open beams, pillars, and huge bronze chandeliers.

"Imagine *this* wonderful space," Hef said, "*and* forty rooms."

"Enough for Ali Baba," I said, "and all his thieves."

He laughed, maybe even finding that funny. "So . . . can you fix me up with security, while we're remodeling?"

"Sure. I have people we use."

Within months, as the new decade began, the mansion took shape. He added suits of armor to guard either side of the entrance to the grand living room that the ballroom became, adorning its paneled walls with massive modern art pieces by de Kooning, Pollock, and others (seemed the boy cartoonist preferred abstract expressionism these days).

The bedroom and apartments were refurbished lavishly and most had fireplaces. Hef's master bedroom had a round, rotating bed, its headboard home to controls for the latest in TV and stereo. He told me he got more work done there than the office; I said, "I'll bet."

Below the former ballroom he put in a palm-bedecked swimming pool, with a small, waterfall-protected, recessed grotto. A sunken bar whose primary light source seemed to be backlit framed centerfold photos provided a massive window on underwater swimmers, who were mostly shapely young women in — and sometimes out of — bikinis.

I was by no means a regular, but the weekly parties — starting in the spring of 1960 — were attended by several hundred guests: show business types, upper-echelon magazine staff, pro athletes, plus occasional politicians, novelists, poets, journalists, and other liars.

And of course beautiful young women, Playmates who now worked for Hef's company, some as receptionists and secretaries, others as traveling *Playboy* PR ambassadors, quite a few employed as "Bunnies" at his new, very successful Playboy Club, on nearby Walton Street, for key-holders only. The Bunnies wore one-piece satin swimsuit-like outfits, lots of bosom and thigh exposed, plus cute rabbit ears, bow tie, cuffs, and a tail fluffier than Bugs Bunny's.

I picked up a few at these parties, and dated one or two. Some were stupid, some smart, some in-between, but all were lovely and most were cooperative — neither hookers nor nymphos, just girls looking for opportunities. Marriages and movie contracts and various other arrangements blossomed for them at the mansion and the club.

Though Hefner spent a fortune on food,

drinks, and help at his weekly shindigs, the entertainment cost him nothing, coming courtesy of his showbiz guests — folksingers and stand-up comics from Mr. Kelly's, always, big-name acts over from the mobbed-up Chez Paree, usually.

Right now, September of 1960, I was seated on a sofa next to Hef, who was in a continental-style tuxedo, pipe going, occasionally sipping a glass of something that might have been a mixed drink but was probably Pepsi.

"Just nine months ago, Nate," Hef was saying with his wide thin smile, eyes as bright as these of a ten-year-old who just got a train set for Christmas, "my baby didn't exist."

"Nine months is about right for a baby," I said.

I was in my own After Six tux, and most of the men here were similarly dressed, though a few were in business suits. The look for both sexes was fairly formal, though in a surrealistic touch, dripping-wet couples in bathing suits and towels would come sloshing through at will, laughing, presumably heading somewhere to dry off.

Sitting on the arm of the sofa with her arm draped around Hef was a lovely blonde girl in her early twenties wearing a sort of obscene pink prom dress, her full bosom half out, white-blonde hair in a sprayed bulletproof bouffant. She had a very innocent face, and he was calling her Cynthia; she wasn't calling him anything — we'd been sitting ten minutes and she hadn't spoken. But her smile was swell, and her laugh created memorable jiggling.

The music was a little loud — a black combo Hef had recruited from the South Side, in sky-blue tuxes with black lapels and cuffs, was playing and singing "The Twist." Not long ago, rock 'n' roll was a subject of much derision here. But "The Twist" had changed that. Or anyway the way Hef's female guests did the Twist had changed that.

"You know some people look at this," Hef said, waving his pipe like a wand, "and all they see is sex."

I was watching a dark-tanned, busty brunette in a blue bikini, her hair a beehive tower, do the Twist with a fiftyish guy in glasses eyeing her the way a dog does a squirrel. He was some kind of associate editor at the magazine.

"How did they get that idea?" I asked.

He ignored my sarcasm, or maybe didn't pick up on it over the loud music. There was considerable chatter, as well — we were near the endless buffet table. Food smells were pleasant. Bunnies were circulating taking drink orders.

I said, "I had a few people over the other night myself. Would have called you but I'm particular."

"You don't think I know I'm the luckiest human being in the world?" He painted the air with his pipe smoke. "But I'm also *doing* the world, this *modern* world, a favor — people who work hard should get to play hard. You get one time around this merry-go-round, and if you don't make the most of it, who do you have to blame?"

"Now you're a philosopher."

"This is a new decade, Nate. Pretty soon we're going to have a new president." He grinned, and his eyes danced with manic delight. "I think we know who that's going to be."

"Nixon's ahead in the polls."

"Tricky Dick won't win. What *Playboy* represented in the fifties was my personal dream — sexual pleasure, material abundance, without guilt. But now it's time to break down other barriers — take civil rights, for example . . ."

Shrill, giddy laughter and applause rode over Hef's speech, and "The Twist" ground to a halt. Tonight's guests of honor had arrived, fresh from the Near North Side's Chez Paree — Frank Sinatra, Dean Martin, and Sammy Davis, Jr. (Joey Bishop and Peter Lawford weren't on the Chez bill), moving past the suits of armor down into the living room, stopping to talk to men they knew and girls they wanted to know. Somebody was doing the fingers-in-the-teeth whistle: Hef's bouncy blonde.

Everybody crowded around a little performance area adjacent to a piano, bass, and drums, where a trio of musicians awaited, and without preamble, the Summit (they didn't call themselves the Rat Pack) went into an abbreviated version of its Vegas show.

First Dean went out to sing while the other two faded back to a nearby liquor cart. After drunkenly asking what all these people were doing in his room, the big well-tanned handsome crooner, in a tux with loose crossover tie, did a lighthearted "Volare," then several song parodies ("You made me love you . . . you woke me up to do it"). He was delivering a straight "June in January" when Davis, sans tux jacket, strode over, mimicking Martin's ex-partner Jerry Lewis (*"Deeeeeeean!"*) and Dino responded accordingly ("Jer — you've *changed!* But at least you're still *Jewish. . . .*"). The two walked off arm in arm and Sinatra took their place.

It was always a surprise how small Frank was, and even more surprising how quickly you forgot that when he sang. His tux tie was still snugged in place, but he was loose as he did a jazzy "Chicago," getting the expected wild response, then "Luck Be a Lady," which played surprisingly well without a big band.

Then Dean carried Sammy out in his arms and presented him to Sinatra as a token of appreciation from the NAACP, and this got howls, particularly from Sammy.

The little Negro — and he made a giant out of Sinatra — was probably the most talented of them, and he sang a very earnest "Hey There" (a hit of his) and then "Birth of the Blues," doing some flashy dancing. Finally he went into "The Lady Is a Tramp" and had lapsed into a Sinatra impression when the other two came out and shut him down.

The three together did a bunch of comedy that had most everybody in stitches, but I have to admit I would rather they'd kept singing. Maybe it was because I'd seen this act — with Bishop and Peter Lawford mixed in — three times, and knew all the "improvisation" was written.

And a lot of it played on Sammy being

colored. Racial stuff that was so stupid, they were spoofing it, so hip and cool they could get away with it. Sammy laughed hard, bending over and slapping his thighs, at Frank and Dino's darkie stuff (mostly *Amos 'n' Andy* references), but I always noticed you didn't actually hear Sammy laughing. . . .

They were doing a "Guys and Dolls" medley when somebody came pushing through the crowd — it was Peter Lawford, also in a tux.

"Fellas!" he said. "How could you start without me?"

Sammy said innocently, "We were gonna wait, Pete, but nobody could remember what it is you do."

This got a big laugh, then Sinatra and Martin mugged while Lawford and Davis did a little soft-shoe bit — the expatriate Britisher had after all been a star in musicals at MGM — and finally Lawford held his hands up to the crowd.

"The real reason I waited to come on this late," he said, with that barely there British accent, "was so I could introduce a new member to our little Summit."

Sammy said, "Bobby Darin?"

Sinatra raised a fist and gave him a comic glare.

"No, no," Lawford said, with that nice big winning smile of his. "Ladies and gentlemen, the next president of the United States — and I *don't* mean Hugh Hefner. . . ."

Gasps blossomed everywhere as all eyes went to the presidential candidate gliding effortlessly through the crowd in a brown suit with a red tie, straight from some political event, tanned and handsome, his brown bangs slightly tousled. Everyone knew he was in town, campaigning for this crucial state, but his presence here was a surprise.

By the time he reached the little performing area, the applause was ringing in the big old remodeled ballroom. It was dying down when Kennedy said to the pianist, who was doing a jazzy "Hail to the Chief," "I, uh, want to thank you for your positive outlook."

When he finally spoke, in that distinctive halting Massachusetts way of his, he was casual and gracious. "I didn't come around, uh, to spoil the party with a campaign speech. I just want to thank my friend Frank, for, uh, the great work he's doing. You've *heard* his jingle?"

Laughter and clapping and a few whoops indicated they had — a specialty version of "High Hopes" that was running in radio and TV ads.

With a smile, the candidate turned to Sinatra and said, "You know, uh, Frank I think you may have a *future* in this recording business."

Sinatra made a dismissive gesture, but he was beaming.

"And, uh, I have to thank our host, Hugh Hefner. He represents a breath of, uh, fresh air in our rather stale culture . . . but don't quote me. Jackie doesn't approve of the centerfolds."

As laughter rang, front-row Hef grinned and shrugged, pipe in hand.

"And, uh, Hef . . . if I may, without embarrassing you . . . I'd like to thank you for your, uh, generous financial contributions. And all of you very, uh, prosperous-looking individuals, I know my campaign would be grateful for, uh, any help you might still give. We're coming down to the wire now. And don't miss the first of, uh, three televised debates, coming soon to a living room near you. Should be exciting. I understand, if things don't go well for him, Dick Nixon may be, uh, reprising his famous Checkers speech."

That got a huge laugh. He gave a little wave, and Sinatra and company sang the "High Hopes" rewrite as the presidential hopeful mingled. This was the kind of hip group that gave even the likes of JFK some space. I didn't see a soul ask for an autograph, and soon he'd disappeared.

I spotted him with Lawford in the sunken bar, where the window on the swimming pool glowed hypnotically with subdued lighting and unsubdued female flesh. A lot of smoke swirled in here, and Lawford had lighted up, but not Kennedy.

The candidate was nestled in a booth, and I knew he had a terribly bad back — sometimes wore a brace — so I motioned for him not to get up, offering my hand to shake, which he did, flashing that famous smile.

"My favorite private eye," he said. "Is it, uh, true James Bond was based on you?"

"No, it's just the tux," I said, and nodded to Lawford, exchanging smiles. "But I would like to get some of his action."

Kennedy grinned. "Who wouldn't?"

Absently, flicking ash into a tray, Lawford said, "You know, they offered me that part. Money was poor, and I turned it down. They're going with an unknown."

"Too bad for them," Kennedy said. "Uh, Peter — could I have a word with Mr. Heller?"

"Most certainly," the actor said good-naturedly, sighing smoke, then sliding out of the booth.

I took his place. A Bunny came over, but Kennedy already had a mixed drink of some kind going; me, too — a vodka gimlet.

"You know, Nate, I, uh, always look forward to seeing you."

"Why's that?" I didn't figure we'd ever exchanged more than a dozen sentences.

"You're not a bore," he said, and twitched half a smile. "And you're not a yes-man. I have so many of those."

"That's because you like it that way."

Which made him laugh. "See? Exactly what I mean. You know, Bobby, uh, thinks the world of you."

"I like him back. He's a bulldog. Reminds me of a friend of mine."

"Oh? Who's that?"

"*Late* friend of mine. Eliot Ness."

"On TV?"

"No, the real man. He was shorter than Robert Stack, but a better actor."

Kennedy grunted a little laugh. "Funny to think of somebody like that — so much larger than life? Actually existing. Walking around. Just a man, like the rest of us."

Like the rest of us.

"What can I do for you, Jack?" I felt I could take the first-name liberty — I mean, he wasn't president yet; and anyway, I was the guy who made his first marriage go away. And I wasn't even pope.

"You, uh, know how stubborn Bobby is about his, uh, his passion."

"I'm not sure." I should have known what he meant, but in my defense, half-naked Playmates nearby were bobbing up and down underwater.

"The, uh, issue you worked with him on, years ago."

"Organized crime. Teamster corruption. I wouldn't call it an issue. But your brother's passionate about it, all right."

He sipped his drink; his eyes no longer met mine. "Bobby doesn't always, uh, understand the waters we must swim in."

Again, in this context, that could be taken wrong. Wasn't that Miss January?

"What are you saying, Jack?"

Now his gaze rose. If his voice had been any softer, the piped-in jazz would have covered it. "I may need, uh, from time to time, the, uh, help of an intermediary . . . a liaison . . . with certain types of individuals."

"Mobsters, you mean. Isn't that what Sinatra is for?"

Kennedy's smile was faint. "Frank's a good friend, but he, uh . . . he's a public figure, and he has a temper, and can be . . . controversial."

As in, everybody from Hoboken to Hollywood knew Sinatra had mob ties. That hadn't stopped the Kennedys from using Frank's fame to their benefit in this campaign.

I said, "You're saying you may need to get the occasional message to guys like Johnny Rosselli or Sam Giancana, and may need someone reliable to handle that."

"Yes. But, uh, Nate, let's not use specific names."

I had a sip of gimlet. "If you win this thing, you'll have the Secret Service, and the FBI, and —"

He held up a hand. "The Secret Service needs, I think, to steer clear of such matters, if possible. And the FBI, uh, well — you've had your *own* run-ins with J. Edgar Hoover, I, uh, understand."

"Yeah. Told him to go fuck himself, back in '34. Before that kind of thing was fashionable."

He liked that.

"Jack, I'm glad to help, but if I could put in my two cents . . . ?"

"Throw in as much as you like, Nate. The, uh, campaign coffers can use it."

"I hear you got some help in West Virginia."

The story was that Giancana had pulled

strings in that state and pumped in money, some of it from a Teamster pension fund. That made Jack beholden to both Giancana and Hoffa, two of his brother's least favorite people.

"It was a, uh, tough primary."

"Not as tough as the general election'll be. And if it's Illinois that puts you over the top? And Giancana is, or even just *thinks* he's the one who made it happen? Well . . . those *are* dangerous waters, Jack."

"*Those* are dangerous waters," he said, smiling at an underwater nymph ogling him and waving. Then he looked at me. "In politics, Nate, we make, uh, all sorts of promises. All sorts of strange bedfellows. We make deals with people who are, uh, also giving to the other side, covering their bases, because that's, uh, how it works. They hope for a little consideration. Sometimes you give it to them. But it's not a quid pro quo situation."

"Just my two cents."

"Well, uh, I appreciate that, I really do, Nate, and your willingness to help out. . . . I'll be in touch. If and, uh, when the time comes."

We shook hands again.

I'd been dismissed. Lawford, who was at the bar, saw me departing, nodded, smiled, and slid back in across from his brother-in-law.

Upstairs, I had a brief nonpolitical conversation with Sinatra, who I'd done a few jobs for. I didn't know Martin or Davis very well, but we exchanged pleasantries.

Hef — holding court back at his couch, surrounded by guests and girls — gave me a happy-kid look. Kennedy's presence meant a lot to him, though no reporter would cover tonight — a direct link between Hef and JFK might be embarrassing, and the press boys liked and protected this candidate. They also liked getting asked back to Hef's parties.

The next hour I spent in the pool, in a bathing suit, chatting up Krista, that twisting bikini brunette I'd spotted earlier, a twenty-year-old who'd recently quit her bank secretary job to be a Bunny. She was from Los Angeles and originally from Sweden and had been in the magazine early last year.

Odd to see her in that skimpy bathing suit and already know that her breasts would be a pale pink against the dark tan and her nipples dark as that tan and rather large and puffy. We flirted, and I used the private eye angle to impress her — she had big brown eyes and a very white, very fetching smile, and a ridiculously sexy accent. We'd been tangling tongues at the edge of the pool for maybe ten minutes when I suddenly realized the tent I was making would be visible from the window in the bar, and suggested we make use of that grotto behind the waterfall.

But when we got in there, somebody was already standing in the waist-high pool with his back to its edge, his body reflecting the shimmering lighted-from-below waters in the cave-like surroundings.

Bad back be damned, there was Jack Kennedy, his chest tan, a goofy smile going, his hands underwater, somebody splashing as he held that somebody's head under. As if trying to drown whoever it was.

Krista gave me a look and I gave her one back.

"Well, uh, hello again, Nate," Jack said. "Who's your lovely friend?"

Hands kept pushing down. More splashing.

"This is Krista. Jack, you better let that —"

"Be damned," he chuckled. More splashing. "Wouldn'ta taken *you* for a spoilsport, Nate."

And he let the person up — not surprisingly a girl, a lovely Liz Taylor–ish brunette with a mouthful of something, probably not water, which she swallowed, and then shoved her hands at him, half playful, half angry.

She scolded, "I told you not to *do* that anymore, Jack!"

"Don't you trust me, Judy? . . . Nate, do you know Judy?"

"Yeah. Yeah. We've met."

I'd met Judith Campbell before.

She was Sam Giancana's current squeeze, and most anybody who was anybody in Chicago mob circles would know that.

Dangerous waters was right.

It was a little unsettling. What did the golden boy need with me as go-between, with Judy in the picture? Still, it didn't stop me from sneaking upstairs like a thief with Krista and finding an empty room among the forty.

CHAPTER 5

The Lawfords lived in what Hollywood types would call a beach house but anybody else would call a mansion. The rambling marble-and-stucco neo-Spanish dwelling on Palisades Beach Road had been Louis B. Mayer's, once upon a time, visited by — and making an impression upon — young Peter Lawford, back when he was a contract player at MGM.

It could still make an impression, though from without it was just another (if large) Santa Monica beachfront property like those of the neighbors, doctors or lawyers or agents; usually not movie stars, who preferred Malibu or Beverly Hills. Like Marilyn, who lived barely ten minutes away, the Lawfords cared more about comfort than status. When you're the president's sister and brother-in-law, status isn't an issue.

Despite the size of the place — taking up

two lots — you could park right in front of it, pulling in like you were at a roadside restaurant. I stepped out into the cool ocean breeze of late afternoon, shadows just starting to go to work, the pound of surf making foamy music.

I'd come right over from my encounter with Roger Pryor and his TV repair van, and had spotted two similar vans (though not ones I recognized as Roger's) parked within a quarter mile of the fenced-in Lawford estate.

Slipping my Ray-Bans in my sport-shirt pocket, I was about to knock at the front door when two guys in black suits and black ties and black sunglasses materialized and made bookends of themselves. The one on my right was a little older — thirty-five? — and took the lead: "May we help you, sir?"

This was with the warmth of a UNIVAC spitting out a punch card.

"My name's Nathan Heller," I said, and got my wallet out and let the windows flip down, displaying my array of investigator's licenses: Illinois, Los Angeles, New York State. "I'm a friend of Mr. Lawford's, and of the president and the attorney general."

That got something that might have been a smile out of the older one. I wondered what branch they were. Was there a permanent fed detail attached to keep an eye on the presidential relatives who lived here?

The younger one, who hadn't said anything, departed, heading to a black Ford Galaxie parked two down from my Jag.

"Black suit," I said to the guy on my right, "black tie, black sedan? You guys really know how to blend in here in sunny Cal."

"Who says we're trying to blend in?"

"Well, the sunglasses are a start. What if I asked to see your credentials?"

"You could ask."

I didn't.

But it only took five minutes for me to be cleared, and I didn't even have to knock again, as a smiling and slightly chagrined Patricia Kennedy Lawford opened the door on us.

"Mr. Heller," she said pleasantly, offering a hand for me to take and shake. "Nate. Nice to see you again."

Pat Lawford wasn't beautiful — too much Kennedy in her face — but she was certainly striking, tall, slender, not yet forty, fetchingly casual in a blue-and-white striped top and matching blue capris with white Keds.

"Sorry to stop by without calling, Mrs. Lawford. It's important I see Peter."

"Certainly, and it's Pat, of course."

She opened the door for me, and nodded

and smiled tightly at the men in black.

"See you at the company picnic," I told them, and then the door was closed on them. "Are they always here?"

"Sometimes they're here," she said, with a smile that had just enough crinkles in it to say that was none of my business.

I had been inside this house before. I knew it had a dozen rooms and yet managed to have a nice lived-in, comfortable feel while reeking of money.

The Lawfords had intimate parties two or three times a week, dinner and games and cards, with poker usually reserved strictly for "boys' nights in." I was not a regular, by any means, nor was I stranger. I'd been here often enough to know Pat made a great beef stew, and Peter's specialty was liver and bacon with Brussels sprouts. The latter dish was enough to make some invitees inquire on the phone who tonight's chef would be — Pat, Peter, or their cook.

Also, I was aware Pat could be moody. I'd seen her warm, I'd seen her hostile, I'd seen her indifferent. And I'd seen all that just being here maybe half a dozen times in three years. Today — despite being unsure whether to call me "Mr. Heller" or "Nate" — she was gracious, moving through the spacious, curving living room with windows

99

on the ocean and French doors to wrought-iron balconies.

"Is Peter expecting you?" she asked, glancing back at me.

"No. This is something that just came up. I wouldn't be so rude as to drop by this late in the day if it wasn't important."

"Don't be silly. We haven't even made dinner plans yet."

I noticed she stopped short of inviting me to be part of them.

She guided me outside, down some steps onto the generous skirt of an enormous marble swimming pool separated by a fence from the Pacific, whose tide was rushing in just yards away. Down the beach, the voices of young people, teenagers probably, laughed and shouted, distant, like memories.

In a yellow polo shirt, white slacks and sandals, wearing sunglasses, Peter Lawford was semi-reclined in a lounge-style deck chair next to a small white metal table. He was reading *Ship of Fools* by Katherine Anne Porter. That was my first clue to something being amiss — like me, he was more the Harold Robbins type; that had to be Pat's book.

On the white table was a pitcher of what was probably martinis, but the only glass was in Lawford's hand. Maybe he was thirsty. The guy did put away a lot of booze, I could testify.

"Well, Nathan Heller," Lawford said, with a sudden dazzling smile, tossing the book without marking his place, scrambling up to greet me, "this *is* a pleasant surprise."

Always Nathan with him, not Nate.

We shook hands, pump-handle style. The last time I'd seen him, I'd taken two hundred bucks off him in poker, so this welcome was warmer than need be. This felt mildly staged, and I had a hunch I knew why.

Lawford looked typically tanned and slender, befitting his recent run as TV's *Thin Man;* gray was coming in at the temples, but that was a full head of hair. Not exactly the biggest star in Hollywood, he still had the looks, and a certain grace, though he looked older than his mid-thirties. A limber six feet, he walked me over to a larger white metal table and tossed his sunglasses there — his eyes were as dark as the shades — where two chairs awaited under a white umbrella. Giddy laughter echoed up the beach. Surf rumbled. Sea birds called.

Pat brought over the pitcher of martinis, identifying it as such and asking if I'd like her to bring me a glass, or she could make me something else?

101

"You're a gimlet man, if I recall," she said.

Vodka gimlet, but damned close. I was getting waited on by the president's sister. Wasn't *I* special?

"No, I'm fine, Pat. Thanks. Shouldn't be here long."

She smiled tightly; her eyes weren't as friendly as the rest of her face. "Well, then. I'll leave you boys to it."

And she went briskly inside. There was something military about it.

Lawford looked after her fondly. "I'll never know how I managed that," he said.

"None of us will," I admitted, knowing the word was they were desperately unhappy. "I'm going to tell you something off the record."

"Of course," he said. He got a gold cigarette case out from his breast pocket, found a lighter in his pants, and lighted up. He didn't offer me one — he knew I didn't smoke.

"I can't give you details without violating the trust of my client," I said. "There won't be any details. So don't ask. All you get is a general warning."

Now he was frowning. "What is this about, Nathan?"

"If my client wasn't already compromised, I don't think I'd even be here. This is a tricky one."

"All right. Come on, man. Out with it."

I met his eyes and held them. "I've heard the rumors about your brother-in-law and Marilyn."

"Jack, you mean?"

Well, I didn't mean Bobby.

He was shrugging and saying lightly, "You know this town, Nathan. The rumor mill. Half of it is nonsense."

"This is part of that other half. I have it on reliable authority that Jack and Marilyn have been intimate. In fact, that they've been intimate" — I jerked a thumb toward the nearby sprawl of Spanish beach mansion — "in one or more of those four bedroom suites of yours."

His smile was a little too broad, and he seemed about to wave it off, but finally my unchanging deadpan got to him.

"People do things," he said, with a different kind of shrug. What he said next came with a twinkle in the eye and the lilt of a British accent that made it no less crude: "If you were the president, wouldn't *you* fuck Marilyn Monroe, if you had the chance?"

"Me being president," I said, "doesn't come up that often."

"I suppose not," he granted.

"Peter, I don't know if you know it, but from time to time, I've done jobs for your wife's family. For Jack, and his father. And Bobby and me, we go way back. To Rackets Committee days. All the way back to that asshole McCarthy. *That* fucking far."

"I'm aware, Nathan. Why do you think you're sitting here?"

"Why do *you* think I'm sitting here?"

That threw him off balance. His chuckle got mixed up with a cigarette cough. "Well . . . I, uh . . . *assume* it's to be of help."

"Marilyn is a friend of mine. I really like the girl."

"So do I! She and Pat are tight — they're like schoolgirls together."

That sent a disturbing if not entirely unappealing image flashing through my mind, but never mind.

"So was it a fling?" I asked. "Was Jack just putting another notch in the Kennedy boys' belt?"

Lawford's smile crinkled, then curdled. He was looking for words and not finding them. Actors, especially mediocre ones like Peter, need somebody to provide lines.

"Those two together just once," I said, "is plenty to make a lot of this administration's enemies happy. I know for a fact, from my own very special point of view, that certain friends of *your* friend Frank are not thrilled with Bobby making a hobby out of them at the Justice Department."

Frank was, of course, Sinatra, and those "friends" included Sam Giancana and James Riddle Hoffa.

His smile almost disappeared. "Frank and I aren't as close as we once were."

"Yeah. I heard about Palm Springs."

That seemed to goose him, mildly. His eyes tightened. "*What* have you heard?"

"Just that Frank remodeled his place there, hung up a 'President Kennedy Slept Here' plaque in advance and everything, spending a small fortune turning it into a kind of Camp David, Hollywood-style."

Lawford's expression turned melancholy. "That is true."

"And Bobby put the brakes on with Jack, told him no matter how hard Sinatra'd worked for him, the president of the United States could not be seen hanging out with a known associate of gangsters."

". . . Also true."

I sat forward. "But, Christ, Peter — did Jack *have* to stay with Bing Crosby instead? The only competition in Frank's class?"

Lawford reached for the martini glass, saying, "And a Republican, old boy."

A Republican old boy was right.

"Sometimes," I said, "I think Bobby gets carried away with this do-gooder nonsense. Where does he think Old Joe's money came from?"

Lawford grunted something that was not quite a laugh. "That is the *point,* Nathan. One must purge one's self of the sins of the father."

"Tell that to Jack before he picks out his next movie actress to bang. Or at least tell him to pick one less famous, and less temperamental, than Marilyn."

Lawford sighed. "Bobby was right, and you're right, too, Nathan. It wasn't so much Sinatra himself, you see, or even his associates. Hell, in our nightclub act — you've seen it?"

I nodded.

He was smiling, remembering. "Joey would say, 'Tell them about the *good* things the Mafia's been doing, Frank.' And the audience would roar, and Frank would, too. I mean, it's a joke. It's kind of . . . sexy. Naughty fun."

I'd been around gangsters in Chicago since I was a kid. And I admit I never thought of them as "naughty fun."

"Something made Bobby put the kibosh on it," I said.

106

"*Giancana* had stayed there — there in Palm Springs at Frank's place. Old J. Edgar has the photos in a file. And one could not have the president bedding down where the boss of the Chicago Outfit once slumbered. Could one?"

"Frank could always get a bigger plaque and put both names on."

He gave that the raspy laugh it deserved, and pressed on: "Jack is a great man. He has a huge heart, and a mind that to me is unfathomable in its brilliance. And the *pain* he's in — do you know, Nathan, that he almost always wears a back brace?"

"Yeah. Except when he's fucking, which is a good deal of the time. I also know he's got Addison's disease, and was given the last rites four times before he ran for Congress. Public has no idea of the state of his health. The VD, for example."

Lawford looked pale despite the tan. "How do you know these things, Nathan?"

"Hell, who do you think covered them up? Answer me, Peter — is it a fling, or is this affair ongoing, Marilyn and Jack?"

"It, uh . . . *was* ongoing. It's either over, or tapering off. Fling doesn't quite cover it. It goes back farther than you might imagine, Nathan — unless you already know that."

"No. Nobody hired me to cover this up. Yet."

Lawford was staring, but not at me. "Started back in the fifties. I was at the party where she flirted with Jack and Jack flirted with her and DiMaggio just *fumed*." He sipped the martini and smiled. "I'll tell you something funny, Nathan . . . about Palm Springs?"

"Sure. I can always use a laugh."

"At Bing Crosby's? *Marilyn* was *there*. Openly with Jack. Playing goddamn *hostess*. My God, how the word hasn't gotten out, I'll never know."

I didn't shock easily, but I admit this news threw me. "Bobby forbids him to sleep at Sinatra's, but it's okay to screw Marilyn at Der Bingle's? You have any aspirin, Pete?"

"I keep myself well-supplied in painkillers."

"Maybe Crosby should put a plaque over *that* bed." I shifted on the metal chair. The sun was setting fire to the ocean. "Why is Sinatra pissed at you?"

"You know Frank and his temper."

"I know Frank and his temper, but I also know Frank sees you as his entrée to the Kennedys."

He winced. "I'm afraid that relationship is strained at the moment, as well — not *over*, merely strained. Anyway, *I* was finally *elected* for something in this family."

"What?"

His expression was wry. "To deliver the bad news to Frank."

My eyebrows went up. "That Jack was going to stay with Crosby, not him?"

"Yes."

"And he took it well."

Lawford studied the remains of his martini as if reading tea leaves. "I understand he took a sledgehammer out to the cement helicopter pad he'd had constructed for the president, and broke it up into little pieces."

That made me smile.

"It's not funny, Nathan."

"It's kind of funny, Peter."

He sighed. Took another draw on his cigarette, then sighed again, with smoke this time.

"What else?" he asked.

"I really am here to help," I said. "That's why I'm telling you that Marilyn's place has been bugged."

I'd expected more of a reaction, but all I got was him twitching a sort of noncommittal smile.

"Really," Lawford said. "Well, that's interesting. Who by?"

So that didn't worry him. But he *was*

interested.

"Apparently," I said, "everybody but the Boy Scouts of America, and I haven't ruled them out. Maybe by you or your in-laws, I don't know. But I'm here to pass along one of those words to the wise you hear so much about."

"All right."

"Tell that reckless son of a bitch in the White House to use some discretion for a goddamn fucking change."

Lawford chuckled dryly. "As if he'd listen to *me*. As if he'd listen to *anyone* . . . But Nathan, I do thank you for this."

He started to rise, assuming I was done, but I waved him back to his chair. He frowned and drew on his cigarette.

"Something else?" he asked.

"Yeah. But maybe I can spare myself the bother of telling this twice."

"How so?"

"I think I ought to share this with your houseguest."

He half-smiled again, but the eyes weren't twinkling. "And what houseguest would that be?"

"I don't know. It's either Jack or Bobby. Was that Secret Service or FBI out there?"

CHAPTER 6

"Jack has always had a fascination with show business," Bobby Kennedy said, "that I just don't share."

We were standing at the edge of the ocean, hands in our pockets, slacks rolled midway up our calves, bare feet in the foam, watching the orange of the sun fight the blue of the ocean in that twilight time that Hollywood calls "magic hour." Sorrento Beach was known for volleyball, but nobody was playing this late afternoon.

He gave me that boyish, almost bucktoothed grin; he looked like a college kid in the blue polo and rolled-up chinos. Well, a tired college kid.

"For a fella like Jack?" he said, and chuckled soundlessly. "Having Peter for a brother-in-law, well, ah, that's your classic kid-in-the-candy-store situation, isn't it?"

The cadence echoed his famous brother's, but with fewer of the characteristic hesitations; also, his voice was higher-pitched, the words coming quickly.

He looked like a condensed edition of Jack, a well-tanned five feet nine or so compared to the president's six one, his eyes bluer than Jack's gray-blue, his hair darker and more tousled. Not as handsome, though by no means homely. He was intense and intensely shy, but he had a temper and could strike like a viper, if so inclined.

After Peter Lawford had fetched his brother-in-law, Bobby and I had a brief, smile-and-handshake reunion — Bob was not the warmest guy, even with a friend — at which point Lawford suggested we repair to his den, and the comfy couches there.

I had suggested that what I had to say was best for Bobby's ears only, leaving it to the attorney general's discretion just how much (if anything) he wanted to share with his actor in-law.

Who took no offense, waving, smiling, retrieving his sunglasses (but leaving *Ship of Fools* behind), and disappearing inside the mammoth beach house.

"Shall we, ah, talk here by the pool, Nate?"

"Why don't we take a stroll instead?"

Bobby's eyes slitted, reading my hesitance to be even this close to the house. "Uh, yes. Nice afternoon for a walk on the beach."

So we ended up with our feet in the soothing surf, walking slowly along, stopping a while, then sloshing back, with black suits shadowing us from well up the slope of the beach, far enough away that we could talk freely.

There had been a little small talk. Just enough to pass for us both being civilized. He asked about Sam, I asked about his growing brood. Then we got to it.

I said, "I don't think Jack understands that movie stars are people. He comes out here and it's all make-believe to him. Fun and games."

That grin flashed again, but beneath the brown bangs, the eyes were troubled. "You're preaching to the choir, Nate. I was sent to put an end to this silly dalliance. I've spoken to Marilyn about it, personally."

"Really?"

"Yes, and, uh, I feel confident she'll be cooperative."

In a way, this was typical — Bobby cleaning up after Jack. For years, the middle brother had operated as the family hatchet man. Old Joe had groomed him for it.

"I didn't know you were acquainted with Marilyn."

"I met her earlier this year, right here at Peter's, at a party. Ethel found her quite

charming. We spoke current events —
surprisingly knowledgeable girl. I even
danced with her. You haven't, uh, lived till
you've seen Marilyn Monroe do the Twist."

"As long as I don't have to see you do it,
too, I'm interested."

He smiled politely.

"You need to be careful, Bob. You're dealing with a very intelligent woman who has
an ego as big as it is fragile. Cross her at
your own risk. She's a star among stars."

He shrugged. "I know she's famous. I said
before she's intelligent. Also creative and
well-informed. But there are dangers here
besides the, uh, potentially embarrassing
presidential indiscretions."

"Such as?"

He gave me an awkward glance. "Don't
laugh, Nate. But she has Communist affilia-
tions."

Only I did laugh. "Is that the ghost of Joe
McCarthy I see, haunting us all of a sudden?"

His tone grew defensive. "No, she really
does. Her psychiatrist, her doctor, too, and
even that housekeeper of hers, go way back
with the party."

"This is not a Peter Lawford party we're
talking about now, is it?"

He frowned; for a young face, it could

really rumple. "Christ, man, she was married to Arthur Miller! If we hadn't pulled strings for the guy, he'd have gone to jail for contempt of Congress."

"This makes Marilyn Monroe a Commie?"

"No, it makes her naive and vulnerable, and potentially useful to the other side."

I presumed he meant the Russians and not the Republicans.

He was saying, "Did you know that just recently Miss Monroe spent time in Mexico with a colony of left-wing expatriates?"

"She was buying furniture, Bob."

"She's a security risk, Nate."

"What kind of pillow talk is Jack indulging in, anyway?" I gave up a disgusted grunt. "This bears the delicate bouquet of J. Edgar."

"Yes it does," he admitted, eyebrows up, then down. "And, ah, the director has indeed met with Jack several times of late, sharing . . . information. And concern."

"Concern about the Commie angle? Or the sex?"

Bobby grimaced. "Both. The director seems convinced that Marilyn might go public and embarrass the administration. He actually said that her doing so would 'serve the Communist agenda.' "

"You kids do know there's a difference between undercover and under covers? Tell Jack to stop loaning J. Edgar his Ian Fleming books."

"It's no joke, Nate."

And it wasn't.

I frowned, stopping, water slapping my ankles. "The press boys have always steered clear of Jack's extracurricular activities . . . but they'd have a hard time resisting this. And if she *did* go public, in a press conference format —"

"That's exactly what the director claims she's threatening." Bobby shook his head; he looked very young and very old all at once. "Why are these actors so difficult to deal with?"

"It's because they're damaged goods, Bob. They're talented, often gifted, but they live out of suitcases and pretend to be somebody they aren't, for a living. You know — like politicians?"

He showed no reaction, looking out at the ocean again. He wasn't known for his sense of humor.

"Think of them this way, Bob — they're carnies."

That did get a faint smile out of him. "You're saying Laurence Olivier and, uh, Peter O'Toole and Audrey Hepburn are *car-*

nival people."

We started walking along the shore back the way we'd come. We moved up onto the sound because we'd hit a patch of brown seaweed that the rising tide thoughtlessly littered.

"Yup. Hardworking folk in the entertainment business, but a breed apart." I painted the air with a hand. "Suppose you needed a new driver for the presidential limo. Would you choose a nice young chauffeur with a Secret Service background check? Or would you look for a guy with four teeth and six tattoos who hasn't shaved in three days and chain-smokes whose prior job was tending the Tilt-A-Whirl?"

Deadpan, he said, "Your point?"

Tough room.

"You tell your brother that there are plenty of nice young girls with nice young bodies who would be happy as hairy little clams to make his back *and* his front feel good. Secretaries and stewardesses and staffers, oh my. But fooling around with Hollywood's reigning sex symbol? That's reckless even for him."

For all of that effort, I got a simple nod.

Bobby had a reputation as the family's prude, the guy who wouldn't even stand for a dirty joke, who adored his wife and his ever-increasing family. And that was true, as far as it went.

But he had the same womanizing tendencies as his older and younger brothers — hard not to, when your old man defines marriage as, "Find a nice girl from a good family, have lots of babies, and screw as many other women as you like."

Robert Kennedy (before and after becoming attorney general) had affairs and one-night stands, but was never stupid or careless about it, and I found it ironic that a guy who messed around himself spent so much time cleaning up his two brothers' messes, never needing to clean up his own.

"Bob," I said, "Jack is going to screw himself out of office, if he doesn't start being careful. You're goddamn lucky nothing came out *last* election."

He kicked at the water, childishly. "You think I don't know that? Anyway, it's over. Jack and Marilyn haven't been together since after the Garden."

He meant the birthday bash at Madison Square Garden, weeks ago.

"It's . . . over?" I said.

"They had one last night together, and out."

"Does *she* know that?"

"She's been told. No uncertain terms."

"By you, or Jack?"

"By me. I told you, Nate, I'm handling this personally. Anyway, she hasn't been able to reach Jack. He, ah, changed his private number, and —"

"She was calling the *White* House?"

"Yes."

"Jack gave her a direct number to him there?"

"Yes, but it's been changed."

"How could he be so goddamn dumb?"

"Nate, it's Marilyn Monroe. What man doesn't want to talk to Marilyn Monroe?"

"Your brother *Jack,* at the moment. And talking isn't the issue."

He stopped, and the water sloshed us.

"Nate. Listen to me — I told her, in no uncertain terms —"

"What uncertain terms exactly?"

"I gave her both barrels. Told her that she was just another lay to Jack. This talk of being First Lady, and living at the White House and so on, it had to stop."

I felt like I'd been smacked in the face with a carp. "She was entertaining thoughts of becoming First Lady?"

"Ah, I'm uh . . . afraid so. She, ah, doesn't seem to know much about the Catholic Church."

"What the hell was she thinking?"

Of course, she did manage to marry the most famous ballplayer in America, and when she was done, snagged our greatest living playwright, though I have to admit I fell asleep in *Death of a Salesman.* Why *not* be Mrs. Jack Kennedy? If they thought Jackie's tour made a great TV special, wait till they got Marilyn's remake.

"Nate. We're *handling* this. *I've* handled it. That chapter is over, Jack and Marilyn."

Then why was Marilyn putting a bug on her own phones? And should I tell Bobby? Where did my loyalty lie?

What I heard myself saying was, "Telling Suzy Secretary she needs to know her place, or even giving her ten grand to go back to college, that's one thing. Literally fucking around with a famous actress like Marilyn . . . it's suicidal and it's stupid and it's arrogant."

He could see I was steamed and did something surprising. He touched my arm. "I don't disagree with you. But I can't blame Jack, really. She is a lovely girl."

"Really, Bob? Marilyn Monroe is a lovely girl? Stop the goddamn presses." I sighed. "I assume when Peter went to find you — wherever you hid out when I showed up unannounced — that he let you know why I came around this afternoon. And shared

120

what I told him — that Marilyn's new house has been bugged?"

"He did."

Like Lawford, he didn't seem unduly alarmed by this news.

"Well, here's the rest of it," I said. "So is *Peter's* house."

Bobby's eyes widened; he turned ashen, despite his tan. "Shit you say. For how long?"

"I don't know."

"Who by?"

"Now, that doesn't require much effort to figure, does it? You really need an expensive detective like me to figure that out?"

He said nothing.

"Giancana ring a bell, Bob? How about Hoffa? Same two people who're having *Marilyn* bugged, by the way, although the LAPD intel boys are in on that, too — *you've* got friends there; maybe they're surveilling her on your say-so."

He was shaking his head firmly. "No. If Chief Parker's boys are on it, they're not on it for us. Maybe the studio. One-industry town, you know."

"Know who *else* wants to hear Marilyn fornicate? Your friends at the CIA. Whether those spooks are in on the Lawford surveillance, too, who can say? I spotted a couple of panel trucks down the road that could be doing remote radio stuff."

He moved away from me and began pacing at the edge of the surf. From a distance it might have looked playful. Didn't look that way from where I'd backed off onto higher, drier sand.

Finally he stopped and looked up at me. "This is really, really unfortunate."

"One way to put it. Back in the service we'd say, 'Fucked up beyond all repair.' "

"Nate . . ."

"Of course, you could always have your friends in the dark suits sweep Pete's place for bugs" — I nodded up the hill where the men in black were keeping watch — "but if they're FBI, they may have already planted their own bugs. For J. Edgar's collection."

Bobby said nothing.

"There are tapes of your brother fucking Marilyn," I said softly, almost whispering, pointing toward the house where they'd done that, "that are probably already in the hands of Giancana and Hoffa. Bedsprings and moans and groans and love talk from two of the most famous, easily recognizable voices in America. It'll make a better party record than Shelley Berman or Lenny Bruce."

His forehead was knit in thought, eyes

sparking. "These are *illegal* wiretaps."

"Yeah, *there's* a threat that'll shake them in their shoes. What's that, a misdemeanor? This is *Giancana.* This is *Hoffa.* You know what that means, Bob. You know what this is really about."

Hands in his pockets, back to the sun, he nodded gravely.

"I told you," I said grimly, "and I told your brother, that when you deal with people as crooked as the Chicago boys, you *have* to play it straight. They gave you West Virginia. They gave you Illinois. And what have you given them?"

He was shaking his head, solemn as a gravestone. "There were no promises, Nate. They knew who they were dealing with."

"So did *you,* Bob! And I don't even want to *mention* Operation fucking Mongoose, because I wish I'd never heard of it."

He swallowed thickly. "That's good, because I don't want you mentioning it, either."

Operation Mongoose: the top secret CIA plan to use the mob to assassinate Fidel Castro. A civilian like me shouldn't know about it. And I wouldn't have, if I hadn't made the first contact with Giancana for them.

"You are in bed with these fuckers, Bob. You have been since 1960. And *how* many organized crime convictions did you rack up last year?"

Bobby flicked a smile — defiant. Proud. "Around a hundred."

"And this year?"

"We'll do better."

It wasn't just Jack who was arrogant. The only reason Bobby was attorney general was that Old Joe insisted, and the reason Joe insisted was that he knew there would formal actions claiming Jack stole the election, and no matter who bitched about Bobby being underqualified, and no matter how many hollered nepotism, Robert F. Kennedy would need to be in a position to shut those actions down.

Which he had.

I moved very close to him. "It's not a good sign that Hoffa and Giancana are together in this. Jimmy was very pissed indeed when Giancana raided Teamster coffers to help put your brother in office. For months and months, Jimmy didn't like Giancana very much for that, being a Nixon man and all. But now they're together again . . . isn't it grand? Ain't it touching? And guess what? They have a new hobby they share — hating you."

"Feeling's mutual."

"Yeah, play it tough, Bob. Jesus! This wholesale wiretapping, they've probably already gathered enough concrete evidence about Jack and Marilyn to blackmail you into oblivion. And if the mob and the Teamsters aren't enough, there's the FBI. Maybe that's why you're unconcerned — you're used to being blackmailed already, thanks to Mr. Hoover."

He gave me a smile that was supposed to calm me down. "Come on, Nate. Take it easy. What are you so angry about?"

"What *aren't* I angry about? You put *me* in bed with these guys, too. If Hoffa ever figures out I was on your team back in the old days, and not *his,* I'm fucking dead. And if Giancana gets irritated because the Kennedys have double-crossed his guinea ass? He may just look around for the middleman who helped set him up, and guess what? I'm fucking dead *again.*"

He spread his hands as if the ocean at his back were his. "Nate. Don't be ridiculous. You'll be fine. *We'll* be fine. I have the entire Justice Department behind me."

"It'll be behind you, all right. Your brother will be a one-term president, and you will be a private citizen, an out-of-work mouthpiece who'd better hope the Republicans have enough of their own dirty laundry so that you and Jack can ride into the sunset."

If his face had been any longer, it would

be melting. "You know I respect you, Nate. There aren't many people I would let talk to me this way."

"There aren't many people who know where this many bodies are buried. I respect you, too, Bob. Just don't dump dandruff on me and tell me it's Christmas."

He put a hand on my shoulder — a fairly uncommon gesture, coming from him. "Nate — I'll do right by you."

Our shadows were longer and darker, and magic hour was dwindling.

"Do right by Marilyn, Bob. She's a good kid." I pawed the air. "Screw that, she's a *woman,* an intelligent, talented woman, but like all of us carnival people, she's damaged. Just don't you damage her any further."

He moved even closer and, at his most intimate, said, "Everything'll work out fine. You have to trust me on that."

"I know I do," I said. "What other choice do I have?"

"Nate," he said, and he tilted his head and gave me that shy puppy-dog smile. When he held out his hand, you know I had to shake it.

Then I headed up the slope of the beach, toward my car, but stopping where I'd left my shoes and socks. I was sitting on the sand, putting them on, and Bobby was waving as he headed back to Lawfords.

Never did get a dinner invite.

CHAPTER 7

Marilyn Monroe's chief malady, insomnia, has never afflicted me. I'm one of those lucky asleep-when-my-head-hits-the-pillow types. But last night, I had tossed and turned, and been up and down, pacing about inside and out of my Beverly Hills Hotel bungalow. This must have been what life was like for people with a real conscience.

The only conscience I normally relied on was an ancient nine-millimeter Browning automatic, which I kept well-oiled and in good repair. It had a special resonance for me — the gun my radical leftist father killed himself with on the occasion of my making it onto the graft-happy Chicago PD back in the late '20s. I rarely carried it anymore, and didn't even have a shoulder holster along. Right now the nine-millimeter was serving as a decorative touch on the night-stand next to the little radio alarm clock and two empty Coke bottles. The caffeine in that soda pop had been an accomplice in my sleepless night.

Conflict of interest didn't begin to cover my situation. Marilyn was my client, and while I hadn't betrayed the specific job I was doing for her — tapping her own phones — I had passed along to Bobby (and to a lesser degree Lawford) certain incidental information I'd obtained.

Specifically, that I had learned from Hollywood's favorite electronic eavesdropper, Roger Pryor, that everybody and his duck were already bugging Marilyn's little Fifth Helena hacienda. But I hadn't shared that information with my client. On the other hand, she hadn't told me she was planning to be First Lady.

Marilyn had attracted the attention of my friend Bobby Kennedy's worst enemies, including Sam Giancana and Jimmy Hoffa. Over the years, I had gone to considerable lengths to make Giancana think I was, if not a friend, at least not an adversary, just as Hoffa remained unaware I'd secretly been in Bobby's employ.

Added to that were the contacts I'd arranged between the Kennedy and Giancana camps to help get Jack elected. Plus, of course, facilitating deals with various devils in an effort to remove the one mutual enemy of the Kennedys and the mob — the prime minister of Cuba, a certain Fidel Castro.

My involvement in the Castro affair had been limited, if pivotal. The idea was that mobsters — not just Giancana of Chicago but Santos Trafficante of Miami and Carlos Marcello of Louisiana — still had people on the ground in Cuba, despite having had their casinos and drug-running operations shut down by the new (and very Communist) regime. So getting close enough to Castro to permanently remove him from office shouldn't have been tough.

Only it hadn't happened yet, despite some farcical attempts including poisoned food, lethal fountain pens, and exploding cigars — apparently somebody thought the way to take down a Marxist was to employ Marx Brothers techniques. In the meantime, less amusing events had challenged Cuba–United States relations, like the Bay of Pigs fiasco and the missile crisis. All in all, I was happy not to have played a bigger part in any of these travesties and tragedies.

Only now my unhappy role as an occasional intermediary between the warring Kennedy and organized crime camps had been stirred up to the surface by Jack

Kennedy's frat-boy lust, giving me a sleepless night worthy of the object of that lust.

At least Hoffa was safely in Detroit and couldn't summon me to his presence. With Giancana you never knew, since he had his own Hollywood fixation and was lately banging the cutest of the cloying McGuire Sisters, Phyllis.

I don't know when I finally got to sleep, but I didn't wake up till almost noon, so I skipped breakfast and went straight for lunch at the Polo Lounge. By the time I parked the Jag downtown in the garage near our office, it was pushing 2:00 P.M.

At the Bradbury Building, on the southeast corner of Third and Broadway, we had expanded to four suites on the fifth floor. Two were for our agents (the current term for operative), another for my partner, Fred Rubinski (who ran the branch), with my office in back and a conference room in front. We'd done away with the open bullpen approach for our eight male and two female agents, who used cubicles now, to give clients some semblance of privacy.

We certainly could have afforded more modern accommodations — the five-story brownstone dated to 1893 — but I dug the old digs. In fact, the baroque Bradbury was so perfect for our line of work that Hollywood kept using it for crime pictures. We had rented out my office, which sometimes sat vacant for months anyway, for half a dozen films, including *I, the Jury* and *Double Indemnity* — the latter a laugh because my partner looked like a bald, slightly less homely Edward G. Robinson.

Directors and cameramen loved the interior of the Bradbury with its ornamental wrought-iron stairwells and balconies, globed light fixtures, open brick-and-tile corridors, and caged elevators with all their ancient mechanical innards on display. My favorite touch didn't show up in black-and-white (they never seemed to shoot color here): a huge skylight that for much of the day would bounce golden white light off the echoey lobby's glazed floor.

I looked like a business executive in my lightweight gray Botany 500 suit and coffee-colored Churchill snap-brim; but the ancient Bradbury almost made me feel, at least momentarily, like a private eye again.

We were looking to add two more agents, and Fred had been interviewing prospects all morning. When I got there, he corralled me to join in on four more interviews, after which we sat in my office and reviewed the notes and files on the candidates and settled on two, neither ex-LAPD. One was late of the military police and the other had been on the San Diego force. We had standards.

I was behind my desk, and the windows were open, except for one hugging a bulky air conditioner, currently silent since the day was nicely cool. The office reminded me a little of my first office at Van Buren and Plymouth in Chicago. All that was missing was the El noise.

Cannonball Fred, in a dapper brown suit and brown-and-yellow striped tie, not narrow enough to suit current fashion, was plopped on my couch blending in with the brown leather. His feet were up on the armrest and he was contemplating smoke rings he was blowing, courtesy of a fragrant cigar.

"Somebody should kill that fuckin' Castro," he said.

I blinked. "What?"

His eyes locked onto me, unblinking in his homely mug. "Do you know how much these smuggled Havanas cost me? Ten bucks apiece!"

"I'm glad we're doing well enough to support your habit."

He blew another ring and watched it dissipate. "You have business left to do out here? If you're in the mood, I can line you up with a famous client or two. They all

133

want you on the case, since that *Life* magazine spread."

"No," I said. "I'm already doing a little job for Marilyn."

"Miss Monroe?" His grunt had something lascivious in it. "You've always had a thing for her."

"Who doesn't? I'm using Roger Pryor on it."

"Wanna tell me about it?"

"Naw. Nothing. Wants her phones tapped. She's having studio trouble."

Fred's smirk gave him a froggy look. "Yeah, so I been reading. Those cocksuckers in Fox publicity are tearing her down better than they built her up in the first place."

"My money's on Marilyn."

"I dunno. Never bet against utter bastards."

He grunted again as he hauled his squat self off the couch, and shooed cigar smoke toward an open window. I didn't mind the expensive smell and told him so.

"So when are you heading back?" he asked, at the door to the conference room.

"Not sure. Few days maybe."

"If you change your mind, I can always use you around. Just take meetings with our more illustrious clients, then we'll turn the real work over to the youngsters."

"I'll let you know," I said.

Fred nodded and trundled out, shutting the pebble-glassed door behind him.

I guess I sat there for half an hour trying to figure out if there was anything I should be doing for Marilyn, and not getting any farther than I had in my insomniac state last night. Maybe it was time to book my flight back to the land of stockyards and deep-dish pizza. But first I reached for the phone to call my ex-wife, and arrange to see Sam one more time before heading home.

The girl manning our phones next door informed me there was no answer, and I was hanging up, glumly, when two big guys in dark brown suits came in, hats in hand. They were both at least six foot, and together were working on a quarter ton, beefy but not fat, with perpetual five o'clock shadows. They had frequently broken noses and ears that stopped short of cauliflower but showed signs of battering.

Yet I had a hunch neither one had ever been a prizefighter. And I didn't suppose they were extras from some crime picture being shot here, either, wandered in looking for the catering table.

You told them apart mostly by their hair

— one had a butch and a bright expression while the other had what the Vitalis commercials called greasy kid stuff, slicked back. And dumb eyes.

The bright-looking one stepped forward.

"We didn't make an appointment, Mr. Heller," he said apologetically.

His voice was surprisingly mellow, just as his suit was surprisingly well-pressed and not cheap. His friend with the dumb eyes was similarly well-attired.

"No breach of protocol, gents," I said, rising behind my desk. "I don't have a secretary out here. This is just an office I use when I'm in town. What can I do for you?"

The leader said, "We wondered if you would be available sometime this afternoon to meet with somebody."

His associate chimed in: "We can wait till five, should you want."

They looked like thugs, yes, but nicely dressed thugs, and if I was being taken for an old-fashioned ride, this was the most polite attempt ever.

"Would you like to sit down, boys?" I asked, gesturing to the client chairs. "And tell me about it?"

"No thanks," the leader said. "We got a parking place right out front. We can wait."

"Fellas, I'm confused. . . ."

The wide forehead beneath the butch crinkled. "Uh, could I ask you something, Mr. Heller?"

"Okay."

"Is it safe to talk in here?"

Truthfully, at this point, I wasn't sure. I motioned him over with a curled finger, and — after tearing off a page with a couple of scribbled phone numbers — pushed my scratch pad across, then pointed to the pencil nearby.

He nodded, took it, and on the pad wrote two words: Mr Hoffa.

So much for safely in Detroit.

I motioned for him to return the pencil, he did, and I wrote: Wants to see me?

And he nodded. The guy with the dumb eyes was frowning, as if this entire exchange had been something mysterious.

Did I mention I didn't even have my shoulder holster along? Not that it mattered, since my nine-millimeter had moved from the nightstand to between shirts in my suitcase, to prevent alarm on the part of Beverly Hills Hotel housekeeping.

"I'll be glad to go," I said, getting out from behind the desk, "right now. But you don't have to chauffeur me. I have my own wheels."

The two men exchanged troubled glances.

I said, "You can either write down the address where I'm supposed to go, or I'll come around to where you're parked and you can lead me."

The guy with dumb eyes was shaking his head, not at me but at his associate, who was thinking it over.

"Fine," the leader said finally, ignoring his associate's vote. He got the pad and pencil again. "I'm gonna write it down, but you might wanna follow us over, like you said. We should escort you up to the suite."

"All right," I said.

I was still enough of a private eye, I guess, to resist getting in a car with a couple of muscle boys, even if they weren't going to bother pulling a gun.

As it turned out, the pair were probably just being helpful, since the suite in question was at the Ambassador Hotel, which was home to over twelve hundred rooms. The massive, many-winged hotel had been refurbished a few years ago, and modernized, but it still resembled a palace that had somehow been dropped from the sky near Wilshire Boulevard, on a lawn as well-manicured and vast as Forest Lawn.

From the parking lot I was ushered like a dignitary with bodyguards through a massive lobby awash in yellow, with pillars, leather furnishings, and scattered ferns, all set off by red-and-black carpeting. Fairly elegant surroundings for the roughneck boss of the Teamsters union, but Jimmy never liked to deny himself, when he was on the road, anyway.

The room at the end of a golden hall on an upper floor was a case in point — the presidential suite, with richer shades of gold and elegant French gilded furnishings and creamy wall-to-wall carpet. In a massive parlor with a chandelier and plush drapes, and a stereo and television that shared an improbably antique-looking cabinet, a kidney-shaped writing table had been turned into a paper-strewn desk by the small, broad-shouldered man at work there.

Well-tanned, about fifty, Jimmy Hoffa was barking into the phone, "I can't get away now. It'll have to wait. . . . You want me to send *who?* No way. That son of a bitch could start a war in a vacant lot. . . . I'll be there tomorrow. Do what the fuck you have to! You're not a child!"

He said a quick good-bye, all but slammed the phone down, then looked up, grinned at me, waved my chaperones away (they went out), and rose to his full five feet five, extending his open hands as if in welcome to a prodigal child.

"Nate Heller!" he said, moving like a friendly gorilla across the expanse of carpet to meet me halfway. We shook hands, and his grip, as usual, was a vise. "How the hell long has it been, a year, two years?"

"You know what they say, Jim, about time passing fast when you're having fun."

"I don't believe in fun. I believe in hard work, and to me I guess *that's* fun. Let's see if we can find someplace comfortable to sit in this dump."

He was wearing a nice enough blue gabardine suit, off the rack, but his trousers were highwater-style, exposing the white socks that were part of his everyman persona ("Colored socks make me sweat"). His dark hair was glossy, cut short, standing up like the quills of a pissed-off porcupine. There was something vaguely oriental about his rough-hewn, heart-shaped face, and that he exuded that mystical quality called charisma could not be denied.

I was half German Jew and half mick, and he was Dutch-Irish, which from the start had given us a bond. And my father's unionist activities had been a big plus, back when I went to work for the Teamster boss.

Jimmy was your classic roughneck made good. His coal-miner pop had died young, and his mother had polished radiator caps in an auto plant. By sixteen he was earning fifteen bucks a week unloading fruits and vegetables for a grocery chain, getting paid only for time worked and not time waiting for freight trains. He addressed that with a wildcat strike, earned the attention of the Teamsters, and had been on that payroll ever since.

The Teamsters was the only life he knew — he even met his wife on a picket line. In 1957 he became president of the International Brotherhood of Teamsters, replacing Dave Beck, who got busted for tax evasion. Hoffa, who never drove a truck, more than doubled the IBT membership, bringing in everybody from cafeteria workers to zookeepers. But the AFL-CIO expelled the union because of Hoffa's ties to organized crime.

These ties I'd known about for a long time — the guy Hoffa put in charge of the union's pension fund, Allen Dorfman, was Outfit through his stepfather, Red Dorfman, a onetime Capone crony and current Giancana one.

The McClellan Committee, with Bobby Kennedy as its chief counsel and John Kennedy as a member, had made a crusade out of nailing Hoffa over his mob connections. They'd gotten indictments on charges of trying to steal committee documents and bribing a staff lawyer — I'd been in the thick of that, but Hoffa hadn't known I wasn't on his side.

Anyway, somehow Hoffa beat it, though Bobby had been so confident about his case, he bragged he'd jump off the Capitol dome if he lost. Jimmy won. And sent Bobby a parachute.

"Tell me about Sam, Nate," he said. "Did he play football last year?"

And we talked about my son, and my problems with Sam's mother. One of Jimmy's best qualities was his ability to remember people he'd met and spoken to at any length, and care (or anyway seem to care) about everybody and their families and problems — health, financial, what have you.

If you walked around with him in union circles in Any Town USA, he would stop and talk on a first-name basis with dozens of rank-and-file members. With anybody in leadership, he had personal histories down cold, chapter and verse.

"What brings you to Tinseltown, Jim?"

We were sitting on a spectacularly uncomfortable brocade couch.

"Hell, Nate, I been on the road all this month and it's just starting. Negotiating

God knows how many contracts, dealing with this latest bullshit case against me, this Florida thing? And, of course, lining up support for the big contract."

"What contract is that?"

He cackled. His rather tiny eyes danced in the wide, rugged face. "The contract that has Bobby Kennedy's asshole puckering! We've been working for months, for years, on a nationwide master contract, a bargaining agreement that'll stop commerce in this country with a single strike order."

"A single phone call from you, you mean?"

He grinned like a demented pixie. "That's right. What do you think your old man would think about *that?*"

Jimmy always talked about my father like he'd known him. And I never broke it to Jim that my father would likely have considered him a monster and a disgrace to the unionist cause.

On the other hand, it was hard to deny Jimmy Hoffa was an effective labor leader, and that he'd negotiated generous contracts for his members.

"Listen," he said, and he leaned over and patted my knee. "I know you're a busy guy, important guy out here, not just in Chicago, these days. I'm proud of you, kid."

We were roughly the same age, but he'd

always called me "kid."

"Thanks," I said.

He hunched his shoulders in a Cagney-like way, a recurring mannerism. "Thing is, I just don't want you to think I'm sticking my nose where it don't belong."

"How so, Jim?"

His eyes all but disappeared into folds of flesh. "I need a personal assurance from you. That is, of course, if I'm not overstepping the bounds of our friendship."

"Oh-kay. . . ."

The eyes tightened. They were hard and cold now. "I know you ran into somebody, the other day, who is doing some work for me."

I shouldn't have been surprised by this. What else would Roger Pryor do but run to Jimmy? What would I have done in his situation?

"Roger, you mean," I said.

"Yeah. You recommended him to me, or anyway your partner, Rubinski, did. I used Pryor a couple of times now and he seems reliable. He *is* reliable, Nate?"

"Far as it goes. He's for hire, like all of us."

He hitched his shoulders. "Well, Pryor told me you saw where he was parked and looked over his setup and guessed right away that he was, uh, doing a little eaves-dropping on a certain female, who is I understand a friend and maybe a client of yours."

"Marilyn is a friend, and a client."

"Roger says he made you aware of the fact that our glorious president is fucking her. And I think maybe his brother is, too."

I blinked. "What, you mean Ted?"

"No! Bobby."

My head bobbed back, like I'd taken a punch. Then I almost laughed. "That's just silly, Jim. Bob's a family man. You know that."

"You want to see the list I got of the women he's screwed since January?"

"No thanks." Knowing this was hateful wishful thinking on his part, I said, "So then — you got Marilyn and Bobby on tape, too?"

His face scrunched into a cagey mask. "Maybe. I don't think that's really your business."

He'd brought it up.

But why press it, and anyway, this was horseshit. I just wasn't in a position to tell Jimmy what I knew to be true — that Bobby's only role here was to shut down the JFK/MM affair. A typical Kennedy family hatchet-man assignment.

Jimmy waved a hand, smiled, shrugged. "Let's not get off the track, kid. You want a beer or a Coke or anything? There's a wet bar, too."

"No thanks, Jim."

He leaned forward — what was that, Jade East? "The question I want to ask, one friend to another, is whether you have told your client what you know."

"You mean, have I told Marilyn that her house is bugged?"

Anxiety clenched his features. "That her house is bugged, yes."

"No. It doesn't strictly speaking have anything to do with the job she's hired me to do, and Roger is a colleague and, out of professional courtesy . . . no. I haven't told her."

But I might. Hadn't decided. Had been all up night thinking about it, but hadn't decided. . . .

Jimmy was grinning his Chinaman grin again. "That's good, Nate, that's good. Now here's what I want you to do, kid. I want you to stay in touch with little Miss Seven Year Itch. I want you to stay friendly."

"Well, we are friends. But I'm heading back to Chicago."

He waved a finger, like a cross schoolmaster. "No. You are not. You are staying out

146

here and cozying up to that immoral little broad and seeing what she has to say about Bobby and his cunt-hound brother."

"Jim — you've got the place bugged already. . . ."

His voice, already hard, hardened, and words machine-gunned at me: "Listen, she's not stupid. If she's having her own phone bugged — yeah, Roger told me; don't be naive — then she knows there's a possibility of being eavesdropped upon. So she probably will spend time with you elsewhere. Maybe at your bungalow at the Beverly Hills Hotel. Maybe outside her place at her swimming pool. But if in some part of the house that ain't bugged, like where the washing machines are, she starts talking while they're churning? She spills anything incriminating about Bobby and Jack, I want to know."

"Jim — please. She's my friend. Like you're my friend."

"Some things are bigger than other things." His mouth moved as if he was tasting something foul. "These two privileged pricks, never did an honest day's work in their lives, have singled *me* out as some kind of fucking cancer, rich kid bastards. And that cocky little shit, Bobby? You've seen him go out of his way to embarrass me in public, you know how he dogs my ass, it's a goddamn *vendetta,* and it's got to stop. It is *going* to stop." He worked at removing his scowl, and shrugged. "This is a harmless thing, anyway, what I'm suggesting."

"Harmless?"

"Yeah. We get information on what kind of sorry immoral lowlifes these two brothers are, and we either embarrass their ass out of office, or they straighten up and honor agreements and deals they have made with certain individuals, myself included. You know a little about the Castro situation. Was I a good American on that one, Nate, or was I good American?"

"You were a good American," I said.

"You should *hope* this works because otherwise it could get ugly." Very quietly, he said, "I damn near killed Bobby's punk ass a couple years back, remember?"

I remembered. I'd stopped it. But Jimmy didn't know that.

His upper lip peeled back and his smile was a skull's. "Next time I'm going after the brother."

The casualness of that was chilling. "But why Jack? Bobby's the one causing the trouble. Bobby's the one you hate."

"You gotta cut off the head of the snake to get rid of the rattle, kid. That lecherous liar Jack, if he would do us the favor of ceasing to exist? You *really* think a President *Lyndon Johnson's* gonna hang onto Bobby Kennedy as his attorney general?"

He straightened without standing, digging his hand in his pocket. Christ, was he going for a gun or a knife or something?

No — he was peeling hundreds off a fat roll. "Here. Off the books, the way we both like it. A thousand as a retainer do the trick?"

The son of a bitch was going to pay me to betray a client, and a woman I very much liked. I should have shoved the bills down his damn throat.

"Thanks, Jim," I said, and found a place for them in my wallet. "Anything else?"

Chapter 8

So I decided to stay on a while in Hollywood. My partner Fred was thrilled at the prospect, and my son Sam seemed pleased, too, though neither of them factored into my decision.

Keeping Jimmy Hoffa happy did. With surveillance in play, I'd need to see Marilyn a few times to justify the thousand I'd taken from the labor leader.

Not that I'd wanted to take it, nor did I have any intention of betraying Marilyn to Hoffa or anybody else. I'd been provided the number of an LA attorney to whom I was to file my reports — these would be bogus, of course, but I'd have to make a few. The point was to stay alive, and seem to be cooperating.

Beyond that, I wanted to get Marilyn alone, or anyway in some area of her home where a conversation would not make it onto tape — by the pool or in her garden, maybe.

The morning after the Ambassador con-fab, Roger Pryor put in *my* phone tap, Marilyn having arranged for both Mrs. Murray and handyman Norman to be away. So early that afternoon, I called her private line — if a line tapped by its owner and Christ knew how many others might still be called private — and said I'd like to stop by and check up on the work my subcontractor had done.

"Oh, please come, Nate!" a very upbeat Marilyn said. "I have so much to tell you."

"Things are going well, then?"

"Wait till you hear."

This time when I tooled the Jag down the dead end of Fifth Helena and pulled up to the double wooden gates, they stood open, and I was able to roll into the small court-yard and park next to a two-tone green Dodge and a BMW. The latter wasn't Mari-lyn's — she drove a Caddy, which was prob-ably in the free-standing garage — so she had a visitor. Last time I'd come casually dressed, but the lady of the house was a cli-ent now, so today I was in a light-olive Cricketeer suit with a darker green tie and yellow button-down shirt, though I dis-pensed with a hat.

The ocean breeze was ruffling the stand of eucalyptus trees that made the second line of defense after the two-foot-thick, seven-foot-high walls. I went up the flagstone walk toward the whitewashed, scarlet bougainvillea–splashed exterior of Marilyn's Spanish-style hideaway.

When I knocked at the front door, the dowdy little bespectacled housekeeper — in another shapeless housedress, this one with amoeba-like blobs of yellow and green on white — looked up at me with no recognition. She said nothing, as if her bug-eyed stare behind the cat's-eye glasses could catch enough sun to reduce me to ash.

"Nate Heller?" I said. "Miss Monroe is expecting me."

"I'll ask," she said, and shut the door on me.

I sighed. If they ever remade *Rebecca,* this broad was a shoo-in for Mrs. Danvers.

At least a minute passed before the housekeeper returned, her expression consisting of equal parts contempt and lack of interest.

"She's just finishing up with Dr. Greenson," she said. "Would you like to wait inside?"

No, I figured I'd climb a tree and watch for ships.

"That would be nice," I said.

She deposited me on a white-upholstered

affair better suited for a formal living room than the rest of the living room's studiously casual if arty Mexican theme. I had a nice view of the fireplace and an expressionist painting of a seated guy playing the guitar.

I only waited fifteen minutes or so — where Marilyn was concerned that hardly counted — before she entered from the direction of the dining room. In a white short-sleeve blouse, blue jeans, and bare feet, she looked about sixteen — platinum hair lightly brushed, just a touch of lipstick, freckles on display.

She was leading an average-sized, slender guy, maybe fifty, who wore a dark sport coat, narrow gray-and-black striped tie, and gray knit slacks. His hair was white and thinning but his mustache was black and full; his oval face was home to the kind of sleepy eyes that don't miss a thing.

"Romy," a beaming Marilyn said to him, "this is a dear friend of mine — Nate Heller! He's been in *Life* magazine. That 'Private Eye to the Stars' you've heard about."

She made making *Life* sound like a big deal — she'd been on the cover, what, a dozen times? I got two pages.

Dr. Ralph Greenson's smile was as deceptively lazy as his eyes. I'd gotten up off the sofa and met them halfway and he was leaning forward to shake my hand.

"Pleasure meeting you, Mr. Heller," he said, with a faint Viennese accent; it was like Central Casting sent him to audition for psychiatrist. "I have indeed heard of you."

"And I'll do you the favor of not calling you the 'Shrink to the Stars,' " I said.

"I hope you're not investigating *me,* Mr. Heller," he said, and the smile broadened.

"Well, Romy," Marilyn said, "it's only fair — you've been playing detective inside my mind, for how long?"

She seemed to be enjoying the sight of two of her men meeting for the first time, her hands behind her as she rocked on her heels, a happy kid.

"I'm just doing a little job for Marilyn," I explained. "This Fox nonsense."

He nodded, frowning. "Ah, I'm afraid I know more of that deplorable matter than you might think."

Marilyn was nodding, too. "Romy's been my chief go-between with the studio. Practically acting as my agent. Tell him what they did, Romy."

Greenson sighed. "I was negotiating with the studio heads in good faith when, behind our backs, they were already drawing up the dismissal papers, and filing the lawsuit against Marilyn —"

"Half a million," she cut in. "Did I mention that? That they're suing *me?*"

"It was in the papers," I said.

A phone began ringing elsewhere in the house, but our hostess didn't acknowledge it. My God, she looked pretty; so bright-eyed and girlish.

The psychiatrist continued: "Here I was, arranging terms for Marilyn to return to the set, with assurances that I could help her get there every day and on time, and they were acting in the *worst* faith imaginable." He shook his head. "That foul media campaign of theirs — they were preparing to launch that, even as we were negotiating. Reprehensible."

It didn't seem my place, or maybe just not the right moment, to ask what the hell a shrink was doing acting as an agent, or how the hell he could assure Fox his patient could be on set.

The stout housekeeper materialized at my side. How did she *do* that?

"Telephone, dear," she told her charge. "It's Mr. Rudin."

"Thank you, Mrs. Murray," Marilyn said with a smile. Was there something strained in it?

Then the housekeeper was gone, and

Marilyn was making an apologetic gesture, moving off herself, heading toward the bedrooms, saying, "I have to take that. Romi, thank you for coming over!"

"Always my pleasure," he said.

When we were alone, I asked the doctor, "Do you have another appointment to get to, or could we talk?"

"We can talk. I usually spend several hours with Marilyn, but today only took half an hour. Come with me."

Greenson seemed very much at home in Marilyn's place, and he showed me to the sunroom, where he fixed himself a Scotch and soda from the liquor cart (I passed) and settled onto a cushioned wicker chair while I took the wicker love seat opposite.

The space was bright, thanks to the uncovered windows, with a view of the kidney-shaped pool, where the blue surface twinkled like a Hollywood special effect. Two walnut bookcases were home to an eclectic collection of books, everything from Hemingway and Camus to Thurber and *The Little Engine That Could*. Mexican touches prevailed here, as well — an Aztec tapestry on one wall, and wirework musicians in sombreros on another.

"What kind of job are you doing for Marilyn, Mr. Heller?"

"She's my client. That's confidential. Sort of like doctor and patient?"

He upturned a palm. "You were the one who suggested we talk, Mr. Heller. Anyway, I'm merely interested in knowing if you feel she is displaying any . . . how shall I put it?"

"Mental illness? Symptoms of paranoia?"

"Call it signs of stress."

"Working for Twentieth Century–Fox, who wouldn't? This is only the second time I've seen her lately, but she seems fine, particularly considering what the papers are saying about her."

"She presented you as a friend."

"I met her in 1954. Another Chicagoan, Ben Hecht, introduced us — he was ghosting her autobiography, which was never published." I shrugged. "I've done the odd job for her, time to time."

"Finding her father, for example?"

I grinned at him. "If you're going to use information you garnered from sessions with your patient, Doc, I'll have to cry foul."

He patted the air with his free hand; his drink was in the other. "Perhaps I overstepped, Mr. Heller. It's just . . . I feel confident, based upon what I do know about you, never mind the source, that you have Marilyn's welfare at heart."

"Swell. She obviously thinks the world of

you. What's this 'Romy' stuff?"

His smile made the mustache twitch. "My real name is Romeo Greenschpoon. Anglicizing one's name is very common out here, of course. But I changed mine, legally, long before I came west."

"Where, at Ellis Island?"

"No. I'm a Brooklyn-born Russian Jew, Mr. Heller. But I studied for many years in Vienna, and that explains the accent."

Or the affectation.

"Greenschpoon is a mouthful," I admitted, "and I guess if I had a wife and she was going to a shrink named Romeo, it might give me pause. Probably a good call, changing it."

His smile froze. He wasn't sure what to make of that.

"Tell me," I said, "if *I'm* not overstepping — am I right in thinking that Marilyn's doing pretty well right now? For the blow she got, from those pricks at the studio, she ought to be reeling. But she seems to be thriving."

Nodding, he said, "She is. She's in excellent shape. One of her problems, and this I think is fair for us to discuss, is that for a long time she was seeing many doctors — most of whom did not know of one another's existence."

"So she could get prescriptions from a raft of them. It's an old dodge."

He nodded grimly, then gave me a half smile that seemed almost a smirk. "Right now she has only two doctors, her internist, with whom I work closely, and myself. I completely weaned her off all of these drugs — my God, Mr. Heller, when we first met, she was on a laundry list of medications . . . Demerol, Sodium Pentothal, phenobarbital, Amytal, Nembutal . . . and currently she is clean. She uses a little chloral hydrate for her insomnia problem, but that's all."

"This internist — what's he giving her? I assume you know."

"Right now, Dr. Engelberg is giving her injections of vitamins and liver extract. This is strictly for her sinusitis." He shook his head. "You know those bastards at the studio, they were giving her what they call 'hot shots' — God knows what was in them, methamphetamines certainly."

"During the shooting of *Something's Got to Give,* you mean?"

"Yes." His expression turned bitter. "I was out of the country during much of the filming, unfortunately, having booked speaking engagements far in advance. I delivered her into their arms clean, and they turned her dirty with drugs again."

"But now?"

He sipped his Scotch, shrugged. "She's fine. She has amazing recuperative powers, this child."

"Marilyn told me she was blessed with a rare ability to go cold turkey without suffering the usual heebie-jeebies."

The half smile again, and it was definitely a smirk. "I might put it somewhat differently, Mr. Heller, but yes. She's a remarkable woman."

"Yet she needs a shrink."

"She needs psychotherapy, yes she does."

"And you're providing it. You make a habit of making house calls to your famous patients?"

"No, Marilyn is a special case."

"How special?"

"You know I can't get into that. I *will* tell you, Mr. Heller, that I have made myself available to her on a twenty-four-hour basis."

"Really? How often do you see her?"

"As often as every other day."

"My God, can even *Marilyn Monroe* afford that?"

"She cannot afford to do otherwise. Mr. Heller . . . she is not just a patient to me. She's like . . . a member of the family."

That was weird.

"So then what's the family rate?"

He thought about whether he wanted to answer that. After several long seconds, he did: "I charge her half of what I regularly bill my patients."

He was making me work for it.

"What's your *regular* rate?"

"One hundred dollars an hour."

"So what's Marilyn's normal monthly bill?"

"Really, Mr. Heller. . . ."

"Okay. That *was* overstepping."

But if he was seeing her every other day, for say two hours a session, that worked out to something like fifteen hundred bucks a month.

Suddenly Marilyn was leaning against the door frame. "So *this* is where you boys went to. Getting along?"

"Famously," I said, and gave her a reassuring smile.

Greenson said, "Your friend Mr. Heller has been probing to see what makes me tick. He would make an excellent psychoanalyst himself."

"We're both snoops, Doc," I said with a shrug.

Marilyn smiled at that, but I could see in her eyes that she was wondering if we'd been trading secrets. Her secrets.

The psychiatrist rose. "I should be getting back."

As we moved through the kitchen, where Greenson placed his empty glass in the sink, Marilyn glanced my way.

"Dr. Greenson mostly works out of his home, you know. You should see it! It's a dream. Like a hacienda out of some wonderful old movie."

"Really?"

Did that explain the house she'd chosen for herself?

Marilyn stayed framed in the doorway while I spoke briefly with Greenson as I walked him to his BMW.

"Our approaches may differ," I told him quietly, "but I'm going to take you at your word — that we both want what's best for Marilyn."

"I hope so, Mr. Heller," he said. He offered his hand, and I shook it. "I hope so."

Inside, Marilyn hooked her arm in mine and whispered, "Do you want to inspect your accomplice's gadget?"

"Sure," I said.

She took me to the fitting room, shut us inside, and pointed to the phones. "They don't look any different, do they?"

"No, they wouldn't. The gizmo's inside."

"But look at this."

She walked me to a small closet. Several hatboxes were stacked on a high shelf. On tiptoes, she handed them to me, one by one, and I stacked them on the floor. When she was done, she had exposed a tape recorder.

"The reels aren't spinning now," she said, pointing up at the machine. "Because it's voice-activated, your man said. He was very nice."

"Yeah, Roger's okay." I thought he'd be operating from his van, but didn't say anything. What she said next explained it, though.

"He said he could make the recordings," she said, "from a distance? But I wanted to be able to listen to them myself. And collect them myself."

I had no comment. I helped her put the hatboxes back in place and she gave me a wicked little smile.

"This spy stuff is fun, isn't it?"

"Not really," I said.

I crooked my finger and she frowned, but followed me as I led her through her house and back into the living room, where I slid open a glass door onto the pool area. She stayed right with me as I slid the door shut.

I pointed to the black wrought-iron chairs on the opposite side of the pool, she nodded, and we went over there.

She perched on the edge of one chair, her arms draped between her open legs, hands folded. "You're acting funny."

"Marilyn, something's occurred to me."

"What has?"

"If you've thought about tapping your phone, somebody else could have done the same."

Her eyes widened as her forehead tightened. "Did your associate say they were *already* tapped?"

"No. I'm just saying . . . if things are serious enough in your life, for *you* to take this step . . . somebody else could have taken that step, too . . . only not with your best interests in mind."

"You think my phones may already be tapped?"

"It's possible. And you can just about bug an entire house through nothing but the phones. I mean, you can hear not just phone conversations but things being said in the room, even other rooms."

Alarmed, she whispered, "Are you saying my house is bugged?"

"I'm just saying it's possible."

"God." Her hands were fists now, tiny and white. "What should I do?"

"Just take care about what you say, and where you say it. If you're going to have a conversation that nobody else should hear — such as this one — then find a safe place to talk."

She pointed to the cement at her feet. "Like here."

"Like out by the pool. In your yard. Away from this house."

She thought about that. The furrow between her brow only made her look prettier.

"All right," she said. "That's good advice."

"Yes it is. Now. Is there anything else you want to share with me?"

"Huh?"

"Anything else going on in your life that worries you."

"Besides the studio."

"Besides the studio." If I'd sat forward any farther, I'd have fallen off the chair. "Marilyn, I'm somebody you can tell things to. I'm not Greenson, that's not what I'm talking about — I don't need to hear chapter and verse about your childhood. But stuff going on today? I can protect you in ways your good doctor can't."

She smiled. "You mean, because you're a big bad private eye."

"Yeah. I'm not as young as I used to be. But I am still big and bad. If you need protection — and I don't mean to scare you, honey, but if you need a guy with a gun?

I'm that guy."

She frowned again, more confused than worried or scared. "You have a . . . gun?"

I smiled, shook my head. "Not on me. But yes. Back in my bungalow at the Beverly Hills."

Her chin was crinkling with amusement. "So I'm safe, if somebody attacks me . . . in your bungalow at the Beverly Hills."

"Yeah. Unless, of course, it's me who's attacking you. But I promise only to do that in the most friendly way."

She laughed softly. Touched my face with her hand. "You don't have to attack me. Just ask, Nate. Just ask."

I kissed the hand and gave it back to her.

"I'm serious," I said.

"You're sweet." She shook her head and the tousled white-blondeness bounced and her smile was bigger and better than in CinemaScope. "But Nate — don't you know that everything's turning around for me? Have you *seen* the interviews?"

"Yeah. That was a great one you gave Flo Kilgore. I loved where you said when a studio executive gets a cold, he can call in sick, but not a star. That you'd like to see a top executive act in a comedy with a temperature and a sinus infection."

Her eyes sparkled and her smile made

dimples. "From sources inside the studio, I know for a fact that thousands of letters and telegrams of support have come in from my fans all around the world."

"Doesn't surprise me."

"And Fox thinks *they* know how to work the publicity mill?" She started ticking off on her fingers: "How does this grab you? *Vogue, Life, Redbook, Cosmo* — articles or interviews, all with full photo spreads. Top photographers. I'm shooting one tomorrow with Bert Stern, and I'm busy all next week."

I had to grin at her. "They didn't know who they were messing with."

"And Peter Levathes — you know who he is? He's the head of the studio — he wants to come over next week to talk to me, here at the house."

"What for?"

"For the terms of my reinstatement, Nate! They've already offered me a two-picture deal — we'll finish up *Something's Got to Give,* then we do a musical, *What a Way to Go!*"

"That's great."

"Guess how much per picture? Just guess. Half a million each! My first million-dollar contract. Let Liz Taylor stick *that* up her fat ass!"

There was just enough of the comedienne in that delivery to make me laugh.

I reached out and took both her hands in mine. "I am so pleased for you. And I think you're doing the right thing, putting the focus on your professional life."

Her head tilted; she was smiling but not quite following me. "What do you mean, Nate?"

I gave her back her hands. "Well, uh, all I mean is, sometimes we focus on our personal lives, other times on our professional, and I think for you, now's a good time for . . . *not* personal."

"What are you talking about?"

I was talking about Jack Kennedy, and her dreams of being a First Lady, and threats of woman-scorned press conferences; but I couldn't bring myself to spell it out. Not even safely away from any likely bugging devices.

The troll who tended Marilyn's toll bridge stepped out from the living room onto the skirt of the pool opposite where we sat. Her sleepy voice echoed across the pool: "Someone here to see you, dear."

"Who?"

The guest answered that question himself.

Joe DiMaggio, wearing a cream-colored sport shirt and tan slacks, looking as tanned as any movie star, not counting his creamy pale ex-wife, waved shyly.

Marilyn leapt to her feet and clapped her hands in delight. "Joe! You came!"

She instantly forgot all about me, and ran like a schoolgirl around the pool and into the arms of the big, rather goofy-looking lug who had been called our greatest living baseball player, as well as the Yankee Clipper, Joltin' Joe, and, for a time, Mr. Marilyn Monroe.

They were talking, and I overheard him saying, "I woulda got here sooner, babe, but I was in London."

"Doing PR for those PX people," she said, nodding.

I learned later that DiMaggio had been working for a corporation back east that supplied American military post exchanges. But at the moment what she said sounded like gibberish to me.

"That's right, babe, but when I heard about your troubles, I quit 'em on the spot, and now here I am."

"Oh, Joe . . . you're the *best*. . . ."

She was hugging him. In her bare feet, she looked very small, compared to her ex-husband's six foot two. His dark brown hair had gone largely white, but otherwise he was still the rugged, boyish-looking slugger.

169

I came around and joined them, giving them plenty of space.

"Joe," I said with a nod. "Good to see you. Nate Heller."

Marilyn moved to one side, but remained under a protective DiMaggio arm, and he grinned awkwardly and held out his hand. It was the firm grip you'd expect, but he didn't overdo.

"I remember you, Nate. Nice seeing you."

I'd helped him out of a jam once, though it had almost got me in dutch with Marilyn.

Of course, by now I was that celebrated third party in a three's-a-crowd scenario. Even Mrs. Murray had had the sense to do her disappearing act.

So I said brief good-byes and headed through the house and out to my Jag.

I got in and just sat there a while, trying to digest my conversations with first Greenson and then his patient. I caught a glimpse of Marilyn, arm in arm with DiMaggio, showing him around the grounds, pointing out flowers she'd planted, telling him what she'd done, and what she planned to do.

It was as if they were the happy, domestic couple Marilyn's ex had always hoped they'd be. Except instead of a picket fence, they had a stone wall.

How happy would Joe be, I wondered, if

he knew his competition for the once and maybe future Mrs. DiMaggio was the president of the United States?

Plus, I was pretty sure DiMaggio was a Republican.

CHAPTER 9

The voice on the phone was unmistakably Marilyn's, but not the upbeat girl I'd left at Helena Drive, what, five hours ago?

"Nate," she said pitifully, "can you help me? I need your help. Please help me."

She was slurring, either drugged up or drunk, but the plea was genuine.

"You bet, baby," I said, sitting up straighter.

I'd been in my bungalow slouching on the sofa with my feet up on an ottoman, watching *Love That Bob* (ironically, Joi Lansing was on, doing her Marilyn shtick), and had turned off the TV with one of those remote gizmos when the phone rang next to me on the end table.

I said, "Where are you, honey — home?"

"Yes. Home. No one else is here. Mrs. Murray isn't here tonight. I couldn't reach Dr. Greenson. I thought of you. You can help me, can't you?"

She sounded like somebody either going into or coming out of a coma.

"I'll be right there," I said. "Just take it easy."

"Thank you. Thank you. You are so sweet. Bye-bye. . . ."

"Be right there."

I hung up, grabbed my suit coat, and didn't bother snugging the well-loosened tie. But I did make one small addition to my wardrobe: from my suitcase I got the nine-millimeter, and stuck it in the beltless waistband. I left the suit coat unbuttoned, because it hadn't been tailored to accommodate a Browning.

Maybe I was being melodramatic. But with Giancana and Hoffa hovering in the wings, being armed seemed a sensible precaution. More likely this was something else, the kind of emergency where a firearm was useless.

I'd heard and read stories about Marilyn and drugs and overdoses and even suicide attempts, though I felt fairly confident that if Dr. Greenson ever broke doctor-patient confidentiality, he'd say the latter were of the cry-for-help variety. Anybody who self-medicated to the degree Marilyn had over the years knew just how many pills to take to cry wolf, or to play dead forever.

Mid-evening was busy along Sunset Boulevard, and under such conditions the trip between the Beverly Hills Hotel and the Fifth Helena hacienda should take maybe fifteen minutes. I was aggressive enough to make it in twelve, though I hadn't broken any speed limits, since I really did not want to get sidelined when Marilyn was calling out to me. Especially not carrying a nine-millimeter, even if it was licensed.

The scalloped-topped wooden gates at the dead-end of Helena were ajar, with her leaning between them — she'd been waiting and watching for me. Still barefoot and in the same white shirt and jeans. She opened the gates wide, and the Jag slipped in, and she closed them behind me.

If she had any yard lights, she'd turned them off, and precious few windows glowed in the house. But there was a nice chunk of moon and the night was clear enough that I could see pretty well.

The moment I got out of the car, she was in my arms, and she was sobbing. I held her close, but didn't hug her, because I had glimpsed something on the white blouse — dark spatters that might be dried blood.

"I don't know if I can stand for you to see me," she said into my chest. "I don't want anybody to see me."

"Are you hurt?"

"Yes. But . . . no . . . I'm all right. But, yeah, I'm hurt."

Okay.

"Honey," I said, "there's nobody else here?"

"No. Is that . . . your gun?"

"Maybe I'm just glad to see you."

That didn't get even a nervous laugh out of her; she seemed too dazed for my charm and wit to do any good.

I held her gently away from me and she turned her head to one side, but I'd seen what she didn't want anybody to see — beneath her eyes the skin was black and blue, and an oval bruise colored her left cheekbone like a terrible oversize beauty mark.

"Who did this to you?"

"Nobody. I fell in the shower."

So DiMaggio had slugged her. I'd heard about his fucking abuse from Whitey Snyder. I had never liked the guy and, since I am not much of a baseball fan, his celebrity never moved me.

"Really, I slipped," she said, her eyes hooded above the bruising. She was not bothering to avoid my gaze any longer. "It was a stupid accident. I fell in the shower. On the tiles."

I'd been in that bathroom. Billy Barty couldn't have fallen in that shower, much less hit his face on the tile flooring.

A guy in my line has heard dozens of wife-beaters' wives lie for and stick up for the no-good bastards, and it never makes for easy listening. You want to shake the babes till they tell you the truth, but that would rather be missing the point.

"What kind of pills have you taken?"

"Little Demerol I had squirreled away. And I been drinking champagne. It helps some."

If nothing else, makes for a festive mood.

"Let's go inside," I said, and we did, hand in hand, like teenagers.

Just inside the door, she got on her toes and whispered in my ear: "Do you think my sunroom is bugged?"

Then I whispered in her ear: "Probably not. It's probably your bedroom."

She drew away and said, out loud, "Are they snoops or dirty old men?"

"There's some overlap."

So we wound up in the sunroom, where I'd spoken to Dr. Greenson just hours ago. She was lugging a bottle of Dom Pérignon, picked up along the way — I hadn't noticed where she got it from, since after all I was only a detective.

We both sat on the little wicker couch for two and I slipped an arm around her. She offered me the bottle of champagne, like it was a Coke we were sharing, and I took a swig, just to be a good sport.

"I need your help," she said. She seemed to be slurring a little less. A little. Would it disgust you if I said I found it sexy? If so, consider — Marilyn Monroe half in the bag and with a bunged-up face was still very much Marilyn Monroe.

"Which shower stall was it?" I asked.

"Well . . . mine of course. Why?"

"So I know which one to beat the shit out of."

That made her smile. Her first smile since I got here.

"I have a number I want you to call," she said.

"All right."

"It's a doctor. Plastic surgeon." She touched her nose, and I was impressed she could do it. "He took the bump off my nose, a long time ago. And fixed my chin a little."

"I should beat him up, too."

"Why?"

"Because he's the one who made you perfect. Before that, I might have had a chance."

She looked up at me with exquisite sadness, her eyes lovely despite the black and blue beneath, shining with tears, and she kissed me, very sweetly, very tenderly.

"You came," she said.

That was what she'd said when she spotted DiMaggio across the pool this afternoon. She really had to stop trusting men.

Marilyn had already written the number down on a piece of paper, which she got out of a jeans pocket, and then she told me what she wanted me to say. Why she couldn't have made this call herself, I wasn't sure. Perhaps because it was the doctor's home number, and a doctor's wife might answer, and raise suspicions real or imagined. Maybe she didn't think she'd be taken seriously in her slightly inebriated state.

Anyway, I didn't get a wife, I got the doctor, and I explained the situation and, while a long-suffering tone came into his voice, he agreed to accommodate his famous client. We would have to come to him, however — he might need to make an X-ray, so a house call was out of the question.

Half an hour later, in an alley in downtown Beverly Hills — somehow it was surprising Beverly Hills even had alleys — I helped Marilyn out of the Jag. I stuffed the nine-millimeter in the glove compartment, then joined her at the anonymous-looking door.

She was in an ordinary black suit, not the work of some top designer, with a full, flowing black wig and black sunglasses. Anywhere but this part of the world, or maybe certain parts of Europe, the sunglasses would have attracted attention this time of night.

The doctor — who had put a white jacket over a polo shirt and chinos — answered her knock immediately. I doubted this was a rarity, attending a celebrity patient after hours; certainly using the rear door wasn't, since this was the top plastic surgery clinic in Beverly Hills, and gossip columnists were known to keep an eye on comings and goings.

His name was Dr. Michael Gordon, and he didn't look old enough to have been the doc who gave Marilyn her minor plastic surgeries at the start of her career, in the late 1940s; but then he was a plastic surgeon, and probably had a few connections, should he want some work done.

He was tall, dark, and blandly handsome, but his aqua-blue eyes were an attractive feature that nobody but God had a hand in.

Ignoring me, he made a little pleasant small talk with her as he guided her into an examining room. I stayed out in the hall, unable to translate the muffled conversation behind the door, pacing like an expectant father. Among the things on my mind was wondering how Joltin' Joe would like being on the other end of a Louisville Slugger.

Maybe fifteen minutes later, the doc emerged, and shut Marilyn within — I'd caught a glimpse of her sitting up on the end of an exam table on the usual crinkly white paper. She looked small and frightened, like a kid in for a tetanus shot.

Almost whispering, the doctor asked, "Is Miss Monroe under the influence of drugs this evening?"

"I think she had a Demerol or two. And a lot of champagne."

"Explains the slurred speech." Then the eyes hardened. "She says she was in her shower, and slipped and fell."

I held up my hands in surrender. "Whoa, Doc — I'm not the culprit. I can guess who is, but she wouldn't want me to say. I'm just the friend she called for a ride here."

He studied me, as if he could diagnose whether I was lying or not.

I showed him my credentials, which he studied for maybe half a minute.

"I've heard of you," he said with a nod.

"And I've heard of you. So how is she?"

"Well, her injuries *might* have been the result of a fall. But it's more likely she was struck in the face. Probably in the nose, although she isn't bruised there. When an injury is sustained to the nose, any bleeding under the skin shows up in the soft tissue under —"

"Doc, that's okay — I been punched in the nose a few times."

That got a wry smile out of him. "Anyway, the good news is that her nose isn't broken. I could find no evidence of fracture and saw no need to take X-rays."

"She's hoping to go back to work soon. She has some photo shoots next week. . . ."

"Miss Monroe may be fine as soon as Monday. A little makeup should take care of anything the healing hasn't."

I shook his hand, and he released Marilyn to me — she gave him a hug before we left, and I'm sure the doctor appreciated it, but I had a hunch it wouldn't get her a discount.

"I'm taking you back to my bungalow," I said, leading her to the Jag.

The Beverly Hills Hotel was minutes away.

"I'd like that."

"Have you eaten anything?"

"No. Not since breakfast."

"Could you eat?"

"I don't know. I could try."

She did pretty well, actually. We ordered room service, and on trays had a Polo

Lounge Caesar Salad for two with shrimp. I vetoed champagne and she settled for sparkling water. I had the same.

That she might not have to postpone next week's photo shoots made her happy. She had taken off the suit jacket and was in a white blouse (not the blood-spattered one) and the dark skirt, her legs bare, her kitten heels kicked off; her hair was disheveled as hell, once the wig was discarded, but I thought she looked great just the same.

We sat on the couch like an old married couple and watched television — no tiny portable sets for the Beverly Hills Hotel, this was one of those big twenty-four-inch numbers — with her curled up beside me, my arm around her, her head nestled against my chest.

We watched *The Tonight Show* and I said I wasn't sure this new Carson kid was going to work out, but Marilyn disagreed, liking him better than Jack Paar, who she said was an obnoxious jerk. I wasn't aware she'd acted with him in an early picture of hers.

Finally the late news came on and I switched off the set. The lights were otherwise out, though hazy illumination filtered in from the hotel grounds through the sheer curtains, the heavier drapes pulled back.

"Okay," I said, "so what really happened?"

". . . You have any smokes?"

"I didn't know you still smoked."

"Sometimes when I get nervous."

"I don't smoke."

"I thought all detectives smoked."

"I did in the service."

"You were a Marine, weren't you?"

"Yeah. I can ring and have some brought around."

"I might have some in my purse."

It was a little black thing she'd tossed somewhere. She went and got it, and found some smokes and lighted up using hotel matches. Then she paced in front me, moving in and out of the filtering light, the little amber eye of the cigarette bobbing along.

"I was showing Joe the herb garden I planted. Along that little brick path, between the guest cottage and the kitchen? We were talking about, you know, happier times. We did have a lot of good times together."

"You weren't married very long."

"No, we weren't, but even after, he was always there when things got tough. He'd come find me and he'd just be there. Like last Christmas? He knows how tough Christmas is for me, if I'm alone. He made sure I wasn't alone. That was back in New York. Today was the first time he'd been to my new place."

"Sounds friendly enough."

"It was fine, as long we talked about what used to be. But, you see, from what he heard and read, he got the wrong idea. He heard about me getting fired and he just dropped everything, walked away from a really good job, because he thought things were going to be different now."

"In what way?"

"He said he wanted to get married again, now that my — this is what he said, Nate — now that my career was over." She laughed once, a bitter little burst. "That was always the battle between us, you know — he married me thinking I'd give it all up, the movies, the money, the fame, to be a good little Italian housewife and raise lots of Catholic babies. Well, I'm not Italian and I'm not a Catholic, and when I said this was just a bump in the road, that the press was full of lies and exaggerations, that I was going back with Fox for big money, and that nothing was more important to me than my career . . . he started getting angry."

"And he hit you then."

"Not then." She shook her head. "Not then. It was . . . it was about something else."

And there was the opening.

I said, "Maybe he'd heard the rumors."

"Rumors?"

"About you and Jack Kennedy."

The cigarette stopped bobbing.

"You've heard about that?"

"Yeah." Suddenly I felt defensive. "You're not the only one around here friendly with Pat and Peter Lawford. And, you know, I worked for Bobby, back when he was on the Rackets Committee —"

"You know about *Bobby,* too?"

That hit me in the gut.

Suddenly I recalled Lawford responding to my question about his brother-in-law and Marilyn, and he'd said, "Jack, you mean?" Because I could also have been referring to Bobby.

And Bobby telling me he was handling the Marilyn problem "personally." Personally was right.

And Jimmy Hoffa making what seemed a crazy statement about both brothers fucking Marilyn. Not so crazy, after all.

I worked to keep my voice calm, not accusatory: "Marilyn, what is going on with the Kennedys?"

Not what the hell is going on . . . just "what."

The amber eye began to bob again.

"The thing with Jack is over. He really is kind of a louse. I mean, a great man, but a lousy guy. I'm really disappointed in him. Do you know that he changed his phone number, just so I wouldn't call him?"

I didn't know what to say.

"Anyway, Bobby is much nicer. Much smarter. His intellect is . . . really quite incredible. He's going to make a much better president than his brother someday."

"But you *were* with Jack. . . ."

Her silhouette shrugged and she paced and the amber eye floated as she gestured. "I go way back with Jack. First time Joe got jealous of him was, oh . . . '54? He was a lot of fun, Jack. Not much of a lover, no romance, just in and out. But fun, funny, charming, smart. And then he sort of sent Bobby to see me and do his . . . dirty work. But Bobby felt really bad about it. Very sweet, really sweet. When I was angry and saying how Jack changed his phone number, what did Bobby do? Gave me his! Such a wonderful listener. He and I get along really well. I think it surprises him, how much I know about things. The questions I ask. It's funny."

"What's funny?"

"The things they tell me. In the dark. In bed? Both of them. I know such *crazy* things, things I really shouldn't. Some of it I have to admit I really don't approve of — like trying to kill Castro. I mean, that isn't right! They don't call it assassination, they

186

call . . . what did Jack call it? 'Executive action.' That's wrong, killing the head of state of another country, just because you don't agree with them. What do *you* think, Nate?"

I think men will say a lot of things to impress a woman in bed. But the Kennedy boys had topped us all.

I said, "I think . . . you should come sit next to me."

She did. She leaned across me to stab the cigarette out in a tray on the end table. I couldn't see it there but apparently she could.

She snuggled against me again. "Someday he's going to leave her."

"Who is?"

"Bobby! He doesn't love her. That Ethel. I don't like her at all. Do you think she's attractive? I certainly don't."

"Marilyn, stop."

"What?"

"This afternoon — did you talk to your ex-husband about this?"

"Oh, Joe knew about Jack. I don't know how, but he did. He also knew it was over, Jack and me. It was . . . I told you, it was hearing about Bobby that made him flip."

I had no urge to hit her, but I got why DiMaggio had. The inside of his head must have gone redder than marinara.

"Marilyn, this is what I was trying to tell you earlier today — you need to focus on your professional life. You're an actress, a gifted actress. And not just a movie star — they're calling you a superstar. So popular they had to make up a new word to describe it. You need to make that be enough for you."

But she was barely listening. "Nate, it's so exciting, being with Bobby. It was exciting with Jack, but this is so much better. So much deeper. Can you imagine? Me in the White House?"

"No. That won't happen, that can't happen. Bobby won't leave his wife and family for you, just like Jack wouldn't. Not because they don't want to, but because they are politicians who want votes and Catholics who want to go to heaven and a dozen other things that mean this is one dream, Marilyn, that you don't get to have come true. They're good men, in their way, but they use people. Hell, they've used *me* often enough."

"I don't want to hear this."

"I don't want to have to say it."

She was looking away from me, staring into the dark.

I asked, "Mad at me?"

She shook her head, blondeness bouncing. "No. I called and you came."

"That's right."

Something little girl came into her voice, possibly contrived, maybe not. "What if I promised you I'll take your advice?"

"I'd be very pleased. These are dangerous waters, Marilyn — that Cuba stuff, you can't ever talk about that again. To *anybody.* In these times of electronic eavesdropping, and with Bobby's enemies including everybody from mobsters and the Teamsters to Soviet agents and the FBI, you have to grasp that these are treacherous fucking waters. Please, baby. Stick to make-believe."

"You came."

"Promise me you'll take my advice."

"Why can't I love a guy like you? Just a normal everyday guy?"

That's me — Nathan Heller, normal everyday guy.

"Go ahead and try," I said. "I won't stop you."

She found a shaft of light coming in through the sheer curtains and when she stepped out of the skirt — she of course wore no panties — and got out of the blouse — no bra, either — she was naked as the day she was born. Of course, she hadn't been born with that gallbladder scar, or the black-bruise circles under her eyes or the nasty purple bruise on her cheek. But she hadn't been born with those perfect breasts, either, still full and pert despite her thirty-six years and God knew how much drug abuse and alcohol.

She was a creamy goddess who knelt before me, and unzipped me, and if you think the revelations about the Kennedys and their sexual trifling with her, and the dangers that were lurking out there, from Giancana to Hoffa to J. Fucking Edgar Hoover, if you figured all that would make it tough for me to get aroused, well, to paraphrase Bugs Bunny to Elmer Fudd, you don't know me very well, do you?

On her knees, smiling up at me with in-nocent wickedness, she took me in her hands and fondled and kissed and sucked me and slid me into the famous face until it was almost too late. She knew it, too, laugh-ing a little, waggling a scolding finger at me, and then she led me into the bedroom by the part of me extending from my fly and she undressed me, like she was stripping a department store dummy, and then pushed me onto the bed, onto my back.

She mounted me and she moved her hips slowly, the breasts swaying, the hair an abstraction of white, her face lovely in the dim dreamy light, the bruises hidden by darkness, and when her hips had accelerated until I was again at the edge of that wonderful cliff, she slipped off me and onto her back and that mouth whispered, "Love me," and I got on top of her, pushing up on the heels of my hands so I could see her, and entered her and again it was slow, in rhythm with her continued pleading demand, "Love me . . . love me . . . love me . . . ," which gathered speed and so did I until finally she was saying "*Fuck* me . . . *fuck* me . . . *fuck* me," and I did, I did, I did, understanding now how the leaders of the free world might risk it all for this.

She'd said it before, hadn't she?

She called.

And I came.

Chapter 10

Two weeks later, more or less, I was sitting in a booth at Sherry's with my son, the occasion being I was heading back to Chicago tomorrow.

The restaurant had once been among *the* "in" nightspots on the Sunset Strip, especially after hours. But Ciro's had closed in '57, the Mocambo in '59, making a dinosaur out of Sherry's, its brightly lighted interior, glass-and-chrome decor, and Cole Porter–playing pianist suggesting a yesterday that seemed forever ago.

Nonetheless, my teenaged son loved to come here. It wasn't the celebrities, a good number of whom had stayed loyal, though you were more likely to see Susan Hayward than Sandra Dee, Robert Taylor than Troy Donahue. For Sam the appeal of Sherry's was simple — I always let him order the lobster tail. Apparently his big-shot producer stepfather was too cheap to spring for the four bucks.

You see, I had a piece of Sherry's. Fred Rubinski was the restaurant's principal owner, and had let me in on what had at the time been a good investment. It might still be a good investment, if Fred ever realized he needed to throw in the towel and sell this valuable hunk of real estate.

We'd had the soup and salad and were waiting for my son's lobster and his father's filet. Sam was in the required suit and tie, looking very Sunday school though this was a Thursday evening. I wore a blue plaid Palm Beach sport jacket with a pale blue shirt, navy tie, and navy slacks, cool in more than one sense of the word and suddenly out of place in my own restaurant.

"Tell me how Marilyn's doing," my son said.

Sam knew nothing of anything I'd done for her (much less with her), but like everybody in the world, he was aware of her woes from the papers and TV.

"She's doing fine," I said. "She's renegotiated with Fox, and has been doing all sorts of photo shoots and interviews."

Sam nodded, sipped his glass of iced Coke, and said, "That's called a media blitz, Dad."

"I'll try to remember that."

Actually I hadn't seen Marilyn since that night at my Beverly Hills Hotel bungalow. We'd spoken on the phone a number of times, usually but not always initiated by me. Funny thing was, she didn't make any reference, not even veiled, to that evening. This was a little troubling, since she'd indicated she would take my advice and close the chapter on the Kennedy brothers, and the last thing I wanted out of her right now was selective amnesia.

But, from our phone chats, I could tell her focus was her career, just as I'd suggested. So I felt all right about it. Not great, but all right. And, anyway, her phones were tapped, weren't they? Naturally she would watch what she said.

Most of my time these past couple weeks had been taken up by agency work, Fred talking me into booking a number of client meetings, on matters ranging from divorce to home security. I even went out to several celebrity homes to check out possible security problems — these were people you've heard of, but as they have nothing to do with this narrative, we'll respect their privacy.

The thousand-dollar retainer from a certain labor leader had been dealt with as well. I had twice called the attorney whose name Hoffa had provided, and informed him that Marilyn had privately confirmed that she'd indeed had affairs with both Kennedy brothers. I also shared that she indicated both men were history, as she was going full-speed ahead with projects ranging from two films, a television special (a new version of the old whore-versus-man-of-God play, *Rain*), and possibly a Broadway show, the latter obviously Lee Strasberg getting into the act.

Passing along this stuff, garnered from that night at my bungalow and our handful of phone calls, was no betrayal of Marilyn. Hoffa had already known about Jack's and Bobby's respective dalliances, and almost certainly had the tapes to prove it. And the showbiz stuff was in the press or soon would be.

So everything was fine, considering — I'd even had a medical checkup that came out A-OK. At Nate 'n Al's for breakfast after my night with Marilyn (whom I'd driven home around 2:00 A.M.), I had considered ruefully the distinction of my morning worries — that I was fearful of having caught VD from Marilyn Monroe because she'd been sleeping with the president of the United States.

But I had a clean bill of health, and Marilyn seemed to be buzzing happily along, causing no international incidents that I was aware of. I was in the company of my son, who loved me — I was buying him lobster, remember — and tomorrow I would be back in that more familiar lunatic asylum known as Chicago, Illinois.

So I was in a good mood, until I noticed the two men dining in a booth across the way.

One was Frank Sinatra, who was nice enough to frequent the restaurant (probably the biggest star who still did) and his presence was not what put me off my filet. It was his companion, a gent named Johnny Rosselli, who should have known better than to grace our premises. Had he not been with Frank, someone would have said something — if Fred Rubinski had been here, he might have even with Sinatra present.

Back in '49, Sherry's had been the scene of a failed but bloody attempt on gangster Mickey Cohen's life. A cop had almost died, and one of Mick's bodyguards did die. The botched hit got lots of press, and the wrong kind of publicity, except where morbid tourist trade was concerned. So Fred had sent out word that we were no longer friendly to that breed of customer.

Not that Rosselli looked like a hood. You might take him for a successful agent or producer, with that perfectly coiffed silver-gray hair, deep tan, cool blue-gray eyes, and flashing smile. His chocolate-brown jacket hadn't cost more than your average used Buick, his crisp yellow button-down shirt with green striped tie looked plenty smart, and that watch catching the light and winking at me would almost certainly be a Rolex.

I knew Johnny fairly well. He was a guy who'd been around in mob circles, aligned with this group and that one, and had even been described as a gangland ambassador, who could mediate problems and pave the way for alliances.

Mostly, though, he was Chicago, with strong Outfit allegiances, and his history with Hollywood went back to the days of Frank Nitti's attempted takeover of the movie unions. This had led to Nitti's suicide (or maybe murder) and jail sentences for such top Outfit guys as Paul Ricca, Louis Campagna, Phil D'Andrea and . . . Johnny Rosselli.

Before the indictments, Rosselli had been a big shot around Tinseltown, wining and dining studio bosses, hitting the nightspots, dating actresses, winding up married to one for a while. They called him "The Hollywood Kid" in those days. Now, as an elder mob statesman, he was "The Silver Fox."

And he didn't live in Los Angeles anymore, at least not full-time. Since '57, he'd been Giancana's man in Vegas, and was the entrepreneur behind the Tropicana, whose owners were a who's who of mob bosses from New York's Frank Costello to Florida's Meyer Lansky, from Louisiana's Carlos Marcello to, yes, Chicago's Giancana.

Sliding out of the booth, I said to my son, "I need to talk to a couple of people."

"That's Frank Sinatra sitting over there, isn't it?"

"Yeah. I need to pay my respects."

"Don't tell him I'm an Elvis fan."

"I'll try not. . . . Listen, when you're finished with that lobster, order yourself the biggest, nastiest dessert on the menu. I may be a while."

"Deal," he said, dunking lobster meat into melted butter.

I went over and both men smiled at me. Sinatra had a great smile, of course, a kind of beacon in that ravaged face; but Rosselli could beat him at that game — the Silver Fox had a dazzler, wide and seemingly sincere. He waved the hand with a few thousand in diamond rings and bid me join them in their half-circle booth between two empty ones. Not an accident. I got in next to Rosselli.

They had eaten and were working on after-dinner drinks — Sinatra his usual martini, Rosselli his trademark Smirnoff on the rocks. I flagged a waitress down and ordered a gimlet.

Sinatra was in a blue sport jacket and lighter blue shirt with a yellow-and-blue tie. He looked sharp, but next to the immaculate Rosselli, he seemed an overage college kid.

"Charlie," Frank said (that was the name he used for all of his friends), "is that big galoot your son?" He was nodding toward Sam.

"Yeah. Good kid. His mother hasn't ruined him, which speaks well for his character."

Frank twitched a half smile. "Yeah, I know the creep your ex married. I did a picture for him once. He should only drop dead, twice."

Rosselli said to me, "You spend a lot of time with the boy?"

"Whenever I can. I don't live out here, you know. He usually has holidays with me, back in Chicago."

With a thoughtful frown, the smile gone, Rosselli said, "Very important, family."

I wasn't sure what "family" he meant.

"Listen," the silver-haired gangster said, that endless smile back again, his manner good-natured, "it's a nice coincidence, running into you. I've been wanting to talk to you."

I gave him a smile — maybe not a dazzler, but it would have to suffice. "Lucky, too," I said, "because I'm heading back tomorrow. I can take about a month out here and then I get the urge to date a female who doesn't want to be in the movies."

He chuckled at that. Then he turned to Sinatra and said, "Didn't you have a phone call you had to make?"

"Yeah. That's right, John. Thanks for reminding me." The singer stubbed out his cigarette in a glass Sherry's ashtray, and disappeared faster than Claude Rains. Nobody pushed Sinatra around, but if a mob guy said go fuck yourself, he would ask which hole.

That's when I knew it wasn't a coincidence.

I said, "So, you called the restaurant to see if I had a reservation?"

The gray-blue eyes twinkled. "Actually, I called your partner. I said I wanted to see you, and he said I better hurry because you were about to go home. And he was good

200

enough to say I might catch up with you here."

Great knowing my partner would pass along my whereabouts to any gangster who asked. Particularly when I was with my son.

"Johnny," I said, "do we have any business? I don't recall us having any business, not for a while."

He lighted up a cigarette. Yeah, a Rolex.

"Nate, I need you to take a message to your friend Bobby."

I didn't suppose he meant Darin.

"You have an inflated idea of my importance," I said. "I've seen him once in the past six months."

"But you can reach him. And you need to take some responsibility here. This is about the Caribbean matter, Nate."

He meant Cuba, of course.

"Johnny, I am no part of that. I set up a meeting. That makes me the guy that introduced the happy couple — but I had nothing to do with the baby."

He leaned nearer; he smelled good, redolent of some cologne I didn't recognize because I couldn't afford it on sixty grand a year.

"You put this in motion, Nate, and I appreciate that, because it's something I want to do. I hate the fucking Commies and I'm a good American. I'm a proud immigrant to this great country, which is partly why I am pissed off."

There was nothing pissed off in his tone, however; he was genial, and smiling lightly. Those at the table nearest us couldn't have guessed that the dapper gangster was enraged.

He continued: "Your friend, I won't say his name again, is working on getting me deported. Could you let him know that it's difficult for me to deliver on what I promised, where Mr. Castro is concerned, if I have been fucking deported? And the IRS harassment, that's got to stop. And the phone taps, and the shadowing."

I pushed the air with my hands. "This is nothing to do with me. I don't know anything about it, and I don't want to know anything about it."

He ignored that. "Do you have any idea, Nate, what your friend is putting Mooney through?" Mooney was Giancana. "They're pulling that lockstep routine on him."

Round-the-clock surveillance.

"They follow him into restaurants," he was saying, "they follow him into church, they follow his ass onto the goddamn golf course. Mooney's had to shut down protection and gambling, back on your turf, Nate.

He's thinking of suing the FBI for harass-ment."

"If you or Mooney have FBI troubles," I said, shifting in the booth, "that isn't neces-sarily coming from Bob. That prick Hoover has a mind of his own. Anyway, talking to me about this is useless."

The smile broadened and the gray-blue eyes turned cold — not twinkling now. "You tell your friend that his brother is still fuck-ing Judy Campbell. Tell him that."

I almost asked if she was also still fucking Giancana, but let it pass.

Rosselli, still good-natured, smiling, soft-spoken, touched his chest. "I own Judy Campbell. I introduced her to Mooney. And I have her in my pocket. She will spill if I tell her to spill."

"Johnny. . . ."

"You inform your friend that I am a good American, a patriot, and I am happy to perform this Cuban service for my country. I have asked for no money. Did you know that, Nate?"

I raised surrender hands. "I didn't, and I don't want to. Listen, you must have a spook contact."

After all, this was a CIA setup all the way — they were the point men on this Opera-tion Mongoose. I was fine with somebody killing Castro; I just didn't want in on it. Christ, how had I allowed myself to get on even the fringes of such dangerous shit?

"I have a contact," he said, after a healthy sip of Smirnoff, "but that agency has more layers than a devil's food cake. And *he* tells them what to do — he's the president's brother, and the president put him in charge of it."

"If you say so."

"Heller, Bobby's *your* friend. You used to work for him."

Funny thing was, Rosselli was tight with Hoffa, too. And Hoffa thought I'd only pretended to be Bobby's pal, to spy on him and spread disinformation for my *real* buddy, Jimmy; but Hoffa had been good about keeping that to himself. Layers was right. Devil's food was right.

Rosselli chuckled, and from a distance he might have seemed to be relating a funny little story.

"Here I am," the Silver Fox said, "helping the government, helping my country, and that cocky runt of a son of a bitch is breaking my balls. . . . Will you excuse me, Nate? I need to visit the little boys' room."

He gave me the warmest smile anybody ever gave anyone, patted my shoulder in a convivial manner, and slid out of the booth on the absent Sinatra's side.

When I was alone in the booth, my son glanced over at me, and I just shrugged. He gave a little "no problem" wave, and dug into his dessert. Would be a nice touch if it were devil's food, but Sherry's specialty was "imported" New York cheesecake. They made it for us over at Canter's.

Sinatra returned alone and said, "Johnny asked if you would excuse him. He just remembered he had another engagement."

Before he'd got back into the booth, I said, "You want to join my son and me?"

Sinatra shook his head and waved off that suggestion, then slid in, and edged over onto Rosselli's spot. He lighted up a cigarette with a gold FAS lighter.

"I'll say hello to the boy, on the way out, if you like," he said. "But you and I should talk first."

"He's an Elvis fan, anyway."

He gave me half a smile. Those blue eyes were at least as winning as Rosselli's gray-blue ones.

"Listen, Charlie," he said, and his mouth curved in that familiar way, "I wanted to ask you about Marilyn. About how she's doing."

"You're one of her favorite people. Just call her and check for yourself."

He waved that away, too. "Not that long ago, we got kind of serious, Zelda and me."

Frank often called Marilyn "Zelda," her own favorite pseudonym that she often traveled under: Zelda Zonk.

"But she's got too many problems," he said, "and too many needs. . . . She's a beauty, at least when she takes time to clean herself up, and she's Hollywood royalty, no question. But the last thing an eighteen-karat manic-depressive like yours truly needs is being attached to somebody more screwed up than he is."

"She doesn't seem that screwed up to me. I don't know her as well as you, Frank. I've done a few jobs for her, and spent some time with her now and then, and never saw this drunk, drug-addict, messed-up girl everybody talks about."

"Oh, that messed-up girl's real, all right. But so is the one you're describing. It's just . . . I really care about that kid, only, shit, she attracts tragedy like blue serge does lint." He shivered. "I don't think I can handle her melodrama anymore."

Did he mean the Fox firing? Or did he know about Jack Kennedy?

I took it nice and easy. "Look, she's very intent on getting her career back on track right now. I saw her a couple weeks ago, and she was lining up what my son says is called a 'media blitz.' "

He grinned. "I've seen some of that. She's been fighting that garbage those studio clowns have been putting out. Good for her."

"My understanding is Fox has offered her a new contract. To finish that picture she was making with your buddy Dino, and then another one after that. Understand, I'm not saying she doesn't have any love-life problems."

"What kind of love-life problems, Charlie?"

"If you want to know, you should call your Rat Pack pal Lawford and ask him."

He stabbed the cigarette out on the table-cloth. I'd forgotten he hated that Rat Pack term . . .

. . . but that wasn't it.

"That limey bastard," he said. "I've about had it with his no-talent ass. We got two pictures lined up, me and Dean and Sammy and Joey, and Lawford's supposed to be in them, too. I am *this* fucking close to pulling the chain and flushing that four-flusher. You know what the Seal and his brother-in-law did to me?"

The Seal was Lawford (aka "Charlie the Seal" for his cigarette cough) and I was tempted to hear the whole Palm Springs story from Frank's side, but decided he might set fire to the tablecloth this time.

"I know about the president canceling on you and going to Crosby's instead," I said gently. "I'd call that somewhat ungrateful."

"You're goddamn right, after all I did for them! But I don't blame Jack, really — I mean, I talk to him on the phone all the time, he's had me to the White House for lunch . . . never when Jackie's around, 'cause that bitch hates my Italian ass, but that fuckin' Bobby. It's *his* doing."

I shrugged. "You think he's screwing *you* over — look at Mooney."

"Tell me about it! Do you have any pull with that bucktoothed bastard?"

"Not really. I saw Bob a few weeks ago, at Lawford's, and had a conversation along similar lines. Tried to make the point that you don't make deals and then welsh. Not with anybody, but certainly not with guys like you."

"Or *Mooney*," Sinatra said, eyebrows high, the baby blues wide. It was like he'd heard a smart guy say the world was flat.

"I'm sure Marilyn would appreciate a call," I said off-handedly. "She still goes to sleep to the sound of your voice. Hell, during the day she plays your albums, too.

You're her sound track, when Lionel Newman isn't around."

"She's a sweet kid, in her fucked-up way," he said wistfully. He finished his martini. "You want me to say hello to your son? I ain't Elvis, but I sold a few records."

"That would be cool," I said.

And we went over and Frank was great to Sam, signed a Sherry's napkin for him; then he split, moving through the restaurant at a brisk pace to avoid any more autographs.

"He seemed nice," Sam said.

"Yeah. He can be."

"That other guy looked nice, too."

"Yeah. He looked nice."

CHAPTER 11

I had returned to Chicago confident that Marilyn's problems were safely half a continent behind me. But a month later, I found myself again advising her, as we sat watching the shimmer of Lake Tahoe from a balcony at Cal-Neva Lodge.

Or, as it was now called (on napkins, ashtrays, and menus, anyway), Frank Sinatra's Cal-Neva. The same Sinatra who was opening tonight in his own Celebrity Showroom, and the last person I'd have expected to hear from regarding Marilyn. As you may recall, he'd told me at Sherry's he was through with her "melodrama."

Yet he was our host. And at his request, and Marilyn's, I was here in the role of her companion or bodyguard or something-the-hell. How did this transpire, you ask?

First, the travel-brochure stuff: with its only access a long winding narrow mountain road, the rustic Cal-Neva sat high above

Tahoe's northern tip, its sun-sparkling lake a blue jewel in a lush green setting. The lodge was a rough-hewn castle dominated by an oversize wigwam of an entrance; guests not in the main building could choose between cabins, bungalows, and (high-rollers and celebrities only) chalets, the latter scattered about the slope below the lodge, among granite outcroppings, sporting magnificent views.

Long before it became the Tahoe home-away-from-home for the Rat Rack and various Vegas and Hollywood stars in Sinatra's orbit, the resort had been a favorite hide-away of bootleggers like Joe Kennedy, who'd loved the place. So had Baby Face Nelson, Pretty Boy Floyd, and other outlaws who dug the fishing and gaming retreat's unique location.

The state line bisected Lake Tahoe, south to north, up the hilly, rocky shoreline through the hotel's central building, fire-place, and outdoor swimming pool. Before Nevada legalized gambling in '31, the gaming tables were on rollers, pushed, on the occasion of a raid, across the wooden floor to whichever state the law didn't represent. Same was true for a wanted criminal: the Nevada coppers couldn't touch you on the California side, and vice versa. These days, food, drink, and guests lived in California, with the casino way over in Nevada — across that fabled dark line on the wooden floor.

For several years now, Sinatra had been the principal owner of the Cal-Neva, on paper anyway. That the singer's hefty percentage included Sam Giancana's silent-partner investment was an open secret, Mooney being on the Gaming Commission's list of "excluded persons" who must never set foot on the floor of a Nevada casino, much less own one.

Anyway, just the day before, Sinatra had called. I'd been sitting behind my desk in the venerable Monadnock Building in the Loop. The A-1 had a large corner suite with a bullpen for our ten agents and private offices for me and my semiretired second-in-command, Lou Sapperstein, now in his spry early seventies.

I was going over a contract to take on all of a major downtown bank's credit checks when the call came in through our switchboard.

The girl said, "He says he's Frank Sinatra."

"Who does he sound like?"

"Frank Sinatra."

"Then let's chance it."

And it was indeed Sinatra, as brash and breezy as one of his album covers (not the one where he was a sad clown).

"Okay, Charlie," he said. "Drop your bird. I'm opening at Cal-Neva tomorrow night, and you're invited."

"If I hop on my bicycle now, do you think I'll make it?"

"It's a no-shit paying gig, Charlie."

"I didn't figure you sang for free."

"Maybe I didn't explain so good — I'm hiring you. I'll have a first-class ticket messengered over. You'll fly into LA, we'll take my private jet to Tahoe. Gonna be a gasser."

"As it happens, I'm free this weekend. Let's go back to the you hiring me part."

"All expenses paid, nice room, crazy meals, all the booze you can guzzle, and two grand for your trouble. You should be back in Chi-Town by Monday, latest."

Incidentally, nobody from Chicago calls it Chi. Just so you know.

"This sounds agreeable," I admitted, "and I might come hear you sing for half that. Am I wrong in thinking there's an actual job buried somewhere in all that Italian ham you're serving up?"

"There is, in fact. It's, uh . . . Look, I love you and everything, but it's Marilyn's idea."

"Marilyn's idea what?"

"That you come along. She wants you to help celebrate."

"Sure. Celebrate anything special, or just being alive?"

"Listen, Charlie, you can call her and ask her herself. I'm sending that ticket over to you. No arguments."

He clicked off.

I sat and thought for a while. Everything lately about Marilyn in the papers (and on radio and TV) had been positive, thanks to her own efforts. Several columnists had leaked the news that she would likely be returning to Fox to complete *Something's Got to Give* and do at least one more picture.

So I called the private number she gave me. I figured my odds of getting her were lousy, but maybe I could leave word with that bridge troll in the cat's-eye glasses.

Only it was Marilyn who answered: "Hi! It's Marilyn Monroe," she said to whoever the hell was calling.

Which was me, so I said, "The actress?"

I could almost hear her smile. "Nate Heller? The smart-ass?"

"Speaking. What's this about Tahoe?"

"Well, Frank wants to celebrate. I'm signing the new Fox contracts Monday, and he's going to be in the next movie, *I Love Louisa*."

"I thought it was called *What a Way to Go!*"

"I hope it still will be. But that's what they're calling it for now. It's going to have a whole bunch of top male stars, possibly Paul Newman and Dick Van Dyke and Gene Kelly and maybe Dean again . . . but for sure Frankie."

"That's very exciting. But I figured you'd have signed that new Fox deal by now."

"Well . . . I shouldn't talk about it on the phone."

"Okay. But why do you want me along? I'm glad to have the chance to see you, honey, but Sinatra's flying me in from Chicago for this. At your request, or so I'm told. Why?"

"I shouldn't talk about that on the phone, either."

That made two things she didn't want her own phone tap picking up.

"If you want me there," I said, "I'm there."

"You'll be sort of my . . . bodyguard. You do make a good bodyguard, don't you?"

Huey Long had no complaints. Neither did Mayor Cermak.

"Sure," I said.

It had been whirlwind. Like I'd blinked

and there I was on Sinatra's fancy little private Learjet, *Christina,* with its wall-to-wall carpet, fancy wood paneling, full bar, and piano, which incidentally nobody was playing. We were on facing couches, with seat belts that after takeoff the pilot gave permission to unbuckle. The company was interesting, even illuminating as to why I was present.

Marilyn was next to me, with Sinatra next to her. Across from us were Pat Lawford and her husband, Peter.

That's right — seated directly across from Frank was Charlie the Seal himself, the hated presidential brother-in-law, the messenger who'd been shot for delivering the news that JFK was bunking at Bing's in Palm Springs, not Frank's.

Yet here the late Lawford sat, fully resurrected. That a certain awkwardness was in the air couldn't be denied; nor that his attempts to make conversation with his host were met with only limited success.

But there they both were — Frank and Peter, together again.

What had it taken to reunite these two? A selfless wish to congratulate their mutual friend Marilyn on her triumph? A sudden realization that their friendship had been deep and meaningful, and sorely missed?

No. And no.

This had "Kennedy family" stamped all over it — a nervously toothy Pat making the smallest talk imaginable, while Sinatra tried not to pout and Lawford babbled, and Marilyn just sat and drank champagne served to us all by Sinatra's cute brunette-bouffant stewardess Joni (that's how her little silver-wing name tag read, anyway).

Was it early for champagne? That depends on whether you consider eleven in the morning early for champagne. None of us seemed to have a problem with it, though Sinatra was substituting Jack Daniel's on the rocks.

Not that you could trust *my* frazzled judgment. That fancy first-class ticket had been for a red-eye last night, and I'd been cooling my heels in the airport lounge since 8:00 A.M. until Sinatra and his guests showed. I felt overdressed in an olive hopsack blazer and gray trousers — everybody else was in the most casual wear, knit sport shirts and slacks, including Pat, though Marilyn looked sportiest in a lime-green blouse, sunglasses (not so dark you couldn't see her eyes), and white capris.

Pat sat forward, hands clasped, and told Marilyn how happy she was that the studio had come around. Marilyn said she was thrilled to be finally working with Frank, and Frank said the script could be better, and Marilyn said it can always be better. Peter joked about wondering if there was a part for a slightly graying child star, only he probably wasn't joking.

Anyway, that was the level of repartee, and I didn't get a moment alone with Marilyn until we were checked in, having been taken to the lodge by limo from the private airstrip near Crystal Bay, on the California side. She was in Bungalow 52 and I was in one of the standard cabins, but only a walk of two minutes to her little light-brown "chalet," which was actually nothing fancy, bedroom and bath, but had a stunning lake view from its overhang porch-like balcony.

There, seated in patio chairs, she was still in the lime-green blouse, scarf, and sunglasses, while I'd gotten comfortable in a polo, shorts, and sandals. She was sipping champagne again, to my knowledge only her third glass of the day. Frank went on at nine, with dinner seating in the showroom at seven thirty.

"It's five," I said checking my wristwatch. "How many days do you need to get ready?"

She gave me a smile that looked like a kiss. "You think I can't be on time? You think I can't get ready without my entourage?"

"No," I said.

"Ha! I'll show you." She reached over and touched my arm, and her voice warmed. "Thank you for this. Thank you for coming."

"My pleasure. Why am I here?"

She sipped champagne. Looked out at the lake, which the sinking sun was painting a shimmering gold.

"Don't you want me to answer your other question first?"

"What other question is that?"

"Why I'm not signing till Monday, when I've had the Fox deal in my lap for weeks."

"Any time you mention your lap, I'm listening."

She giggled. Maybe it was my wit. More likely the champagne. "I put off signing until the coup was over. Zanuck and Skouras? They have control again. Those Wall Street lawyers are oh-you-tee."

"Then you've won."

She was smiling like a princess. "Yes I have. . . ." Then the smile dissolved. ". . . But I'll always wonder."

"What will you wonder?"

"Did Bobby help me or hurt me? He and his family had connections with the studio chairman of the board — the one that Zanuck just unseated? Bobby *said* he was helping. But I'll always wonder — was he behind that smear campaign? Did he only pretend to call his friends at Fox and try to get me reinstated?"

"Why would Bobby want to smear you?"

She laughed soundlessly. "I'm disappointed in you, Nate."

". . . To discredit you generally, in case you decided to go public with what you know about him and Jack."

"So you're not just a dumb redhead."

I sat forward and allowed an edge into my tone. "Listen, Marilyn, we've talked about this — people on this level, they're dangerous. Hell, *Frank's* dangerous. You know who co-owns this joint, don't you?"

"Certainly I do. That awful little man, Giancana. I've met him." She shivered. "Makes my skin crawl."

"One of his girlfriends is named Judy Campbell, did you know that? An ex-playmate of Frank's. She's also one of Jack's girls."

"I thought Giancana was in love with Phyllis McGuire."

My eyebrows went up. "Marilyn, this may be a tough concept for you, but some guys go with more than one female at a time."

She said nothing. The breeze rustling the lush firs and the gleaming blue-burning-orange lake provided a languid ambiance. Otherworldly. Time had stopped. But problems marched on.

"Why am I here, Marilyn?"

"That's not the question."

"What is?"

"Why am *I* here?" Her smile crinkled. "Can you tell me? Is it to celebrate working with Frankie?"

"Probably not."

"Right. What then?"

I sighed heavily. "I think at some point, this weekend, in and around the fun and the frolic? They're going to sit you down for a good talking-to."

"So do I," she said. Her eyes were on the lake again, which had gone bloodred.

"Have you been staying away from Bobby?"

". . . I've made a few calls."

"Where to?"

"You know . . . the Justice Department. Once to Hickory Hills."

"Hickory Hills? His *home?*"

She shrugged. "Just once. I got Ethel. I didn't say anything to upset any apple carts."

"Well, that was wise. You and Pat Lawford, you seem friendly. . . ."

"We *are* friends."

"She'll probably carry the ball, if they corner you. I won't likely be invited to this little family talk."

"No. But you'll be here. Here, if they get . . . I don't know. Rough with me."

"I don't think they're going to work you over. Not with billy clubs or anything."

She sipped champagne. "No. Just words. But if I need somebody to be on my side? That's where *you* come in. Somebody who can take me home, if I decide I've had enough."

"Marilyn, I don't even have a car up here."

"No. But you're my big bad private eye. I bet you brought your gun."

I had.

"Maybe," I said. I gave her a serious smile. "You won with the studio, honey. Embrace that. Don't you know you can't win this one?"

She shrugged again.

"You don't really still want to be First Lady . . . ?"

She frowned. "I wouldn't marry Bobby, or Jack, if they were the last Democrats on earth."

So when the right Democrat came along, she might *still* be First Lady. . . .

I asked, "Then what *do* you want?"

Her eyes were surprisingly hard behind

the gray sunglass lenses. "Not to be taken for granted. Not to be abused. Not to be taken for some dumb —"

"Redhead?"

She flicked me a smile, then nodded. "I might not win. I don't think there's a way *to* win . . . but I *will* be respected. They will know I was here."

"I think they already know that."

"Not really. Not down deep." She got up suddenly, like toast popping from a toaster. "Now, shoo. I do need a *little* time. . . . Even putting on a modified Marilyn takes *some* effort."

She looked great at dinner — a hairstylist named Sebring had helped her out, and she proved capable of doing her own makeup to perfection. She'd even been right on time when I picked her up to walk her over. The showroom was Vegas modern in orange, beige, and brown (Sinatra's favorite colors), and the seven-hundred-seater was packed.

We were ringside, and Marilyn — wearing a clingy black gown that showed off her current, more streamlined figure — drank a little too much champagne but was fun, laughing company. At our small table, tuxedo-sporting Lawford was on my one side and Marilyn on the other, next to Pat, who wore a lovely but simple blue gown. I had on a white dinner jacket and black tie. When comic Pat Henry came on to open, Lawford put a hand on my shoulder and whispered, "Could we speak?"

We left the showroom and found a corner of the lobby.

He stood close enough for me to smell his lime-scented cologne. It was almost enough to put me off gimlets.

"How does Marilyn seem?" he asked.

"She seems fine."

"Have you seen her take any pills?"

"No. She's off the pills."

"Are you sure?"

"No, I'm not rooming with her. She's hitting the bubbly pretty good tonight, but isn't it a celebration?"

"Not entirely. Listen, old chum, are you aware of what she's been doing?"

"You mean taking Twentieth Century–Fox to the woodshed?"

"Not that — she's been calling Bobby, or trying to."

"I heard something along those lines."

He sighed; he was a handsome devil, but looked closer to my age than his own. "She's phoned the Justice Department switchboard perhaps a dozen times, screaming at them when they won't put her through. Then somehow she wormed Bobby's home number out of Jerry Wald — he's producing the *Enemy Within* picture, you know — and got Ethel on the line, and, well, Bobby is just *furious.*"

"Want to know what I think?"

"What?"

"Bobby needs to deal with this directly. He needs to speak to Marilyn, probably in person, and treat her respectfully. Essentially apologize for his bad behavior, and Jack's."

"Are you mad?"

"Don't knock it, it got me out of the Marines. But if what you're planning is to sit her down this weekend, so you and Pat can do Bobby's dirty work, well . . . how did that turn out for you with Frank?"

His expression turned defensive. "I'm *here,*" Lawford said. "And Frank and I are like this again." He held up forefinger and middle finger entwined.

I did the old gag: "I bet I can guess which one is you. Is this the first time you've spoken since the Palm Springs fiasco?"

"Maybe it is."

"No maybe about it. You and Frank and the Kennedy boys all know how lousy this will look if Marilyn goes public."

His eyes and nostrils flared. "You're telling me! She's talking to Sidney bloody Skolsky about this, and just about every other columnist — they're being gentlemen about it, even the ladies, but what if she holds this press conference she's threatening? What then?"

"She's not a baby. She's not stupid. She's not a bimbo, either, even if Jack and Bobby treat her like one. She's a genius, in her way, and a very important person."

"I know. . . . I know. . . ."

"They're users, Peter. They've used me. And they've used you. But I'm just a two-bit private eye who lived long enough to get respectable. And you aren't exactly Brando or Olivier, are you? So they can get away with using us. But you don't use Marilyn Monroe and toss her aside like she's Jayne Mansfield."

He looked alarmed. "How did you know that?"

"What?"

"That Jack and Bobby had Jayne Mansfield, too?"

What could I say to that?

I just held up my hands in surrender and went back in to hear Sinatra sing.

And it was a great show — a fantastic big band playing so hard and loud, it enveloped you, with that living legend teasing, delighting, seducing, and beguiling an audience that was the real instrument he played, those mature pipes tossing off songs like he was making them up as he went: "Come Fly with Me," "One for My Baby," "Luck Be a Lady," "I've Got You Under My Skin," the son of a bitch was a genius.

Like Marilyn.

But for that brief intermission with Lawford, the evening had gone well, I thought. Marilyn hadn't really had all that much champagne — if she'd eaten more than just a salad, she might not have shown the effects of those three or four glasses.

Then things got weird.

Right after Sinatra's closer, "Chicago" (had that been for me?), when we were still seated, after the lights had come up and before Frank could come out and join us, somebody else did.

Standing between Marilyn and me, like an evil dwarf, was Sam Giancana, elegant in his continental formal wear, well-tanned and ugly as hell, his hair dark going gray and thinning, his oval face home to tiny dark eyes, a lumpy nose, and a sideways slash of a smile.

"I just wanted to welcome you to the Cal-Neva," the Outfit boss said to us all. "Mrs. Lawford. Miss Monroe. Nathan. Peter."

Nobody knew what to say.

Finally I managed, "Pleasant surprise, seeing you, Sam. But I didn't think you were allowed at Cal-Neva."

His smile could darken up any room. "Ah, but I'm on the California side, Nate. It's Nevada where I'm persona non grata. . . . Don't mean to interrupt." He nodded to one and all, then looked right at Marilyn, who had a stricken expression. "Have a lovely weekend, Miss Monroe."

He was moving away. No bodyguards. I found myself following him, catching up with him halfway out.

"Sam — what's the idea?"

"Nothing's the idea, Nate." He was still moving, but not that quickly. The showroom was crowded, and exiting took a while, though some guests lingered for an after-dinner, after-show drink.

I was at his side. "Did Sinatra know you were going to be here?"

"Why, did you think he sang 'Chicago' for you?"

I pretended that didn't deserve an answer. We kept moving.

I said, "Is the point to scare Marilyn shitless? Because I think it worked."

"I hope it did. She needs to concentrate on what she's good at. Posing. Acting. Fucking."

That was ungracious, but I didn't point it out; I think he knew.

"She's not going to cause any trouble, Sam."

"You guaranteeing that, Nate? Putting your personal assurance on it?"

"Well . . . no."

He stopped. He bestowed another awful smile on me, even put a hand on my shoulder.

"Just know that I appreciate you being here," he said, looking up at me in a fatherly fashion, "and helping us corral this crazy cunt."

He patted my shoulder, and moved on.

I didn't follow him.

When I got back to the table, Sinatra was standing there, tux tie loosened, smiling, asking his seated guests if they'd enjoyed themselves. Lawford was forcing a smile — not his best performance — and Marilyn looked pale and sick. Almost as sick and pale as Pat Lawford. Apparently Pat had recognized Giancana, which was interesting in itself.

I went up to Frank and he, too, put a hand on my shoulder. Gave me a grin so dazzling it rivaled Johnny Rosselli's.

"Dig the show, Nate?"

I gave him my coldest look, which is pretty

fucking cold.

"Which one?" I asked.

CHAPTER 12

Nobody argued when Sinatra invited everybody to join him in the cocktail lounge. It
was one of the resort's most popular spots,
with a big circular bar under a colorful
stained-glass dome. Frank had reserved the
section by the tall windows overlooking the
lake, whose surface was playing mirror for
the sickle-slice moon. There, on stools, sat
the Lawfords, Sinatra, Marilyn, and I — no
sign of Giancana, but then green-felt tables
lined the periphery. Definitely the Nevada
side.

The drinking was heavy and the talk was
light, dominated by praise for Frank's show
(Lawford's fawning got fairly sickening).
Resort guests who said hi to Frank would
get nods and smiles, even if he was in the
midst of conversation; he was a convivial
host unless somebody overstepped.

One guy in his forties with a thirtyish
female on his arm came right up and said,

"Frank, I want you to meet my girl."

Sinatra gave him a snarl of a smile and said, "You want me to meet your girl? Does she want to meet me? Can't she speak for herself? Who are you to do the talking? Is she deaf and dumb, this girl of yours?"

The couple froze in shock, then melted away.

Peter, finding a little spine somewhere, said, "For Christ's sake, Frank, why *do* that?"

Sinatra shrugged and returned to his martini. "I don't know. I can't help it. Some people are just so goddamn dumb."

A few celebrity types stopped by to pay their respects to the Chairman of the Board — a nickname bestowed on Sinatra when he thumbed his nose at Capitol Records, who'd revived his career, and started his own label, Reprise.

The respect-payers included singer Buddy Greco, between shows in the Indian Lounge, and restaurateur Mike Romanoff and his wife, Gloria. Greco was a talented guy and cocky, and treated Sinatra like an equal, which was dangerous. Romanoff was that well-liked fraud who pretended to be Russian royalty, a dapper, homely little septuagenarian with a mustache and a beautiful brunette wife many decades younger.

I knew Romanoff only slightly, from his restaurant, and his wife not at all; but they were close friends of both the Lawfords and Sinatra, because "Prince" Michael had been part of Humphrey Bogart's original Rat Pack, of which Frank's current crop was an extension.

As they gabbed, Marilyn probably appeared bored or even in a haze to onlookers; perhaps that was why no one, famous or otherwise, came over to talk to her, just acknowledged her with a smile. Even resort guests didn't speak to her or ask for an autograph, merely moved slowly by, gazing, as if at Mount Rushmore.

I knew she'd been shaken badly by Giancana's presence. And in forty-five minutes or so, she'd put away enough champagne for a small wedding party. She'd spilled some, and it shimmered on her black dress like embedded jewels.

I whispered, "Want to get out of here?"

She just nodded, and gathered up her little black purse.

I went over to Sinatra. "I'm gonna walk Marilyn home."

"Walk her all the way to Brentwood," he said unpleasantly, "far as I care. I hate a sloppy broad."

I gave him a look.

He gave me one back. "You think I arranged that? I didn't know Momo would be here. He comes to a lot of my openings. You're not calling me a liar, are you, Nate?"

"Not while you're my client," I said. "Maybe off the clock, next week, I'll have a different opinion."

He decided to laugh at that.

I went over and took Marilyn by the arm and walked her out into a warm but breezy night. The occasional splash of neon and the shrill sounds of gambling and drink were at odds with the beauty of the Cal-Neva grounds, the fir trees, the rocky hillsides, the shelves of granite, touched lightly by moonlight.

"That awful man," she said, and shuddered. She was clutching my arm as if afraid to fall from a height.

"I don't suppose you mean Romanoff," I said. She might have meant Sinatra. But I didn't think so.

"You know who I mean. He has a lot of names. Mooney. Gold. Flood. Giancana. Frank calls him Momo. What kind of name is that for a man — Momo?"

"I'm surprised you know him by any name," I said.

"I *don't* know him, really. But he's a friend

of Frank's. So I've met him. He's not supposed to be here, is he?"

"No."

"Did Frank invite him?"

"Maybe. Or maybe he just showed. The
guy *is* a co-owner of this place."

"He's also a killer, isn't he?"

"He used to be."

"Why, can you stop being one?"

Damn good question.

Suddenly she put on the brakes and
clutched my arm even harder. "I need you
to stay with me tonight."

"Well, sure." Some men might turn down
an offer like that from Marilyn Monroe, but
I wasn't one of them.

"Only . . . we need to stop by your cabin
first. Isn't that your cabin? Right there?"

My nod affirmed that.

"Well, I want you to go get your gun."

"What?"

"I want you to go get your gun and you're
going to protect me." She wobbled. "You're
my bodyguard, aren't you?"

"Sam Giancana isn't going to come shoot
you, honey. Or send anybody, either."

Her inebriation had her overenunciating,
the way she did in comedy roles. "I am a
threat. I am a threat to ev-ery-body. Haven't
you been paying attention?"

"Sweetie, the last thing Giancana or your friend Frankie would want is a dead body turning up here on their premises. A *famous* dead body would be even worse. Your famous dead body, particularly."

She had started shaking her head halfway through that, her platinum tresses struggling to free themselves of their hair-sprayed helmet. "Get your gun. Get your gun. Get your gun."

I got my gun.

She came in and peed while I traded my formal wear for a polo and chinos and sandals. The nine-millimeter, extracted from my suitcase, I stuffed in my waistband. My toothbrush I stuck in my pocket. A man with a gun and a toothbrush can go anywhere.

We made it up the stairs onto the balcony of her chalet, despite her stumbling a little. She found her key in the purse and let herself in, and I followed. It was a fairly standard if nicely appointed motel room, similar to mine, somewhat larger, same beige walls and rather small bathroom. The only extra touch was a round bed, like Hefner's (minus the gizmos), with a pink satin bedspread. In the corner, angled to face the door, was a white, overstuffed chaise lounge.

She pointed at the lounge. "That's your post."

"Okay." But I didn't take my position just yet. "Gonna hit the hay?"

It was about 1:00 A.M.

She was over by the foot of the bed, or where the foot would be if the thing weren't round. "I think so. I'm reading some scripts." A pile sat on her nightstand. "I may take a few sleeping pills."

"Just so you don't overdo."

She headed toward the bathroom. "I'll be fine. Just a little chloral hydrate."

"In my business we call that a Mickey Finn."

"In mine," she said, pills in her mouth, water running, "we call it Marilyn's little helpers."

I went over to the chaise lounge and stretched out. Comfy. Nearby, a floor lamp provided the only illumination. The nine-millimeter nudged me in that half-sitting position, so I placed it on the floor to my right.

She came out in a sheer bra and nothing else, her amber tuft nicely unruly.

"If I'm not being ungentlemanly," I said, "why a bra and no panties?"

She cupped her breasts. "Pussies don't sag."

Wasn't that a mystery novel by A. A. Fair?

She clicked on her bedside lamp and suggested I switch my light off, unless I wanted to borrow a script to read. I declined, and she got under the covers and read for a while, and in maybe five minutes was asleep. I went over, put the script on the nightstand stack, turned off the lamp, and returned to my post.

I was fairly tired, and maybe a little drunk, though nowhere near as tipsy as Marilyn had been. So I might have fallen asleep quickly if my mind hadn't insisted on tormenting me with various nasty thoughts, the first of which was that I had brought a gun into the motel room of a woman notorious for suicide attempts.

If Marilyn used my nine-millimeter, at some despairing point in the night, I might as well use it on myself, too, for how little career I'd have left.

Then there was Sinatra. I didn't believe for a second that Giancana's presence wasn't his idea, to remind Marilyn just how deep and dangerous were the waters she was swimming in, and I didn't mean Lake Tahoe or the kidney-shaped pool.

But Giancana's presence could cost Sinatra his gaming license, and guaranteed a weekend presence at the lodge of FBI agents, male and female, racking up fun expenses on Uncle Sam's account. This, at the very time Marilyn — a Communist sympathizer in J. Edgar's view — and President Kennedy's sister were also Sinatra's guests at Cal-Neva.

I couldn't imagine Pat Lawford had been thrilled to find her brother Bobby's nemesis playing host. But she was complicit nonetheless — this weekend wasn't about celebrating MM's new Fox contract, was it? It was about Peter and Pat putting the pressure on Marilyn. A real three-ring circus, and Sinatra was providing the tent.

But confronting Frank was pointless. First, the damage was done — Giancana had shown his lizard-like face and spooked Marilyn, and whether he was still around tomorrow was a moot point. Second, Sinatra was my client, and while I was Marilyn's bodyguard, the Voice was paying the freight.

Don't think it wasn't tough work for a guy, trying to get to sleep in a lounge chair with a mostly naked Marilyn Monroe a few feet away. She was snoring a little, but that didn't help, because even her goddamn snoring was sexy. . . .

When the knock came at the door, sunlight was edging around the drapes.

Mouth thick, I glanced at my wristwatch

— ten o'clock.

The knock wasn't insistent, sort of tentative, but I went to answer it fast, because Marilyn was still sleeping, stretched out on her tummy with her dimpled fanny up and uncovered, and I didn't want to disturb her. Or spoil the view.

While I knew it was ridiculous, I took my gun with me. Stuffed in my waistband again, but in back this time.

I cracked the door and looked over the night-latch chain at Peter Lawford. He looked quietly sporty in a black pullover and gray slacks.

"Nathan? Is Marilyn all right?"

I undid the latch, slipped out and onto the balcony. The sun was bright and glancing off the lake in golden shafts that cut through the green of firs.

"She's fine," I said softly, almost whispering. "Sleeping. She had a lot to drink last night. Let's let her sleep it off."

Lawford was smoking, nervously. "Do you believe that guy?"

He meant Sinatra.

"You mean, you don't think having Giancana drop by to goose Marilyn was a fun party idea?"

He sighed, shook his head. "You have no idea what I've been through."

I took a wild stab: "Your wife tore you a new one?"

He rolled his eyes. "Did she ever. From now on, when I sit upon the throne, it will be multiple choice, which orifice to use. But at least Frank has shooed that creature away."

"Mooney's gone?"

Lawford nodded, dropped the cigarette to the balcony floor and ground it out with a sneaker toe. "I think Frank realized he'd taken things too far. Do you have any idea, Nate, the ramifications of that man's presence?"

"Sure. FBI for one. Your wife's reaction, for another. Irony is, I don't think Marilyn, in the long haul anyway, scares so easy. You'd think Frank would understand that even though your brothers-in-law don't."

"How so?"

"Marilyn isn't just another lay, Peter. That's how Jack views her, and maybe how Bobby views her, although he's got a naive enough streak to really fall in love with her, temporarily."

Lawford was slowly nodding. "Actually, I agree. Marilyn is like Frank. She's on that level of fame, of importance. As someone wise once said, it's Frank's world — we just live in it."

"Right now he's living in Marilyn's world."

"I can't disagree." The president's brother-in-law lighted up a cigarette and flashed that winning smile of his. "All right, friend Heller — I'll tell one and all that Marilyn's doing fine. You were with her all night?"

"Yeah."

"No excess pills?"

"Nope. She didn't even order an extra champagne bottle from room service. She was a good girl."

Lawford frowned as he exhaled smoke. "Are *you* doing her, too, Nathan?"

"Not last night."

And I went back inside.

By the time she woke up, around 1:00 P.M., breakfast had long since passed.

I had watched a little television, with the sound way down, and on the news picked up on a tidbit of interest: Bobby Kennedy was in Los Angeles, giving an address to the National Insurance Association. Was Bobby's being in LA this weekend another reason for spiriting Marilyn out of town? If Marilyn heard about this — make that *when* she heard about this — beauty would turn into beast. . . .

Anyway, I managed to order up a light

room-service breakfast for Marilyn, despite it being well into lunch hour, and had them bring me a Cobb salad. We ate on trays and said little, though Marilyn seemed in good spirits.

She got dressed, getting back into the lime-green top and white capris, tying a white scarf over her messy hair. All I needed was to brush my teeth, having slept in the polo and shorts.

On our way to the pool area, we made a stop at my cabin, where I returned the nine-millimeter to the suitcase and the tooth-brush to a glass in the john. Marilyn was standing by my unused bed patiently, sun-glasses on, looking less like a movie star than some tourist getting over a hangover.

I said, "That killer we spoke about has taken a powder."

"You just love to talk like a private eye, don't you?"

"Why, didn't you know they based the guy on *77 Sunset Strip* on me?"

She smirked prettily. "Who, the one who parks cars and combs his hair?"

As it happened, I was combing my hair, having wet it down since I had morning cowlick. "Don't you know Efrem Zimbalist, Jr., when you see him? Anyway, Giancana is gone. Should be smooth sailing, rest of the weekend."

Unless she found out about Bobby being in LA.

It wasn't far to the pool area, a short walk up a gravel incline. Buddy Greco was swimming and being gregarious, and a bare-chested Sinatra in shorts was sitting quietly, maybe even sullenly, reading *Variety*. Lawford was perched on a higher stool near Sinatra, like a good-natured bird of prey, trying to prove to the world and himself that Frankie and Charlie the Seal were still best of buddies.

Marilyn posed for a few pictures and was in giddy good spirits. At one point she went over and kissed Sinatra on the lips, kind of a loud smack.

"What was that for?" he said, looking up at her with a grin.

"It's because I love you, anyway."

The grin went away and something vaguely hurt took its place. "I'm always looking out for you, Zelda. I hope you know that."

"We shoulda got married, Frank. We really should. That would've given them something to talk about."

The grin returned. "Yeah," he said, "for the three or four weeks we'da lasted." Then he waved her off and returned to his paper.

Soon Marilyn was over talking to Greco and a shapely brunette with a bouffant that made for a sort of Martian look. I was told the brunette was Roberta Linn, who was opening for Greco in the Indian Lounge, though I'd never heard of her. Not that she didn't have a shape worth knowing.

Anyway, they were laughing and talking, and Greco was pretending he was going to throw Marilyn in the pool. I went over and took the deck chair next to Sinatra. Lawford had wandered away — maybe because his idol wasn't paying any attention to him.

"I hear our friend Momo checked out," I said.

"Yeah. He had another engagement."

"Nice of him to support you like that, opening night and all."

"Are you cracking wise, Charlie?"

"Not with Jilly and the other chipmunks around." I nodded across to where several of Sinatra's bully boys sat in bathing suits, in their own deck chairs, sunning themselves like big dead fish on a beach.

Frank gave me a foul glance. "You think I like this?"

"Being king of Cal-Neva? Sure. You love it."

He grunted a non-laugh. "I mean helping these jackasses handle Zelda. She's too good for them."

"Then why help?"

His eyebrows rose. "You have any idea the trouble that broad could cause, with what she knows?"

"Sure I do."

"Anyway, I couldn't use the grief." He shook his head. "Not that I haven't about had it with these damn Kennedys."

"You get asked to the White House, don't you?"

"Through the side door." He said "fuck" silently. "This is all Bobby's fault. Snotty little prick. Why did Old Joe have to get a fucking stroke for Christmas, anyway? Gonna give *me* one."

That comment resonated — it confirmed my suspicion that Sinatra had dealt with Joe Kennedy, not Jack and certainly not Bobby, when he arranged for Outfit help in the West Virginia and Illinois presidential sweepstakes. The old boy's stroke last December had put his two oldest sons in charge of their own destinies. His reckless, arrogant sons. . . .

Lawford and his wife, who wore a tan sport shirt and matching slacks, strolled onto the pool's cement skirt hand in hand — and wasn't *that* suspicious — and went over and spoke to Marilyn, who was sitting at the edge of the pool with her sneakers off, kicking idly at the water, her conversation with Greco and his opening act having passed.

Soon Lawford was leading Pat and Marilyn — chattering like schoolgirls — away from the pool area. The trio went into the lodge, to do what, I had no idea.

"Peter and Pat's suite is in there," Sinatra said, nodding toward the rustic main building that hovered over the pool area.

"What's up?"

"I don't know. I'm not in the inner circle, Charlie — are you? . . . Listen — something you *should* know."

"What?"

"Marilyn's ex showed up last night, trying to get in. How he knew she was here, I have no fucking idea. But we were booked up, and when I found out the bastard was around, I made sure he wouldn't be allowed in, if somebody canceled."

"Which ex?"

"Which do you think? DiMaggio."

Sinatra and DiMaggio and I had a history together. Back in '54, *paisans* Sinatra and DiMaggio were drinking buddies, and one drunk night, they called up a detective attached to the A-1 Agency — not me; I was back in Chicago — and hired him to go check up on Marilyn, who Joe was sure was cheating. The detective promptly delivered them to the wrong apartment, kicked the door down, and some middle-aged gal got the shit scared out of her, only to later settle out of court. Marilyn was in a nearby apartment. *Confidential* magazine made this minor incident famous, dubbing it "The Wrong Door Raid."

Where I'd come in was a year or so later, when that detective got caught up in a statewide inquiry into shady practices in the private eye game. We had long since fired this jerk, who claimed Sinatra and DiMaggio had kicked the door down personally, when actually Sinatra stayed in the car, blotto as hell, and DiMaggio looked on, in full-blown ballplayer stupidity. Anyway, to help out the A-1 Agency's rep, as well as my friend Sinatra and his friend DiMaggio, I looked into it, and through various witnesses and the discrediting of other witnesses, cleared them both.

Luckily for them, Marilyn had mostly been amused, and both Sinatra and Joltin' Joe had eventually wormed their way back into her good graces. But the two Italians had come out of the affair hating each other, though I never really understood why.

"Just keep an eye out for that jerk," Sinatra said. "My whole staff knows he's on my shit list, and we can get a small army of bellboys to bounce his ass, if necessary."

"Okay," I said. I was with Frank on this, considering what I knew about Marilyn recently "falling in the shower."

Then Frank went back to his *Variety*.

Me, I spent the afternoon gambling. I could count cards well enough to make blackjack worthwhile, and by five or so had turned twenty bucks into one hundred and twenty. I figured we'd be going to the Sinatra show again, and went back to Marilyn's chalet and knocked at her door, not sure she was in there.

I had knocked enough times to decide she wasn't, when she startled me by answering, her eyes red, her face streaked with tears.

"Honey," I said, "what's wrong?"

She was still in the lime-green top and white pants but the head scarf was gone and so were the sunglasses.

"I hate them," she said, her lower lip quivering. "I hate them!"

I stepped inside and shut the door and she flung her arms around me and held me tight. I was patting her back and soothing her and doing the "there there" routine, when she turned her face up to mine and her mouth settled on my mouth and her tongue did things. She pulled away and looked at me desperately.

"Make me feel better," she said, and she slipped out of her capri pants. No panties, of course.

She went over to the bed with the lime-green top on and all that flesh below the waist flashing, and she got on her back and planted her heels in the mattress and opened her knees and spread the petals of the flower between her legs. That her top was still on was crazily sexy and I went from three inches to seven in record, throbbing time.

As I was getting out of the shorts, deciding to leave my polo on so we could make a matched set, she was saying impatiently, "Make me feel better! Make me feel better!"

I went over there and did my best. She was moaning and crying and how much of it was me and how much was whatever she'd just been through, I had no idea. But her nipple tips poked at the lime-green top and her neck flushed scarlet and her eyes rolled back in her head as I drove myself into her with friendly fury.

Then, out of breath, wondering if a man in his fifties could die like this but not really caring, I rolled onto my back and she cuddled against me.

"I feel better," she said. "I feel better."

I waited to see if maybe she'd fall asleep, but I could tell she was awake, so I broached it.

"*Who* do you hate?" I asked.

"Pat and Peter. They took me to their suite and they sat me down like a child and they lectured me. They fucking fucking *fucking* lectured me!"

"I bet I know what subject."

"They said my relationships with Jack and Bobby were over. No more contact. No more phone calls, no more visits, no more cards, no more letters."

"Are you surprised?"

"Aren't they *men?* Jack sent Bobby to send me packing, and now Bobby sends his big sister? And do you know what those two had the nerve to tell me?"

"No."

"That I had to do this for America. Because someday Bobby would be president, and someday — you'll love this — someday Teddy will be president, and Teddy has a tough race right now, in Massachusetts? For senator? And bad publicity right now would just spoil everything."

"Did you fight with them?"

"You mean argue? No. I just listened. I just nodded. I don't remember saying

anything. Then I came back here and I . . .
I bawled my fucking eyes out. That's where
you came in, remember?"

"I just hate coming in late on movies."

That made her smile, and she kissed me.
It was messy, snot and tears and saliva, but
it was still wonderful. For about fifteen
seconds, I thought she loved me. Maybe she
thought so, too. For fifteen seconds.

"What now, kiddo?"

She sighed. "Just get through this goddamn weekend. You think this dump has
enough champagne to help me do that,
Nate?"

"I should think so. You want to skip
Frank's show tonight?"

"No! I don't blame him for this."

Apparently the Giancana infraction was
forgotten.

"Anyway," she said, "I always listen to
Frankie before I go to sleep. You come pick
me up at seven thirty."

I said fine, and was halfway out the door
when she called: "But I'm not sitting with
those two traitors!"

She meant the Lawfords.

"Get us a table for two," she said, "in
back."

I made all that happen, and the Lawfords
knew she was upset, though she was polite

to them, saying she just didn't want to be in the spotlight tonight, since she wasn't doing the "full Marilyn."

Full or partial, she was lovely in a white satin dress that clung nicely to her lithe figure. She'd combed and arranged and sprayed her hair to decent effect, and the light touch of her makeup I thought looked swell. You could even make out her freckles under the light layer of powder.

As for Sinatra, he did an almost completely different line-up of songs, and dedicated one to his "friend Zelda Zonk" — "My Funny Valentine." Maybe he was less than a good man, but he sure was a great artist — "Goody Goody," "Imagination," "I Get a Kick Out of You," and the sheer beauty and sensitivity he brought to "Moonlight in Vermont" was bewildering, if you knew the guy.

As promised, Marilyn drank a lot of champagne that evening. I held it to a couple of gimlets, because I had a hunch she'd need some tending. We skipped the post-show cocktail lounge bit and I dropped her off at her chalet.

"Stay again," she said in the doorway. "I want you here all night."

"Can I leave my gun behind?"

"That depends on what you mean by 'gun.'"

I smiled. Kissed her nose. "I'll be back in five or ten minutes."

At my cabin, I got out of my evening clothes and into another polo and some H.I.S. slacks. Grabbed my toothbrush again, and the phone rang.

"Heller," I said.

"Nate," a rough, familiar voice said. "This is Joe. I'm glad I finally got you."

Joe DiMaggio.

"Listen, that prick Sinatra won't let me in there. I wanna see Marilyn. I wanna talk to Marilyn."

"Where are you?"

"Not far. I got a room at the Silver Crest Motel. It's practically next door. She's there, right? They say at the desk she isn't registered, but that housekeeper of Marilyn's told me she was coming up there, to be with Sinatra, that lousy son of a bitch."

This was the most words at one time I'd ever heard him string together. And by the way, you could always count on Mrs. Murray, right? What a gal.

"You came to the wrong guy," I said. "Kind of like when you and Sinatra went looking for Marilyn, that time?"

"Huh?"

"Slugger, you're the last person on earth I'd put in touch with Marilyn."

And I hung up on the bastard.

When I got to her chalet, Marilyn was watching television. It was a little console that she could see from the round bed, but she wasn't under the covers, she was sitting on the edge of it, still in her white satin dress.

Her eyes were wide. Whites showing all around.

But she wasn't doing a dumb-blonde Betty Boop shtick — oh, no. She was pissed off. Truly, royally pissed off.

She looked at me with those eyes staying wide but going crazed. "I just caught the late news. Guess what? Bobby is in LA this weekend!"

"Really?"

"He gave a speech to a bunch of goddamn insurance agents. And he's in to talk with executives at Fox, where he's trying to get a movie made from his book."

"*The Enemy Within.*"

"Yes. They say he's going to be a regular Eliot Ness in the picture. Eliot Ness! Wasn't he fictional, like Dick Tracy?"

"Not exactly. Are you all right?"

She got up, charged over to the set and hit the on/off switch with a little fist. *"That's* why they brought me up here! Sure, to lecture me like a bad little girl . . . but mostly to get my ass out of the way, so I didn't do anything *embarrassing!*"

"I'd say you're right on the money."

"He was in LA, Nate! He could have come to see me! Personally! To talk to me, and tell me *himself* it's over. Maybe tell me he still loves me, but it's a far better fucking thing than he has ever fucking done before! Does he have a spine, your friend? Does he have balls?"

Now Bobby was *my* friend. That wasn't fair.

"Honey," I said, "they're a bunch of self-centered, self-interested bastards."

"And bitches! And *bitches!* Don't forget Pat!"

A knock at the door.

"Get that!" she ordered.

I got it — it was a bottle of Dom Pérignon in an ice bucket. I took it from the kid, gave him a half a buck and sent him on his way.

"Somebody sent you champagne," I said.

"Right. Somebody who loves me. Me."

We sat on the bed, backs to the headboard, sipping champagne. Or anyway I sipped it. She pretty much gulped. She told me in detail about her relationship with Bobby, how many times they met, how many times they'd made love, all of the elaborate promises he'd made, including leaving Ethel for her. In Bobby's defense, if Marilyn Monroe is in your arms, any man is probably going to want to leave any woman named Ethel.

Then she got up and walked around the room, pacing, stalking, describing everything she was going to say and do in public. Telling me about notebooks she'd kept and how she had Bobby on two of the tapes, thanks to my wiretap. Shit, and I'd warned him! Finally she got tired and came back with a glass in one hand and the champagne bottle in the other.

"What kind of notebooks?" I asked.

"Spiral kind. Started when I would get help from Romy and from his son, Danny, to come up with good questions to ask Bobby. I'd write those down in a spiral. Bobby's an intellectual. I know current events okay, but not enough to talk to the General."

That's what she called Bobby sometimes: the General.

"So," she was saying, in her comic overenunciated way, "I'd come home and write down the things he'd say. Answers to my questions. Wouldn't like some of that to come out, would they? Cuba, for instance?"

She was too drunk to reason with, so I just agreed with her.

It was probably around two or maybe even later when she passed out. I lifted her like a bride about to be carried over a threshold, and somehow maneuvered the covers back and nestled her in there.

I slept on the chaise lounge again, considering this bodyguard duty. I'd had my reward this afternoon.

The next morning, she woke before I did. In fact, she jostled me awake.

"Nate? I'm getting some air. Sorry. Go back to sleep, sugar. Didn't want you to wake up and see I was gone."

She was in a white bathrobe and slippers. I watched her slip out, like a ghost, then got up. Like yesterday, I was already dressed. I took time to pee and brush my teeth.

My watch said 6:00 A.M. Fog was settling in along the lake shore. I found Marilyn sitting at the pool again, her sandals off, kicking water gently, like a very small child. But her eyes were on a nearby hillside, a patch of green and granite up between cabins, including my own, where a figure stood like a sentry.

It was a guy in a red sport shirt and blue slacks, the colors making him pop out of the wilderness setting. And even from a distance you could tell it was Joe DiMaggio. They were staring at each other.

Fuck it. I went in to see if I could get myself some breakfast. No matter what I thought of the guy, they deserved their privacy.

And he was far enough away he couldn't swing on her.

We flew back that afternoon, on Sinatra's jet. She had spent the rest of the morning in her chalet. I offered to stay with her but she told me, very sweetly, she needed to be alone.

Pat and Sinatra did not make the trip back. Mrs. Lawford flew to San Francisco, to make a connection that would send her to Hyannis Port; and Sinatra still had performances to give at Cal-Neva. I had my usual bungalow at the Beverly Hills Hotel booked ahead, since I wanted to take advantage of this Frank-funded trip to do some business and see my son again.

So it was just Lawford, Marilyn, and me on the plane. Very little conversation ensued. Both Peter and Marilyn were quite drunk, the former napping, the latter having even more champagne, courtesy of Joni, Sinatra's stewardess, whose number I snagged.

I didn't bother Marilyn, but as we were about to land — darkness had fallen in Los Angeles — I told her I'd be in town for a week or so.

"What we talked about last night," I said softly, Lawford snoring up a storm across from us, "you need to just forget all of that, and move on. With your career. Your life."

The beautiful face, bearing only lipstick and light powder, was an expressionless mask. "Are *you* lecturing me now, Nate?"

"No. I'm just a friend who wants the best for you."

"I know." Almost a smile. "I know."

When the wheels touched noisily down, Lawford woke up briefly, then settled back to sleep as we taxied.

"With this Fox thing settled," I whispered, "you want me to stop by and take out that wiretap?"

"You're free to stop by," she whispered back, and squeezed my arm. "But leave the wiretap."

"What for, honey?"

"You're not always around, Nate. And I may need protection."

A limo was waiting for her. There'd been rain earlier, and she was in her bare feet, tiptoeing toward the vehicle, lugging a red leather cosmetic case and matching bag.

She was in her head scarf but no sunglasses, still in the trusty lime-green top and white capris. The driver opened the door for her, and she got in.

Then she was just a pretty face smiling at me from the window, tiny hand waving, disappearing.

■ ■ ■ ■

Two:
What a
Way to Go!
August 5–12,
1962

■ ■ ■ ■

CHAPTER 13

The banging at the bungalow door alternated with the doorbell's ding until the racket had given up on trying to work itself into my dream and instead roused me from a deep, pleasant sleep.

Saturday had been a great day for me — I'd taken Sam to Grauman's Chinese, where we got to watch Sophia Loren bend over and put her hands in cement (no bad angle on that) and took in the matinee of her latest movie, *Boccaccio '70,* one of those arty foreign jobs that made little sense, but also had Anita Ekberg and Romy Schneider in it. The European landscape, with its rolling hills and inviting valleys, was lush enough to hold the interest of a teenager and his old man.

That evening I'd taken a starlet out, to take in Bobby Darin at the Cloister supper club on the Strip — I'd done a Chicago job for Darin, and was able to get my date backstage for an autograph and some harmless flirtation. She was an attractive redhead of twenty-three who made a point of not putting out on the first date. Fortunately this had been our third.

Anyway, she was long since back in her Studio City apartment — I loved it when they had their own car — and I was enjoying the big roomy double bed when that racket ensued.

Despite my good mood, I took time to get my nine-millimeter out of the suitcase. There was no real reason to suspect anything was amiss, and this wasn't twenty or thirty years ago when unfriendly people with weapons occasionally dropped in on me in the middle of the night, or rather pre-dawn morning.

But I took it along just the same, padding out into the living room in my shorts, T-shirt, and bare feet. I cracked the door, looked past the night latch, catching my visitor poised with raised fist, about to deliver yet another knock.

"What the hell?" I said.

It was Roger Pryor, who I'd last seen in a "TV repair" van in Brentwood.

"Let me in, Nate," he said, breathing hard. His breath was lousy; of course, so was mine. "For Chrissake, lemme in. . . ."

I let him in, and closed the door behind him, reapplying the night latch.

He looked like hell — his thinning blonde hair uncombed, his eyes bloodshot, his bland, deeply creased boyish face reddish, his phony 24-HOUR ELECTRIC jumpsuit rumpled.

"What's that for?" he blurted, pointing at the gun in my left hand.

"People don't usually drop by at five in the morning," I said. "You know what they call guys from Chicago who aren't para-noid?"

"What?"

"Dead." I motioned to the couch. "Can what it is wait till I pee and get my trousers on?"

He swallowed and nodded, then stumbled over to the couch and flopped, while I headed to the john, then back into the bedroom. I returned the gun to my suitcase, swapping it for a fresh polo and some slacks. I stayed barefoot.

When I joined him, pulling a chair around so I could sit facing him, Pryor had a sick look, the red replaced by fish-belly white. I thought he might paint the carpet.

"You okay?"

He swallowed. "It's just the fuckin' diabetes. Why don't *you* age, Heller, like the rest of us?"

"Clean living. To what do I owe this honor?"

Another swallow, then an earnestness came into his face, and a little color. "This is a job I was working for *you*, remember — you aren't my *only* client, but you're *in* this. You *are* in this."

"Roger, what the hell are you —"

"You invited yourself in!" His defensiveness crackled like electricity; maybe it was the jumpsuit. "*You* tell *me* — when I told you who I was working for, the multiple clients? Did you keep that to yourself? Or did you run over to Lawford's goddamn castle, and spill?"

Was that a guess?

With neither sarcasm nor rancor, I asked, "Are you sick? Do you need a doctor? Food? Drink? There's twenty-four-hour room service here, and it's not just a scam written on the side of van." Well, some sarcasm in that last part.

He was tasting his mouth; he didn't seem to like the flavor, yet he kept tasting. Still, he did not request a room-service alternative, merely stating flatly, "She's dead."

"Who is dead?" I asked.

Knowing.

He glanced all around, including up and down. "Is this place . . . safe?"

"You mean is some asshole bugging it? You tell me."

". . . It's Marilyn."

The sigh I let out took a while.

His eyes were as moist as they were red. "Looks like a drug overdose. There's people all over that place. Cars. Ambulance. Christ knows."

"But do the *cops* know?"

His eyes popped. "*Some* know, all right. Jesus shit, man, I was asleep in the van. Shorthanded working a double shift." The shaggy eyebrows went up. "Heard some very interesting stuff in the late afternoon. Very interesting. You want to hear?"

"Eventually. For now, skip ahead."

"Okay. Early evening, I was monitoring, you know, in the headset, and it was just . . . normal shit. Dull. Nothing going on. Far as the phone went, couple of calls to Lawford, about some party over there she decided not to go to."

"Go on."

He shrugged, his eyes staring past me as he collected and ordered thoughts. "She talked to DiMaggio's son for a while — kid had broke up with a girlfriend or something, and Marilyn said she was glad, didn't think the girl was right for the boy. Just a friendly, social call. Anyway, dull shit. I took off the headphones and went over and crawled on my little sofa. She was in bed, getting ready to go to sleep — why shouldn't I? Nobody was over there or anything."

"Not Mrs. Murray?"

"That witch? Yeah, well, she was there. She was sleeping over. She didn't *always,* but she did tonight . . . I mean, last night? Christ, is that the sun?"

"Seems to be."

He leaned forward, frowning, the shaggy eyebrows trying to meet. "Look, Nate, my boys and me, we seldom monitor the tapes after a subject's bedtime. We check them later, of course, but . . ."

"Then how did you know she was dead? You must have heard something."

"I'll *tell* you what I heard — somebody banging on my door and waking me the hell up!"

I could relate.

"I mean, inside that van?" He shook his head. "It sounded like cannons going off, scared the fuck out of me, somebody slamming their fist against the metal. I bet they goddamn *dented* it."

"So who was it?"

"Intel." He gave the word the ominous

tone it deserved. "I don't know their names. Hamilton wasn't with them. But they were *intel,* all right."

Los Angeles Police Intelligence Division. Captain James Hamilton was Chief Parker's man in charge. And if I can think of something good to say about Hamilton, you'll be the first to know.

"What did they do, Roger?"

"Right off, they cuffed me. But they didn't drag me out and stuff me in a car, they just pushed me onto that little sofa I got in there. The cuffs were behind my back and it was goddamn uncomfortable, I can tell you. Anyway, it was two white guys and a spic. They got a couple spics on the PD now and even a few colored."

"Skip the sociology."

"Sure. They showed me their badges and told me wiretapping was illegal in Los Angeles County, and they took every tape. Every fucking one of 'em."

"Every tape, meaning . . . ?"

"All of the August fourth tapes were there in the van. You know, the ones that I knew the contents of, the morning and afternoon stuff. But also the tapes that started about the time I fell asleep."

"Meaning, her death might be recorded on *those* tapes."

"I guess. But what was there to hear? She probably took pills, right? She wouldn't fuckin' narrate it. She'd just swallow them." He shrugged a single shoulder. "If she puked, you'd hear that, probably."

"If she puked," I said, "she might not be dead. You haven't said how you know."

"Know . . . ?"

"That Marilyn is dead."

"Oh." Another shrug, a full, sour-faced one. "Those pricks *told* me. 'Marilyn Monroe killed herself tonight,' one of 'em says. 'Overdose,' he says. 'Had to happen sooner or later.' White guy with bad pockmarks and capped teeth, like an actor. 'And you were eavesdropping. How's that gonna be for business?' Something like that, anyway, is what he said."

"And they just left you there?"

He nodded once. "When they had what they wanted, they uncuffed my ass. Hell, I was glad just not to be dragged to some basement and beat on like a redheaded stepchild."

"And that was it?"

"Before they left, the other white guy, skinny character with orange hair and blue eyes, he says, 'Your best bet to stay in business is forget you had this particular job. You were never here. Get it?' I got it."

I frowned. "How do you read this?"

He rolled his eyes. "Shit, man, I don't know. Chief Parker and Hamilton are pretty chummy with the Kennedys. They say Parker is up for Hoover's job, someday. Maybe the intel boys were cleaning up for the K's. But I don't put it past the intel boys to be working for the Outfit, or hell, even the Company. All the interested parties, which is to say my various clients, have plenty of money to spread."

"Maybe even enough," I said dryly, "to corrupt such fine public servants."

That made him laugh. Nervously, but he laughed.

"Christ, Nate, where does that leave us?"

"Us?"

"You're one of my clients! I was tapping Marilyn's line for *you,* remember."

"Yeah you were. Among how many others?"

He spread his hands, and the shaggy eyebrows climbed his forehead. "You got to ask yourself — you want this in the papers? When the cops come around, *not* the intel boys, but whatever *real* cops catch this case, do you want to tell them you were bugging Marilyn's bedroom?"

"At her *behest,*" I reminded him.

"At whoever the fuck's behest! You want

to be in the middle of this?"

I was afraid maybe I already was.

But I asked, "Why are you here, Roger?"

"Because . . ." He swallowed and made his tone less defensive. ". . . First of all, we need to cover for each other."

"Cover how?"

"By neither of us telling more cops or FBI or for shit sake the papers or *anybody* else about the wiretap job we did for Marilyn."

"The cops'll know she's been tapped."

"I don't think so."

I studied him. "*Why* don't you think so?"

He was trembling. Not a lot, but noticeably. His eyes were no longer meeting mine, instead moving with the search for something to say to me that wouldn't get him slapped.

Finally he said, "Maybe I *did* go in there."

I slapped him.

"Fuck! What was *that* for?"

I grabbed the front of his electrician's uniform, just as I had the TV repair one in the van at the beginning of this goddamn fucking mess.

"I'm gonna more than slap you, Roger, if you lie to me again. Every word from your mouth, from here on out, is going to be a shining beacon of truth."

He wrested himself away, only because I

let him. "What the hell's wrong with you, Heller? We're in this *together.*"

Calm now, or anyway pretending to be, I said, "I liked that woman, Roger. If this isn't suicide, I'll probably kill someone. And it won't be myself."

"It was suicide, all right," he said, waving that off.

"How did you get in?"

". . . I have a key."

"You said the place was crawling."

"That was later."

"What about Mrs. Murray?"

"She was talking to somebody in the kitchen — that doctor of Monroe's, Greenson, the shrink? Saw them through the sun-room window. I went around and slipped in the front door — it's right by where the hall goes to the bedrooms, you know. Her bedroom was just . . . right off there."

"I know. And you, what? Took your device off that phone?"

He was nodding. "Yeah. I can do that in, like, under thirty seconds, with my trusty screwdriver. Trickier getting rid of the wires to that tape recorder in her closet, though. Let the tape recorder be, because why *shouldn't* she own one? So a recorder was on a shelf in her closet, so what? And I had a transmitter in the overhead light to remove, too. Snagged that, and left."

"But you got them all?"

"Yeah."

"Wasn't there a tape in that machine?"

"No. And no stack of tapes, either. The intel boys must've beat me to it."

I looked at my watch: five twenty. "What time was this?"

"Maybe . . . two hours ago. She looked beautiful."

"What?"

"She was on her tummy. Face against her pillow. Hand on the receiver. Very sad. There was some, uh, lividity, of course. I mean, she *was* dead. But beautiful."

My stomach was hurting. Not with hunger.

I asked, "All this went down *after* your fun and games with the intel boys?"

More emphatic nodding. "Yes. Yes, that's how I knew she was gone, 'cause they told me. Like I said, I was sleeping, not monitoring. Don't look at me like that. If I'd been monitoring, would it have turned out any different?"

"Probably not," I admitted.

He smoothed his electrician's uniform shirt with a palm. "I think you owe me an apology."

"No. Time to tell me what you heard."

276

"I fuckin' *told* you! I wasn't —"

"*Earlier* that day. You said some 'very interesting stuff' took place."

"Yeah. It did." One shaggy eyebrow rose, and he lowered his voice, as if maybe somebody *was* listening, besides me. "Your friend Bobby Kennedy and Lawford dropped by. . . ."

"What?"

"You heard me. Marilyn was fussing with Mrs. Murray over some spread of food. Guacamole she'd made, some other Mexican-type stuff she'd bought for the occasion. She was all excited about 'the General' coming by to see her — 'personally.' Then Kennedy and Lawford showed up, around three fifteen. But I didn't hear much of Lawford. I think they sent him outside or something."

"What did you hear?"

"They were in the living room. It started out normal conversation level, and I couldn't make it out. That's not unusual. I mean, I had the master bedroom wired, and like I said before, it was right there off the living room, but the entryway is tiled, you know, and everything was kind of echoey and . . . at a distance."

"Understood."

He leaned forward. "But then their voices

got louder — they were obviously arguing about something. Something about 'broken promises.' And their voices grew shrill. Especially that Kennedy, man, when *he* gets pissed off, hell, he sounds like an old lady, all high-pitched and screechy."

"Were you getting words?"

"More . . . just the gist. She said, at one point, 'I feel used, I feel passed around.' Toward the end, Kennedy was wanting her to give him something — he kept saying, 'Where is it?' Or maybe it was, 'Where *are* they?' This he said over and over — they'd talk and argue, then more of this 'Where are they' shit."

"But what that *pertained* to . . . ?"

"No idea. Tapes? Anyway, Lawford must've heard them — I would guess he went out by the pool, to give them some privacy, but the pool is just off those glass doors in the living room, so he must have heard the yelling and got concerned. Because suddenly I could hear him talking."

"Peter got in the middle?"

"Exactly. That actor voice of his was easy to tag. He says, 'Calm down! Calm down!' to both of them. Then he was saying something about 'important to the family' and I definitely heard him say, 'We can make any arrangements you want!' Then Kennedy

278

said something, too muffled to make out, and Marilyn got very pissed — I think maybe things became physical, because there was this banging, flopping sound. Finally she was screaming at them, ordering them out of the house."

"And?"

He shrugged. "And they left."

"What happened after?"

"Next call of Marilyn's was pretty soon, maybe ten minutes later. She called that Greenson character and he came right over. He was there several hours."

"You hear any of their conversation?"

"No. I'm guessing they were talking in that sunroom. That's where they usually consulted. He's hardly been on any of these tapes over all these weeks. And that sunroom, it wasn't bugged. No other rooms were — just the phones themselves and the master bedroom."

I drew in some air and sat and thought. He let me do that.

After a while, he said, "Will you cover for me, Nate?"

"If you mean, am I willing to forget about the wiretap job Marilyn had us do . . . *what* wiretap job?"

He grinned. Nodded.

Now I leaned forward. Friendly. "But,

Roger — you need to lay low. This thing, death of a superstar like Marilyn? It's going to be big, and over the next few days, even weeks, nothing will be bigger."

His eyes were tight. "I know, but if we —"

I had silenced him with a raised hand. "Think about it. You've talked to me — one of your clients. And you talked to the intel boys, who were also your clients, right? But I bet you haven't talked to Sam Giancana or Jimmy Hoffa or any CIA spook, or any of their minions. Like Johnny Rosselli, for example, who could represent any one or all three."

His eyes were wide and his jaw slack as the pieces came together. "And . . . and *I* gave their tapes up."

"And you gave their tapes up. Here's the best part — you gave them up to the cops. The intel boys, granted . . . but that still counts as cops." I sat back. Shrugged. "I may do some minor poking around this thing — as I say, Marilyn was my friend — and until this nasty affair has shaken down, I would suggest you, as I said . . . lie low."

"Where?"

"You're not married, right? Not any-more?"

"Not anymore, right."

"Still got that little house in the hills?"

"Yeah."

"Don't go there. The tapes from before last night — where are they?"

"In my bank deposit box. I keep several boxes for sensitive material like this. Until delivery to the client, that's how I routinely handle it."

"No dupes or anything at your office?"

He shook his head. "No. Nothing. Not even any paperwork. Not on a deal like this."

"Good."

I got up and went into the bedroom, then came back with three C notes. "Go buy yourself a few clothes and supplies — groceries and sundries."

"What? Why?"

"So you don't get yourself killed. I'm calling Fred Rubinski. He'll come over with a key to our safe house, and directions. You stay put a while. I'll let you know when I think it's okay for you to reapply to the human race."

He didn't argue. He just sat there and took the bills, rather absently, and then nodded and said, "I appreciate this. For a guy who's kind of free with the physical stuff, you're okay, Nate. But why help me out?"

"Because, like you said, we're in this together. The same people looking for you might come looking for me, particularly if they found you first, and you made me popular with them."

"You think I'd rat you out."

"I know you'd rat me out."

Roger didn't argue the point.

So I called Fred, who bitched about being woken up blah blah blah, but when I said Marilyn was dead, and we needed to hide Pryor away for a while, my partner quickly got on board.

I didn't wait for him, though. I got dressed, leaving the gun behind, and halfway out the door said to Pryor, "Fred'll be here shortly. In the meantime, watch the place. Like, make sure nobody bugs it."

"Where are you going?"

"Brentwood. Fifth Helena Drive."

He was chewing on that when I shut the door and went out into windy warmth and a dawn throwing long shadows. My stomach hurt. I didn't feel anything like grief yet, not even simple sadness.

But I did feel sick.

Chapter 14

The morning was bright and remarkably clear for smoggy Los Angeles, pleasantly warm thanks to desert winds, though experience said by midday we'd have a scorcher.

It was pushing 6:00 A.M. when I followed a cream-colored, somewhat battered Ford van down the dead-end that was Fifth Helena Drive. The vehicle's side panels said WESTWOOD VILLAGE MORTUARY — no Roger Pryor fake-out, this was the genuine article, and a potentially nice piece of luck for me.

The van nosed through a gathering crowd of press and gawkers at the scallop-topped wooden gates. Two uniformed cops were on sentry duty and immediately opened up for the mortuary wagon, my Jag practically kissing its rear bumper. My window was down and the young cop I passed gave me a look as I glided by.

I nodded, said, "Coroner's office," and he

nodded back and returned his attention to the swarm of neighbors and reporters.

I'd spotted a few familiar faces in that crowd — Tommy Thompson, *Life*'s Beverly Hills man; showbiz columnist Jim Bacon of the Associated Press; Flo Kilgore, the *New York Herald Tribune* Hollywood correspondent. Flo was a brunette in her forties with pretty eyes, a weak chin, and a nice shape — I'd been out with her a few times, between husbands (she had just ditched her fourth). Wasn't sure if she'd made me, as I passed through the Fifth Helena portals.

But her presence, and that of those other famous ink slingers, was no surprise to me. On the radio on the way over I'd already heard the following: *"Marilyn Monroe is dead of suicide at age thirty-six. We grasp at straws as if knowing how she died will bring her back. Not since Jean Harlow have the standards of feminine beauty been so embodied in one woman. Marilyn Monroe — dead at thirty-six."*

For a news bulletin, that had been pretty studied; but with Marilyn's history of overdoses and other melodrama (as Sinatra put it), all the news services would have obits on file and even squibs like that, ready to go.

What really disturbed me was that flat pronouncement of suicide. If I was following a mortuary wagon in, then the body was still in the house. A little early in the game for a verdict, even from the newshounds.

I backed the Jag around so I'd be facing out if I had to beat a hasty retreat. For a moment my path was blocked by a pudgy guy in a suit walking Marilyn's little white mutt off somewhere. But I still managed to follow the two mortuary reps across the brick courtyard and into the house. Both wore the expected black suits and ties, slim, nondescript messengers of death — one shorter, fiftyish, Brylcreemed and bespectacled, the other a beanpole no more than twenty, with a flattop and his mouth hanging open.

Except for a quartet of milling uniformed cops, who just nodded at us as we came in, the living room was empty, Marilyn's Mexican-flavored decorations doing nothing to make the occasion less somber. Muffled conversation came from the direction of the dining room — I thought I picked out Pat Newcomb's voice, and maybe the indistinct murmur that characterized housekeeper Murray.

The two mortuary reps paused, probably to ask where the bedroom was, and I pitched in: "Just to your right." Making the turn into the nearby hallway, we saw two uniformed cops posted in the hall, one at her door. Nobody questioned it when I followed the black-clad duo inside the master bedroom, stepping over the long phone cord that led back to the fitting room.

A sheet had been pulled over Marilyn's body, with just tufts of her hair visible against a like-colored pillow. The older mortician carefully drew back the sheet and gathered it at the feet of the naked woman who was lying facedown, diagonally, toes bottom right, head top left and turned left, right arm bent, legs straight. Against her pale flesh, the bruising of lividity was stark.

"She's been moved," I said to the mortician.

He expressed no opinion.

Not that it was a matter of opinion: blood pools in the body when the heart stops pumping. If you die facedown, blood will settle along your chest. And she showed that distinctive bruised look on her face and neck, so had probably died facedown. Okay. Then why was there also lividity along her back? And the back of her legs and arms?

It takes four hours for lividity to reach a fixed state. Any movement of the body within that time frame would result in that bruised look. She seemed posed, as if to show she'd been talking or trying to get somebody on the phone, a hand hovering off the bed over a dropped receiver on the carpeted floor.

But if she'd overdosed on barbiturates, she would have suffered convulsions, and died in a contorted position. Not this gracefully tragic one, which was as studied as that radio bulletin.

Her entire body, save for the lividity-touched areas, had a bluish cast, as if she'd frozen to death, and her nails looked dark and dirty, probably from gardening.

The rest of the underfurnished space was a mess, much messier than I'd seen it on prior visits. A drinking glass on the floor near the bed, the phone and receiver (near her left hand), clutter on the nightstand (though pill bottles stood like little soldiers), letters and books and magazines on the floor, purses against one wall, very junky. No sign of her spiral notebooks, though.

Had the room been tossed?

"Rigor's set in," I noted.

This time the mortician replied: "Advanced."

"Time of death, educated guess?"

He adjusted his glasses and checked his watch; his mouth moved silently with math.

Then he said, "Between nine thirty and eleven thirty last night." He shook his head, giving the naked, bruised body a sorrowful look. "It'll take a while to straighten her out and get her on the gurney."

The young mortuary guy said, "Jeez, Pop, she just looks like some girl. Not Marilyn Monroe."

So it was a family business. That was heartwarming.

Pop was getting a paper bag out of his pocket and brushing the pills into it; they were rattling, the bottles mostly full, apparently.

"Hey!" I said. "What the hell are you doing?"

"Collecting evidence for the coroner, Detective."

I guessed "detective" would do fine as a designation for me. Anyway, it was too late to stop him; maybe that sweeping motion had preserved some fingerprints.

Father and son were starting the grisly task of bending the dead woman's stiff limbs into the desired position, and I'd had about enough. Before I left, I noticed something odd — Marilyn's black-out curtains were brushed aside, revealing that a window had been broken, and some boards haphazardly put up on the outside.

In the hallway, I asked the uniformed guy what the deal was with the window.

"Marilyn's shrink had to break in." He gestured with a thumb at the door he was leaning against. "This was locked."

"Really?" I took a look at the keyhole lock. "So who cleaned up the glass?"

"Huh? Nobody cleaned up the glass."

"Well, if he broke in from outside, there'd be glass on the floor. There isn't any."

He just shrugged. "That's for you detectives to scope out."

Everybody thought I was a detective. I guessed I *was* a detective. Here I thought I was with the coroner's office. . . .

The dining room turned out to be the holding area for people waiting to be questioned. Under a swag-chained star of frosted glass and leaded copper, at a big rustic round wooden table with a handcrafted look, sat four people who might have been attending a séance.

Shell-shocked Pat Newcomb, her dark blonde hair a mess, wore sunglasses and pajamas under a tan raincoat. Jowly, dark-haired, dark-eyed Mickey Rudin (Marilyn's attorney as well as Sinatra's) looked professional and put-upon in a brown suit and loosened tie. A somber horse-faced guy about fifty (Dr. Hyman Engelberg, I later learned) wore a sport coat and no tie. And Ichabod Crane–ish handyman Norman Jefferies, in a dark sweater over a dark button-down shirt, sat with hands folded, like he was saying grace.

Two detectives had set up a temporary HQ in the nearby kitchen. A young plain-clothes dick, taking notes, had borrowed one of the wooden chairs from the dining room table, and positioned it several feet away from the trestle table by the window that served as a breakfast nook. Another plainclothes cop, seated on a bench at that table, had his back to me as I entered, and across from him sat Mrs. Murray, looking like your least favorite grade-school teacher.

It wasn't at all secure — you could hear some of what was being said out in the din-ing room, I'd noticed, although with whis-pery Mrs. Murray you didn't get much. You barely picked it up in the room with her. She was wearing a sort of Aztec-pattern poncho (almost certainly a gift from Marilyn) over a simple cream-colored dress.

I moved to the Hotpoint fridge where I could get a side view of the detective doing the interview. I was pleased and relieved to see that these officers were not intel — likely from the West Los Angeles Detective Divi-sion, since the guy asking the questions was Lt. Grover Armstrong, who ran it.

Armstrong I knew, but the younger guy

no, and he climbed out of his chair and demanded who I was, since after all I was just somebody who'd wandered unbidden out into the kitchen. He didn't look bright, a crew-cut former jock, but I gave him credit for being the first person to really question my presence.

I didn't bother answering the kid. I just waited for heavyset, fortyish Armstrong to swivel his bucket head and recognize me. We weren't friends, but we weren't enemies, either.

Mildly irritated by the interruption, he excused himself to Mrs. Murray and slid off the bench onto his feet and faced me, hands doing Superman on his hips. His suit was brown and baggy but his tie was fresh and crisply knotted.

"What are you doing here, Nate?"

"I was on a job for Marilyn. I heard about this and came over."

"How'd you get in?"

"I lied."

That seemed an acceptable answer to the seasoned copper. "What kind of a job?"

Over in the breakfast nook, from behind her cat's-eye glasses, Mrs. Murray was gazing at me with undisguised contempt, certain I was about to betray Marilyn.

"Helping out on security," I said.

The younger officer already didn't like me. He said, "Yeah? Helping how?"

"That gate out front? My idea."

The kid was staring at me, searching for sarcasm. He wasn't that good a detective.

Armstrong was studying me. Then he said, "You know these people?"

"Some of them."

"You want to sit in on the interviews? If something strikes you, you can even ask a question."

"I'd like that."

He gestured to his side of the bench. "Come on in, then."

I sat next to him, and Mrs. Murray made a point of not looking at me as she said, "He's not a policeman."

"No," Armstrong said, right across from her, "but he's a professional detective and Miss Monroe hired him in that capacity."

That's all he gave her.

"I need to back up," Armstrong said. "You told the first officer on the scene, Officer Clemmons, that you discovered something was wrong with Miss Monroe around midnight. But the police weren't called till four twenty-five A.M."

"I was mistaken," she said with the kind of patient little smile a grandmother gives a really stupid grandchild. "This was upsetting to me, and I must have lost track of time. It may have been closer to three thirty that I noticed a problem."

Armstrong's eyebrows hiked. "You lost track of three and a half hours?"

The smile, ever more inappropriate, turned up at the corners. "You know how it is."

Armstrong gave me a sideways glance. Neither of us knew how it was.

"So what time," the lieutenant asked, "did you call Dr. Greenson?"

Speaking of which, where *was* Greenson? I didn't interrupt to ask.

"I believe I called him at three thirty-five," she said. She had her usual withdrawn, otherworldly air; but there was something else, too — was she frightened?

"When did he get here?"

"Oh, Dr. Greenson lives close by — he must have arrived five or ten minutes later."

Armstrong glanced at the young cop taking this down. The cop showed no reaction to any of this. A witness had just carved three and a half hours off a statement made to another officer only an hour before.

"All right, then," Armstrong said. "Now that we've . . . corrected the time frame, let's back up and go over how you first got concerned about Miss Monroe."

The vague, whispery voice continued: "Certainly. I went to bed about ten o'clock. I'd noticed the light was on under Marilyn's door, and assumed she was talking on the telephone with a friend, which was not unusual, so I went to bed. I woke up at midnight, and had to use the bathroom. The light was still on under Marilyn's door, and I became quite concerned. She'd been in bed since late evening and should have been asleep by now. I tried the door, but it was locked, you see."

"Locked?"

"Yes, from the inside." She shifted primly, her hands in her lap. "I knocked, but Marilyn didn't answer. So I called her psychiatrist, Dr. Greenson, who as I say lives nearby. When he arrived, he too failed to rouse her with his knocking, so he went outside and looked in through the bedroom window. He saw Marilyn lying motionless on the bed, looking peculiar. He broke the window with a fireplace poker I provided, and climbed inside and came around and opened the door. He said, 'We've lost her.'"

"And after that?"

"Dr. Greenson called Dr. Engelberg. Marilyn's internist. He arrived shortly and pronounced her dead."

This she had delivered with the emotion

of a grocery clerk requesting payment.

"What did you do after finding the body?"

She tossed her head girlishly. "Oh, so many things. I realized there would be hundreds of people involved, and of course I had to dress." She touched the gay poncho. "All *sorts* of things to do. I called Norman Jefferies, a handyman employed by Marilyn. I called and asked him to come over immediately and repair the broken window."

Which he had done by hammering a few boards over it. *Before* the police arrived.

"Then," she was saying, and gave a little wave, "I was doing other things. You know how it is."

"What kind of things?"

"Getting my own possessions together. Why, I've practically lived here most of the time these past months, and I have many personal items besides my clothes. There's a laundry basket of mine here, and I filled it with my things. I really don't know what else there is I can tell you."

Marilyn's housekeeper/companion folded her arms, her sad, sick smile continuing. She had spoken her piece.

"Well — thank you, Mrs. Murray."

She smiled and nodded, slipped off the bench from behind the trestle table and exited with studied dignity, back into the dining room.

Armstrong sighed, got up and slid in where Mrs. Murray had been, so he could face me.

"Well?" he asked.

"You want to start?"

"No," he said wearily. "Take a run at it."

"First of all, how prepared does that story sound? Marilyn was 'motionless' and looked 'peculiar' . . . who talks like that?"

He didn't bother answering.

"And this business about 'Norman Jefferies, a handyman employed by Marilyn.' He's Mrs. Murray's damn *son*-in-law."

"You missed the part," Armstrong said, almost groaning, "where I tried to get Monroe's activities for the day out of her. She was vague, downright evasive."

"Possibly lying. Go take a look at the carpet in that hall — it's wall-to-wall. The door is flush to it. I may be wrong, but I doubt any light could show under it."

"I hadn't noticed that."

"I take it there was no suicide note."

"No."

"Did you find a key in that bedroom?"

"No."

"I didn't think so. Lieutenant, this is an old house, with old-fashioned doors and locks. I bet the keys are all long gone. That break-in was staged — how exactly did Dr. Greenson look into a bedroom with black-out curtains over the windows and see a goddamn thing? Plus, no glass on the floor. Was there glass on the ground outside?"

"Yeah." He gave up a heavy sigh. "So we agree the scene was staged. What do you make of it?"

"Well, it's probably not murder. Marilyn has a history of this kind of thing. Suicide attempts, girl who cried wolf stuff, but also going overboard with drugs."

"You see her recently, Nate? Did she seem depressed?"

"I saw her a few days ago. Her career was going great guns."

"I read she got fired. . . ."

"She just got rehired, and at a big pay boost." I shrugged. "She had a few personal problems. In the love-life department. And anybody with that kind of problem can have a bad night and decide to cash it in."

"Is that what happened here?"

"I'll be honest, Lieutenant, I hate to think of it ending like that. She was flawed, a cross between a genius and a little girl lost . . . but she was one of a kind, and I really thought she had a shot at making it over the long haul. It's small solace, but I think the more likely answer is that she misjudged her self-medication."

"My understanding is Miss Monroe was a heavy user who knew exactly what she could and could not get away with, in the pharmaceutical area."

"Normally. But she was clean. She cleaned up for that movie, and — except for sinusitis she was fighting — was healthier than ever. Sure, she had a champagne binge now and then, but as of this last week, the only pills she was on were sleeping pills. Light dosage. Insomnia was the problem, you know."

He leaned his chin into an elbow-supported hand. "So she had trouble getting to sleep, misjudged, and took too many pills."

"That's my guess, Lieutenant. But it's not a wild one."

"So not a murder."

"Probably not a murder."

He sighed, dropped his hand, shook his big head. "What's going on, then? The housekeeper first saying 'around midnight,' then it's three thirty. . . ."

"What do you *think,* Lieutenant? The docs called the studio when they found her dead — 'cause dead or alive, she's a star and a property, *Fox's* property, and the studio wants to stage-manage the scene. If there was a note, they destroyed it — recently they smeared her in the press, and now they'd prefer an accidental death to a suicide where they come up the villain. You've been there before — this joint was probably swarming with studio cleanup crew."

Armstrong knew I was right. "Fucking one-industry town," he groused. "Waltz into crime scenes and treat 'em like a goddamn movie set."

"No," I said. "They respect movie sets. Movie sets they leave alone. Screws with continuity."

Next up was Mickey Rudin. Milton. I knew him to speak to, but he'd never done any business with me personally or the A-1, either.

The attorney wasn't exactly fat but it was an effort to get himself squeezed into the nooklike area formed by the trestle table and its benches. His jowls had five o'clock shadow — well, 5:00 A.M. shadow, anyway.

He didn't wait for a question, just started right in.

"Last evening, eight four sixty-two, my message service received a call at eight twenty-five P.M. that was relayed to me at eight thirty P.M. I was to call Milton Ebbins, an acquaintance of mine who is an agent. Around eight forty-five P.M., I called Mr. Ebbins, who told me he'd received a call from his client Peter Lawford, who stated he had called Miss Monroe about a party she was to have attended at his home on the beach. But Miss Monroe's voice seemed to fade out, and the connection was broken. Mr. Lawford's attempts to call her back were unsuccessful, the line busy, and Mr. Ebbins requested that *I* call Miss Monroe and determine that everything was all right. Short of that, I was to attempt to reach one of her two doctors. At about nine P.M., I tried to call Miss Monroe and the phone was answered by the housekeeper, Mrs. Murray, who assured me that Miss Monroe was all right. That, Lieutenant Armstrong, is all I know."

After that performance, I damn near expected him to take a bow. But he just gave Armstrong a nod, ignoring me, and worked his way out of the nook, like a piece of shrapnel finding its way through flesh.

This gave the lieutenant time to ask, "Mr. Rudin — what are you doing here now?"

"Dr. Greenson called me. I thought I might be needed."

Then he was gone.

"Fucking lawyers," Armstrong said.

I couldn't disagree.

The young cop ushered Pat Newcomb in next. She almost staggered in, still wearing the sunglasses. She took her position across from Armstrong in the nook, freezing when she saw me. I guess she hadn't really noticed my presence before.

"Nate Heller?" she said, as if not sure I was me. "What are you doing here?"

There was nothing accusatory in it.

"Just trying to help out, Pat. You can talk freely to Lieutenant Armstrong. He's one of the good guys."

Armstrong gave her a serious, supportive smile. "How are you feeling, Miss Newcomb?"

"How the hell do you think I feel, losing my best friend?"

And she began to cry.

I told the young plainclothes kid to get her some Kleenex; he gave me a look that said he didn't like being ordered around by a private detective, even if that private detective was older and wiser. But he did it.

When she'd gathered herself, Pat said, "I . . . I'm sorry. That was uncalled-for. What can I tell you?"

I didn't know whether that last was in the vernacular — as in, *what can I say?* — or a genuine offer to the investigator.

"How did you happen to be here, Miss

Newcomb, when we arrived?"

Her reply seemed, at first, a non sequitur: "I was home sick. I was here yesterday — slept over. Marilyn knew I wasn't feeling well, fighting a bad case of bronchitis, and offered me a sort of sanctuary. Typical of her, that kind of concern for a friend. 'You can sun in the back,' she said, 'and get all the rest you want, and forget about going to the hospital.' "

"What was her state of mind?"

"She was in wonderful spirits. Very good mood — very happy. Friday night we had a nice dinner at a quiet little restaurant near here. Saturday she was puttering around the house, just getting things done — this was the first home she ever owned herself, you know. It was all apartments and rentals before, and . . . she was excited, a little girl with a new toy."

"Can you remember what time you left? And what was her mood then?"

"Probably . . . five forty-five? Six? Her mood hadn't changed. She smiled at me from the door and said, 'See you tomorrow. Toodle-oo!' "

"And you went home?"

"Yes. To bed. Took some medicine. Slept till a phone call woke me, from Mickey Rudin, uh, Milton Rudin. He's Marilyn's attorney, but then you must know that, and he's also Dr. Greenson's brother-in-law."

That last I hadn't known, nor had Armstrong, apparently, based on our exchange of glances. Immediately it explained where the chain of phone calls had begun.

"Mickey . . . Mr. Rudin . . . said Marilyn had . . . had accidentally overdosed."

Again the lieutenant and I traded looks.

"I came over here and met with my boss, Arthur Jacobs. I'm Marilyn's publicist. Did I say that? Her publicist. Mr. Jacobs is my boss. It's his agency."

"Mr. Jacobs was here?"

"Yes."

Armstrong frowned. "He was gone by the time my sergeant and I arrived."

"Well, I know Arthur will cooperate in every *way.* . . ."

We heard a commotion in the dining room and then a big craggy guy came barging into the kitchen, a bull in search of a china shop. He wore a gray suit, somewhat rumpled, though not as rumpled as his face.

Pat Newcomb jumped a little, and I might have smiled if our uninvited guest hadn't been Captain James Hamilton.

"What the hell is this cocksucker doing here?" he demanded in an unmusical baritone, giving me the Uncle Sam Wants You point.

Then his football-sized head — with its slicked-back black hair, small eyes, long knobby nose, jug ears, and Kirk Douglas dimpled chin — acknowledged Pat Newcomb with an apologetic nod.

"Sorry, ma'am," he said. "Well? What's this cocksucker *doing* here, Lieutenant?"

"Mr. Heller was working security for Miss Monroe," Armstrong said, looking back at the superior officer and holding in his anger. "I asked him to sit in on the interviews. He knows some of these folks, and is familiar with the circumstances."

"Well, whoop-de-doodly-doo," Hamilton said. "On your feet, Heller. Thanks for your help, get the fuck out. Lieutenant, Intelligence Division is taking over this investigation."

"Sir?" Armstrong said, swinging out of the bench and onto his feet before I could get to mine.

"Have you got statements from all these people?"

"Yes. Preliminary ones. This is the second round. I'm trying to flesh —"

"I said on your *feet,* Heller! . . . Lieutenant, release these people, and you and Sergeant Byron turn your notes over to my men. We'll take over from here."

"Yes, sir." Armstrong moved past me, and Pat slipped out of the nook, quickly, exiting like a thief after a smash and grab.

Hamilton turned his dark little eyes on me, and his Sen Sen breath, too. "Are you still here?"

Twenty years ago I'd have made a wise-crack. Thirty years ago I'd have tried to goad him into laying hands on me so I could collect a few teeth.

"Just going," I said.

Much as I found Hamilton's presence odious, that he was here spoke volumes — as the commander of intel, he rarely showed at any crime scene, much less a suicide and never a possible accidental death. Yes, it was Marilyn Monroe, but, still — what brought Chief Parker's top dog to Fifth Helena?

I was afraid I knew, and it was not anything I'd brought up in my otherwise frank discussion with Lieutenant Armstrong, who'd had a short run indeed as the cop in charge of the Monroe investigation.

We were all escorted out the kitchen door by an intel sergeant whose pockmarks and capped teeth identified him as one of the dicks who'd rousted Roger Pryor in his van.

Then, as we came around the house, we got a last look at Marilyn. . . .

It was 6:30 A.M. when she was wheeled over the *Cursum Perficio* tiles and onto the bumpy brick courtyard. She was shrouded in a blue woolen blanket I remembered from her bed, nothing of her showing, though you could make out the shape of her hands folded across her stomach. She appeared tiny. Leather straps held her down by the feet and waist.

The gates were opened by the cops on guard, just as the gurney was being loaded up and into the nondescript van by the father-and-son mortician team. Photographers and reporters rushed in, like a tide taking the shore, and questions were hurled at all of us, overlapping into chaotic unintelligibility, against the strobing of flashbulbs.

Pat Newcomb, reacting to the flashes about as well as King Kong, shouted, "Keep shooting, vultures! Keep shooting!"

Possibly the first time a publicist had ever told the press what she really thought.

As the barrage of shouted questions continued, Pat was getting in on the passenger side of the two-tone green Dodge that either belonged to Norman, who was helping her, or Mrs. Murray, who Norman next guided into the back. Finally the handyman came around and got behind the wheel.

I beat them out, again tailing the mortuary wagon, nagged by a stray thought: hadn't Pat Newcomb said she'd driven over here? Then where was *her* car?

Right before I got through the gate and onto Fifth Helena, I caught Flo Kilgore's knowing smile and a tiny finger-point shooting gesture, *Gotcha,* that told me I'd be hearing from her soon. There were worse fates to suffer.

Where the little alley of a street emptied onto Carmelina Avenue, Marilyn went one way, and I went the other.

But all the questions her death raised rode with me.

CHAPTER 15

By mid-morning, Sorrento Beach — the sun high and hot over white sands blemished only by that distinctive seaweed the tide insisted upon delivering — had been invaded by skimpy-suited girls and boys and brightly colored umbrellas and beach chairs and, of course, volleyball nets.

A Top 40 station was doing a live feed from a kiosk, loudspeakers bombarding the kids with rock 'n' roll. Right now those who weren't knocking a ball across a net were twisting right there on the beach to "Irresistible You." Plenty of girls had the sort of platinum hair and stylized makeup Marilyn had made famous. Plenty of others were doing the Liz Taylor *Cleopatra* bit, before anybody knew if that movie would ever get finished, much less released.

A surprising number of kids were sitting on the sand reading a newspaper — not something you saw on this or any beach every day, but this wasn't just any day, was it? Some were even handling the papers with care, when finished reading, folding and covering them with a towel or putting them inside a side pouch of a bag with other precious items like suntan lotion, insect repellent, or cigarettes.

Both the *Herald* and the *Times* had put out EXTRA! editions, first time since the Bel Air fire last year. The *Times* headline said it all, in eighty-six-point type: MARILYN, DEAD. I had to give them points for style — somehow that comma provided punch and poignance, separating MM from death, making her bigger than mere mortality.

Viewing all this from behind the comfort of my Ray-Bans, I'd been walking the beach, up and down, in a tan Ban-Lon sport shirt by Puritan, white Levi's, white Keds, and no socks. For a guy almost three times as old as most of these infants, I looked young as hell; I'd been out here enough this summer to display a nice tan, if I kept my clothes on. The DJ was playing "The Wanderer" now, and that was about right. Since maybe nine thirty, I'd wandered this stretch of beach, and even found enough appetite for a hot dog and Coke at a stand, half an hour ago.

I'd returned to my bungalow at the Beverly Hills Hotel just long enough to decide against going back to sleep or having breakfast. I did call Fred Rubinski, who cursed me out for waking him up again but then stayed awake a while to say he'd helped Pryor out, and that the guy should be ensconced in our safe house by now. Fred also sat still for a rundown on what I'd seen and heard at 12305 Fifth Helena.

Typically gruff, he asked, "Then you figure it was an accidental overdose?"

"Yeah. But despite what I told 'em, I'm not with the coroner's office. So we may want to wait for another opinion."

"Here's an opinion — definitely a cover-up. Studio . . . or . . . ?"

"Don't say it."

He didn't. "You finished with this? Satisfied?"

"Don't know. We gotta get a handle on what's going on, or we'll be putting Roger Pryor up in that cottage till Christmas."

"Suppose so. These are dangerous waters, Nate."

I'd used those very words with Marilyn.

The waters looked not dangerous at all right now, the blue-green tide rolling in lazily. Not good surfing weather. But a fine day to walk along the beach or play volleyball or do the Twist on the sand near a

310

radio station kiosk that was maybe five hundred yards from the sprawling Lawford beach house.

The curtains were drawn on the big old place. Even the picture windows onto the ocean were covered, shuttered, unusual for summer. No sign of life, no flurry of activity here. I knew the mistress of the house, our president's sister, wasn't home — she'd left Cal-Neva for Hyannis Port and was still out there, with various other family members, though Bobby wasn't one of them. The paper said the attorney general was in San Francisco — had a speech to give on Monday to some other lawyers.

I walked up between houses where suddenly the Palisades Beach Road loomed, shockingly close to the beachfront properties. My Jag was parked up here, but I wasn't going to retrieve it yet. I had a call to make.

The bell and my knocking weren't getting a result, but I kept it up, alternating, until the Lawfords' Negro maid — in a tan uniform the color of my sport shirt — finally answered. She did not look happy.

"We're not receiving nobody today," she said, and started to close the door.

I inserted a Ked-shod foot, and the door caught it, making me long for Florsheims. I pushed my way in, and she stumbled back and had a frightened look, but I slipped off my Ray-Bans and calmed her, patting the air with a raised palm.

"Honey," I said, "I'm not a threat, and I'm not a reporter. I've been here before, remember? Or do we all look alike? Tell Mr. Lawford that Nate Heller is here to see him. Do it now."

But she recovered her dignity and held her ground. "No. Mr. Lawford isn't seeing nobody today."

"Is he still in bed? I know where the bedroom is."

Her eyes and nostrils flared, and she said, "Mr. Lawford is up but isn't, as I clearly stated, receiving nobody."

"Then I'll just wait here till he does." I leaned against the door behind me. "Let me know."

She had no idea how to deal with that, and — huffing a little bit, muttering under her breath — she finally went off. A good five minutes passed and I figured maybe she called the cops. There were certainly no Secret Service around. Then I heard footsteps and thought maybe Lawford himself was coming, but it was just her.

"He's in the den. Come with me."

"No, that's okay. I know where it is."

The den featured big windows and a collection of comfortable chairs and couches and walls with built-in bookcases that were also home to some fancy hi-fi equipment. But no music was playing and the windows were covered, and Lawford — in a blue polo and white deck pants — was slouched in a dark brown leather overstuffed couch with his sandaled feet up on an equally padded ottoman. One small lamp was on, on a distant end table, and the room was damn near dark.

I took a matching chair opposite him. To one side of the ottoman was a low-slung, mostly glass coffee table with *Esquire, Gentleman's Quarterly,* and *Playboy* magazines scattered, as well as a big glass pitcher of what might have been tomato juice but was probably equally vodka, a stalk of celery stuck in it. The coffee table was also home to a box of Kleenex, which had given birth to scattered wads of used tissues, some on the coffee table, others on the floor.

Lawford's berry-brown face looked terrible — deep grooves, flesh that seemed to have been frozen in the process of melting. His eyes were mostly red, half-hooded, and his graying hair was uncombed. Little dark splotches on the sport shirt indicated he had occasionally spilled a bit of Bloody

Mary on himself. A glass of the red stuff was in one hand, threatening to pour itself onto the Oriental carpet.

"Nathan," he said, and he smiled, though it was among the sadder smiles I've witnessed. "Glad to see you, old boy."

He got more British when he was sloshed.

He pitched forward and stuck out a hand and I shook it. To say it was a limp-fish shake would be to insult a limp fish. Then he flopped back.

"So kind of you to come. So kind. . . ." He sipped the drink. "Would you like one? There are glasses over there, or Erma Lee can fetch you something else . . . ?"

"No thanks," I said.

"She's dead, Nate. That poor girl's dead. And it's all my fault. All my *fault*. . . ."

Then he began to cry. To sob. Spilled some drink on himself but managed to put the glass on the coffee table and then just rolled up in a ball and bawled, right there on the couch. It went on for several minutes. I didn't comfort him.

When he seemed to have it out of his system, I said, "*Was* it?"

". . . What?" He righted himself. Looked at me like he'd forgotten I was there. Tears were all over his face, and snot, too. I pushed the box of Kleenex toward him. So

I guess maybe I did comfort him.

"Was it your fault, Peter? *Is* it your fault?

His lower lip trembled as he frowned. He had wiped his face and nose clean, and added another little wadded-up ball to the floor. "You . . . *you* don't blame me, do you, Nathan?"

"I don't blame anybody," I said. Yet. "I don't even blame Marilyn. I was at the house this morning, early this morning — saw them wheel her out."

He closed his eyes. Shuddered. "I'm glad Pat's not here. She would be . . . I know she *is* taking this hard . . . but at least her family's there . . . around her."

"I sat in on some of the police interviews, before the Intelligence Division came in and took over."

"Did they really? Hamilton and that bunch?"

"Yeah. How drunk are you?"

"I'm . . . all right. We can talk. I can tell you want to talk."

"Good." I crossed my legs, got comfortable. "I heard Mickey Rudin say you were the one who initiated the phone calls that led to Marilyn being found. You'd invited her to a party, and you checked on her, and were . . . concerned?"

He drew in a breath. Nodded. Then he

straightened up, sat more erect, clearing his mind, apparently. Of course, part of that process included finishing his current Bloody Mary and pouring himself another.

"I . . . I may have been the last person to talk to her alive," he said.

I managed not to point out the unlikelihood of anyone talking to her dead.

"What the hell happened last night, Peter?"

He shrugged his eyebrows. "Saturday afternoon, I mentioned to Marilyn that I was planning an informal barbecue for about eight o'clock that evening, out on the lanai. You know, people are in and out of here all day, in swimsuits, going to the pool, and generally enjoying themselves. So I was having a few friends over. Eventually we just had Chinese delivered. As it turned out, I was, uh . . . a little too high to manage an actual barbecue."

"Where does Marilyn come in, Peter?"

"I called her about seven, seven thirty . . . to see if she was coming. She said no . . . she was already in bed. She sounded terrible, very slurry. She almost seemed to be . . . slipping away."

"If she'd taken some chloral hydrate," I said, "she would be."

"Yes, I know, but I sensed she was . . . I

could feel her . . . the depression rolling in on her. Moving in. Like . . . like bad weather. Sometimes she couldn't understand what I was saying, and I started really *talking* to her, almost shouting . . . sort of a verbal slap, to wake her up."

"Peter, if she'd had sleeping pills —"

"You don't understand. Some of what she was saying . . . I didn't think she was saying good *night*, Nathan — I thought she was saying good-bye."

"Good-bye."

He nodded, took a swig of Bloody Mary, and said, " 'Say good-bye to Pat,' she told me. 'Say good-bye to Jack, and say good-bye to yourself . . . because you're a nice guy.' "

That last seemed like wishful thinking to me. She hadn't thought Lawford was a very nice guy at Cal-Neva, after he and his wife sat her down for a good talking-to. I'd say she hated him then. And that was just days ago. . . .

"I had a party under way," he was saying. "I do try to be a good host, and I didn't want to bother any of them with it."

"Who was there?"

"The Naars . . . a couple we've known for years; Joe's a TV producer. Bullets Durgom, the agent. My agent, Milt Ebbins, was supposed to come but begged off. Small group. Anyway, fifteen minutes, half an hour later, I was just not able to shake the feeling something was wrong . . . so I called Marilyn again, or tried to. I got a busy signal."

"How many numbers did you have of hers?"

"Just the one."

He may not have had the personal line. He may have been calling the phone in the fitting room, not the one with her in the bedroom.

Lawford was saying, "I called the operator, said I was concerned about a sick person at this number, and could she see if anyone was speaking on the line. No one was. The phone was either off the hook or out of order."

"Then what did you do?"

"Well, I tended to my party, of course . . . but I was still bothered. Still worried."

But apparently not enough to drive over there. Marilyn lived mere minutes away.

He dealt with that next: "I called Milt, my agent, and told him about the phone call, and not being able to reach her after that, and said I just had to go over there, and check on her. Milt told me absolutely not. He forbade me go. He said, 'For Christ's sake, man, you're the president's brother-in-law. If something has happened, how would it look?' Obviously, he had a point."

". . . And that was it?"

"That was it, Nathan. My understanding is that Milt called Mickey Rudin, who checked up on Marilyn. I believe it took a while, because Mickey was out, and the call came into his answering service . . . but eventually he got ahold of that housekeeper, who said she checked on Marilyn and that Marilyn was fine."

"Do you know the time frame of any of those calls?"

"No. Only of the calls I made, and I am somewhat vague there, as well. I mean, after all — I had no idea that there would be importance to any of this."

"Come on, Peter. You say you thought Marilyn was killing herself."

"*Threatening* to kill herself. That was commonplace with her, *you* know that. Rudin himself called me, Nathan, and said, 'Marilyn does this all the time.' He said if there was any reason to be alarmed, he would know about it — because Mrs. Murray would have called his brother-in-law, Greenson."

Lawford, apparently finished with his story — and it *sounded* like a story to me, an alibi — sat back and let out a chestful of air. He suddenly looked smaller. And older.

"You've been talking pretty freely," I said.

"Well, yes. Why would I hide anything from you, Nathan? We're friends, aren't we?"

That was overstating it, but this was no time to go into that.

"Peter, what I'm asking is — How freely *can* we talk in this room?"

His eyes widened — my God they were red, like Christopher Lee in *Horror of Dracula*. Then he smiled for the second time since my arrival.

"Oh, the entire house is quite secure, old boy. Thanks to your tip, we had the place, uh, I believe the term is 'swept' — and we do so once a week now."

"Well, that's swell. Now let's talk about Bobby."

Despite the tan, he went ashen. "What does Bobby have to —"

I raised a hand. "You need to *not* lie to me. I have no desire to embarrass my friend Bobby or his brother. I am willing to be discreet. But I won't be lied to, and I won't be used. Any questions?"

He shook his head.

"You'd better refill your glass. You're going to need it."

He did, immediately bringing the bright

red liquid back up to his lips.

I said, "I know Bobby was at Marilyn's yesterday afternoon."

"Bobby was in San Francisco!" he blurted.

"No fucking lies, Peter."

"It's not a lie, it's —"

"It's a lie of omission. He's been in San Francisco since Friday afternoon. I read the papers. I have access to television. He's there now. But he flew down here on Saturday. Secretly, but he flew. I am guessing that Marilyn, knowing Bob was going to be in California, pressed for that face-to-face meeting she'd been wanting."

Lawford raised an eyebrow. "She was calling around for him. She . . . she called Hyannis Port. Talked to Pat, who did *not* give Marilyn the number of the Bates ranch, where he and the family were staying, but did tell her that Bobby would be at the St. Francis Hotel, off and on, through Tuesday. He has a speech to give there tomorrow night."

"So Marilyn was still making waves."

He nodded glumly. "I took Bob over to Fifth Helena in the afternoon, three or so. I didn't hear much of what was said. She handed me a glass of champagne and I just went out to the pool and waited. I did go in when things got heated, and tried my best to settle them down. I think we'd all, Marilyn included, thought this meeting could once and for all settle things. Cool it all down. But it went badly. They yelled at each other. A terrible mistake. Bob flew right back to San Francisco."

"How did he manage that, without attracting attention?"

"Helicopter. Flew into Fox and out again."

Fox again. He was developing his *Enemy Within* picture there, and had plenty of support, even after the Zanuck coup.

"That sounds like the truth," I said, knowing it matched up with what Pryor had reported hearing.

"You can see how important it is," Lawford said, "keeping Bobby out of this. If it were known he saw Marilyn, the afternoon of her death . . ." He shivered. ". . . The ramifications are unimaginable."

"Not if you can imagine the end of the Kennedys in politics. What do you know about Hamilton's role in this?"

"James Hamilton? The policeman?"

Calling James Hamilton "the policeman" was like saying Marilyn Monroe "the actress." No one short of Chief Parker himself wielded Hamilton's kind of power and influence. The intel commander knew where the bodies were buried — sometimes, because he'd buried them.

"I told you Hamilton took over the investigation at Marilyn's," I said. "And he goes way back with Bobby, to racket-busting days. Is intel looking after Bobby's interests in this?"

I didn't feel Lawford needed to know about Roger Pryor and the tapes that had been seized by Hamilton's boys.

"Nathan, I'm afraid you have me out of my depth. . . ."

"Chief Parker is looking for J. Edgar's job, and Hamilton is his Siamese twin. He's also the guy in charge of security for Jack or Bobby, when either brother comes to town. What do you *know,* Peter?"

"Well, I *don't* know the answer to that question. I truly don't." He swallowed, looked around nervously as if not sure his pronouncement of no bugs had been correct. Eyes narrow, he pushed up from the couch and somehow managed to get on his feet. "You wait here, Nathan — you wait here."

I had no clue what this was about. I got up and went over to a window and pulled back the curtain enough to watch little Marilyns and little Lizs run and laugh and bobble prettily along the white beach.

Finally Peter came in with a white phone

in his hands. He plugged it in somewhere and dragged it over to me and set the base on the coffee table and handed me the receiver. He gave me a raised-eyebrow look that said, *Take it.*

"This is Nate Heller."

The voice accompanied by long-distance crackle was distinctive: "Nathan — Bob. Peter told me about your concerns. I, uh . . . we are getting some support from the LAPD Intelligence Division, yes. Nothing extralegal, mind you. Just . . . support."

"Bob, the detective that Hamilton replaced was a good man. I'd already talked to him about Marilyn."

"Is that right?"

"Yeah. I had him pretty well convinced that the oddness of the scene — and it was odd, Bob — had to do with Twentieth Century–Fox performing cleanup work. That kind of thing has gone on since the beginning of Hollywood."

"So I understand. I feel terrible about this."

"You should. Do you want to know what I observed at the scene? What I heard various parties say to the police?"

". . . No. Do you have a feeling about this?"

"I may be kidding myself, but I don't

324

think Marilyn intentionally took her life. She was clean of drugs, relatively clean anyway, and it would have been easy for her to misjudge."

"She, uh, *did* need pills to go to sleep."

"That's right. Easy to see where she could take some pills, wake up, take some more, maybe repeat that. Possible she didn't know how to self-medicate when she was cleaned up."

". . . Very sad. A tragedy."

"Right. Anything I can do to help?"

"The biggest favor you can do me, Nate, is to just stay out of this."

"Really."

"Let this matter run its natural course. How is, uh, Peter doing?"

"How do you think? He's a goddamn mess."

"Too bad. Too bad. It might be better if Pat were there, but she's . . . she's taking it rather hard, I'm told. She and Miss Monroe were close."

Miss Monroe, huh? Had he forgotten he'd been screwing her? I let it go.

"All right, Bob," I said. "I hear you."

"Thank you, Nate. We'll get you out to Hyannis one of these days, and show you a good time. Get you out on a sailboat. Small payment for your loyalty."

"Sounds great," I said, but couldn't muster much enthusiasm.

We said good-bye, I hung up, and Peter was right there, like a big eager hound.

"Well?" he said. "Everything straightened out?"

"Oh, yeah," I said. "It's fucking perfect. Can I give you a piece of advice? It's free."

"Certainly."

"Getting plastered won't bring her back or undo anything. Go to bed and sleep it off."

"I'm sure that's excellent advice."

I left him there, pouring himself another Bloody Mary.

Outside, as I slipped the Ray-Bans back on, the urge hit me to walk back down on that beach and strip off my clothes and show these kids how a real man took a swim, and wait for the police to come take me away. Somehow I resisted. Maybe I was afraid it would be Hamilton.

Driving back to Beverly Hills, I couldn't stop thinking about two things.

What Bobby had asked: *The biggest favor you can do me, Nate, is to just stay out of this.*

And that I wished he hadn't.

CHAPTER 16

Lawford was among Marilyn's celebrity friends whose reaction made the papers.

"Pat and I loved her dearly," he said. "She was probably one of the most marvelous human beings I have ever met. Anything else I could say would be superfluous."

Maybe not. Fred Rubinski had already heard Lawford was ducking the police, and hadn't given them even the briefest statement.

As for the ex-husbands, DiMaggio refused to talk to the press, and went into seclusion. Arthur Miller said the tragedy was "inevitable," and volunteered that he would not be traveling west for the funeral — "She's not really there anymore." Her first husband, police officer Jim Dougherty, wasn't quoted anywhere I saw.

Among the movie stars who shared their thoughts, two were particularly interesting. When a paper called him with the news,

Donald O'Connor blurted, "Not Marilyn! No, she's too alive — she's not the kind of person just all of a sudden to be gone." And *Gentlemen Prefer Blondes* costar Jane Russell succinctly said, "Sounds like dirty pool."

Of the insiders, Sinatra said he was "deeply saddened," and would miss her very much. Lee Strasberg went on the record, and somewhat controversially.

"She did not commit suicide," he told the *New York Herald Tribune.* "If it had been suicide, it would have happened in quite a different way. For one thing, she wouldn't have done it without leaving a note. Other reasons, which cannot be discussed, make us certain Marilyn did not intend to take her life."

By "us" he meant himself and wife Paula, the star's final acting coach, the dreaded "Black Bart."

The statements in the press from key witnesses — Dr. Hyman Engelberg, Dr. Ralph Greenson, housekeeper Eunice Murray, publicist Pat Newcomb, attorney Mickey Rudin — were sketchy and contradictory, painting no real picture at all.

Dr. Theodore Curphey became the pudgy, bespectacled, mustached bearer of official tidings. The coroner — whose horror-show, vermin-infested morgue was the most underfunded and understaffed of any major city — sat before a bank of microphones and a rapt sea of reporters, local, national, international.

"Marilyn Monroe," he said, "definitely did not die from natural causes. She may have taken an overdose of pills. Her death will be probed not just by my office but by the Los Angeles Suicide Prevention Team, the independent investigating unit of the Los Angeles Suicide Prevention Center at UCLA."

The papers quickly dubbed this group the "Suicide Squad," and to the public their appointment seemed to indicate local government's intention to treat the Monroe tragedy with the special care and attention it deserved.

But something was missing.

And on Tuesday, I said as much to Flo Kilgore, who asked me to meet her for an early lunch at the Musso and Frank Grill on Hollywood Boulevard.

When she'd caught me on the phone at my desk at the A-1 Monday afternoon, she hadn't said what the eleven o'clock meeting was for; but I knew. I mean, it had been months since we'd seen each other, so her spotting me at Fifth Helena Sunday morning meant this was Marilyn.

For a Hollywood landmark, Musso and

Frank was fairly unassuming in appearance if pretentious in execution, a typical dark-paneled, men's club kind of restaurant-with-bar, similar to Binyon's back in Chicago. Though the steaks were among the best in town, Musso's real claim to fame was its longevity — Hollywood's oldest such establishment, dating to 1919, though in fairness the facility had moved in 1934 all the way from 6669 Hollywood Boulevard to 6667.

The mostly Mexican waiters and their bright red jackets, echoed by the red of the leather inside the mahogany booths, had been here almost as long as the restaurant — Jesse Chavez maybe before there was a Hollywood — and to my knowledge Jean Rue had always been the chef. I figured when he died, they wouldn't bury him, they'd serve him.

Flo was already there, working on a martini, which was her idea of breakfast, seated in number one, the front corner booth and the only one with a window, though the blinds were drawn.

This was at once the most prominent spot in the place and the most private — all the booths were high-sided, but this had only one neighbor, currently vacant. This had been Charlie Chaplin's booth, before people decided he was a Communist cradle robber, and prior to that Rudolph Valentino's, who I guess left it to Chaplin in his will. Right now it was ours.

The columnist wore a simple black dress and pearls and looked attractive enough, but I found the bouffant hairdo unflattering, exposing more forehead than her weak chin could handle. That was her only really bad feature — the big blue eyes and flawless porcelain skin worthy of many an actress' envy, as was her curvaceously slender, leggy figure.

I slipped into the other side of the booth, dressed for business in a lightweight black-olive Fenton Hall suit with a green-and-black Wembley tie. But *was* this business?

We made a little small talk, and Jesse took our order, fairly obsequiously (it was the tourists who got the snooty contempt). Flo ordered a shrimp cocktail and I went for the Tuesday special, corned beef and cabbage. It was too early but the cocktails were goddamn good here, so I asked for a gimlet.

"Marilyn came here fairly often," Flo said, finally invoking the reason for our meeting.

Her voice was soft and rather high-pitched, girlish for so powerful a journalist.

Flo was saying, "She liked to tell the story about being at the bar with Joe and seeing some fans come rushing up, and dreading having to deal with them . . . but nobody even looked at her. They all wanted Joltin' Joe's autograph."

"Must have been very young boys," I said.

She smiled; it was a nice, thin-lipped, pixieish smile. "Would you care to tell me what you were doing there?"

She meant at Marilyn's house Sunday morning.

"Would I? Hasn't every reporter in town written 'thirty' on this one? I mean, it's all human interest now. Now that there's a verdict."

Her smile was impish and the big blue eyes flashed. "You're being clever again, aren't you?"

"It's a bad habit. Do you think anybody but the two of us noticed what really was put over?"

She sipped her martini.

Then she said, "You mean, that there isn't going to be an inquest? That the coroner said Marilyn 'may' have taken an accidental overdose, then turned the inquiry over to a civilian group? No more police, no one interviewed under oath, nothing that can become part of the public record?"

Flo was right.

Right that I already had noticed all this, and right that the coroner — faced with doubt about cause of death — was abandoning his public duty to impose an inquest with subpoenaed witnesses, and launch a full-scale investigation.

"I thought the cutest part," I said, "was handing this over to that 'Suicide Squad.' That tells the public it's suicide, without having to go to the bother of actually finding out. The very name pre-supposes she killed herself — they don't determine *if* there's been a suicide, but try to determine *why* there's been a suicide."

Her smile had some sneer in it now. "I've done a little *digging* on the three members of the so-called squad — all of them are associates of Dr. Ralph Greenson."

"I don't know if that's significant." Jesse dropped off my gimlet, I thanked him, and he bestowed a nod. "Doctors out here are bound to know each other, have professional associations."

Flo didn't argue the point. "*Do* you think it was suicide?"

"No. That's not impossible, but I was with her a little over a week ago, and she had some personal problems, sure, but also a lot going for her."

Her smile turned up at one corner. "I know all about the 'personal problems.' " Then her expression sobered. "But I'm afraid I may have provided the . . . the spark that ignited this tragedy."

"How so?"

Her thin eyebrows arched quizzically. "You don't know? You didn't read my Friday column?"

"If I say I didn't, does that mean I have to pick up the check?"

She laughed a little. I didn't have much trouble making her laugh, even in serious circumstances.

"No, Nate, I'm on expense account." Flo leaned forward, spoke softly, though still no one was in the adjacent booth and I was pretty sure none of the waiters here really understood English. "I've been chasing this story for weeks, talking to everybody from chauffeurs to society reporters, even Fox publicists."

"What story?"

"Please. The two Kennedy brothers, sharing Marilyn's charms? Jack passing her to Bobby like a basket of these French rolls?"

So she knew that much. Not surprising. She'd started out as a crime reporter in New York for Hearst in the late thirties, and was much more than just frothy columns and game show appearances.

She cocked her head. "What I said, more or less, was this: 'The appeal of the sex goddess of the 1950s remains undiminished in the sixties. Marilyn Monroe has proven vastly alluring to a handsome gentleman with a bigger name than Joe DiMaggio in his heyday.' "

"And you think *that* sparked Marilyn's . . . what? Suicide?"

"We won't use the right word just yet. But understand that that little squib was only the tip, with an iceberg to come." She leaned forward, eyes on fire. "I was working on the story of my career, trying to get some kind of response from the Kennedy camp. I decided to nudge them with that little blind item . . . which is, in my opinion, what caused Bobby to visit Marilyn on the day she died. To tell her it was over and to lay off and . . . you can guess how she must have taken it."

Of course, I didn't have to guess. How did she know this?

"Your little Flo," she said, dealing with my unasked question, "was pretty fast out of the gate on this one. I even did my own legwork, too."

"Well, they're nice legs."

"Don't change the subject. What would you say if I told you Peter Lawford's neighbors are upset about a helicopter touching down on the beach, in back of the villa, early

Sunday morning? Made a heck of a racket and blew sand into all the neighbors' little swimming pools. Making them walk clear across their backyards to the ocean for a swim. What would you *say,* Nathan?"

But I didn't say anything.

"And how would you react if I told you Peter and Pat Lawford's next-door neighbor says he saw a Mercedes pull up, late Saturday afternoon, and Bobby Kennedy and Peter Lawford step out, and go on into the house."

"A Mercedes *and* a helicopter? These Kennedys do have dough."

"The helicopter is Fox's." Her smile grew dimples; she was proud of herself. "I've confirmed that via Fox studio logs."

"You need a job? We're hiring at the A-1."

With a shake of her head that damn near moved the bouffant, she said, "You ain't heard nothin' yet."

"I hope you're not going to sing 'Mammy.' "

She giggled. "Stop."

I have to say I liked that about her. We're talking about life and death and still she has the time to laugh at my dumb jokes. Maybe I could be her fifth husband. Now that Marilyn was gone, I was available. And a guy can always use a rich wife.

"Let me back up," she said. "I've jumped ahead a little. The first interviews I did were in Marilyn's neighborhood, there in Brentwood. How about this? One neighbor says she saw Robert Kennedy walk up to Marilyn's gates and go in. Some time mid-to-late afternoon — the neighbor lady was playing bridge, and glanced out the window, and just saw that famous face walking by."

"Interesting, I guess. Is that it for neighbor witnesses?"

"No! Several complained of hearing a woman screaming and, later, a hysterical woman — maybe the same one, maybe not — yelling, 'Murderers! You're *murderers!* Are you satisfied? Now that she's *dead?*' "

I wasn't sure that rang true. Sounded a little melodramatic. But I asked, "Have they told the police?"

"Have they? You know who took over the investigation, don't you?"

James Hamilton.

"But now," she said, "even *he's* off the case. The 'Suicide Squad' is in charge! But he did his share, on the few days he worked — did he ever. Did you know that Richard Boone played him in the *Dragnet* movie?"

"What, Paladin?"

"Yes. Mr. *Have Gun — Will Travel.* But in my opinion the real Hamilton is even uglier, and lacks Boone's charisma."

Flo just couldn't stop writing her column, could she?

"Anyway," she was saying, "he's certainly no modern-day knight. After canvassing the neighborhood, the next thing I did was go to the phone company. I have a . . . contact there. I asked him to make me a copy of all the numbers on Marilyn's billing tape."

She finished her martini and waved at Jesse and he scurried over to get her a refill. I'd barely touched my gimlet.

"You know what my phone company contact said? He said, 'All hell's broken loose down here. Apparently, you're not the only one interested in Marilyn's calls.' "

"That *is* something."

"Isn't it? He said, 'The tapes and toll tabs have all disappeared. Men in dark suits and shiny shoes impounded them.' Word was, he said, somebody 'high up' ordered it."

"With all the formalities these days," I said quietly, "should take something like two weeks for an ordinary cop to get that stuff."

"An ordinary cop. Is James Hamilton an ordinary cop, Nate?"

Our food arrived. Despite the early hour and the grim subject matter, I was hungry and dug in. When you're half Irish and half Jewish, corned beef and cabbage makes the perfect compromise.

She nibbled at a shrimp, then said, "You know what I think, Nate? I think Captain James Hamilton is the ideal candidate to cover up the circumstances of Marilyn's death."

"I don't disagree. But who's he covering it up for?"

I thought I knew, but I wanted to hear her say it.

"For Chief William Parker, who wants to be J. Edgar Hoover when he grows up — he's been *training* for the job long and hard enough, using Hamilton to build a file cabinet full of secrets, for blackmail and general influence. So that means Hamilton's working indirectly for Bobby Kennedy."

"Maybe directly," I heard myself saying. "Hamilton and Bobby and Jack are tight. Bastard runs security on all their LA trips."

She nodded as she chewed, then swallowed shrimp. "And, too, he and Bobby go way, way back, to Teamster-busting days."

I said nothing. Had a bite of corned beef and cabbage and potato all at once; very nice.

But she was looking at me, the fire in the blue eyes replaced with ice. "And *you* go way, way back, don't you, Nate? You worked for Bobby and his Rackets Committee. So maybe I'm taking a chance, talking to you."

"Why?"

"Maybe I'm talking to a Kennedy clan insider, and not a friend of Marilyn's."

"Can't I be both?"

She said nothing. Dipped a shrimp in bright red cocktail sauce, and held it up to study its scarlet glimmer. Then she said, "Maybe once upon a time, you could. But I think that time is about over. . . . I have *more* for you, but I think we should finish eating first."

"Yeah?"

"Yes. You see, I have a contact in the coroner's office, too. And I don't think we will want to explore this subject till after lunch."

We returned to polite conversation and good food. Her son and daughter were both in their teens, so talk of them and Sam took us through the meal.

But for dessert we talked autopsy.

"Marilyn died of a massive overdose, according to the toxicology report." Flo had a little notebook out and was referring to it. "Four point five milligrams percent of pentobarbital and eight point oh milligrams percent of chloral hydrate in her bloodstream. Her liver contained thirteen milligrams percent pentobarbital —"

I cut in: "Nembutal. That's the brand name of pentobarbital."

"Right — and we're talking about an abnormally large concentration of the stuff." She referred to her notes again. "There were eight prescription bottles found at her bedside, including an empty container for twenty-five Nembutal. Also, a chloral hydrate container with ten pills remaining."

Jesse had brought coffee and I sipped some. "I assume Curphey performed this autopsy himself . . . ?"

"No. A young fellow, Noguchi, fairly new. There's only three full-time pathologists on staff."

"Did this Jap call it a suicide?"

"At first. Then, when things didn't add up — *literally* add up — he sent tissue samples for further analysis. Kidney, stomach, urine, intestines. Those aren't back yet, my contact tells me."

"What do you mean, literally didn't add up?"

The columnist folded her hands. "For Marilyn to have overdosed — whether accidentally or on purpose — she would have to have taken fifty to seventy chloral hydrate pills, and seventy-five to ninety Nembutals."

I couldn't find anything to say.

"My contact quotes Noguchi as saying

there were enough drugs in Marilyn Monroe to kill any three persons." She again leaned forward. "Nate, do you think she could have taken — physically taken — a minimum of *one hundred twenty-five pills?*"

"No," I said flatly. "She'd have had to take them very, very quickly — mouthfuls, swallowing, gulping them and still manage not to . . . puke."

That last word was spoken softly, as this was a restaurant, after all.

I went on: "And if she'd taken them a few at a time, she'd be unconscious, or maybe dead, before swallowing enough to reach the extreme level of barbs you're talking about."

Flo gave me a crisp nod, then said, "Thing is, she only *had* twenty-four Nembutal in the house, at most — that was her prescription, which she'd filled on Friday."

"And there were ten chloral hydrates *left* in that pill container," I said hollowly. "Could she have injected herself?"

She shrugged. "Well, Marilyn died in a locked room, supposedly, and no hypodermic was found."

"I don't think it was locked. Somebody else could have injected her."

"Maybe." Her eyes narrowed, blue glittering from the slits. "Here's a small mystery. I call it 'small' because I do think it can be cleared up. Noguchi claims to have gone over every inch of her with a magnifying glass, and saw no injection marks. But there are several problems with that."

I nodded. "There are plenty of places hard to detect an injection — on an existing bruise, for example, and she was splotched as hell, with lividity. She may have had existing bruises. Also under the arm, bunch of places."

"And Noguchi just didn't *see* it, magnifying glass or not."

I leaned toward her. "*Something's* not right, because I know Marilyn was getting regular injections from this character Engelberg, for her sinus and cold problems. Liver extract and vitamins. She almost certainly had an injection within a day or two of dying."

"Are you *sure* that's what the injections were?"

"No," I admitted. "Far as I know, Engelberg could be one of these Dr. Feelgoods. Enough stars and politicians take magic shots from quacks to make that a possibility."

"But Engelberg didn't get there till *after* Marilyn was gone."

I shrugged. "How do we know? Who the

hell can say how many people were running in and out of there, all night? What little I heard Sunday morning was riddled with lies and half-truths."

Like Pat Newcomb saying she left Marilyn's place late in the afternoon, and that Marilyn was in great spirits. But I knew Marilyn was unhappy as hell then, because of her fight with Bobby. Unhappy enough to have her shrink make an emergency house call.

And Mrs. Murray had been playing tricks with time that H. G. Wells might have envied.

"There's one more really interesting item," Flo said. She was having another martini, and sipped it. "Noguchi found almost nothing in her stomach. A small quantity of liquid, he said. No sign of heavy drugs or sedatives."

"No pill residue? Don't they call those Nembutals 'yellow jackets' — for the yellow in the gelatin? Shouldn't there be yellow dye?"

"Yes. But there was *no* residue. No evidence of pills in the stomach or small intestine. No . . ." She checked her notes. ". . . No 'refractile crystals.' Whatever that means."

"I think it just means any sign of reaction." I shifted in the booth. "Okay. Yeah, well, this smells."

"Funny you should say that, because it *doesn't* smell. Not of what it should smell — victims who ingest chloral hydrate give off a powerful pearl-like odor. Noguchi notes its absence. What he *doesn't* note is what that absence of odor strongly implies."

"Death by injection," I said.

She sipped her cocktail.

I sipped my coffee.

Then she smiled at me; not a broad smile, just a small, friendly one.

"So, Nate — whose friend are you? Mine? Bobby's? Marilyn's?"

". . . You've told me a lot, Flo. But you haven't told me *why* you're telling me. . . ."

No smile at all now. "I want to hire you. I can only do so much myself, and I don't want to use any other reporter on this. Anybody seasoned could steal it out from under me. Anybody who's green isn't good enough. I'm going to run after this on my own pretty legs, but I need help. And you know *why* I need help — we're already behind the clock."

With every day that passes, an unsolved murder is more likely to stay that way. The first twenty-fours are critical, and we'd lost those. After the first week, your odds drop precipitously.

"You know it's risky, using me," I said. "Maybe Bobby's already hired me to help cover this up."

The biggest favor you can do me, Nate, is to just stay out of this.

"Cover up what? If this is about Marilyn and Bobby having a fling, and Marilyn getting depressed and killing herself, that's a big story. Yes. Might even cost the Kennedys the next election. Might. But if it's a *murder,* and the Kennedys are covering it up . . . which would imply that the Kennedys made that murder happen . . . Well, Nate, whose friend are you?"

You could picture it, the beautiful blonde sitting at the wood-and-glass bar next to her famous ballplayer husband, and some fans come up and they don't even care about Marilyn. Funny. Absurd. Fucking comical.

But somebody had to care about Marilyn.

"Can you afford a retainer of two thousand?" I asked her.

She made out the check.

CHAPTER 17

The Will Rogers Memorial Park in Beverly Hills provided a beautiful little oasis forming a triangle between busy intersections at the north end of Rodeo Drive. The landscaping was lush, the fountains bubbling, the trees majestic, the flowerbeds plentiful. And for a meeting with Sergeant Jack Clemmons of the LAPD, the location couldn't have been more convenient for me — the park had once been the five-acre front lawn of the Beverly Hills Hotel.

With a gentle wind whispering through the copious trees, Clemmons and I sat with the sun at our backs on a wrought-iron bench near the big central fountain, where colorful Japanese fish provided a touch of the exotic.

The off-duty cop did not look in the least exotic, or even like he belonged anywhere near Beverly Hills in his short-sleeve red-and-black plaid shirt and Levi's. I was still in the suit I'd worn to Musso's, albeit with tie loosened, as this meeting was taking place in the early afternoon of that same day.

Flo Kilgore had provided me with Clemmons' home number, warning me she hadn't reached him yet, but I got lucky and caught him right away. He worked midnight to eight, and normally slept from about nine till 4:00 P.M., but I'd reached him much earlier.

"Haven't been sleeping so good last few days," he'd told me on the phone. "So, then, what? You're working for the Monroe estate?"

"No," I said. "I don't even know who that would be. Marilyn's mother is in the loony bin and she has a half sister somewhere."

At no time in this investigation did I tell anyone I was working for a reporter.

I went on: "I was doing security for Marilyn, and looking into some things for her. She was my client and I feel like I owe it to her to ask a few questions that nobody else seems to be."

There had been a long pause. If he was caught up in Captain James Hamilton's cover-up, this was where Clemmons would have hung up on me. A good sign when he didn't.

And now we were sitting on that iron bench. On a weekday, there were more squirrels than people here, and the frothing fountain provided nice noise to cover up our conversation. So did horn honks and other car sounds from nearby Sunset Boulevard.

My companion was a cop right out of Central Casting — about forty, square-shouldered, square-jawed, flinty-eyed, with a narrow line for a mouth, speaking in a no-nonsense second tenor.

"I came on duty as watch commander at the substation at midnight," Sergeant Clemmons said.

He sat comfortably, nothing tense about his body language, though his eyes were tight and his tone carried an edge. Only occasionally did he look right at me, mostly staring into his thoughts.

"Routine night," he was saying. "Slow as hell. Had my feet up when the phone rang well after four A.M."

Clemmons said he didn't understand the caller at first, a male with "a European accent."

"Guy is agitated, talking real fast. I ask him to calm down, slow down. He says all right, and there's this pause you coulda hung a hammock in. And then he tells me

Marilyn Monroe is dead. That she'd committed suicide. Well, that woke me up, all right. But my first thought is, it's a damn hoax. So I ask him to identify himself."

The caller said he was Dr. Ralph Greenson, "Miss Monroe's psychiatrist." Clemmons asked for the address and said he'd be right over.

"My mind was racing," he said, with the tiniest smile. "I mean, you can imagine — if this thing was on the level, all hell would break loose. So I go out there myself, and don't waste any time about it. No need for a siren, though — streets deserted, and if she really was dead, Marilyn Monroe wasn't going anywhere."

When he turned down the little dead-end alley of Fifth Helena Drive, he found the gates open, and pulled into the brick courtyard. A few cars were there, and he apologized to me that he didn't spend any time committing their makes to memory or writing down any license numbers.

"But then, there were no lights on at all outside the Monroe house," he said. "Porch and garage all dark. Not even pool lights, and damn few on in the house. Only sounds were police calls from my radio and a dog barking."

Maf, Marilyn's poodle, most likely.

"So I go up and knock on the door. I can hear footsteps, more than one person whispering, but I must have stood there a full minute before the porch light comes on and that Murray woman answers." He shook his head. "*She* was a hell of a character — all whispery and nervous and afraid of her own shadow."

"How did that strike you, her odd demeanor?"

"To me, she seemed dishonest right off the bat. I couldn't put my finger on what was wrong, Mr. Heller, not right then . . . but I knew *something* was off about the woman."

Immediately the housekeeper led the police sergeant to the bedroom, "very near the front door, actually," where a sheet-covered body sprawled across the bed. A shock of platinum-blonde hair poked up onto a pillow.

"The two doctors were waiting for me in there," Clemmons said. "This taller doc, Engelberg, distinguished-looking fella, he'd pulled a chair up and was sitting near the bed. The other doc, smaller, with a mustache, was standing over by the nightstand — that was Greenson. He introduced himself. He was the guy on the phone, all right, with the Dr. Freud accent."

The psychiatrist simply said to the officer, "She committed suicide," then pointed out an empty container of Nembutal at the woman's bedside. "She took all of those."

The sergeant drew back the sheet revealing what proved to be a naked Marilyn Monroe, but "with no makeup, and splotched with lividity."

"She was lying facedown in what I call the soldier's position," he said. "Her face against a pillow, arms by her side, right arm slightly bent. Legs stretched out perfectly straight."

What I'd seen.

I asked, "And how did that strike you?"

"Hinky as hell. If she OD'ed on barbs, she'd be all twisted up. I've seen dozens of them. Wrong. Dead wrong." He shifted on the bench. "Then I asked 'em if the body had been moved. You could tell from the dual lividity she had been. And these lying bastards, both of them, say no, she hasn't been moved. *This* is how they found her."

"Both said that."

"Yeah. Well, the little guy, Greenson, he kind of took charge. The taller guy seemed in a real funk. Not talkative at all. Whereas this Greenson character . . ." He shook his head, smirked humorlessly, and for once looked directly at me. ". . . He was cocky, almost daring me to accuse him of something. I kept thinking, 'What the hell's wrong with this guy?' It just didn't fit the situation."

"What's your take on the scene itself?"

"That it was the most obviously staged death scene I ever saw. The pill bottles were arranged in neat order and the body deliberately positioned. It all looked too damn tidy."

"Tidy? Really?"

"Yeah. Everything was neat. I of course looked for a suicide note, but there wasn't one, weren't any documents, no scripts, no notebooks, nothing like that."

But just an hour later, I had seen a very messy bedroom, with plenty of scripts and books — although, perhaps significantly, I had not seen any of Marilyn's spiral-bound notebooks.

Had somebody searched the place, and then tidied it? And someone later searched it again, and messed it back up? Or even worked on the scene to make it look less staged, so a pro like Clemmons wouldn't pick up on it? Curiouser and curiouser.

Clemmons had then asked the doctors if they'd tried to revive her, and they both claimed it had been too late. Neither would hazard a guess what time she took the pills.

He was looking at me again. "If you're a private detective, Mr. Heller, I assume you're an ex-cop. Am I right?"

"You're not wrong."

"Well, in your experience, at a death scene where the victim's doctor is present, whether accident, suicide, or even murder, weren't the doctors helpful? Trying to be as informative as they could?"

"That's pretty standard."

"Well, these two had to be interrogated like goddamn suspects."

Maybe that's what they were.

"Something else strange — there was no drinking glass in that bedroom for her to have taken a single damn pill, let alone handfuls."

"There was when I visited the scene, maybe an hour after you did."

"Then it was planted. But that's not the *really* strange thing — her bathroom? Where she would run a glass of water to take those pills? There was plumbing work in progress. You know, she was having a lot of repairs and remodeling done on the old place."

"Right. Plumbing work. So what?"

"So the water in her bathroom was off."

I gaped at him.

"It's the truth, Mr. Heller. Turned off. She couldn't have run a glass of water to save her life, never mind take it. She couldn't use that bathroom, if she had to pee, either — she'd have to run down the hall."

"Did you ask the doctors whether Marilyn took injections?"

"Yeah I did. Greenson never gave her any, but she *was* getting some kind of vitamin shot from Engelberg, had done so the day before she died, in fact. Both claimed she didn't inject herself. And I didn't see any needles around."

He fell silent.

I prompted him: "Was that it? Did you search the house?"

"I gave the place a quick look," he said with a gloomy shrug. "I was the first officer on the scene, but I'm not a detective. Didn't spend much time doing it, and didn't check the guest cottage, either . . . though, and this may sound crazy, I had this kind of sixth-sense feeling there were people out there. And I would have checked, but I got sidetracked."

"Sidetracked how?"

"By seeing light coming from the garage, where I *did* check when I went looking for Mrs. Murray."

"Looking for her?"

"Yeah. The biddy slipped away while I was questioning the docs in the death bedroom.

So where do I find her? Out in the garage, the door up, where the washer and drier are. And she's washing a load of clothes! She'd already washed one load and folded the linens and is doing a second, preparing a third!"

"Do you think the sheets on the bed were changed?"

"Maybe. Maybe the poor girl soiled them. Lots do, when they die. Maybe it was out of some sense of preserving a star's dignity. I don't know. And I'm embarrassed to say I didn't think to ask, I was so flummoxed by it."

"But you did question Murray, right?"

"Oh yeah, right there in the garage. While she folded fucking towels, pardon my French."

The story she'd told Clemmons mirrored the one she had told Lieutenant Armstrong Sunday morning in Marilyn's breakfast nook, but with one significant difference.

"Mrs. Murray said she found the body around midnight, and that she immediately called Dr. Greenson, who arrived about half an hour later."

"Did she say why she checked on Marilyn at midnight?"

"Yeah, and that also was odd. She said the light was on under Marilyn's door, and the phone cord was running under, all the way down the hall from this spare bedroom where the two phones were. Okay, now first of all —"

"The thick-pile carpet prevented Murray from seeing a crack of light under the door."

"Right! And second, not thirty seconds before, Mrs. Murray had said how Marilyn often kept one of her phones in there with her at bedtime — to make late-night calls when she couldn't sleep."

"Which was most nights."

"Right, which was most nights. So what was suspicious about the phone cord under the door? It was typical, not unusual. Mrs. Murray also said the door was locked, but I didn't see any keys around."

Murray had told Clemmons the same tale she gave to Lieutenant Armstrong about Greenson having to break in the window.

"Even while she was fidgeting with that laundry, nervous as hell, she's speaking in this soft, even, precise little voice. And everything she gave me seemed prepared, rehearsed as hell. Anyway, I went back to the bedroom, where the doctors were still keeping the body company."

I gave him half a grin. "Let me guess. You wanted to ask them why they waited four hours to notify the police."

"*Oh* yeah. Well, this Greenson, in this smart-ass tone, says, 'We had to get permission.' And I say, 'Who the hell from?' Not terribly professional, but it was getting to me. And he says, 'The studio publicity department. Twentieth Century–Fox. Miss Monroe is making a film there.' Like I should know better than to ask."

"Told you this right out."

He cut the air with a hand. "Right out. I've heard about this kind of thing, but I was dumbfounded. And when I asked those docs what they'd done during those four hours, they told me — you're gonna love this, Mr. Heller — they said, 'We were just talking.' "

"About what in hell?"

"Oh, when I asked them . . . they shrugged. Cop at the scene of a suspicious death, they *know* it's a coroner's case, they *know* they have to notify the police in such an instance, and *right away* . . . and what do they do? Just shrug."

Greenson had then told Clemmons of discovering Marilyn's body in a manner perfectly consistent with Murray's version.

"His only additional touch," Clemmons said, "was saying he removed the phone receiver from the woman's hand. Said she must have been trying to call for help."

"Calling for help?" I asked. "With her housekeeper down the hall, ten feet away?"

"I know. But it wasn't my job to investigate, was it? I was there to take down the initial report. Record what I saw and heard. Then I was relieved by Sergeant Iannone."

"Good man?"

A shrug. "Good enough, I'd say. Only one thing about Marv I'm not crazy about — he's in tight with Hamilton's crowd."

"Works for intel, you mean?"

"No, but works *with* them, time to time. They like him. One of his special duty assignments is kind of interesting, in light of things."

"Interesting how?"

"Well, whenever the president or the attorney general visits the Lawfords, Iannone gets the assignment from Hamilton to work the beach house."

Neither of us said anything. Colorful fish swam by, swishing their tails, the kind of display they invented Technicolor for. The fountain bubbled. Squirrels scampered.

"I filed a report when I got back to the substation," he said. "For all the good it did. Then I called Jim."

"Jim?"

"Marilyn's first husband — Jim Dougherty. He's a cop on the LAPD, y'know.

We're old friends. He said two things that both got to me. I think they've been keeping me awake more than anything else."

"What did he say?"

"Well, first he said he was surprised. And then he said, 'There's no way Norma Jeane killed herself.' No elaboration. Just those two things."

Traffic sounds from Sunset Boulevard provided a dissonant reminder of the city surrounding.

"I appreciate you telling me this," I said.

"It has to stay off the record," he said.

"I know."

"I could lose my job, this gets out. They've clamped down tight on this, Mr. Heller."

"Then why talk to me?"

"Because that woman was murdered."

We shook hands, and he headed home. Maybe he could catch a nap before he went on at midnight.

Maybe.

I didn't have an appointment with the boss at the Arthur P. Jacobs agency on the Sunset Strip, not caring to risk one. Instead I waltzed into the posh, modern offices, and told the attractive brunette at the amoeba-shaped reception desk that I was Nathan Heller, had no appointment, and was here to see Mr. Jacobs.

She of course asked if she could tell him what it was about, and I told her Norma Jeane Baker.

I had barely got nestled in my curved space-age chair, preparing to read the front page of *Daily Variety,* when another attractive girl (this one blonde) appeared, and walked me up some winding, exposed stairs out of a science-fiction movie to Mr. Jacobs' private office. She delivered me to his receptionist, a redhead (all bases covered), and buzzed me on through.

His office wasn't ostentatiously large, no more than twice mine back in Chicago, but it had a modern, empty look that made it seem bigger. One wall was all windows onto the strip, though the view was obscured by black vertical blinds. The other walls were bone-colored, with sleekly framed black-and-white portraits of stars he represented, Marilyn prominent among them; several framed one-sheet posters (including *Bus Stop* and *Let's Make Love*) hung opposite the window wall.

Jacobs sat in the recession of a kidney-shaped, black-topped, metal-legged desk arrayed with phones and stacks of paperwork and a scattering of pens, a black enamel ashtray, a black enamel box or two, and no family photos. Behind him was a big built-in black wall cabinet with doors below and shelves stacked with books, screenplays, and piles of magazines, a working library at odds with the sterile modernity of the rest of the office.

He looked small for so important a man, and in the publicity game, Arthur Jacobs was among Hollywood's most powerful. This former MGM mail-room clerk now ruled an agency with New York, Hollywood, and London offices.

His suit was dark gray and tailored, his tie black, narrow, and silk, his hair dark, just starting to gray, and cut in Caesar bangs. His oval face had intelligence despite simian grooves, and he might have been handsome if the nose had been shorter and the ears smaller.

He gave me a practiced smile and stood behind the desk and held out his hand for me to shake, saying, "Nate Heller. You're lucky — you caught me toward the end of my day."

His handshake was just firm enough — it was practiced, too — and I said, "Arthur, I don't need much of your time," and sat down in one of the two leather director's chairs opposite him.

We were on a first-name basis, it seemed,

though we knew more *of* each other than actually knew each other. He'd been to Sherry's with clients a couple times when I was on hand, and I'd seen him at this event and that one, exchanging a few friendly social words, mostly because of shared friends and acquaintances. Like Marilyn.

Anyway, I was here to run a bluff, so I got started.

"Listen, Arthur, I guess you know I was helping Marilyn with security at her home. She had me wiretap her place, but by the time I got there Sunday morning, the tapes were gone and so were the gimmicks in her two phones."

"Really," he said, his longish face trying to decide whether to stop smiling or not.

"And I'm glad of that, as far as it goes . . . but I wondered if *you* knew what had become of them? The tapes, I mean. Pat Newcomb said I'd just missed you at the house."

"She did? Well, I don't know anything about those tapes, Nate. Or the phone 'gimmicks.' Sorry."

I shrugged, crossed a leg. "Well, I don't know what's on the tapes, so whether it's a problem for anybody, who can say? I'm just trying to do right by Marilyn. And you know, I wouldn't mind helping Bobby and

Peter out. Wouldn't want to see them get pulled into this."

His mouth kept smiling but his forehead frowned. Then he shot a finger like a gun at me and said, "That's right — you're a friend of Bobby's, aren't you?"

"Yes. Go way back. We played Untouchables together in the fifties." I raised my hands in surrender mode. "I'm not working for him, understand. Quite the contrary — when I offered to help out, he just said I should stay out of it as much as possible."

"Not bad advice."

"I do feel I have a responsibility to Marilyn in this. As I'm sure *you* do."

Jacobs opened a black enamel box on the desk. It contained cigars, and they smelled fine — Havanas, I would wager. He slid it over by way of offering me one and I didn't decline. Then I slid the box back, and he selected a plump specimen and lighted it up. I got mine going. It took a while. It does, with Havanas.

I drew in the thick, rich smoke and tried not to choke. Then said, "If I'm not overstepping, I'm assuming you're walking point on this — I'm sort of on the fringes, but I'd like to know the party line."

He nodded, let out some smoke he'd been holding in. "We were all upset when this suicide story got out."

"Yeah. Hell, I heard it called that on the radio on my way to Fifth Helena!"

The publicist frowned, shook his head in irritation. "Stupid. Very stupid. How can we market Marilyn, if she's a tragic suicide? Now — an *accidental* death. That's a tragedy we can work with."

"Right. Are you planning a press conference?"

"Hell no! No press releases. Everything oral. We're working hand in hand with Fox on this thing. Very delicate. Very controlled."

I sat forward, rested the cigar in the ashtray. Thing tasted great but was so strong I thought I might pass out.

"Arthur, I've managed to duck the cops so far. I had a lucky break of sorts when that Captain Hamilton showed up. He and I have a love/hate relationship — he loves to hate me. So instead of questioning me, he threw my ass out."

Jacobs chuckled. "Well, the good captain has his uses."

"So what *is* the story line? What do we say . . . I mean, what do we *think* . . . happened to Marilyn?"

He gestured with an open palm. "Simple. Marilyn took a normal dose of sleeping pills and dozed off. Then she woke up a half hour later and took another dose. Then a half hour later, she did the same, and so on, until it all added up. To tragedy."

"Okay." I showed him an open palm. "You know, I hear the autopsy tells a different story. She'd have needed to take a wheelbarrow full of pills."

Jacobs smiled patiently, putting his cigar next to mine in the tray; we were sharing. "Nate, that doesn't matter. I don't know what happened to Marilyn. What does it matter what happened to Marilyn, really? What counts now is her legacy. Suicide is sad and weak. An overdose is accidental and tragic. Like James Dean in that smash-up. Look how big Dean still is. They re-release his three pictures every few years."

"Ah. So what's the full story, then? The official story?"

He leaned back in his swivel chair; tented his fingers, looked at the ceiling, which was high above us. "Three thirty, Eunice Murray notices that Marilyn's bedroom light is still on, and knocks. Marilyn doesn't answer. Murray runs outside, looks through the window and sees Marilyn looking strange. She phones Dr. Greenson, alarmed. Greenson rushes over and finds his patient already gone. Dr. Engelberg comes right over and pronounces Marilyn dead at four A.M. The police are called shortly thereafter." He took his eyes off the ceiling and sent them my way. "The end."

"Okay," I said, nodding. "But I heard the housekeeper told the first cop on the scene that she found Marilyn at midnight or earlier."

"Doesn't matter. That first cop isn't in charge. Your 'friend' Captain Hamilton is."

"Which must mean Chief Parker's given his blessing." I shook my head. "Must've been wild, those four hours or so, before the police were officially called. Fox fixers crawling all over the joint, making sure nothing unflattering turned up. House getting searched stem to stern. You and Pat Newcomb and those doctors and, Christ, trying to help that flaky Murray woman get her story straight and *keep* it straight. And somebody must have been looking after Bobby's interests. Don't tell me you had FBI stepping on your toes, too. Must have been crazy."

Well, this time I *had* overstepped.

Jacobs was looking at me with eyes turned unblinking and cold. He even stamped out that expensive, barely smoked cigar.

I risked half a smile. "If I've said too much . . ."

"Mr. Heller, why are you here?"

"I told you. For Marilyn's sake." I dropped the pretense. "So what time did you get there, Art?"

"Who says I was there at all?"

"You didn't deny it earlier, when I brought it up. Pat Newcomb told the West LA Detective Division boys that you were there — I heard her. So it's in their notes and records. Maybe you better warn Hamilton to take his eraser over there."

Scorn met defensiveness in his tone. "Not that it's any of your business, Mr. Heller, but I was at the Hollywood Bowl Saturday evening, with my fiancée, till quite late. The Henry Mancini concert? I was seen by hundreds of people."

"I don't remember saying you needed an alibi."

His eyes left me and he was straightening a pile of papers in front of him. "I do have a few more minutes of work I need to get done today, Mr. Heller. Anyway, you were just going."

"Yeah," I said, getting up. "I was." At the door, I threw back: "Does Bobby know you're smoking Castro-brand cigars?"

That wasn't the best exit line I ever came up with, but probably better than nothing.

And *much* better than nothing was the piece of luck I caught (rivaling my having

368

gotten a parking place on the strip) just as I was exiting the glass-and-steel building.

I practically bumped into her. About to go in was a lovely strawberry blonde with light-colored eyes and freckles and a great smile. She was wearing a simple yellow dress that her slender yet curvy figure did wonders for.

But seeing a great-looking girl in her early twenties didn't require any luck on the Sunset Strip. Running into Natalie Trundy, Arthur Jacobs' young fiancée, did, especially since we knew each other a little. I had dated a girlfriend of hers.

"Nate!" she said. "You're looking well."

"You look gorgeous. Which is par. Going in to see Arthur?"

I maneuvered to keep her out on the sidewalk, just outside the building. The sidewalk was wide enough for a conversation without interfering with beautiful out-of-work actresses and actors strolling by.

"Yes," she said. "Art and I are having an early dinner. We have to take in a premiere tonight for one of his clients."

I snapped my fingers. "Say, didn't I see you at the concert the other night? At the bowl?"

"Well, I was there. I don't remember seeing *you,* though."

"I waved. Thought you had. Anyway, that Mancini's great, isn't he?"

"Oh yes. And with Ferrante and Teicher, those *dueling* pianos! Really wonderful, and in the open air. Of course, we missed the last part."

"Oh?"

"Yeah." She gave me a you-know-how-it-is shrug. "Art got a phone call and had to go."

I nodded knowingly. "Sure. Marilyn thing."

"Right." Her eyes narrowed. "You *know* about that . . . ?"

"Uh-huh, I was just in talking with Arthur about her. Comparing notes. I'd been doing some work for Marilyn lately."

Another shrug. "All I know is some guard came and got Art, and he came back and said he'd got a call from Mickey, saying poor Marilyn was dead, and he had to go handle it."

"Marilyn's lawyer, Mickey Rudin, you mean?"

Her head bobbed, making the strawberry blonde locks shimmer. "And then we were out of there like a shot. I was home by eleven and didn't see Art till the next evening."

"A hell of a thing."

"*Terrible* tragedy. I liked her. Really *liked*

her. Art and I spent a lot of time with Marilyn, trying to support her through some . . . some tough times."

I gave her a worldly-wise nod. "I know all about Bobby."

She smiled bravely, crinkling her chin; her eyes were moist. "Poor thing really thought she'd be First Lady someday. But I agree with Arthur."

"Yeah?"

"She didn't commit suicide. It was accidental. *So* tragic. . . . Nice to see you, Nate. You know, Melody got married."

"I heard. I was too old for her anyway."

Her smile was teasing. "That's funny. She said she found you immature."

She and her delightful smile went inside to meet her fiancé. At least *he* was mature. Twenty years more mature than she was, anyway.

I headed to the A-1 and filled Fred Rubinski in, but just the broadest outlines.

"I don't want you or the A-1 directly involved in this," I said to him in his office.

Behind his desk, Fred was smoking a cigar that he wished was a Havana. He wrinkled up his Edward G. Robinson puss and said, "Nate, you *are* the A-1. Christ, after all these years, are you gonna finally manage to get yourself killed?"

"Don't be stupid. But I guess I might as well use some of our agents for simple legwork stuff. Fact-checking. Like trying to locate the guard at the Hollywood Bowl who paged Jacobs for that phone call."

"Sure. We'll just keep the boys blissfully ignorant of context. You can pay for it out of the Kilgore dame's mazuma."

"Damon Runyon is dead, you know."

"I heard."

By the time I got back to the Beverly Hills Hotel, I was feeling pretty cocky. My investigative skills seemed intact, after several years of mostly PR and management duties.

I stepped into the darkened bungalow, reaching for the light switch, wondering why housekeeping hadn't left a goddamn lamp on at least, when a hand clamped onto my right suit sleeve, followed by a hand on the other side doing the same with my left.

I moved forcefully forward and walked out of the suit coat and left the two big boys holding onto either empty sleeve, like they were fighting over a sale item. The guy who'd grabbed me first — they were both just dark shapes, but big dark shapes — I swung my elbow around and caught on the left side of his face. As he was going down I flat-kicked him in the stomach like I was putting out a fire.

The other one was coming at me from behind and I gave him a backward elbow sharp in the chest. His pal was still doubled over and deciding whether or not to puke, and Christ I hoped he wouldn't because that smell would linger, when the other one, who'd taken a couple steps back, got a gun out from somewhere, off his hip I guess, and showed it to me. It was dark in there but not that dark. I knew a .38 revolver when I saw one. Even in silhouette.

When the bad moment passed — the one where I wondered if it was my last — the guy who almost puked picked up my suit coat and tossed it at me while the other latched onto my right arm and they marched me out into sunshine and to their car, where they threw me in back.

Not thugs. Worse.

One guy was a rangy redhead with blue eyes and the other had pockmarks and actor teeth.

LAPD intel.

CHAPTER 18

We rode in an unmarked car, of course, with both intel boys in front, and me in back like a perp, but no handcuffs. I asked no questions and made no comments, wise-ass or otherwise, not inquiring about my rights or was I under arrest or even what the fuck time is it.

For their part, they had said only one thing — the redhead, anyway, who early on glanced back from the passenger seat to offer: "The captain wants to see you."

Since I'd just assaulted two police officers, however unintentionally, the professional tone and demeanor of the ride did encourage me. Still, it was an inherently unsettling journey.

They could have been taking me anywhere — the Intelligence Division was not known for standing on ceremony — and even in this enlightened age, I might find myself beaten in a basement somewhere.

I'll spare you the interminable trip, and instead provide a touch of background about my least favorite division of the LAPD. Intel consisted of something like forty officers dedicated to keeping out-of-town mobsters out of town. Both Parker and Hamilton made proud public statements about the extra-legal nature of the division's activities. Like the three-man squad who'd memorized every nasty La Cosa Nostra face in their files, and worked the airport full-time, just watching, ready to refuse entry into Parker's closed city.

Intel's files weren't just filled with mob guys. Potential Commies were in there, too, since Chief Parker frequently went on public record about his desire to "protect the American philosophy of life," particularly from the Russians. Parker's man Hamilton and the boys and girls of the Intelligence Division went after such subversives as labor leaders and reporters who'd failed to genuflect before the chief. My favorite was when they gathered intel on mayoral candidate Norris Poulson, trying to prevent his election.

But when Poulson *did* win the election, and the new mayor failed to fire Hamilton and disband the intel division, there were those who scratched their heads. Why would

Poulson hold on to Hamilton and the division that had just tried to smear him? Others understood that the big bad files kept in the captain's big fat safe made changes of administration irrelevant in LA.

There'd been a time when a ride downtown meant City Hall and a dank cellar cell where the likes of Hamilton and his crew would beat out a rubber-hose rhumba on the likes of yours truly. But times had changed. My chauffeurs were hauling me underground, all right — they were driving through a crowded lot toward an underground parking garage.

The seven-story very modern Police Administration Building sat like a big derailed boxcar pointing at nearby City Hall and other Civic Center buildings. Of course, hardly anybody called the facility by its actual name — to cop and crook alike, this was the Glass House, though that moniker had never prevented any stone-throwing, figurative or otherwise.

We took the elevator up to the fourth floor and they paraded me down a narrow, high-ceilinged, fluorescent-lit green hall through a door where a small black sign with white letters said INTELLIGENCE DIVISION, right across from ROBBERY HOMICIDE. The redhead took the lead, with me following, and the pockmarked dick behind me. In case I made a break for it.

The intel bullpen might have been a classroom: pale green walls, blonde-wood desks, white file cabinets and green ones, too, framed maps of the city and sections thereof. The office labeled (white on black) CAPTAIN JAMES HAMILTON had no receptionist.

The redhead knocked, didn't wait for a reply, and stuck his head in. I could hear his muffled: "Got 'im, Cap."

"Send his ass in," Hamilton said. Not so muffled.

The redhead closed the door and came over to me and his partner.

"We'll keep the scuffle to ourselves," he said quietly. "You don't want the captain knowing you swung on his officers, and I don't wanna waste time confirming or denying havin' to pull a gun on you."

I nodded. "Deal."

Behind me, the pockmarked guy said, "I *didn't* agree to this crap."

He was the one who'd taken the brunt of it, an elbow in the face, which had given him a welt, and my shoe in his gut.

The redhead said, "Let it go, Larry. Sometimes when you make an omelet, the yolk's on you."

Har de har har, as Ralph Kramden used to say. Still, kind of nice having one cop crack wise at the other cop, and save me the trouble. And risk.

Anyway, Larry let it go, and the redhead opened the door for me and made an after-you gesture and winked. Smart-ass. Being one, I didn't much care for the rest of the breed.

The chair waiting for me in front of Hamilton's desk was metal with a padded green vinyl seat. The captain was occupied with a file, so I got my bearings.

Not a big office, though not as sterile as some in the Glass House, Hamilton displaying numerous awards, citations, and even framed newspaper clippings on his walls. A big old iron safe — a relic from earlier, grittier days — squatted against the wall at my right, between metal filing cabinets. The fabled repository of the dirt that Chief Parker and his favorite police dog had dug out and assembled on one and sundry. And were continuing to do so.

The safe was not my favorite decorating touch, however — right above it hung a large framed photographic portrait of Chief William H. Parker, one of those pastel hand-tinted jobs that always made its subjects look slightly unreal and the men somewhat feminine. It was like Hamilton was displaying a portrait of his best girl.

I chose not to share this observation with Hamilton, who looked no less big sitting behind a big blonde desk that was arrayed with files, mug shots and circulars, standing family photos, a multi-line phone, and a much-used ash tray. His craggy face had a naturally sorrowful cast, but the small hard eyes seemed strangers to pity.

He tossed aside the report like a wadded napkin and said in his distinctive husky baritone, "I think I made a mistake the other day."

"Nobody's perfect," I said.

"I threw you out over at the Monroe house. I should have been . . . more polite. We should have had a talk."

"I'm here now. Your men asked politely. So I came, even though I don't believe I'm under arrest . . . am I? Not a material witness, or —"

"No. This is voluntary." He smiled. It did nothing to improve the rolling prairie of his face. "I'm sure the fellas made that clear."

"Yeah. They were nice."

He studied me. I don't know how to fully drain the sarcasm out of me, but I can drain it out of my voice, which makes it hard for the recipient to tell, sometimes.

He found a pack of Chesterfields on his desk, offered me a smoke. I declined and he lighted one up, shrugging. "We don't like each other. You don't like me. I don't like you."

"See, you are a detective." Didn't bother disguising that one. He'd asked for it. And anyway, this office, with tinted-cheeked Parker looking on, was no place to conduct a beating.

"We had a run-in or two," he said, sighed smoke, brushed it away from his face, "and I am not naturally enamored of people in your business. It's a shady trade. Sleazy."

"Tacky, too," I contributed. "But it can pay well."

He made a noise that might have been a laugh. "Hell of a lot better than a *real* cop's pay. But I digress. Fact is, you and I . . . we have a common basis in friendship and co-operation, if we just care to admit it."

"Sure. What?"

He gestured with an open palm, his expression telling me the answer was obvious. "You worked with Bob Kennedy back in the old days."

This was no revelation — my first run-in with Hamilton had been back then, when we were both supposedly on the same side. I thought at the time he was an unpleasant cross between a bully and a bureaucrat, and I still did.

"Bob's a friend," I said. "And I know you two get along. So, now . . . you want *us* to be friends, Captain?"

He sighed more smoke. "Let's say I want us not to be enemies."

"Okay. Why don't you make the first move."

He shifted in his swivel chair, then leaned both elbows on the desk, clutter be damned. Rested his cigarette in the tray.

"This Monroe matter is potentially embarrassing," he said. "To our mutual friend."

"Did you say Monroe murder?"

"*Matter.* Matter. It's no murder, Jesus. We all know that poor girl took her own life, and whether intentional or not, it's a sad goddamn thing, but what can you do? Done is done."

Interesting point of view for a police detective.

"Captain, I understand wanting to help Bob out. His younger brother's running for the Senate, and his older brother wants to keep being president. The two of them handing that woman around like a drunken cheerleader after the big game, well, that getting out wouldn't reflect well. Of course, boys will be boys."

The lumpy face glowered. But he said nothing.

"Still," I said, "she deserves better than what you fellas are providing. She was a big star, a public figure, and incidentally a human being. And she doesn't even get an inquest? And you turn the investigation over to some civilians at UCLA?"

"Why don't you drop by the chief's office," Hamilton said, damn near growling it. "I'm sure he'd love to hear your suggestions."

Too bad — our friendship was already strained.

"What I'm saying," I said, "is that within reason, I'm all for keeping the Kennedy name out of the mud. They like to tramp *around* in the mud, which makes helping them tricky. But I'm for it. So what can I do for you?"

The average observer would call his demeanor calm. But those eyes, small to begin with and hooded, were taking me apart the way a kid in biology class does a frog.

"You can stop nosing around," he said simply.

"I don't know what you —"

"Lying to me isn't smart." He jerked a thumb toward the safe. "Your file's already foul enough, Heller. Lie to me, play me, and see what happens."

"I hope nothing goes on my permanent record," I said.

The eyes closed. I half expected steam to come out of his ears, like Yosemite Sam. Why the hell did I insist on needling this bastard? Did I think I'd win him over with laughter?

"Sorry," I said, and waved a hand. "You'd figure at my age I'd have outgrown this case of smart mouth."

"You would figure." He drew deep on the cigarette. Let it out like steam — not from his ears, though. "What were you doing at Fifth Helena Drive Sunday morning?"

I shrugged. "I'd been doing some security work for Marilyn, the last month or so. I heard about her death on the radio and came right over. Felt a responsibility."

The little eyes managed to narrow further. "You were up at five in the fucking morning, Heller? And heard it on the radio?"

"If this is about me needing an alibi, I want my phone call first."

He shook his head. He was struggling, too. Having to talk to me was no fun at all. How Hamilton must have longed for that cellar cell across the street. And a rubber hose. . . .

"Now," he said, making that innocent word a guilty accusation, "I hear you've been

bothering one of our people. Sergeant Clemmons."

I would bet big bucks he hadn't heard it from Clemmons.

"Just trying," I said, no confrontation in my voice, "to fill some things in for my personal satisfaction. Begins and ends there."

"Really. Then why, while my boys are out picking you up, do I get a phone call from Arthur Jacobs saying you were at his office, bothering *him* about it?"

"If that was Mr. Jacobs' impression, I apologize to the both of you. I worked for Marilyn, he's her publicist; I just wanted to know what the official story was."

"Official story?"

"The party line. I feel a certain loyalty to Marilyn. Did I mention she was my client? I want what's best for her."

He grunted a non-laugh. "Nothing's best for her now. You should worry about your friend Bob. He's still breathing."

I sat forward. "Tell me *he* didn't ask you to —"

"No! No." He waved that off; that and some of the smoke he and his cigarette were manufacturing. "I'm just looking out after his interests as best I can."

"Like I am Marilyn's."

384

He sat back. Sighed through his nose. No smoke. He looked like a weary bull wondering whether goring this petty toreador was worth the bother.

"You were seen this morning talking to Flo Kilgore," he said.

Christ — either they were good, or I was sloppy. Had the intel boys been tailing me? And I didn't notice? *Maybe the Musso's waiters were undercover men. It would explain the service the tourists got.*

"Flo and I are friends," I said.

"She was at the Monroe place Sunday morning, looking for a story."

"What newshound wasn't?"

"Just a coincidence that you talk to her this morning," he said, stabbing out the smoke, "and are out and about in the afternoon, poking around."

"Marilyn was my client," I said again. "I'm just examining a few loose ends, to my satisfaction. I'm certainly not trying to cause any trouble for our mutual friend, the attorney general."

He shifted in the seat again, trying to get a different angle on me. "What specifically were you doing for Miss Monroe? Security-wise?"

I knew better than to lie. "She wanted a tap put on her phone."

"Her own phone."

"Yeah."

"Why?"

"She indicated it had to do with that mess with Fox. You know, her firing and the studio politics and all."

"What became of the tapes?"

". . . You don't know?"

"I'm asking."

"My understanding is that two of your intel boys grabbed those tapes from Roger Pryor. That's who was working for me. And, uh, it was those same two detectives, I believe, who brought me over this afternoon."

He was nodding; for the first time this afternoon, my answers were satisfying him. "We've been having a little difficulty locating Mr. Pryor. Would you have any idea where he is?"

Now it was time to lie.

"None," I said. "He isn't A-1 staff, you know. He's a freelance operator."

"Oh, I know." Hamilton checked his watch. Apparently I'd begun to bore him. "Here's what it comes down to, Heller. I want you to stop nosing around."

"Am I breaking any laws?"

"*Are* you? Anyway, consider it a favor to me. Personal request. Now that we're friends." He selected a file from the cluttered array on his desk, thumbed it open, and began reading. Then he looked up as if surprised I was still there, and said, "You can go."

I went.

Nobody offered me a ride, and I wasn't about to ask for one. I figured a cab would do nicely. At the elevator, I was reaching to punch DOWN when a beefy hand slipped in and pressed UP.

Chief of Detectives Thad Brown — a big, balding, bespectacled guy in his early sixties with paunch enough to require his brown suit coat to hang open — gestured for me to get on as the door dinged open. The pleasant face that resided on his egg-shaped head wore an oddly furtive expression.

We got on and he pressed 5.

"Am I invited somewhere, Thad?"

We knew each other a little.

"Don't be alarmed, Nate. I'd like a private chat. If you don't mind . . . ?"

This was one of the three or four most powerful, honored police officers on the force, deferring to my wishes. Raymond Burr had played him on *Dragnet.*

"Glad to, Thad. But I just had a lovely visit with Jim Hamilton. I doubt you'll top it."

The elevator rose.

"Hamilton talked to you, huh? You're lucky."

"How so?"

"Usually he only talks to God and Chief Parker."

The elevator dinged, doors opened, and I followed the bear-like chief of detectives down another narrow green hallway. We paused outside his office, and he waited as several plainclothes officers and secretaries went their various ways.

When traffic had lulled, and it was just the two of us, he walked me down to an interview room, placed the black, white-lettered INTERVIEW IN PROGRESS placard in its slot, and ushered me in.

This was a typical Glass House interrogation room — white soundproof-tiled walls, a blonde-wood desk with a phone and an ashtray, metal chairs on either side, and a big window with its vertical blinds shut, behind the witness chair, which was where Brown gestured me to sit.

I said, "Uh, Thad — or should I say 'Chief'? This isn't official, is it?"

"Anything but."

"This room is wired for sound. . . ."

"So are a lot of rooms in this town, I understand."

He had a point.

The big man sat down and I went around to the other side but didn't sit yet. His smile was as reassuring as his mellow voice. "Nate, this isn't being recorded. This is as off-the-record as it gets."

"Nothing's off the record in these cubicles."

"This is." He shrugged his slightly hunched shoulders. "Look, you don't trust me? Door's unlocked."

I sat. "I see in the papers you're not going to be chief for a while yet."

Years ago, Thad Brown had gone up against Parker for the big job — they'd both been qualified, but Parker had political pull. Everybody figured, though, that when Parker eventually left, the top chair would finally go to Brown.

Who said, "How do you figure that?"

"Front page Monday said Bobby Kennedy has endorsed J. Edgar Hoover. Says as long as his brother is president, Hoover will head up the FBI, meaning Parker has to wait a while, and so will you."

"Interesting," Brown said, with a sideways smile. "Day after Marilyn Monroe dies, Bobby Kennedy suddenly loves J. Edgar Hoover."

"Almost like Hoover has something on

him, isn't it?"

Brown adjusted his glasses, sat back in the hard chair. "Everybody knows you and Bobby are pals, Nate. Going back to the attorney general's first stab at racket busting."

"Yeah. But that doesn't put me on his payroll."

"Didn't figure it would. But you were on Marilyn Monroe's payroll, weren't you? Some kind of security work?"

"You keep your ear to the ground, don't you, Thad?"

"Sure do. Was thinking maybe I wanna be a cop when I grow up. Another thing I hear is you're looking into Marilyn's death. Obligation to a dead client. Which I would imagine is why you were honored with that nice chat in Hamilton's office."

"Yeah, he treats me right. Doesn't shove me in some interrogation booth like a miscreant."

"Don't misunderstand, Nate," Brown said, smiling genially, folding his arms. "I'm not against you looking into what happened to that poor woman."

I admit it — I blinked. "You aren't?"

"No. Because *somebody* should. You see, I was taking an interest in the case myself . . . but I had a talk with Chief Parker this morning, and he has another idea."

I let out a laugh. "Such as, Hamilton can handle it himself, thank you, and doesn't need your help?"

"Something like that. You don't mind if I think out loud, do you?"

"Not at all."

He smiled and nodded his thanks. "See, there's this guy named Bates who's telling the press that Bobby Kennedy visited his ranch near San Francisco. That Bobby never set foot off that ranch except to go to mass Sunday morning."

"Mass," I said. "That's a nice touch."

"Problem is — as I told Chief Parker this morning — I have contacts who saw the attorney general and his brother-in-law Lawford at the Beverly Hilton Hotel Saturday afternoon."

"What kind of contacts?"

"Solid ones. This came straight from my brother. I know you two are like oil and water, but Finis always knows what's going in this town."

Thad Brown was one of the most respected cops on the LAPD, whereas his brother Finis had been for years the department's in-house bookie. Not quite as respected, then, as his celebrated brother, who was nonetheless right about the ability of Detective Fat Ass Brown to be in the know.

"And," the chief of detectives was saying, "I have a report from a Beverly Hills officer who stopped actor Peter Lawford for speeding Saturday evening. The attorney general was in the car. Lawford apologized, but said Mr. Kennedy was on his way to the Beverly Hills Hotel on an urgent matter. The officer let Lawford go with a warning."

"And how did Chief Parker react to this information?"

"He said I was off the case and that it was being handled exclusively by Captain Hamilton. By the way, I happened to see the impounded Monroe phone records on Parker's desk."

I sat forward. "I don't suppose you got a look at them. . . ."

The big bear might have been licking honey out of a comb, he was smiling so big. Bears can get stung that way.

"I was ushered into the chief's office," he said, "when Parker was talking to his secretary about something. I'm afraid, like most cops, I'm a natural snoop. I had a look. All the Monroe July and August phone tabs. Including a number of calls to Bobby Kennedy at the Justice Department."

"Did you ask Parker about them?"

"I did. I pointed and said, 'How did we get these?' He said, '*We* didn't get them —

Captain Hamilton did. And you never saw them.' They're under lock and key by now."

"Why tell me this, Thad?"

"I just want you to know, that as a taxpayer in good standing, you have a friend in local law enforcement."

"That's good information to have."

"One more item — in that limbo between the regular police and intel taking over the Monroe case, one of my men processed her bedsheets. There was a crumpled piece of notepaper among them, which is gone now."

I edged forward again. "Not a *suicide* note?"

"No. It had a phone number on it."

"You gonna make me ask, Thad?"

". . . Robert Kennedy's private line at the Justice Department. Same number as on the phone tabs."

I didn't know what to say.

Finally I managed, "Are you looking for quid pro quo? Am I supposed to empty the bag for you?"

He shook his head. "But if the times come, when you feel the need to unburden yourself, Nate — I'm the priest you should come to."

"Amen, brother," I said.

He gave me a friendly nod, rose and opened the door for me.

As I hailed a cab down on the corner, I was still wondering if there'd ever before been an interrogation like this one . . .

. . . where the guy in the suspect chair just sat there and the interrogator spilled his guts.

CHAPTER 19

At the funeral, Wednesday at 1:00 P.M. at Westwood Memorial Park Chapel, Hollywood luminaries were conspicuously absent. This reflected the guest list as assembled by Joe DiMaggio, who had sat vigil at his ex-wife's casket the night before. (You may have figured out I wasn't invited.)

Among those turned away were Patricia Kennedy Lawford — who'd flown from Hyannis Port especially to attend — and of course her husband, Peter, as well as Frank Sinatra, Dean Martin, and various other luminaries.

While the Hollywood elite were not welcome, a number of Marilyn's associates and coworkers were among the thirty or so in attendance. These included her shrink Dr. Greenson, publicist Pat Newcomb (no Arthur Jacobs, though), lawyer Mickey Rudin, housekeeper Eunice Murray, half sister Berniece Miracle, acting coaches Lee and

Paula Strasberg, executrix Inez Melson (her former business manager), makeup man Whitey Snyder, and hairstylist Sydney Guilaroff.

The handful inside the chapel were surrounded outside by several thousand mourners — men, women, and children of every social class. Fifty LAPD uniformed officers worked crowd control with Twentieth Century–Fox providing forty security guards, but there was no real trouble.

According to the papers, Marilyn's casket was bronze and lined with champagne-colored satin. The open casket revealed her looking lovely in a green Pucci dress and green chiffon scarf, her platinum hair in a pageboy. Makeup man Whitey Snyder had done well by his star, having promised Marilyn years before that if anything happened to her, nobody would touch her face but him.

Lee Strasberg gave an eloquent eulogy, and the organ music added one Hollywood touch, albeit bittersweet: "Somewhere Over the Rainbow."

Only after the procession to the cemetery's Corridor of Memories and final rites did the fans give in to frenzy and go trampling graves and stomping on flowers as they sought souvenirs.

■ ■ ■ ■

The day of Marilyn's funeral I spent mostly at the A-1 on the phone trying to set up interviews when I wasn't taking calls from field agents running things down for me. Flo Kilgore was chasing her list of leads, as we'd divvied up the work. At 7:00 P.M., she and I met at my bungalow to compare notes and share information.

Though she lived nearby on Roxbury Drive, Flo had come to me at the Beverly Hills Hotel, parking in the big front lot and walking through the hotel out onto the grounds where the bungalows nestled amid flowering shrubs, colorful gardens, and palm trees. The polite thing would have been to meet her in the lobby, but I let her make the trek alone, out of concern for discretion and security.

I'm not sure, though, that anyone would have recognized her. When I ushered her into the living room, she looked about half her forty-some years, and while subdued lighting was part of it, she was most of it. The brunette bouffant had been replaced by a long swinging ponytail, her makeup low-key with just a touch of very red lipstick, eyes shielded by oversize sunglasses, and her slender, shapely figure decked out in a short-sleeve yellow-and-white top and white capris and yellow low-heeled sandals. Over her shoulder was slung a big purse, also yellow and white.

I welcomed her in, and she tucked the sunglasses into the purse, which she set on a chair, then curled up on the couch, while I called room service for our supper. She wanted the tortilla soup to start, and wondered if I'd share a Caesar salad with her. The last meal I'd shared with a woman in this room had been with Marilyn, and the menu had been similar enough to provide me a pang.

I pulled a chair over so we could talk eye to eye. "Did you cover it?"

"The funeral? No. Too much of a zoo. Did you know that SOB Winchell made the guest list? Only reporter on the inside. Fucking friend of DiMaggio's!"

"I hear Pat Lawford was turned away."

"And Sinatra and Dino. Can you believe it? DiMaggio has been saying openly that he holds Hollywood and the Kennedys responsible." She shrugged. "Can you blame him?"

"I don't blame him and I don't disagree with him."

She arranged her legs under her and sat

Indian-style. "Are we sure this bungalow is safe for us to talk?"

"We're fine. Fred Rubinski brought somebody in to sweep it just this morning. But you're right to be paranoid. Hamilton has me under surveillance."

I filled her in on my activities yesterday — police officer Clemmons, publicist Jacobs, and the two high-ranking cops. She said little, only asking the occasional clarifying question. I was wrapping up when the food came, and we elected not to talk business while we ate.

After, when she returned to the couch, she sat with her back to an armrest, her bare feet on the center cushion. I sat at the other end, angled to see her better.

"You should know," I said, "I've been using some A-1 agents for legwork. They're trustworthy and don't know enough context to cause any trouble, in any event."

She nodded. "That's fine. Different than me needing to avoid using other reporters. Your worker bees have any luck?"

I told her we'd confirmed Bobby Kennedy's weekend use of a suite at the St. Francis hotel as an office and retreat, in support of his speech at the American Bar Association convention Monday night. A switchboard operator revealed that Marilyn

Monroe had called for Kennedy multiple times, and that messages had been recorded on paper, the slips picked up by aides.

"We asked what those messages were," I said. "The gist was 'You better call me and tell me why I shouldn't blow the lid off. Every reporter in town has been calling me!' Speaking of Winchell, his name and yours were among those mentioned."

Flo hugged her arms as if chilled, though the temperature was mildly warm. Air conditioner was off and windows open. "No wonder Bobby made the trip to LA."

"One of my guys came up with some interesting background research on Eunice Murray," I said. "Turns out she's a trained psychiatric nurse."

She leaned forward. "What? *Really?* That kook?"

"Kooks often have an interest in psychiatry — haven't you noticed? Key thing is, Marilyn apparently didn't know about Murray's nursing background — she thought Dr. Greenson had recommended the woman to be a housekeeper, interior decorator, and companion."

Her big blue eyes got bigger. "So the witch was, what? Greenson's *spy?*"

"That might be a little harsh. Spy, I mean — witch seems about right." I shrugged.

"There's not exactly a Hippocratic oath for private detectives, but even *I* have to question the ethics of secretly placing a nurse at home to monitor a patient's behavior."

Now the pretty eyes narrowed. "Do we know the connection between Murray and Greenson? I mean, how did he come to suggest the woman's services to Marilyn?"

"They're old, old friends. Murray's the widow of one of Greenson's best pals, a military man turned labor organizer. Hell, Greenson lives in a house the Murrays built and formerly lived in. Mrs. Murray sold it to him."

She shook her head, and laughed without humor. "Don't you think this is all sounding just a little bit goddamn incestuous? Murray a longtime associate of Dr. Greenson? Who happens to be Mickey Rudin's brother-in-law, who is coincidentally also *Sinatra's* lawyer? This kind of stretches the 'small world' concept to the limit, huh?"

"Come on, Flo. Do I have to remind you that Hollywood is a one-industry town? It *is* small, in its way."

"Allowing that," she said, raising a traffic-cop palm, "keep in mind Greenson came on board as Marilyn's shrink in the last year or two. Before that, she was with a woman named Kris in New York. Okay. Stay with me now. Is it reasonable to assume Frank Sinatra knew about Marilyn and Jack Kennedy?"

"Yes."

"Is it reasonable to assume Mickey Rudin, her attorney and Sinatra's attorney, also knew?"

"Yes."

"So there's a good possibility Marilyn took Greenson on at Rudin's and/or Sinatra's suggestion."

"I could buy that."

She pointed a gunlike finger. "Then is it too great a leap to suggest Greenson was handpicked by Kennedy insiders to handle Marilyn?"

That hadn't occurred to me.

"I can maybe buy that, too," I said, tentatively. Then it was my turn: "Shall I throw you a curve?"

"Fling away."

"I don't mean to sound like a right-wing loon, but an agent of mine has linked Greenson, Murray, Murray's late husband, and even Dr. Engelberg to various left-wing groups. The *same* groups."

Flo cocked her head. "Marilyn leaned left herself. Why is that significant?"

"Probably isn't. But keep in mind Marilyn has been a bedmate to both the president and the attorney general of these United States. Both of whom appear to have been casual about their pillow talk."

Flo laughed a little. "And, what? Greenson's a Soviet agent?"

"Yeah, I know. It's nonsense. That's the problem with a case like this — once you're down the rabbit hole, every absurdity seems real, and every real thing seems absurd."

She shifted on the couch. "Food for thought, anyway . . . Did you or your little elves come up with anything else today?"

After a sigh, I admitted, "Struck out a lot, frankly. I tried Rudin late afternoon at his office, figuring after the funeral he'd go back in . . . but the receptionist said he was out for the day. His home phone is unlisted, but of course I got it anyway, only he has one of those fancy tape-recorder answering machines. No way to know if he's really out or just screening which calls he takes. Goddamn annoying gizmo. Have to get one of those."

"I have one," she said, dimpling her cheeks.

"Yeah, well, you're rich. I'm just a blue-collar working stiff. . . ."

"With a Jaguar."

"That's the A-1's. I'm so poor I don't even own a car. As for my skills as an investigator, I can tell you I was also unable to get Pat Newcomb on the phone. Or Eunice Murray. The funeral put a crimp in that effort, meaning I had to call in the morning or later this afternoon. Somebody answered for Newcomb, and said she was out, but Murray's phone just rang and rang. Any way you slice it, nobody wants to talk to me."

"Well, they certainly won't talk to me." Her head went back and her little chin stuck out. "Nonetheless . . . I *do* have several interesting things to report."

"Maybe I should give *you* a retainer."

She raised a finger skyward, or anyway ceiling-ward. "Actually, it's not a new source, just fresh information. Remember I mentioned the tissue samples that this young deputy coroner, Noguchi, sent out to try to help determine cause of death?"

"Sure. Are they back from the lab?"

"No. In fact, they're lost."

"Lost? The hell — *That* can't be common."

"It isn't. Guess how many times it's happened before in the history of the LA coroner's office?"

"Half a dozen?"

"Never."

Looked like the long arm of the law could reach way down deep into the coroner's department. That arm belonging to Chief Parker or at least Captain Hamilton.

"There were lab reports on the blood and liver," she was saying, "that indicated death by barbiturate poisoning. But the kidney, stomach, urine, and intestines samples were lost at the lab. That lab, incidentally, is attached to UCLA."

Where Dr. Greenson was an eminent faculty member, and out of which the Suicide Squad was doing their purported investigation into why Marilyn killed herself.

"Those missing tissues, Nate, would have determined without doubt whether this was an oral overdose or an injection. By the way, the death certificate was signed by a coroner's aide, not the coroner."

I frowned. "*That* can't be standard. . . ."

"Of course it isn't. And my contact there says that the Marilyn Monroe death file is shockingly incomplete. Normally it would contain reports, charts, police paperwork, and it had none of the above." Her eyes narrowed again; her head bobbed forward. "Nate, you saw Marilyn's body — did it have a bluish cast?"

"Yes. I noted it — and that was apart from the lividity, too. I remember having a fleeting absurd thought — that maybe she'd frozen to death."

"How about her fingernails?"

"They looked dirty. I figured she'd been working in the garden. And we know the water was off in the bathroom, so maybe she didn't have a shower before bedtime."

Flo shook her head, the ponytail coming to rest over her right shoulder. "The blue cast of her skin, my coroner's office contact says, is something called 'cyanosis' — a prime indication of rapid death."

"Rapid death — such as death by injection."

"Exactly." She changed her position, sitting straighter, hugging her knees to her. "But I've saved the best for last. You'll recall I was to get in touch with Sydney Guilaroff, because he's an old friend."

That had been on her "to do" list.

"Seems Sydney was supposed to fix Marilyn's hair for the funeral, but he passed out at the mortuary. They wound up using a wig from *The Misfits*."

"That's a fascinating footnote, but —"

"Just be quiet for a second, and listen to what a skilled interviewer can get out of a subject. Sydney at first didn't want to say anything. He didn't want to 'sully' Marilyn's memory. Preferred to let her rest in peace. They went far, far back, you know — he did her hair at her first screen test."

"What did your pal Sydney say?"

"Marilyn called him Saturday afternoon or early evening — in 'an absolute *state,*' he said. In tears, upset to where he could hardly understand her. Finally she calmed down and told him that Bobby Kennedy had just been there, with Peter Lawford tagging along. And Bobby threatened her, and screamed at her, and pushed her around."

"There were some bruises on her body," I said, "that might not have been lividity."

"Sydney knew *nothing* about Marilyn and Bobby — he'd known about her and Jack for years, he said, but Bobby was a new one on him . . . and he asked her why on earth Bobby Kennedy would be coming around. She said she'd had an affair with Bobby and everything had gone wrong. Now she was afraid, and felt in terrible danger."

This of course jibed with what Roger Pryor told me he'd heard sitting surveillance Saturday afternoon. Which was information I had not shared with my client Flo Kilgore, hoping to keep it to myself as long as possible.

"Marilyn called him again," Flo was saying, "around eight or eight thirty. She seemed calmed down. More composed, he said, though there was still some fear in her voice. She said one very disturbing thing, however — 'You know, Sydney, I know a lot of secrets about the Kennedys.' He asked her what kind of secrets, and she said, 'Dangerous ones.' "

"What then?"

"Then Sydney told her he'd speak to her in the morning, and she should just try to get a good night's rest. Never imagining he'd never speak with her again. . . . You don't seem very surprised, Nate. This is one hell of a revelation."

"Well, we knew Bobby was probably there, from the digging you did."

"We didn't know about an argument. . . ." A thin eyebrow rose in accusation. ". . . Or did we?"

I came clean. Somewhat clean.

"Flo, I had that same story from another source, but I wanted confirmation before sharing it."

She frowned. "What source?"

"Can't tell you. Don't you believe in that rule about journalists protecting their sources?"

"You're not a journalist! You're a private eye *working* for a journalist."

I raised two palms in surrender. "Cut me some slack on this. For now, be satisfied knowing that Sydney's story is backed up by a second source. Okay for now?"

She drew in a deep breath. Her frown

turned into a reluctant smile. "Okay. I won't deny I knew what I was getting, hiring Nate Heller."

"Atta girl."

We'd exhausted business talk but hadn't yet tired of each other's company, so I ordered us room-service dessert and coffee. The Polo Lounge had soufflés so good they were damn near worth the price — chocolate for her, vanilla for me. Took a while to arrive, and we just sat on the couch and visited. The subject was mostly why we seemed to have a good time together, between her marriages, without it ever amounting to anything more than a friendship. No conclusion was reached.

During the soufflés, which we ate at a table like an old married couple, we returned to business.

"These threats Marilyn was making," she said, licking chocolate off her spoon. "Would she have done it? Would she *really* have given a press conference?"

"I don't think so," I said.

"Really? Why?"

"Just not in her nature. For my money, both DiMaggio and Miller were rats to her, but she never bad-mouthed them in public."

"Then why the fuss with Bobby?"

"For attention. For respect. To be taken

seriously. But I think after all the raving and ranting, she would have immersed herself in her career. I mean — when did she ever attack anybody in public?"

"She defended herself a few times — like when Joan Crawford accused her of looking slutty at an awards event."

"I remember that. But she expressed her disappointment and hurt over the affront, saying how much she'd always admired Crawford. I don't believe there ever was much of a chance she'd go public about the Kennedys. The real danger was if she ever *did* overdose and left embarrassing things behind."

Flo squinted at me. "What kind of things?"

I savored a bite of vanilla, then said, "Marilyn kept notebooks — I saw a red spiral one in her bedroom, on her nightstand, that day she showed me around the place. And later she told me how she wrote down questions she wanted to ask Bobby, then would come home and record the answers, those and other things they'd talked about."

"Surely not political things."

"Yes, political things. International things. Mafia things. Cuban things. Things you don't want to know about, Flo, not even for a scoop."

She pushed the soufflé aside, about two-thirds eaten — either self-control or the discussion had gotten to her. "Then . . . if she *was* murdered, it wasn't the threat of what she'd say, but —"

"But what she'd leave behind. And it looks to me like that house on Fifth Helena was gone through top to bottom, between midnight and around five, and who knows by what people representing how many interests? We know of Fox for sure, having studio reps there to clean up. But who else? Mob? Kennedy cronies? FBI? CIA? Secret Service? Or, to use your phrase — all of the above?"

She swallowed. No soufflé involved. "You're scaring me."

"Good. I'm scared. You should be, too."

"Maybe I should stay here tonight."

"You're obviously welcome to."

I'd thought that was a throwaway, but after I set the room-service tray outside the bungalow door, I returned to find her emerging from the bathroom in a sheer yellow baby-doll nightie she'd conjured somehow, dark sand-dollar nipples and triangular thatch showing through in splendid contrast. For most middle-aged women, that skimpy lingerie would have been a risk. On her it was a sure thing.

I switched off the living room lamp and took her hand and walked her into the next room. She was still in the ponytail, still looking closer to her teenage years than to the half-century mark that was closing in on her.

"You planned this," I said, as I got out of my clothes.

"I tucked a little something in my purse," she admitted, facing me, lifting the hem of the nightie girlishly. "Just in case. I was a Girl Scout. Be prepared."

"That's Boy Scouts."

"Is it?"

She kissed me. The lights were out but the moon was filtering in the sheer curtains on the nearby French doors, touching her with ivory.

We got onto the bed, and she crawled on top of me and she kissed my mouth and my neck, and then moved on down, kissing along the way until she reached a point where her lips circled and enclosed and engulfed me, and the ponytail swung left and the ponytail swung right and left and right, until she sensed she should stop. Then she slipped out of the nightie top, leaving on the sheer panties, her breasts starkly white against tan lines, the nipples as starkly dark against the white flesh, as she positioned herself over me so I could stroke and cup and kiss and suckle those breasts. When she finally mounted me, just moving the panties aside to make room, she began slowly and sweetly and built to a nasty grinding finish that left me drained and woozy and raw.

Soon we were under a cool sheet, and she was nestled against me, lips against my chest, a hand playing in my chest hair. "Nate?"

"Yes?"

"Did you make love to her in this bed?"

"Yes."

"Were you in love with her?"

"Yes. And no."

"Yes and no?"

"I never loved her when I wasn't with her. When we were apart, she was like . . . a city you moved away from. Fond memories but no ownership."

The faint murmur of Sunset Boulevard reminded us a world was out there.

She said, "It's . . . a little intimidating."

"What is?"

"Making love to a man who's been with Marilyn Monroe."

"She's no competition for any woman now."

"Oh yes she is. And she always will be."

Flo fell asleep before long, and so did I.

But mine wasn't a deep sleep — I rarely sleep deep with a woman in my bed. Few ever stay the night, and when they do, it throws me a little. Which is why the faint creak of those French doors popped my eyes open.

The figure was in black, his back to the light from half a moon and whatever illumination was coming from the hotel grounds, making him a silhouette.

But even in daylight, he would have been a silhouette, because he was head-to-toe black: black long-sleeve shirt, black slacks, shoes, and even — and you didn't see this on many August days in Southern California — a black ski mask.

He came in slowly, opening the doors carefully, and I'd heard no click from a key either, the blot of a man just slipping in. He was left-handed, or anyway the gun was in his left hand, an automatic with a noise suppressor. My nine-millimeter was on the nightstand, under a fanned-open *Newsweek*. Sleeping on my back, I could ease my hand over there, and make a reasonably certain grab; but with Flo next to me like this, she could easily be caught in a crossfire.

That was when I saw the glint of the needle.

The guy was not left-handed — the gun was backup — the primary weapon here was the hypo in his black-gloved right hand.

Nasty as this news was, it was good news, too — it meant he was not here to shoot me, rather to shoot me up, which was another, more delicate procedure altogether. He'd given himself a hard job.

The hard job *I* had was waiting.

Waiting while my visitor did a tiny test squirt, and then began to move closer, arching his back, raising the syringe in hand, thumb on the plunger.

Closer.

Closer.

He was less than a foot away when I threw the tackle into him and knocked him back through a half-open French door onto the stone patio.

I was naked, so this was not ideal, but this time *I* was on top, and when I noticed his right hand was empty now, that he'd lost the needle on the trip, I latched onto his left wrist with one hand and onto his forearm with the other, and smashed the back of his gloved hand onto the stone, till the fingers popped open and the weapon jumped and clunked and slid.

That focused attention served me well in disarming him, but not in maintaining dominance, and a hard gloved fist swung into the left side of my face, dazing me, giving him the moment he needed to fling me off him onto the stone floor and into the path of a wrought-iron chair that clipped my forehead.

The blow didn't knock me out, but it jarred me further, and when I rolled over, ready to get back into the fray, buck naked or not, I could see the silhouette running through the palms, and then disappearing between a bungalow and a hedge.

Breathing hard, skinned here and there, I collected my visitor's weapon — a silenced nine-millimeter Beretta — and padded barefoot through the French doors into the nearby bedroom. I shut the doors, locked them, finally getting around to wondering why Flo hadn't reacted in any way. Most women would at least scream, and the kind I ran with would likely have waded in.

Of course, those women would have been awake. She was deep asleep, snoring gently, and smiling, her only concession to the scuffle having been to roll over and face the other direction.

I turned on the nightstand light, slipped into my boxer shorts, put the confiscated nine-millimeter in the nightstand drawer, and got my own nine-mil out from under the *Newsweek.*

Still, Flo gently snored. I am almost tempted to say, at this point, *When Nate Heller fucks them, they stay fucked.* But that wouldn't be gentlemanly.

Neither was trying to kill a guy in his sleep with a hypo full of who-the-hell knew. But soon I *would* know, because I'd have a lab the A-1 used check it for me . . . *if* I could find the goddamn thing. . . .

And I could, and did — on the carpet near the foot of the bed, where my guest had unintentionally pitched it.

"Nate!" Flo said.

I looked up.

An alarmed Flo was sitting there, ponytail draped over a shoulder, her breasts exposed and perky, not that that was a priority right now. "What are you doing? What is *that?*"

She meant the needle.

Flo Kilgore was my client. That didn't preclude me from lying to her, but what the hell.

I told her the truth.

And she understood exactly why I didn't want to call the cops, and why starting tomorrow, over on Roxbury Drive, she would have two A-1 agents as sleepover guests.

Just not with my privileges.

CHAPTER 20

The next day, Thursday, a remarkable exodus began.

Pat and Peter Lawford headed to Hyannis Port for an extended stay at the family compound with the Bobby Kennedys. Under the circumstances, the trip was fairly predictable, but the Lawfords had invited along a surprising guest — Pat Newcomb.

This I learned from Thad Brown, who I'd called to request a no-questions-asked favor involving a certain nine-mil Beretta and noise suppressor — a favor the chief of detectives granted, proving his offer of friendship was genuine.

Mid-morning, at the A-1, when I called the Arthur Jacobs agency to find out when they expected Miss Newcomb back, I discovered something arguably even more interesting than the Hyannis Port trip.

"Miss Newcomb no longer works here," the switchboard girl informed me.

I played a long shot and asked to be put through to Mr. Jacobs, and — even though I'd given my name — he actually took the call.

"Pat is no longer with us, Mr. Heller," he said coldly.

"Might I ask why?"

"Her principal duties were as Miss Monroe's personal publicist. That position has obviously terminated."

"But why terminate Miss Newcomb? Why didn't you just transfer her over to another client?"

He might have said that the Arthur Jacobs agency did not feel obligated to check with local private detectives before making their business decisions. Instead he just hung up.

I got Flo Kilgore on the phone — she was in her office at home — and informed her of the development.

"That puts a new angle on everything we know about Pat Newcomb," Flo said. "And everything she's said."

"I already knew she was lying — saying Marilyn was in high spirits Saturday afternoon. Now we know *why* she lied."

"What you may not know is that Eunice Murray has left town, too," Flo said. "Taking an 'extended European vacation.' "

"On housekeeper's pay?"

"Don't you mean *out-of-work* housekeeper's pay?" She gave me a combined sigh and laugh. "Well, they can't all leave town. I have appointments this afternoon to talk to Washington and Melson."

That wasn't a law firm or a dance act — they were respectively Hazel and Inez, Marilyn's maid at the studio and her former business manager/current executrix. I had told Flo yesterday that my man watching the Fifth Helena house had seen both women there yesterday afternoon.

"Glad to hear they'll talk to you," I said. "But it does seem like we're scraping the bottom of the barrel. I do have one major witness lined up — Norman Jefferies."

"Remind me."

"Murray's son-in-law. The handyman who boarded up the window in that phony suicide rescue scenario. He's been ducking the cops, the press, and my phone calls. But one of my agents caught up with him at a bar around the corner from his apartment in Santa Monica. He's agreed to talk to me today."

"Really? How did you swing it?"

"I offered him five hundred dollars of your money."

I sat with Norm Jefferies on a wooden

bench opposite the Playland Arcade on the Santa Monica pier. This was a weekday but also summer, pleasantly warm, so attendance was fairly heavy. The monumental many-spired Santa Monica ballroom, used for roller-skating now, was off to our right. And behind the row of food stands and gift shops loomed amusement park rides including a big enclosed carousel.

The smell of fried foods was mitigated by an ocean breeze. Teenage girls in belly-baring tops and short shorts, wandering eating cotton candy and nibbling on hot dogs on a stick, made pleasant viewing, and the dings and clangs and buzzers of pinball machines were softened by the rush of tide and wail of gulls.

The lanky, mournful-faced Jefferies wore a frayed dark button-down sport shirt with the sleeves rolled up, tan chinos with knee patches, and scuffed shoes. I'd come in a Ban-Lon polo and white jeans and was munching popcorn.

Jefferies slouched on the bench, legs akimbo, folded hands dangling between them; his voice was soft, medium-range, only occasionally expressive.

"Mr. Heller, couple things we need to get straight right away."

"Okay."

"This is strictly off-the-record. I don't care what you do with this information, as long as you don't attach it to my name."

"All right."

He shrugged. "That's the terms. That, and cash."

I stopped eating popcorn, reached into my right jeans pocket and brought the five folded C-notes out for some air.

When I'd returned them to my pocket, his eyes showed that the money had impressed him; then the mournful expression returned.

"First thing that nobody knows," he said, "is I was pretty much there all day. I was remodeling Miss Monroe's kitchen. Laid new floor tiles, among other things. Funny."

"Funny?"

"Started out so average, such a nothing day. You never know, do you, when it's gonna be the worst day of your life? Well, this one was right in there."

A gull shrieked. A teenage girl laughed. I chewed popcorn.

Jefferies said he'd got to the house on Fifth Helena Drive around 8:30 A.M., and hadn't left until after dawn Sunday morning, the same time I had.

"The first thing out of the ordinary," he said, "was this argument between the Newcomb woman and Miss Monroe. It was about loyalty. About whether this Newcomb gal was loyal to her, or to the . . . you know, the Kennedys."

"How did this come up?"

"I gathered Miss Monroe — it's not disrespectful I call her Marilyn, because she let me call her that — Marilyn, she was expecting Bobby Kennedy — you know, the attorney general?"

Marilyn Monroe — you know, the actress?

"Yeah," I said. "I know."

"She'd been expecting him to come to the house Friday night. And he hadn't showed. Way I took it, the Newcomb woman said she could make that happen, only it didn't. Anyway, she fired her."

"Who fired . . . What?"

"Marilyn fired Newcomb."

"This was when?"

"Just before lunch. Newcomb gal slept till noon. Marilyn, she'd been out gardening in the morning. Also talking to some photographer who wanted to take pictures of her for *Playboy.* The guy was trying to talk her into it, and I guess she must've agreed at some earlier time, and was saying now how she had second thoughts, because of maybe it would make her out a sex object. Is what I gathered."

"Back to Pat Newcomb. . . ."

"Okay, Newcomb. They argue, Marilyn fires her, and then I was doing some work outside and missed why, but for some reason the woman is still hanging around all day."

"Newcomb, you mean."

"Yeah. Only she spends all her time in that room where the two phones are. Like she's just waiting for one to ring, and maybe won something or her lab results are in. And in fact she's still there when Kennedy and Lawford show up, and as far as I know never comes out."

"When was that?"

"Sometime between three and four. Marilyn had this nice spread of food ready, so she must have expected them. Marilyn looked real nice. Not all movie star decked out, but *nice.* You were there at the house a few times, Mr. Heller. You know how good she could look, not trying so hard."

I just nodded.

His eyebrows went up. "Oh, I skipped something that's maybe important."

"That's okay, Norm. Take your time."

"After lunch, I finished up in the kitchen, and I was loading my tools in my pickup. Never meant to stay all day. But Eunice comes out and she looks like death warmed over."

This was her son-in-law, so I decided not to point out that Murray *always* looked like death warmed over.

"She was shaking her head and sighing and so on, and I say, 'What's wrong, Eunice?' And she says, all surprised and upset, 'Marilyn just *fired* me.' "

"Fired her? Mrs. Murray was fired Saturday afternoon, too?"

"That's right. Marilyn wanted her to pack her things and leave, be gone by the end of the day. Which is why I stuck around into the evening."

"I don't follow, Norm."

"Well, Eunice practically lived at that place. She never gave up her own apartment, but three or four nights a week, she'd stay at Marilyn's. So she had a lot of stuff around. I was to stay and help her pack and get her things together. There was more than would fit in her car. So we started loading up my truck."

"Did Mrs. Murray say why she'd been fired?"

"No." He shrugged and gave me an earnest look. "Maybe Marilyn finally figured out Eunice was spying on her."

"Uh, yeah. Maybe that was it."

"So we're packing up the truck, and sometime between three and four, Peter

Lawford comes around and he's got Bobby Kennedy himself along. Big as life. Well, really, fairly small, but you know what I mean."

"Were you around after they showed up?"

"Not very long at all. Mr. Lawford made it real clear he wanted Eunice and me out of there, and told us to go to the market. He gave me some money and said to bring back some Cokes for everybody, but not to hurry. So an hour later, more or less, we come back with a couple cartons of Coke, and their car is gone."

"What kind of car, Norm?"

"Mercedes, I think." He shifted and the wooden bench groaned. "We went in the house and Marilyn looked just terrible. She was just . . . *boiling* mad. Just sore as hell in a way I never saw from her. Weird thing, though, she seemed scared and burning all at once. That's when my mother-in-law called Dr. Greenson."

"Called him because she *worked* for him, right?"

"Yeah. Him *and* Marilyn. Nice work if you can get it — two paychecks for one job? Anyway, Greenson said he'd come right over. And I think he got there around five."

"Had Pat Newcomb gone?"

"No. She did shortly after that. The doc

went in and talked to Marilyn a little while, then came back out and says to Newcomb, who's in the living room with Eunice, 'Marilyn wonders when you're leaving, Pat. When *are* you leaving?' And Newcomb gets up and walks out, just like that. With not one word."

"How long was Greenson there?"

"Maybe . . . till seven P.M.? He comes out and tells Eunice that he's instructed Marilyn to take two Nembutals, and then asks Mrs. Murray to stay overnight and keep an eye on her. With all her belongings packed and everything, Eunice wanted to make sure that 'met with Marilyn's approval,' but the doc said it did."

"Norm, why didn't you leave at that point?"

"Eunice asked me to stay. She was real shaky and upset, over everything that happened, so I sat and watched television with her."

"Where was Marilyn?"

"Never saw her all evening. She was in her room. Some time, maybe ten thirty, Eunice got a phone call. Came back in and said she had to check on Marilyn. We were watching *Gunsmoke,* and I wasn't really paying much attention to Eunice. All of a sudden she comes rushing back and says Marilyn is gone."

"Gone as in dead?"

"Gone as in not in her bedroom. Not in *any* room in the house. So we look outside, and hear that little dog yapping, and right away I notice the light on in the guesthouse. When we go in there — I'll never forget it, try as I might — there she was, facedown, lying across the daybed. She was in the nude. Holding on to the phone with one hand."

"Dead?"

"Looked that way to me. Her color was awful, kind of . . . blue. But Eunice took the phone from her fingers and called for an ambulance. Then she put some kind of emergency call in to Dr. Greenson, who phoned back and said he'd come soon and in the meantime call Dr. Engelberg. I went out to mind the front gates. The ambulance got there before Greenson and Engelberg."

This was the first anyone had said anything about an ambulance.

Well, some neighbors had mentioned seeing one, but none of the primary witnesses. And it made sense. It was Saturday night and both Greenson and Engelberg were out, Mrs. Murray initially getting answering services for both doctors. So what would she do next?

Call an ambulance.

And an ambulance attendant would certainly turn Marilyn faceup to try resuscitation, and if the body had been initially found in the cottage, that explained the dual lividity several times over.

As for Marilyn being in the guesthouse, if she had private phone calls to make, she might have wanted to get away from the prying eyes and ears of Mrs. Murray, who she distrusted enough to have just fired.

"After that, all hell broke loose," Jefferies said. "Police cars, bunch of other vehicles, all kinds of people crawling over everywhere."

"What kind of people?"

"Men in suits. Plainclothes cops, maybe? I think some may have been from the studio. I mean, they were all over the place."

"What about the window, Norm?"

He made an embarrassed smirk. "That suicide thing, breaking in to rescue her? Some plainclothes guy thought that up. There was a dozen of those birds or more. Then, like a magician snapped his fingers? They're gone."

"Could you describe any of them?"

"I don't think so. Maybe the guy who was in charge, or at least in charge of *some* of them. My take was, there were different . . . what would you call it? Groups or . . . factions? Anyway, they weren't all on the same team. They had some shared goals, but they definitely weren't on the same team."

"What did he look like, the guy in charge?"

"Big. Kind of ugly. Rugged face. Funny thing — he kind of reminded me of that guy on TV."

"What guy on TV?"

"Paladin."

Walt Schaefer ran the largest ambulance service in Los Angeles County. He was an old friend of Fred Rubinski's, and the nature of his business and ours meant the A-1 Detective Agency and the Schaefer Ambulance Service were not strangers.

So when I called and said I needed to talk to him, and preferred not to do it by phone, he didn't even ask me why. Just said sure, come on over.

I crossed the nondescript bullpen of dispatchers and on through the open door into Walt's modest office, which had the same cheap rec room–type paneling as the outer area. I shut the door.

A husky, tanned guy in his fifties, Walt was in shirtsleeves with a clip-on tie and you'd never know he was a multimillionaire. Sitting behind a cluttered metal desk, he looked like an overwhelmed junior-high guidance counselor. File cabinets whose tops were piled with folders crowded his work area, and a dozen framed commendations hung crookedly.

He rocked back in his swivel chair and showed off his bridgework. The egg-like shape of his skull was emphasized by seriously thinning, graying dark hair.

"Let me guess," he said in his raspy second tenor. "Somebody needs a discreet exit from the city."

That was a good guess. Just after the war, in addition to running ambulances all over Los Angeles, Walt had established a pioneering air ambulance service. Flying under the banner of medical emergencies, such a service could fly its planes into just about any airport in the world.

Obviously such flights were usually legit. But we had on occasion used his service to spirit clients out of town, and it was an open secret that Schaefer flew clandestine flights for Uncle Sam.

"This time I'm here about an *indiscreet* exit," I said.

"Really? Do tell."

"Just wanted to ask you, Walt, if you're aware Marilyn Monroe's neighbors spotted one of your wagons at her house the night she died."

This near lie (neighbors had spotted an ambulance but had not singled out Schaefer) might have elicited any number of indignant responses. Walt might have asked me what the hell I was talking about, or pressed me for the name of the supposed witness, or maybe said get the fuck out.

But his response was low-key and calm yet dismissive. "We didn't take a call from that residence," he said.

"You handle damn near *all* the calls in Brentwood."

" 'Damn near' is not all the calls. And maybe there wasn't a call. Sorry you made the trip for nothing, Nate. Say hi to Fred."

Then he gave me a thin, cold-eyed smile that meant the conversation was over and the pleasant relationship between Schaefer Ambulance and the A-1 was on shaky ground.

He was doing paperwork or pretending to before I could make it out of his small office.

So I made two stops on my way to the Jag. First, I told the bullpen, in a loud firm voice, who I was, where I could be found, and that I was looking for off-the-record information about the call to Marilyn Monroe's house late Saturday or early Sunday night . . . and that I was renowned for my generosity. I did this going around scattering business cards like confetti.

Then I repeated the operation in the big garage, where half a dozen ambulances were being washed or serviced, my voice echoing with a nice importance. I didn't scatter the cards this time, handing them individually to drivers.

Somebody in the bullpen must have filled Walt in, because he came rushing at me, tie flapping, as I headed through an open garage door to the street.

He blocked my path. "What the hell's the idea, Nate?"

"I'm looking into Marilyn's death."

"Why in hell?"

"Because nobody else is."

"Bullshit! The papers say that Suicide Squad is out questioning people right now."

"Funny, 'cause so am I, and I haven't run into any of them."

Walt let out a frustrated sigh, shook his head, then took me by the arm. Walked me back into the garage, our footsteps resonating like small-arms fire. Put me in the rider's seat of one of the wagons and came around the other side and got behind the wheel. I had a feeling he hadn't driven an ambulance himself in a long, long time.

"I will give this to you off the record," he

said softly, tightly. "If you're working for a client trying to find out if the woman met foul play, I will deny the story to anybody but the cops. If you're working for a reporter, you can't use it, because once you say 'ambulance,' they'll know it's us. Understood?"

"Understood."

He sighed, looked out the windshield at the wooden slats of a closed garage door. "Two of my boys happened to be close, right around the corner practically, when they caught the emergency call. They got there in under two minutes, no siren."

The ambulance driver and his partner were met by a tall man who let them in the gates of the hacienda-style home (obviously Jefferies), and a "frumpy" middle-aged woman (guess who) with a poodle on a leash. She and the poodle led them to a small guest cottage, but stayed outside.

Within, Schaefer's guys got a shock — Marilyn Monroe lay nude, faceup on a folded-out daybed, arm draped toward a phone on the floor.

"She was obviously dead," Walt said, with a fatalistic shrug. "Her body had a blueish tinge, possibly indicating a swift death. So there was nothing my boys could do — we're not a hearse service. As they were getting ready to head out, one of her doctors showed up, this fellow Greenson, I believe."

"Her psychiatrist."

"Yeah, but psychiatrists are MDs. They can pronounce death. So he asked my boys to wait and he went into that cottage and came back a minute or so later. Asked the boys to go in and load her on a gurney and take her to the nearest hospital. Santa Monica hospital."

"But she was *dead*. . . ."

"Which is why my boys, who generally follow doctor's orders in this business, didn't — they just politely turned him down and left. Apparently Greenson, if that's who it was, said he hadn't pronounced her dead and that they should take her, with the suggestion that they would say she expired on the way. That would make it a hospital matter . . . and also a Schaefer Ambulance matter, incidentally, as my boys well knew . . . but from the doctor's vantage, it'd take some of the heat off them there at the house. Is my opinion."

"What time was this?"

"Between ten and eleven."

"Can you check your log?"

"What log?" He shifted in the seat, one hand on the wheel, like an impatient driver in traffic. "By the time my boys left, the other doctor, Engelberg, was there and several cops, too."

"Before midnight, cops were there?"

"Yeah. And one of them was the kind of cop you don't fuck with."

". . . Intel, Walt?"

"I didn't say that." He turned a dour gaze on me. "Now listen carefully, Nate. Eighty percent of my business comes from the city and county, with another ten percent that is very lucrative from the U.S. government. With the Kennedys involved, if I were to speak up about what I know, this business I have worked to build up since nineteen fucking thirty-two would go down the drain. And what do I know, really? That my guys went there, she was dead, and they turned around and came back. Because in case I failed to mention it, we're not a goddamn hearse service."

"What you know, Walt, and what at least two of your people know, is that the official story on Marilyn's death is bullshit."

"And if I come forward, what? Justice will be served? Do I have to tell you what brand of justice gets served up in LA? Chief Parker justice. And by the way, who's the top guy at the Justice Department right now? Let it go, Nate. Let it the hell go."

A siren screamed and made me jump as

an ambulance pulled out.

"Look," Walt said, "she overdosed, we were too late to save her, her own doctor was too late to save her . . . so nobody saved her. The cops have made it clear to me — *clear* — that they aren't interested in pursuing this case. My government clients have indicated, through intermediaries, mind you, that my discretion would be appreciated. Do I really have to tell Nate Heller which way the wind blows?"

"A woman died, Walt."

"And how many women died today in Los Angeles that my buggies picked up? If I don't know, you sure don't. Look. Nate. We never spoke." He shook his head, sighed heavily. "What good hearing this shit does you, I have no idea."

He climbed down out of the ambulance, shut the door, and for a while I just sat there in the vehicle, going nowhere.

CHAPTER 21

Friday morning, I was in a swimsuit and Flo was in a baby blue bikini and we were both in sunglasses, sitting poolside in deck chairs in back of her big white birthday cake of a mansion on Roxbury Drive.

We were working.

I, in fact, had been working since the night before, staying in her house as the inside man with another A-1 agent outside on the street. After the attempt Wednesday night on me (and possibly her) at the hotel bungalow, I felt some precautions were in order. And as for my duties as inside man, I will leave that to your fertile imagination.

In the youthful ponytail again, she was going over notes on a steno pad, her slender tan body pearled with perspiration. As Joe Friday used to say, it was hot in Los Angeles.

"I'm close," she said, tapping the eraser end of a pencil on her pad. "The puzzle pieces are coming together, even with half of the witnesses leaving town. If one of us could just pin Greenson down, that might do it."

"May still happen," I said. "Engelberg would've been nice. . . ."

He was among those who had suddenly decided to take a vacation — or as the doctor's secretary had put it on the phone, "an extended period of time away from Los Angeles."

Flo glanced at me over the tops of her Ray-Bans. "We don't have to solve this mystery, Nate — all we have to do is raise sufficient questions, backed up by facts."

The nature of my business — and the business of my nature — was solving mysteries; but she was right.

"It's tough," I said, "with so much of what we have coming from off-the-record sources."

"Not all. Both Hazel Washington and Inez Melson had no problem being quoted."

The Washington woman — Marilyn's maid at Fox — had seen interesting things at Marilyn's house when she and her husband had stopped by at around noon Sunday hoping to retrieve a card table and chairs they'd loaned the actress. Four clean-cut young men in dark slacks, white shirts, and mirror-polished Brogans were among an infestation that included uniformed Fox security guards, telephone company technicians, police, and reporters.

Hazel's husband, Rocky, was an LAPD detective, so the couple got access where others might not have. As Hazel and Rocky hauled their furniture out, they noticed one of the clean-cut quartet burning a big pile of documents in the living room fireplace. Among them were several spiral notebooks.

Executrix Melson took a similar path. Monday morning she had been going through Marilyn's papers in a file cabinet in the guest cottage, but few papers remained. The file had been broken into, the lock forced, many documents and other items missing. Ironically, one document left behind was a bill from a lock company — in March, Marilyn had changed the lock on the file as well as installed bars on the guest cottage windows.

Flo had called the A-1 Lock and Safe Company of Santa Monica (no relation to the A-1 Detective Agency) and talked her way to the locksmith who'd worked on the cabinet. He told her Marilyn had said in passing she felt things were disappearing from her files.

"Those guys burning papers in the fireplace," I said, "have to be spooks."

"Spies, you mean?"

I nodded. "Yeah, that ilk, anyway. CIA, FBI, Secret Service — they could all have an interest in Marilyn."

"You're not really suggesting the government could have had Marilyn killed."

"More likely killed her themselves."

Somewhere, next door maybe, a transistor radio was playing rock 'n' roll — right now, "Calendar Girl."

"Nate, you can't be serious. . . ."

"Let's talk about another kind of government — organized crime. Back in Capone days, the big boss might have said, 'Bump off that bastard McGurn.' And McGurn would be bumped. But these are more sophisticated, technological times. You never know who's listening, who's watching. So your modern-day Capone says, 'That bastard McWhozit's a real problem. Somebody ought to do something about him.' And somebody does."

"And you think the president or the attorney general has that kind of power?"

I laughed. "You kidding? A woman who has been intimate with both Jack and Bobby, who has overhead top-level, even top secret conversations? Learning things that no one outside the innermost circle should know?"

She shook her head, ponytail wagging. "I

can't believe that."

"You don't want to believe that. The notebooks those clean-cut characters were burning — those were Marilyn's notes on things Jack and Bobby had shared with her. A kind of a diary — the most dangerous kind imaginable."

"So then we're . . . *convinced* it's murder."

"Somebody tried to murder *me*, remember? Maybe murder *us*. That hypo I confiscated from our visitor? Don't get upset, but —"

"Don't get upset!"

"It was filled with pure nicotine."

"*Cigarettes* nicotine?"

"A lethal drug in sufficient quantity that creates the appearance of a heart attack in its victim. A routine autopsy wouldn't turn anything up, and a pathologist would have to know what he's looking for, to spot it."

"You had it analyzed?"

"I didn't taste it."

She sat staring at the blue shimmering water in her pool. "Palisades Park" was coming from the next-door radio. I was fairly certain she was thinking about what a nice life she had, and what a shame it would be to risk losing it, even over the scoop of a lifetime.

"How long," she said softly, almost timidly, "will you keep your people watching my house?"

"Until your story's published. You'll be safe after that. You may be attacked professionally and personally, but your death would be too convenient not to raise suspicion."

"That's reassuring."

"Of course, I could just move in."

"Is that a proposal?"

"I was hoping for kept man."

She laughed. I could always make her laugh.

My relief came on at noon — an agent who would *not* work the bedroom beat — and I headed to the A-1.

No message slips on my desk, but I checked with Fred on the office line. "Nothing from Thad Brown?"

"Actually he did call. So far, the nine-mil is not traceable. Serial numbers filed off. He's turned the Beretta over for possible ballistics match-up with something in their files, but that'll take forever and a day. The noise suppressor is of course a custom job, and that may lead somewhere. More by tomorrow, maybe."

The afternoon I spent on the phone chasing associates of Marilyn's. Makeup artist Whitey Snyder and costume designer William Travilla (one of her personal fashion designers) were glad to talk to me, but had nothing. Her close friend and masseur Ralph Roberts did have some interesting information and insights.

Turned out Roberts and Marilyn were planning to have dinner Saturday evening, and he'd called that afternoon to confirm. He got Dr. Greenson instead, who told him Marilyn was out.

"This Greenson is a goddamn Svengali," Roberts said. "Very controlling. Marilyn and I'd been friends for years, and he advised her to cut me off. She didn't, though, bless her heart. Listen, Mr. Heller, I know she was still seeing Greenson — remember, she was more addicted to therapy than pills — but just the same, she was *not* happy with him. Not for the last couple months."

"How so?"

"She didn't think he was doing her any good — not personally, and not professionally."

"Separate that out for me — 'personally and professionally.' "

"Well, that quack inserted himself into the Fox fiasco, and did her no good at all, playing agent or manager or whatever. What she accomplished, getting that new contract, having Fox come crawling back to her, that was all *her.* She was brilliant, really, and an incredible businesswoman. Greenson was a detriment, if anything. She was going to get rid of him."

"*Fire* him?"

"Definitely. Both him and that awful Murray woman. Did you know Greenson put that woman next to Marilyn just to spy on her?"

"How did you learn that?"

"Marilyn told me."

Another call was illuminating, too, but in other ways.

The chief fix-it guy at Fox was Frank Neill. He was a onetime police reporter and a sort of in-house private eye for the studio, though he called himself a publicist now.

"Say, Frank. Nate Heller. Tying up some loose ends for Marilyn's estate. What time did you and your guys get to the house Sunday morning?"

All right, the estate part was a lie, and the whole approach a cheap shot. But you have to try.

"Wasn't there," Neill said. "Nobody from the studio was."

He hung up. No small talk. No good-bye. No chance for me to point out that the neighbors had seen security guards in Fox uniforms, and Dr. Greenson had told Offi-

445

cer Clemmons at the scene that he had called the studio before the cops. Just a *click* that spoke volumes.

I left my fourth message on Dr. Greenson's home answering machine, then tried his office. His secretary informed me the doctor would not be in next week, and for several weeks thereafter.

He, too, was going on an "extended" trip away from Los Angeles.

This discouraged but did not defeat me. I began calling every travel agency in town, saying I was Dr. Greenson's assistant and needed to confirm his reservations. On my fourth try, I learned that he and his wife would be leaving for London on Monday. That gave me the weekend to corner the bastard.

I was the first one to leave the office, well before five. Closer to four. I wanted to shower and make myself handsome before driving over to my ex-wife's to remind her what a huge mistake she'd made, and to pick my son up for dinner and a movie. Everybody deserves an evening off, right?

Wrong.

I was approaching my car in the underground parking garage near the Bradbury Building, my footsteps echoing in the cavernous cement structure, thinking it was a little eerie to be alone in the underlit catacomb. But when I discovered I wasn't really alone, it wasn't reassuring at all.

Two men in sunglasses, well-tailored black suits with black ties, and mirror-polished black shoes, looking distressingly young and clean-cut, stepped out from between cars and quickly book-ended me. I was still walking. They walked along.

"Mr. Heller, I wonder if you'd accompany us? There's someone who would like to talk to you."

Whatever happened to the good old days, when the guys attempting to kidnap you had cauliflower ears and bent noses and either just blackjacked you or stuck a gun in your ribs and said to get in the fucking trunk?

I of course was not about to go around unarmed, after the needle incident. My suit coat — a Maxwell Street number, tailored to accommodate my shoulder-holstered Browning — was unbuttoned and I had the gun out in a blink and whirled, taking two quick steps back and showing them the long barrel with the black round hole where death comes out.

I was feeling like a private eye again. Peter Gunn. Those *77 Sunset Strip* clowns. Even James fucking Bond had nothing on me.

And then I *really* felt like a private eye,

when a third guy I hadn't seen hit me from behind with something very hard. It didn't put my lights out, so I can't provide anything poetic about black pools I dove into. Instead, I just hung puppet-like in midair, undignified as hell, trying not to piss myself, as the first two clean-cut lads held me by the arms, to prevent my hitting the pavement . . .

. . . before dragging me to a parked car as black as their suits and stuffing me in the trunk.

Maybe these were the good old days.

The ride was short enough to mean we were still in downtown Los Angeles. When the trunk lid opened, all three were standing there — the third was another clean-cut one, but brawnier, a former college athlete no doubt — and I did not leap out at them and clean their young clocks.

The first two politely helped me out, and apologized several times, one even asking how I felt, though I declined to answer on the grounds that I might humiliate myself. Then they decided to help me out on that score, and — after I'd seen only enough to know I was in another concrete parking garage — blindfolded me.

I was walked along into what my keen

sense of hearing told me was an elevator. We went up quite a few floors, and I was guided down what I'm going to guess was a hallway. Here's where this kidnapping differed from days of yore — I was taken into a small infirmary room, where a doctor removed my blindfold and gave me the fastest medical treatment I'd ever received.

He was a middle-aged man with gray hair and gray eyes and the requisite white coat. He checked where I'd been clobbered, did the routine physical things, blood pressure, heart, ears, eyes, and so on, and said, "No sign of concussion." He gave me two aspirin, for the headache that I for some strange reason had, but did not advise me to call him in the morning.

Then I was allowed blindfold-free out into an anonymous hallway in an equally anonymous modern building where the first two of my new friends were waiting, looking more human out of their sunglasses, the brawnier one having gone off to pursue other interests.

"Good news, fellas," I said. "No concussion."

"That's excellent news, Mr. Heller." No irony. No humor. He was maybe twenty-five and had black hair that went well with the suit, and his otherwise bland face bore light blue eyes that were so pretty they were oddly intimidating.

The other one, his twin in blandness, had brown eyes and brown hair that didn't match the suit. He gestured and said, "Come this way."

It was a short trip. I was ushered into a darkened room and placed in a chair at a table — this was a conference room, as I'd been able to perceive, before the door shut behind me and cut off all light. The escorts stayed in the room with me, though I wasn't sure where.

Now the voice of an older man, resonant, God-like, and even more intimidating than my young escort's blue eyes, said, "Welcome, Mr. Heller. Our apologies for the methods."

"It's a new one, anyway. Guys assault you, then take you to the doctor."

"We had no intention of assaulting you. You produced a weapon."

"I didn't produce it, I pulled it. Would I be out of line asking who you people are? Or anyway, who you work for?"

"Mr. Heller, you are here for us to share information with you. But *that* information would not be helpful to either party."

"One party being me, the other party being you?"

"That's correct." He cleared his throat. "It has come to our attention that you've been conducting a private inquiry into the death of Marilyn Monroe."

"Yeah. It's personal. She was my client, and I feel a responsibility."

"I'm sure you do. But the two thousand dollars you deposited in the A-1 Detective Agency's business account, provided you by journalist Florence Kilgore, no doubt gives you an additional sense of responsibility. To Miss Kilgore, that is."

Jesus — how many people had been keeping me under surveillance? How good were they all? How lousy had I gotten?

A loud click announced the throwing of a switch, and at the end of the table, not far from where I sat, one of those carousel gizmos that allowed slides to be shown lighted up, and threw a shaft of white at a screen that revealed itself in the process. Also revealed, in spillover light, was my blue-eyed friend, running the projector nearby.

The radio-announcer voice of my hidden host said, "You are a resourceful investigator, Mr. Heller. You have been involved in an improbable number of important, even famous investigations — the Lindbergh kidnapping, the Huey Long assassination, the Black Dahlia murder. The files on you in Washington are thick and impressive."

That admission was no slip — he wanted me to know this was an official government agency, or people pretending to be part of one. My gut, though, was these were the real spooky deal. Most likely the Company.

"And we have been keeping track of your progress in the Monroe case. Chief Parker hasn't bothered to assign a homicide team to it, instead giving a civilian board a rather nebulous assignment, designed to pacify the public. You alone seem to be seeking the truth — you and Miss Kilgore, that is."

"You're from Washington, so I guess I don't have to explain this whole freedom-of-the-press inconvenience."

"Mr. Heller, we're not adversaries. We encourage you in your efforts."

". . . You do?"

"We just think you could use a little assistance. A nudge in a direction that may prove worthwhile to you."

An image jumped onto the screen — a black-and-white photo, a surveillance photo dating back many years. From the clothing of the man in the photo, I pinned it as the late '30s. And it took me a while to recognize him.

"Dr. Romeo Greenschpoon, now known as Dr. Ralph R. Greenson. Nineteen thirty-seven. An active member of the Los Angeles Communist Party."

Another image leapt on screen: a photograph from the same era that I immediately recognized as of a much younger version of the rather horse-faced Dr. Engelberg.

"One of Dr. Greenson's closest friends, since those early, early days — Dr. Hyman Engelberg. On occasion they have even shared medical offices. Dr. Engelberg has been a particularly zealous Communist, and in his spare time has been an instructor for the Communist People's Educational Center in Los Angeles."

"Excuse me — you have me at a disadvantage," I told the darkness. "You know my name, but I don't know yours."

"Mr. Smith."

"Yeah, well, that's who Capra sent to Washington, right? Look, Hollywood in those days was full of young liberals who got caught up in this Commie stuff. Budding intellectuals who took the Depression as a hint America wasn't perfect. Plus, they dug the cult of secrecy — aliases, underground meetings, double identities. Youthful follies, says I."

Mild defensiveness came into the voice: "Both Greenson and Engelberg were highly active in the Hollywood League for Democratic Action, a well-known Communist front."

I went ahead and laughed at that. "Mr. Smith, that started out as the Anti-Nazi League, if memory serves. This brand of all-American Commie was up in arms about fascism long before Pearl Harbor. I mean, it's your show — I'm your guest, right? But don't hand me peanut shells and tell me somebody stole your peanuts."

That actually got a dry chuckle out of the darkness.

A face flashed on the screen that I didn't recognize, same era, a young guy in a flannel shirt and denim overalls with a hammer in his hand (no sickle, though).

"Meet John Murray. A carpenter by trade, originally. Before the war, he formed a leftist coalition designed to take over the Hollywood locals. During the war, as a colonel, he worked with a young army psychiatrist who was using Freudian-Marxist techniques and philosophies in dealing with mental casualties of war."

A slightly older Greenson, in the uniform of an army captain, popped onto the screen.

"That psychiatrist, of course, was Dr. Ralph Greenson, stationed at Fort Logan, Colorado. To give the devil his due, Greenson had great success with many of his patients."

I must have missed the part where Greenson was shown to be the devil. But I was starting to think I was not a guest of the CIA, rather the FBI. The paranoid, McCarthyesque slant reeked of J. Edgar Hoover.

A more recent photo of Greenson, outside his office, took the screen. Another surveillance photo.

"Greenson, of course, became a successful Beverly Hills psychiatrist. Murray worked and traveled for a company we believe to be a Communist front, most frequently going to Mexico. During the '50s, despite the House Un-American Activities Committee making a target out of Hollywood, neither Greenson nor Engelberg was dissuaded from pursuing their radical beliefs. Communist cell meetings were frequently held at Greenson's home, and also at Murray's Santa Monica home, where he lived with his wife. . . ."

A younger, more attractive photo of Eunice Murray with her husband, John, outside a modest clapboard home, shimmered on the screen.

". . . Eunice."

Another click announced a more recent picture of Engelberg, this a studio portrait.

"Though he had been particularly active

and outspoken, Engelberg finally went deep underground during the rest of the so-called Red Scare years."

I sighed and said, "Marilyn leaned left, but she was no Commie."

"Her husband was and is."

"Her ex-husband Arthur Miller? Far as I'm concerned, he's just another one of these arty dilettantes. Like Marilyn's poet pal, Norman Rosten, and for that matter the Strasbergs. What are you trying to convince me of? That a lot of stars and Beverly Hills doctors are politically naive? Sold. By the way, doesn't your file say my father ran a leftist bookstore on the West Side in Chicago? So obviously I'm a Commie, too, right?"

"These are dangerous people, Mr. Heller. Zealots behind their American masks."

A blurry color photograph came on of a heavyset guy who seemed vaguely familiar. He wore a Mexican-print shirt and was drinking a beer and smiling at somebody off-camera. Then I pegged it: his features echoed Eunice Murray's husband.

"This is Churchill Murray, John's brother, who runs a Communist propaganda radio station in Mexico City. He has countless questionable political contacts, including diplomats from the Cuban and Soviet embassies there."

Now came a color surveillance photo of a balding guy with glasses and a pipe, talking to Churchill Murray outside a cantina.

"Frederick Vanderbilt Field — great-great-grandson of the railroad tycoon. Notorious silver-spoon Communist who was exposed as a Comintern operative and fled to Mexico City. There he was a mainstay of Zona Rosa, a colony of expatriate Americans, Communists mostly, including John Howard Lawson, Dalton Trumbo, Albert Maltz, and of course Churchill Murray — Eunice Murray's brother-in-law."

Wearily I said, "So Marilyn had some extreme leftists in her life. I would imagine that's true of a lot of Hollywood stars."

"I'm sure it is, Mr. Heller. But not a lot of Hollywood stars have had intimate access to the president and the attorney general."

"Now you're imagining Marilyn is a Commie spy?"

"No. A dupe. And we're not imagining anything."

A click announced a very recent picture of a beaming Marilyn at a restaurant table with Vanderbilt Field.

"Field is who Miss Monroe stayed with, Mr. Heller, when she went on her buying trip to Mexico, for new furnishings and decorations for her home, a trip on which Miss Monroe was accompanied by Eunice Murray."

"Okay. So?"

"So, Mr. Heller — Frederick Vanderbilt Field is an active Soviet agent."

I didn't say anything. What had seemed foolish at first had become something real and troubling as hell. Marilyn getting friendly with Field, in the middle of her affairs with Jack and Bobby, had made security risks out of the president and the attorney general.

"We have surveillance tapes in which Field, in the guise of conversation, is heard pumping Miss Monroe for confidential information she learned in discussions with the Kennedy brothers."

"Was Marilyn forthcoming?"

"She was. From her point of view, she was answering questions from an expatriate longing for news of home. Much of what she and Fields discussed was only tangentially associated with politics, her interest in civil rights for example, or her frustration that Jack Kennedy hadn't fired J. Edgar Hoover. But she also talked about what she viewed as her own intellectual shortcomings, her desire to quit show business and change her life completely."

The latter was typical Marilyn, and a daydream she would have under no circumstances pursued, at least not until age caught up with her.

Which now it never would.

"Mr. Heller . . . frankly, we believe Dr. Ralph Greenson, like Vanderbilt Field, is a Soviet agent. Greenson helped form, and then secretly ran, the National Arts, Sciences and Professions Committee, a major force in promoting Communist ideology on the West Coast. Heading up this group, Greenson has influenced sister organizations like the Doctors Professional Group, of which Engelberg was at one time a prominent member."

"I thought the government had stopped looking for Reds under every bed."

"Perhaps under beds, but not in psychiatrists' offices. It is Soviet espionage policy for cell leaders to have psychiatric training, aiding them in the periodic need to interview key cell members, to appraise their state of mind and continuing loyalty. Mr. Heller, psychoanalysts' offices around the U.S. have been regularly used by Soviet agents as safe havens for the transfer of intelligence."

"And I'm supposed to buy that Greenson is one of those?"

"Yes. And to keep in mind that Engelberg is his longtime friend . . . you might say, comrade. Consider, Mr. Heller — how important a Soviet agent might Greenson prove, having access to the mind of a female who often shares the bed of the president? And/or of the attorney general?"

Well, that I couldn't bat away with a flip remark.

"We believe that Greenson, with the aid of Engelberg and Mrs. Murray, created a web of influence around Marilyn Monroe devised to gather information from her relationships with the Kennedy brothers."

"Why are you telling me this, again?"

"To simply aid you in your investigation. Help you avoid going down a blind alley. You see, Mr. Heller, we know that you are a man capable of . . . rough justice. That people in your life who meet with your disfavor sometimes reach a violent if unexplained end. And in other instances, simply disappear."

That thick file they said they had on me again. How much did they really know?

"You'll be free to go, in a very few minutes. Your weapon will be returned to you. First, however, there is something we would like you to hear."

"Like the Commies say — it's your party."

460

I heard footsteps across from me, and when the radio-announcer voice returned, it was closer than before.

"You spoke to Walter Schaefer yesterday, and he told you a story. You will recall that he did not allow you to speak to the ambulance attendants who figured prominently in that story."

Christ, whoever *they were, they were* everywhere. . . .

"We interviewed the driver. His name is James Hall, and you can seek him out for yourself. Whether he speaks to you frankly or not, we can't say. But listen to what he told us. . . ."

A click was followed by the whirring of tape reels.

. . . happened to be close by, right around the corner practically, when we caught the emergency call. We got there in under two minutes, didn't even hit the siren. We were met at the front gates of this Mexican-type home by a tall guy, who let us through. Then this frumpy middle-aged lady, leading a poodle on a leash, met us, and led the two of us into this small guest cottage.

That fit Norman Jefferies, Eunice Murray,

and, for that matter, Maf.

The lady stayed outside when we went into the cottage, and, brother, did we get the shock of a lifetime. It was Marilyn Monroe, naked, faceup on a folded-out daybed. She was alive, but not in good shape, respiration and heartbeat slight, pulse rapid, weak as hell. To administer CPR, we moved her on the other side of this divider into this sort of foyer area. Wanted to get her on the floor, to provide better support, so we did that, put her on her back and, with an airway tube, started resuscitation.

I had a perfect exchange of air going from Miss Monroe, and her color was coming back, and my partner agreed that it was safe to transport her to a hospital. We were heading out to get the gurney when her doctor showed, medical bag in hand. He had me remove the resuscitator and start mouth-to-mouth. I thought this took us in the wrong direction, but you don't keep your job in my business disagreeing with doctors. There were no signs of vomit. No distinctive odors. Chloral hydrate, for example, gives you that pear-type odor.

"So the doctor takes this big old heart

needle out of his bag and fills it with adrenaline. He tries to inject it into her heart, but apparently the angle was wrong. Needle must've hit a rib. Her vital signs were nil at this point, and then the doctor used his stethoscope on her chest, but couldn't get a heartbeat. He told us he would pronounce her dead, and said we should leave.

A questioner's voice:

"Did the doctor give you his name?"
"Yeah — Greenson. Her psychiatrist, I think."

A snap and whirring-to-stop indicated the show was over.
"Well, Mr. Heller?"
"Could be real. Could be a phony. But I can tell you this — the deputy coroner didn't report any sign of a chipped rib, or a puncture in the area of her heart."
"Needle marks are easy to miss, particularly with so much lividity. And a 'Y' incision in the chest cavity might obliterate any such puncture and possibly any chipped bone."
I didn't have a comment.
"That's all we have for you, Mr. Heller."

"Time for the blindfold again?"

"Yes. The literal one. We hope, Mr. Heller, that we've removed the figurative blindfold, and restored your vision."

CHAPTER 22

In the light of the three-quarter moon on this clear August night, the two-story Monterey-style Spanish colonial, with its floor-length cantilevered balcony and thickness of trees out front, played games of light and shade, the stucco cut by dark wood trim, greenery glimmering with a slight breeze, ivory touches here and there, splotches of black elsewhere.

Here, on Franklin Street in Santa Monica, lived Dr. Ralph R. Greenson and his wife, Hildi (their son and daughter off at college); they enjoyed a nice backyard hilltop view of the ocean a few miles west, the Brentwood Country Club and golf course nearby. Maybe they belonged, unless it was restricted.

On a clear night like this, you had a nice backyard view of the Pacific Palisades, too. And I can report this because the back way was how I entered the house. There were glass doors off the garden patio, with an easily picked lock, and if Greenson had an alarm, it was a silent one. I was prepared to take my chances.

The Greensons were out for the evening, though they should be home soon. I'd followed them to La Scala — Marilyn's favorite Italian restaurant, by the way — where their mid-evening reservations indicated they weren't planning to take in a movie. I supposed a jazz or folk music club was a possibility.

Still, I figured they'd be home soon.

No dog greeted me, so the dog biscuit laced with chloral hydrate (a nice ironic touch, I thought) went unused, stuck in a pocket of my black zippered Windbreaker. Which went with my black slacks, black polo, and black Keds — I looked like a cross between a ninja and a tennis coach. The nine-millimeter Browning was in my waistband.

A few lights were on and I was immediately struck by how the living room — with its open rough-hewn-beamed ceiling, big fireplace trimmed in colorful Mexican tiles, and antique wooden table — resembled Marilyn's on Fifth Helena. The decor of the big room, which took up half of the first floor, had clearly influenced her.

The kitchen had more of those tiles, but the den was a small, cozy, predictably book-lined affair, with a massive old desk with wormholes and lots of character. A typing stand beside the desk with a stack of manuscript pages indicated a work in progress. A black couch was opposite the desk along a shaded window. Was this for home visits by patients?

I stretched out on the couch, fairly sure I wouldn't fall asleep. I had the nine-millimeter in my right hand, draped across my lap. Maybe Greenson would find that significant; he'd studied with Freud, after all. But sometimes a nine-mil is just a nine-mil.

The sound of a garage door opening stirred me — despite my confidence, I had gotten drowsy, dangerous for a housebreaker — and I could hear them coming in and talking in soft, muffled tones about nothing special. They were in the living room, just beyond the cracked den door.

His wife said she was going on upstairs to sleep, and Greenson, in that first tenor touched by both Brooklyn and Vienna, said he'd be up soon. He wanted to do a little writing.

To his credit, he didn't yell in surprise or fear, seeing me. Not even in outrage at his home being invaded. He was in a black-and-white houndstooth sport coat, pretty snazzy, a gangster-ish black shirt with white tie, and gray slacks. The tie he'd been in the process of loosening as he entered his den.

"I guess I should have expected this," he said.

"Why? It was just this evening I decided to stop by. I was planning a night out with my son."

"This is about me refusing to see you."

"I never got that far, to be refused."

He shut the door, shrugged. "Well, it's fair to say I've been avoiding you. I know of your reputation, Mr. Heller, but I hardly think you're here to do me any harm."

"Don't be too sure."

"If you were going to kill me, you would not do it where my wife would be an innocent victim in whatever confused scenario you have contrived."

I sat up on the edge of the couch. "Wow. That's very analytical of you, Doc. Have a seat." I indicated his desk with a friendly wave of the nine-millimeter.

"You don't need that gun."

"I was thinking of asking you about that, Doc. See, this is the gun my father used to kill himself. He was disappointed in me for joining the Chicago PD. He was a leftist, a real true Marxist, so you can identify. And ever since, this is the only gun I've carried. I like to call it the only conscience I have. What do you make of that, Doc?"

He had seated himself in his comfortable leather chair, which swiveled and rocked. But he wasn't rocking. The dark eyes in his somber face — made more mournful by the bandito curve of black mustache that provided such stark contrast to his white hair — were trained on me. His hands were folded. He appeared relaxed. He wasn't.

"I don't think you're a good candidate for therapy, Mr. Heller," he said.

"Why not?"

"Because you seem rather too attached to your neurosis. I would say, on some level, in certain instances at least, it provides a sort of engine for your activities."

"Bingo. Do you mind if I get comfortable?"

"Certainly not," he said, dryly sarcastic. "You are, after all, a guest in my home."

I got up, moved the couch around so I could face him more easily, and stretched out again. The weapon in hand I kept against my side, away from the door. He frowned, noting this.

"In case your wife comes checking," I explained. "Just say I'm a patient. Emergency situation."

"I wouldn't be entirely lying, would I?"

"Not really."

He shifted, settled in the chair, somehow found a sardonic smile for me. "Now, what can I do for you, Mr. Heller?"

"You can answer some questions, in a while . . . but first, just do what makes you the big bucks — listen. No note-taking necessary."

He nodded in acceptance.

"Now, you can interrupt or interpose a thought or question at any time. You and I, Doc, we don't stand on ceremony. We share a common goal, or at least we once did."

His eyebrows went up questioningly.

"Marilyn's well-being," I said. "She was your patient, and she was my client. And I believe you did care about her. That you did try to help her. I mean, you are in a sense the hero of this story — you saved her from a number of overdoses, I understand. You weaned her off drugs. You helped build up her confidence and self-worth."

"I'm not a hero, Mr. Heller, but I did do those things."

"Trouble is, you're also an egomaniac, at least as big a one as me — that's a layman's usage, Doc, not a diagnosis — plus you are one controlling son of a bitch. *That's* my

470

diagnosis, by the way. You tried to better yourself through your famous patient. You wheedled and wormed your way into aspects of her life that should have been off-limits — interfering with her movie studio, putting a personal spy in her home, even controlling her interaction with people like Ralph Roberts and Whitey Snyder, who were always supportive influences."

Greenson sighed. "I did those things as well."

Was he playing me?

"And, Mr. Heller, I crossed other boundaries of the patient/doctor compact. I often brought Marilyn into my own home, made my family her surrogate one. This I think may have been ill-advised, but it was, as you say, Marilyn's well-being I sought to nurture."

"I don't see anything wrong with that," I admitted. "She was an orphan kid who always wanted a family. She wanted a daddy. You were it for a while . . . till she fired your ass."

That got a rise out of him. Or a frown, anyway.

"She did *not* fire me as her psychiatrist."

"What then?"

"The last time I saw Marilyn, she informed me she'd fired Pat Newcomb, which

I thought was an excellent decision, incidentally, as well as Eunice Murray, which I considered unfortunate, because Eunice was, to use your word, supportive of her. I suppose I *was* 'fired,' too, in a sense . . . but only as what she called her 'de facto agent.' She was very smart, Mr. Heller. She knew what I didn't, or hadn't admitted — that I was out of my depth, trying to help her in the career department."

"Sounds like maybe she'd finally shaken her worst dependency. And I don't mean drugs."

"You mean," he said quietly, "me."

"I mean you, Doc. She comes to you to cure her insomnia, and you prescribe total dependence on you. You give her twenty-four-hour service. You make house calls. *You* were the drug she was in danger of overdosing on."

The sardonic smile returned. "And . . . as you say — she finally shook that dependance. I believe that last day of her life, though unpleasant, should have been a turning point."

"Well, it *was* a turning point, wasn't it? A turn into Westwood cemetery." I waved off his good intentions. "You called it suicide, Doc. Every interview you've given, whether to the cops or the press, has it suicide."

"And yet it wasn't suicide." His eyebrows were up, but nothing quizzical about it. "You needn't bother making the case for me, Mr. Heller. I *know* it wasn't suicide. I've read the autopsy results."

"So are you prepared to say it's murder?"

He sighed heavily. "I'm prepared to say — I *have* said in my interview with Deputy D.A. Miner and another with the so-called Suicide Squad — that Marilyn was in no way despondent, and that she was a poor candidate for suicide."

"Those statements haven't been made public."

"That's not up to me, is it? Mr. Heller, in the four days preceding her death, Marilyn took three business meetings, bought a ten-thousand-dollar Jean Louis gown, twice ordered deli food, and purchased one hundred dollars' worth of perfume."

Chanel, no doubt.

He was saying, "Over those few days, Marilyn met with me for eleven and a half hours, and they were good sessions, healthy sessions, with the expected ups and downs, but . . ." He shook his head, chuckled glumly. "The bittersweet truth, Mr. Heller, is that Marilyn was finally making spectacular headway in therapy. She was on her way to achieving a degree of security for the first time in her life. And she was ecstatic about the possibilities of the future."

"Was she ecstatic at your last session? *After* her fight with Bobby Kennedy?"

"That was rough. That was difficult. But we are not talking here about unrequited love — no. She had already decided that she was moving on from the Kennedys." He frowned. "Understand, she found it gratifying to be associated with such powerful and important people. But she felt used and betrayed, and she insisted on being treated respectfully. Bobby Kennedy barged in that afternoon, making accusations, demanding she hand over tape recordings and note-books, and generally treating her like . . . chattel."

"So who *wouldn't* flip out?"

"Indeed. But any notion that she would have gone *public* with what she knew about the brothers, well, it's nonsense. So is the notion that this confrontation would send her deep into a well of despondency." He sighed. "Mr. Heller — would you put away the weapon? And would you allow me to play you a tape recording?"

I got up, took a magazine from a stack off a lower bookcase shelf, and folded it open over the nine-millimeter. I also moved the couch into its former position, and sat on the edge, facing him.

He nodded, twitched half a smile, and lifted an upright reel-to-reel tape recorder off the floor behind his desk somewhere, and rested it on the blotter. Then he removed a white cardboard tape box from a desk drawer, which required unlocking (the doctor's security measures weren't much), and fixed the spool in its niche and wound the tape into place.

"In the last few months," he said, "Marilyn made a number of recordings herself. At home."

He was telling me?

"These were stream-of-consciousness sessions, where she could talk to me, though I wasn't present, as frankly and openly as she wished, particularly if I was not available and she wanted to express these thoughts and feelings. I have several hours of these tapes, and if they were made public, the notion that Marilyn took her life would soon disappear."

"What's on *this* tape?"

"Something interesting near the very beginning of the reel. Let me cue it up. . . ."

He did.

And he clicked the machine on, the tape whirring, and a very familiar, soft, slightly halting voice filled the little den.

"To have been loved by John Kennedy only to be rejected so badly is hard to understand. It really is. But Marilyn Monroe is a soldier. And the first duty of a soldier is to the commander in chief. He says 'do this' and you do that."

I could well imagine Jack telling Marilyn to "do this."

"My bruised little ego isn't important. What is important is that these men will change the country. No child will go hungry. No person will sleep in the street and get his meals from a garbage can. They'll transform America like FDR in the thirties."

Greenson made a small openhanded gesture, as if to say, "See? Everything they did to her, and she was still loyal."

"The president is the captain and Bobby is his executive officer. Bobby would do absolutely anything for his brother. And so would I. I would never embarrass him. Or Bobby."

"So much for a press conference," I said.

"But there's no room in my life for Bobby right now. All I ask is that he face me and deal with me directly, like a real man . . . and treat me with a modicum of respect."

He clicked off the machine. Got up, moved it off his desk and onto the floor, then resumed his seat.

"These tapes in toto reveal," he said,

hands folded again, "a woman in command of herself, changing direction in positive ways. She's decided *herself* to end any relationship with Robert Kennedy, she's already fired Paula Strasberg, and soon would do the same with Eunice Murray and, for that matter, me . . . as her manager, that is."

I shrugged. "You don't have to be a shrink to know she doesn't sound suicidal."

"No. She had her sights on new artistic horizons — absurd as it might sound to some, she hoped to one day perform Shakespeare. She had the kind of long-term plans that do not reflect a patient on the verge of suicide."

"You're preaching to the choir, Doc. She was murdered."

This made him uncomfortable. Suddenly the dark eyes were looking somewhere other than my face.

I gave him a friendly grin. "Let's talk about you, Doc. You don't think she committed suicide. You know the accidental overdose verdict is bogus, based on the evidence. Yet you're waist-deep in the cover-up."

Dark eyes beseeched me from under a furrowed brow. "Haven't I given you enough,

Mr. Heller? What more could I have for you?"

"Let's find out. You were there through the night. You know what happened. You know an ambulance came, you know high-level cops from the Intelligence Division were everywhere, all kinds of government spooks, and of course a studio cleanup crew. You let this go on for hours without officially notifying the police. You could lose your license for that, Doc. You don't let a corpse sit for four hours or more before notifying the coroner."

"You said it yourself, Mr. Heller. The police were already there."

"So why did you play along? I have theories. Would you like to hear?"

He shrugged, his smirk stopping just short of disgust.

"Your treatment of Marilyn is riddled with unethical behavior. Whether that rises to the standard of you getting your license yanked, I couldn't say. But you took Marilyn on, even though a lover of hers, a man she nearly married during this period, was already your patient — Frank Sinatra. You took Marilyn on even though Mickey Rudin, your brother-in-law, was her attorney. You placed a former psychiatric nurse of yours, Eunice Murray, in your patient's home as a spy. You inserted yourself into your patient's business affairs, and —"

"Need we go over this ground again, Mr. Heller? I won't argue I may have crossed certain ethical lines, but nothing that would cost me my license to practice."

"Yeah? What if your first loyalty wasn't to your patient? What if you were really working for the Kennedys?"

"What?"

"Frank Sinatra knew about Marilyn and Jack. Mickey Rudin knew. Back around '60, when you took over Marilyn's case, Frank was very close to the Kennedys. Was placing you as Marilyn's shrink a way to keep track of her state of mind?"

Now the disgust was openly displayed. "Perhaps you should return the gun to your hand, Mr. Heller. Because that's the only way I will sit for such insulting nonsense."

"Well, it's actually the lesser of two evils. The other possibility is that you're a Soviet spy."

His dark eyes showed white all around. "Oh, my *God* — you really *do* need to leave, Mr. Heller. I have *tried* to be co-operative. . . ."

He'd asked me to, so I got the gun back in hand. Didn't exactly point it at him. Didn't exactly not point it at him.

"Your Communist ties are well known by Uncle Sam," I reminded him. "You and Dr. Engelberg. I'd like to talk to him, too."

"You can't. He's in Switzerland."

"What, making a deposit? You Beverly Hills Commies kill me. So, with your ties to Eunice Murray and her husband — who I understand built this very house we're in — and ol' silver-spoon Communist Vanderbilt Field and a whole passel of fellow travelers, you've surrounded Marilyn with caring, Communist attention. But what if you have arranged to be Marilyn Monroe's psychiatrist so you can hear the things that Jack Kennedy and Bobby Kennedy shared with this eager-to-learn young woman? And didn't you even help her craft questions to ask Bobby, for her to write the answers down in her notebooks?"

"You can't *believe* this."

I let the gun droop. "Actually, I can't. It is absurd — are you working for the Kennedys, or the Soviet Union? Or maybe Jack and Bobby are Commie spies. Even Ian Fleming couldn't sell this crap. But you couldn't take that chance, could you?"

"What chance?"

"That your very real Communist associations would come out. That's why you had to go along with whatever the Kennedys' favorite at the LAPD, Captain Hamilton of the Intelligence Division, asked. And what was asked of you by the CIA or FBI or Secret Service or whatever mix of spooks came around to haunt Marilyn's hacienda that night. You had no choice. You even, at first, became the spokesman for the suicide crowd. But that finally caught in your craw, didn't it?"

He said nothing. He was looking past me, either at the window or maybe into his conscience. I considered offering him mine — the nine-millimeter one.

"It's not often I have to give a doctor a bad prognosis," I said, "but here it is — today somebody pulled me in and told me bad things about you. Some true, some false or at least exaggerations. I have a reputation, as you noted, for what these gents call 'rough justice.' "

Now his eyes met mine. "I don't follow you, Mr. Heller."

"Somebody, CIA or FBI or, yeah, even Secret Service, grabbed me and tried to sell you to me as Marilyn's killer. Thinking I would do something rash, like break into your house and put a bullet in your brain."

"You can't be serious."

"I do kid around. But not this time. They thought they could play me. Manipulate me into taking you out. Play me a phony tape and watch me dance. Chances are, I would have wound up either dead or arrested for your murder. Maybe Hamilton is sitting out there in an unmarked car, waiting for a gunshot. Anyway, in somebody's eyes, you would make a good corpse and I would make a better patsy."

He thought about that. "What can I do?"

"I would write everything down or record it, essentially a full confession, and let everyone know . . . start with Hamilton . . . that should you have a fatal accident, that information will go public. Public in the way they thought Marilyn was going to."

Now his smile bore no disgust. "That is good advice, Mr. Heller. You may not be as 'crazy' as you seem."

"First, hearing that from a psychiatrist is kind of a relief. Second, I got out of the Marines on a Section Eight, so don't be too sure." I stood, tucked the nine-mil in my waistband, zipped the jacket over it. "You mind if I go out the front door?"

"Please."

"Sorry for the intrusion, Doc."

I was halfway out the den when he said, "There is no way in my lifetime, Mr. Heller, that I can ever make up for this — for aiding the very people who likely took that sweet child's life. . . ."

"You're right. Probably isn't."

"I don't really know if I will ever get over it, completely. And I'll always wonder if there was some way I might have saved her."

I shrugged. "You might try therapy."

And left him there.

CHAPTER 23

At Flo's Roxbury manse, I learned just how hard and fast my little Brenda Starr could work. For all the pampering cocktail parties and press junkets, she proved as hard-boiled a newswoman as Rosalind Russell pretended to be in *His Girl Friday.*

In a home office as messy as she was well-groomed, Flo Kilgore sat in a T-shirt and rolled-up jeans and no shoes, fingers flying at her Smith-Corona, machine-gunning keys, answering each ding with a forceful carriage return. The converted bedroom was filled with filing cabinets, research books, folders of clippings, and haphazardly stacked steno pads, though she never seemed to have any trouble finding in a flash whatever she needed.

I was chiefly a bystander, or sitter, plopped in a comfy chair between a filing cabinet and a worktable, finishing the last couple hundred pages of *The Carpetbaggers.* My

God, did anybody really have this much sex?

Anyway, my presence was needed for the questions and clarifications she would on occasion toss over her shoulder, her fingers frozen over the keys, poised to attack once I had provided whatever tidbit she required.

We started (if I may generously include myself as part of the process) around 10:00 A.M., after her cook fed us corned-beef hash and buttermilk pancakes, and she had a draft of the story by 1:00 P.M.

She handed it to me, saying, "Remember, we don't have to solve the mystery. Just raise legitimate questions, and throw light on the dark areas."

That she had.

Tough but fair, with plenty of confidential sources but a good number going on the record (myself included), the in-depth article made no bones about personal relationships between Marilyn Monroe and both John and Robert Kennedy, and established clearly that RFK had been at MM's house the afternoon before she died.

The scientific impossibility of an accidental drug overdose by Marilyn, and the probability of a "hot shot" injection having killed her (despite the deputy coroner's search for injection marks), was stunningly well argued. The presence of the studio, police, and likely government cleanup crews manipulating the scene and even staging the suicide break-in, all during the early morning hours before the death was officially called in, was firmly established.

"What do you think?" she asked, bright-eyed, her smile tentatively proud.

"Ship it," I said.

But what she did was call it in, and somebody in New York took down the copy word-for-word (". . . period, paragraph . . ."), all twenty-five hundred of them.

We took a late lunch at Nate 'n Al's, both casual, though she'd traded her T-shirt and Levi's for a white blouse and gray skirt. I still had on the lime-green polo and darker green Jaymar slacks I'd worn over to her place this morning. We laughed in the face of death by sharing a huge pastrami and Swiss cheese sandwich.

"You really like it?" she said eagerly.

"I love pastrami."

She giggled. "No. *You* know. . . ."

"I think," I said grandly, Russian dressing dribbling down my mouth, "you will be the first Hollywood columnist ever to win the Pulitzer."

She beamed, her blue eyes bright; her dark brown hair bounced at her shoulders, none of that bouffant noise. "You're not teasing?"

"No. It's a well-substantiated piece. What now?"

"Now I wait to hear from my editor."

"Will he get back to you on a Saturday?"

"For this story, you bet."

But she didn't hear till deep into Sunday. I was back at my bungalow, and Sam had come over to use the hotel pool. I was in my swim trunks and a Catalina pullover, about to follow him out, when the phone rang.

She was in tears. And angry.

"Cocksuckers," she said.

Flo didn't swear lightly, so I knew at once her story had been nixed.

"What did your editor say?"

"He said I did a 'damn good job of research.' But even though the *Herald Tribune* is a Republican paper, this is an election year, and the story would seem a 'gratuitous slap' at the president and his brother. They're killing it."

"Christ, how the hell do you write off exposing a movie star's murder as a gratuitous fucking slap?"

"I think this is more than just editorial policy. I . . . Nate, I *know* it's more."

"What do you mean?"

"I have contacts in the administration."

She wasn't crying now, at least not sobbing, though she snuffled some. "They say the *Trib* sent the story over by telex and asked them to confirm or deny the reporting about Bobby and Jack. They refused to do either, which was bad enough, but you can bet some pressure was put on, behind the scenes."

"Always is. Can you take it elsewhere?"

Her sigh seemed endless. Then: "If a paper as right-leaning as the *Trib* won't print the thing, who will? I might find a magazine to use it, but I would likely lose my job. And I like my job. Anyway . . . I *used* to like my job. . . ."

"I'll come right over."

"No. No, not today. I want to be alone today. We were up very late last night, remember . . ."

I did. We'd been giving those carpetbaggers a run for the money.

". . . and I just have to zonk out. Get some sleep. I'm gonna pop some pills in the glorious Hollywood tradition, and just go away for a while. . . . Bye, Nate."

"Bye, baby."

That was a fitting way for Flo to write -30- on this story, wasn't it? Pop some sleeping pills? Zonk out like Zelda, aka Marilyn Monroe, the former Norma Jeane?

My son overheard this, my end anyway, and he gave me a worried, earnest look, the kind you can summon when you haven't been in the world as long as the grown-ups.

"Jesus, Dad! What the hell happened? You sound really upset."

I just shook a finger at him. "I'm fine. Don't you go using bad fucking language, just because you hear me doing it."

We went swimming.

The moon was nearly full. What its ivory touch could do with a godforsaken landscape was impressive — the narrow, rocky beach, the ribbon of concrete, the barren cliffside with scrubby brush hanging on for dear life. The ocean, as choppy tonight as it was vast, sported waves whose white peaks were like angels dancing on the void.

The two-story beach cottage the A-1 used as a safe house was nothing so grand as the Lawford villa on Sorrento Beach, also on the Pacific Coast Highway. But we were way north of that, between Sunset and Temescal Canyon. The modest clapboard, close enough to the ocean to require stilts, had no immediate neighbors, and was nicely isolated from any police presence.

The beach house had once been Fred's, back when he was doing sport fishing (there was a marina a few miles up the highway). But now that my partner was getting on in years, he rarely went out, and then just for the sun and solitude. So we'd converted the property into one of our safe houses.

Part of the bottom floor was a carport, and I slipped the Jaguar in next to the nondescript dark blue Chevy Impala that Roger Pryor had driven out here. Presumably his employees were making use of the several panel trucks his agency owned. The two floors were set up as individual apartments, in case we needed to use the place for two witnesses or clients or whatever.

To get to the first-floor digs, you came around the side, on a little wooden-plank balcony-type walkway. The night was cool, especially considering how hot the day had been; I was in the ninja/tennis pro getup again, with the Browning nine-mil in my waistband under the unzipped Windbreaker.

I had a key but figured knocking was more polite. Wouldn't want to walk in on the guy jacking off or taking a dump or pursuing some other undignified if necessary human activity.

Roger cracked the door, his blandly boyish countenance creased with worry, his thinning blonde hair looking slept on. He was in a green plaid sport shirt and tan slacks and socks, looking like a high school shop teacher, except for the lack of shoes and the .38 revolver in his right hand.

"Nate," he said. "I thought you'd forgotten me."

He opened the door.

We were immediately in a living room with an assortment of secondhand furnishings — the A-1 did not splurge on its safe houses, knowing that those staying there were generally lucky to have anywhere to camp. But it wasn't unpleasant. Homey, in a road company *Leave It to Beaver* fashion.

The small kitchen, at left (windows on the ocean were at right), was open onto the comfy living room area, with its couch and recliner and portable, rabbit-eared TV on a stand (*Bonanza* was on), all sharing a round braided rug.

Roger rested the .38 on the kitchen table, its Formica modernity out of place against the ancient brown cabinets and a humming Century of Progress–era refrigerator.

"Cold one?" he asked.

"Sure," I said.

"There's just beer. None of that soda shit you go for."

"I'll take a beer. We'll pretend I'm a big boy."

The sounds of the Cartwrights on the

491

Ponderosa were annoying me, so I took the liberty of going in and switching off the set. This made more prominent the sound of surf rushing to shore, not far beyond the windows.

We wound up sitting in the little kitchen. That put the .38 on the table between us. I didn't blame Roger. I'd be cautious, too, if I were him. That's why I brought the nine-mil.

He asked, fairly pleasantly but with a slight edge, "So how much longer am I going to have to be cooped up here?"

"I'd hoped by Monday there'd be a story in the papers," I said, "that would've meant nobody had to lay low on this thing anymore."

With a glum nod, he said, "Yeah — everything out in the open, so what's to hide."

"Right. But I heard today that that story got spiked. The administration is putting the lid on, and everybody's rolling over. But that may be okay."

"How do you figure?"

"Well, it's the next best thing. Either everything's public, or everything's hidden. In either case, you should be able to come out of hiding. That is, if you have any kind of insurance at all."

"What kind of insurance?"

"You've got tapes. Intel may have taken the key ones, from that night, but the rest are in a lockbox, right?"

". . . Right."

I shrugged. "Make it known they'll stay put unless somebody tries to do something bad to you. It's the oldest dodge in the book, but it still works. What the kids call an oldie but a goodie."

He was nodding. "Yeah, that had occurred to me."

"Anyway, I figure you really do have the tapes from that night. Possibly somewhere right here, unless you took the time to put 'em in a bus station locker or something, before you came around to get me out of bed, the night Marilyn died. Morning, I mean."

His forehead was deeply creased. "Is that some kind of offhanded accusation?"

"Not that offhand. You may have handed the tapes off to a client, but as last-moment as this all was, I doubt that. If so, you had enough machines rolling to keep backups."

"What the hell are —"

"Roger, I talked to Captain Hamilton. He's generally not forthcoming to me, but reading between the lines — hell, even reading what was *on* the lines — he didn't have those tapes. Fact, he wanted to know how to get in touch with you. Of course, I didn't rat you out."

His face had gone blank, though his eyes looked tired. He began blinking too much. But he didn't play games.

"How long have you known?" he asked.

"I suspected from the start. I've known for . . . hell, I don't know, probably since I got the time line down. Two things, Roger — when you claim to have waltzed in through the front door, and into Marilyn's bedroom, where you supposedly removed the wiretap gizmos? By that time, that place was crawling with every intel copper and fed and Fox security goon in town."

He just shrugged a little. "Happens, when you have to get your story together early in the game." He sipped his beer — a Schlitz.

I liked Schlitz, which is why we stocked the safe house fridge with them. So I sipped mine, too. The husky whisper of the surf provided a lulling backdrop.

Then I said, "The other thing I learned from the time line — which I grant you is a little vague, because everybody's story seems to float around — is that really only one person had the perfect opportunity, somewhere between nine and ten o'clock, to slip in the front door and kill Marilyn."

"I didn't do that," he said simply.

"No you didn't. What you did actually was easier than going in the front door, though you may have gone in that way *after* you took care of Marilyn. Because at some point you did remove the bugging devices. Or, possibly, you were called in, and came back as part of the tag team cleanup crews that searched that place and stage-managed that death scene and did everything but wax the new kitchen floor."

He grinned. Actually grinned.

"Lawford called me," he admitted with a gruff laugh. "I was back home already and he fucking called me. Wanted me to get over there and get the bugs out. He'd cleared it with Hamilton. So I did."

"Back home, you mean," I said, "after finishing your *first* job at Fifth Helena. If you were in the van, supervising the surveillance taping, how did you get the call?"

Pryor shrugged. "I have a car phone. Like Bogie in *Sabrina.* You know me, Nate. I have all the toys. You gonna ask who made the call?"

He wasn't even looking at the .38 resting on the Formica top. It was like the weapon was a centerpiece or a forgotten half-eaten sandwich.

"We'll get to that," I said. "Anyway, Marilyn wasn't in her bedroom. She'd gone out to the guesthouse, wanting to get away from her own phone tap, and the prying ears of Mrs. Murray. Did you see a light on? How did you know that's where she was?"

"Oh, that guest cottage was wired for sound, too. She didn't know it, of course. I didn't tell you the full extent of what I installed — some of it was hardwired. I was well paid, Nate. Very well paid."

"And by multiple clients. Got to hand it to you. You have always been one savvy businessman. Hope the Chamber of Commerce knows about your initiative. Anyway, Marilyn had taken either chloral hydrate or more Nembutal than she'd recently been taking — she'd had a bad day, and wanted to knock herself out. Not kill herself. And she had a pretty fine pharmaceutical sense, although clean as she was, she might have overestimated what she could handle. In any case, nothing fatal."

He folded his hands on the table. About a foot from the gun. The continuing pulse of surf brushing the beach created an air of timeless unreality, making our conversation seem oddly abstract.

"Still," I said, "she'd taken enough junk to pass out on the phone, in the middle of a conversation, and spook somebody. Enough for her to be dead to the world — but not *dead* — when you came in and gave her that hot shot."

"Now I'm a medic."

"No, you're a guy with diabetes who knows his way around a needle."

"And just happened to have a hypo full of Nembutal handy."

"Not just happened to — you'd had that handy for weeks, Roger, maybe months. One or more of your employers knew that at some point they might have to have this problem dealt with . . . or possibly take an opportunity that presented itself, like a nonfatal overdose that could be turned *into* a fatal one."

A laugh from deep in his belly got caught behind his lips. Then he said, "Now you have me riding around in my van with a needle of poison in my pocket."

"Not riding around. Parked, mostly, near Marilyn's. And anyway, you're capable of riding around with a needle full of poison, right, Roger? Like that needle of nicotine you tried to stick in me?"

He didn't argue. He knew me too well. He just sat there with his young-looking-for-forty face turning older by the second, his eyes hooded and rather moist. I hoped he wouldn't cry. I hate it when they cry.

Or anyway I hate it when they cry and I'm

still telling them the story.

I went on with my once-upon-a-time: "If I'd had any doubt, which I didn't, the capper came this morning, when Thad Brown called me to let me know that noise suppressor came from a guy in Culver City, who specializes in firearms gadgetry. The name meant nothing to Thad, in regard to this case anyway, but I knew it was a pal of yours, a guy you get your custom weapons stuff from."

He was shaking his head, but not denying anything. "I didn't like having to do that, Nate. You been decent to me."

"Yet you got over it. See, Roger, the needles and the poison? That's why I don't need to get you to tell me who had you do this thing. I'm fairly sure I know."

"That so."

"Mmm-hmmm. The hypo is highly reminiscent of the Cuban follies the mob and the CIA have been staging — not with a lot of success, prior to this, I grant you. They have this very special doctor named Gottlieb — and I wish to hell I didn't know his name — who ought to be played by Karloff, twenty years ago. He's the mad doc who builds assassination kits for Uncle Sam. He can whip up a poison or lethal virus faster than your mama can scramble you an egg. So my guess is that the hypo full of Nembutal cocktail came from the CIA. But not the order to remove her. That came from Chicago. Or maybe their local rep — Rosselli?"

He said nothing.

"Here's the thing, Roger. I can't turn you in, because nobody seems to want to arrest anybody in this particular murder case. And if they did, I couldn't turn you in anyway, because you were working for me in this fiasco, so how do I get out of it with the smell of murder not sticking to me?"

His eyes tightened. He was thinking. Was that daylight at the end of the tunnel, or just another train?

I waved it all off. "And I'm not going to kill you, either. You're small fry. You're just a working stiff, like me. What I want are some names. Let's start with Rosselli."

"Wasn't Rosselli. He's in Vegas."

"There are phones between LA and Vegas, I understand. Not car phones maybe, but phones."

"No. Not Rosselli. It was . . . it was Giananca himself."

That made sense. "And who called him? Lawford?"

"I don't know. I honest to Christ don't know. You'll have to climb that ladder yourself, Heller."

Then his brow creased with thought, and he leaned forward and his head almost hovered over the .38, though his hands weren't near it now.

"Or maybe," he said, some desperation finally reading in his voice, "I *can* help you climb. Look. Say I help you. I know you liked that broad, and I had nothing against her either, if it hadn't been me do it, it'd been half a dozen others, some spook, some Outfit guy, fuck, some *intel* fucker. I didn't kill her, the poison somebody *else* provided did. You with me?"

"I'm with you."

"I'll be your inside guy. Trying to get an angle on somebody as high up as Giancana won't be easy. But maybe I can do it. Maybe I can check in, and ask some questions. Maybe I can find out where this thing flowed from."

"I'm thinking Hoffa."

"Definite possibility."

"But Giancana was fine with it."

"Obviously."

"And the CIA went along."

"No doubt."

"Okay." I finished the beer. "Want another cold one?"

"I could use it."

I went to the refrigerator, opened it, shut it, came back behind him, and stuck the needle of nicotine in his neck.

"*Now* you're a working stiff," I said.

And thumbed the shit into him. I wouldn't wear a bigger smile till I was a skull.

Just in case he got ambitious, I swiped the gun off the table and it clattered onto the linoleum floor and, luckily, did not go off. He wriggled around on the floor, clutching his neck like there was something he could do about it, bawling now, which at this point I was fine with.

I went over to the phone out by the couch and dialed Fred Rubinski.

"You can bring the boat around now," I said.

"Check," he said.

I went in to see how Roger was doing. He wasn't unconscious but he had given up. His face looked white and terrible. Good. I retrieved the .38, so he didn't go out in a blaze of glory, ending his misery or mine.

Searching the place, I found the box of small white tape boxes in the closet, up on a hatbox shelf the way Marilyn's tape recorder had been barely hidden at Fifth Helena.

And under some clothes in a bedroom dresser, I found a single red spiral notebook.

Thumbing through, words written in Marilyn's familiar flowing hand jumped out at me: *Bay of Pigs, Castro, CIA, Sam Giancana.*

I gathered all of the material and set it on the couch. Roger was dead, pretzeled on the floor, having shit himself, turning a light shade of blue.

Then I went into the living room, away from the stench, where a recliner awaited. Before getting comfortable, I switched the TV on. Turned the channel. Who the hell wanted to see *Bonanza* in black-and-white, anyway? Jack Benny was on, and I could use a laugh.

CHAPTER 24

That weekend — the one I'd spent helping Flo Kilgore put together an article that would be quashed, chatting with Dr. Ralph Greenson about his famous client, and evicting Roger Pryor from the A-1 Detective Agency safe house — had been a festive one for the Kennedy clan and their circle.

President Kennedy, his brother Robert, his wife Ethel, their many children, Peter and Pat Lawford, and their new best friend Pat Newcomb enjoyed a relaxing weekend at Hyannis Port. Much of Sunday (my really eventful day), they spent on the *Manitou,* a sixty-two-foot Coast Guard yacht. Photos reveal a smiling, happy clan, basking in the wind, spray, and sun.

On Monday afternoon I called the Justice Department and left my name and my number at the Beverly Hills Hotel. Bobby returned the call the next day, about that same time. Our conversation was brief.

"I need to see you," I said. "It's private and it's personal."

"Ethel and the kids are still at Hyannis Port," he said. "They will be *next* weekend, too. But I'll be at Hickory Hill, batching it. Can you join me for lunch Saturday?"

McClean, Virginia, was a labyrinth of macadam roads. I had been to Hickory Hill, the Robert F. Kennedy estate, a number of times, but it was one of those places you always thought you'd missed. Then there it was, up a steep incline back from the road, a big whitewashed brick house in a lush setting of trees and landscaped lawn. The house, dating back to the mid-1800s, had a pool and tennis court. Also horses with the grooms to go with them, gardeners, cooks, nurses, and a butler.

Apparently, like the family, much of the retinue was absent. The dogs that usually roamed the place must have been in kennels, and certainly the butler had the weekend off, because Bobby himself — in a pale pink short-sleeve shirt and tan chinos — met me at the red front door. I was in a polo and slacks, equally casual.

He gave me a big, vaguely embarrassed smile, offered his hand for me to shake, which I did, smiling back at him, perhaps not with as much warmth as before. He led me through the formally furnished home out onto the back terrace. That's where we had lunch — at least one cook was on duty — open-faced steak sandwiches with hash browns. Steaks cooked to order, of course. We both had ours medium rare.

"Pretty strange, isn't it?" he said, with that embarrassed smile, after touching his mouth with a linen napkin. "I feel like a ghost haunting my own house."

"I've seen it livelier."

And, the half dozen times I'd been there, also usually on the weekend, it was. During the day, Bobby roughhousing with his kids, engaging them in touch football, tree-climbing and swimming. At night, social gatherings and outright parties with an eclectic mix, from Harry Belafonte teaching guests the Twist to Kremlin contact Georgi Bolshakov arm-wrestling with Bobby (and losing). Assorted Kennedy hangers-on like Kenny O'Donnell and Dave Powers in push-up contests with Bobby (and losing).

Neither of us wanted dessert, and we had cold bottles of Coke instead of coffee. The sun was high and hot and the bottles sweated and so did we.

The luncheon talk remained small, but after, when he walked with me — Cokes in hand, down past the big hickory with its tree house, usually inhabited by one of the countless kids — he brought up Marilyn, if obliquely.

"Pat is a wreck," he said. "Peter, too."

"Is their marriage going to make it?"

He flashed me a look that said perhaps I'd overstepped. But he answered it, frankly: "Until Jack's been reelected, it will. . . . I think Peter and his friend Sinatra had words." He shook his head. "I've never shared their fascination with that man."

He meant Jack and Peter with Sinatra.

"Frank's one of the few performers on a par with Marilyn," I said. "What they call superstars."

"He's a bully. Little would-be thug."

Coming from the diminutive Bobby, thought by many to be worthy of a similar appellation, this might have been comical. Neither of us, however, was in a light mood. We settled at a white metal table with matching chairs by the swimming pool, the massive white rectangular poolhouse looming nearby like another D.C. monument. Not much breeze, the pool's aqua surface mirror-like, barely rippling.

He twitched the tiniest sad smile. "I don't know what I can say, Nate. I liked Marilyn very much. I'm sorry she's gone."

"She thought the world of you and your

brother. Figured you were going to change everything. That they'd have to carve one or maybe two more heads onto Mount Rushmore."

He broadened his smile, in that endearing bucktoothed way, looking out at the glassy pool. His brown bangs were uncombed, his eyes somewhat bloodshot.

Finally he said, "If you think I'm responsible, you're wrong."

"You're responsible for the cover-up."

"I didn't initiate it." His blue eyes swung earnestly to mine. "Man to man? I accept responsibility for it. People looking after my interests took care of it." He shrugged. "But I had no knowledge."

"You don't disagree with their actions? Your protectors?"

The eyes tensed. "We are talking about what happened *after* Marilyn's death? The search of her house for damaging documents? Of course I don't disagree. It's a national security matter."

"Maybe you should have thought of that before bragging in the bedroom."

He might have taken offense, but instead he just sighed. Stared out at the pool. "I'm not proud of it. Any of it."

I sipped the Coke; warm already. "Maybe I should tell you why I'm here."

Another look, this time sharp. "*This* is why you're here. Unloading recriminations on me." And now a nasty smile. "But, Nate, you make an unlikely conscience."

I almost laughed.

"You know, Eliot Ness was my friend," I said.

"I know he was."

"He wasn't without flaws, none of us is, but he had a kind of ethical authority, a kind of moral vision, the likes of which I never saw in any other man. Half the time I thought he was a fool. The other half I admired him."

Bobby shook his head, brushed bangs away from his eyes. "Pity he didn't live to enjoy his fame."

I nodded. "My point is, when I met you, not ten years ago? I thought I'd met another Eliot Ness."

He grunted a laugh and waved that off.

"No, Bob — really. You took on these Outfit bastards, and were able to withstand whatever they threw at you. You were too rich to be bribed, too stubborn to be scared off, too Irish to give up. I admired that."

He was smiling again, just a little, eyes back on the water. "You were a big help in those days, Nate. You've been a big help since."

"Nice of you to say. Thing about Eliot is, I used to give him hell for appointing himself my personal Jiminy Cricket. It was a running gag with us — the idiot tried to be *my* conscience."

That amused Bob. "Good luck to him."

I grunted a laugh. "So it's funny, ironic, and not a little screwed-up that I, of all fucking people, am sitting here playing *your* conscience."

"I already have a conscience, thanks. Plenty of guilt to deal with. Haven't you noticed I'm Catholic?"

"Without your mess of kids climbing the walls, it's not as obvious. Anyway. The real reason I'm here."

"Which is?"

I grinned at him, swigged some Coke. Then: "I'm turning myself in."

"You're what?"

"You're the attorney general of these United States, right? Number one law enforcement official? Toppest top cop? Well, I'm turning myself in. I killed the son of a bitch who murdered Marilyn."

He sighed, and looked away. "That black sense of humor of yours will get you in trouble someday."

"No joke. He was a guy who worked for me, but he also worked for various other clients, doing surveillance, bugging Marilyn's house. He was at his post when he got a call to go in and take care of the Marilyn Monroe problem."

Now he looked at me. "And you killed him."

"I shot him full of poison, just like he did Marilyn. I'm not going to tell you where the body is. Well, okay, it's in an ocean. Here's a hint. Not this one." I jerked a thumb in the general direction of the Atlantic.

"I don't believe you," he said, but his expression said he was pretty sure he did.

"I wouldn't burden you with this, Bob, but who else can I talk to about it, in a frank, open way? See, I pumped the guy for information before I . . ." I drew a finger across my throat. ". . . And to loosen him up, I said I wasn't interested in small fry like him. That what I wanted were the big fish. But the truth is, I can't go after the big fish. It's vaguely possible I could get close enough to Giancana to put his lights out, but I figure he's living on borrowed time, anyway. And your CIA pals, what's my best course of action there? Go to D.C. and start popping guys in dark sunglasses and black suits?"

"This is lunacy." He was frowning, and

sitting on the edge of his chair, as if about to rise. "You should go, Nate. I'm disappointed in you."

"Disappointed in me? Now there's a laugh. Wouldn't you like to know, just out of a sense of history, how this went down, Bob?"

"No."

"Thought you would." I shifted on the chair. "Peter Lawford calls Marilyn, knowing how she flipped out after you came over and started yelling at her — my God, did you slap her, and push her or . . . ? She was bruised, Bob."

He said nothing. His head swiveled toward the water.

"Calls her once late afternoon, then again around seven thirty, stepping away from his little Saturday night party to make sure she's all right. But she isn't all right — she's saying things that sound like a verbal suicide note. As it happens, she wasn't trying to commit suicide, and she hadn't OD'd — just took a little too much of either chloral hydrate or Nembutal, enough to pass out, which she did on the phone. And scared the shit out of Peter."

"This isn't helpful."

"Now, I'm not sure whether you headed right back to the Bates ranch, or whether

511

you hid out at the Beverly Hilton. My guys couldn't find evidence you'd stayed around town, but that doesn't mean you didn't. And Lawford called you either at the ranch or at that hotel, but in any event told you that Marilyn was in a very, very bad way. Maybe dying or dead, and there might even be a suicide note — and God knows what she may have written about you and Jack. And what did you tell your brother-in-law, Bob?"

He didn't fill in that blank.

So I did: "You told him to take care of it. To get off his lazy ass and take fucking care of it."

Not the faintest flicker of denial.

"And that's all you gave him. That simple order. Vague but not to be ignored. You may have thought Peter would drive over there himself, and deal with it. *Take care of it.* Get her stomach pumped if she'd OD'd, destroy any suicide note if it was too late. And if the latter, put a general cleanup and cover-up in motion, much as what later did take place."

"I didn't initiate anything, Nate."

"But you did, Bob — you said, 'Take care of it.' Only Peter couldn't get off his lazy ass because he was *drunk* on his lazy ass. He could hardly navigate his way across the living room, if his guests that night are to be believed. So what *did* he do? Rosselli was out of town, in Vegas. Might have called him there, but you know who I think Peter called?"

He didn't ask.

"I think he called Frank," I said. "I think Peter called Frank, the superstar who helped elect your brother, remember? Who gave your brother-in-law a new lease on show business life. As he had so many times before, Peter asked Frank for help."

Bobby offered up a skeptical smile. "This is silly guesswork, Nate. Please. Let's not go any further with this kind of speculation."

"Actually, it isn't speculation. Sinatra came into Sherry's last week. That's the restaurant Fred Rubinski and I own, on Sunset. Frank's a fairly regular customer. He was by himself. That's unusual — he's social, there's usually at least one good-looking woman with him, often a whole group of people. He doesn't like being alone. Nobody worships you, when you're alone."

Bobby was frowning. Openly unhappy. His tone grew clipped: "What does that have to do with anything?"

"I sat down with Frank. He gave me this really sad look. He looked like he'd been

crying, Bob. Funny guy, Sinatra. Part heart-
less prick, part hopeless romantic. He didn't
order food. Just Jack Daniel's. Sat in that
booth drinking Jack Daniel's, and when I
sat down, he said, 'I didn't know, Charlie. I
had no way of knowing.' All I said was, 'So
that's how it went — Lawford called you,
and you called Mooney.' He shook his head,
Bob, but he wasn't saying no. He told me
he had no idea it would go that way. No
idea anybody would 'hurt that girl.' And he
said he was finished with Giancana, 'fucking finished.' Never wanted anything to do
with that son of a bitch again."

Bobby said nothing. A mild breeze was
stirring. His hair ruffled, the pool rippled,
the sun glided under a cloud. We sat in cool
blue light.

"Giancana gave the order," I said. "*He*
made the call. But your CIA friends had
anticipated the need, and had provided the
means. This was all part of that unholy marriage you officiated, between the Outfit and
the Spooks. All to kill Castro, and how's
that going, by the way?"

His eyes were closed.

"Once Peter was informed she was dead,
he began making his series of alarmed
phone calls, to get people to check up on
her — so somebody, anybody but *him,*

would find the body. Poor bastard. If ever anybody was in over his head. . . . Still, it was one of his more convincing performances."

Bobby turned to me. He seemed much older than I remembered. Grooves, lines, shadows. His eyes were moist.

"What do you want from me, Nate?"

"Nothing. I guess I wanted to make sure Marilyn dying meant something to you. As your conscience, I like to think you learned something more than just, well, that you'd gotten away with it."

"Goddamnit, Nate, I didn't —"

"Sort that out any way you choose." I waved it off. "The real reason I'm here, all kidding aside, is to ask you to mark me off in your address book. I'm retired from government service. Pass the word to Jack, too, would you? I've allowed myself to get involved with your various ill-advised crusades, from playing double agent with Jimmy Hoffa to your goddamn Operation Mongoose, and I am *not* available for future fun. Understood?"

". . . Understood. I'm sorry it's . . . Nate, I'm just sorry."

I stood, and he did, too.

As we were trudging up the hill, I said, "Just so you know, that red notebook of

Marilyn's? It's safely tucked away."

"Safely tucked away where?"

"Where as long as nothing suspiciously fatal happens to me, it stays tucked away." *Those oldies but goodies.* "So is a set of the tapes of that last night, too, though you can bet the killer turned his machines off before going inside and doing the deed."

"You have the tapes?"

"Yeah. Somebody else may, too. Somebody in your camp, maybe."

I stopped. We were on the terrace now.

"What the hell was Giancana after, anyway?" I asked him. "I mean, I understand the national security implications of Marilyn maybe running her mouth, and how unkindly the spooks might view that. But what good does taking Marilyn out of the equation do *that* wop bastard?"

The wind was kicking in. The sun had stayed under the clouds and it was cool.

Bobby said, "He doesn't want Operation Mongoose exposed any more than we do. Hiring his people out as killers on the one hand, and consorting with the enemy, which is to say me and Jack, on the other." He shrugged. "Maybe he thinks he has something on us now, and I'll give him a free ride." His eyes grew colder than the day had turned. "One thing I can promise you,

Nate . . ."

"Oh?"

"He's going to be disappointed."

Maybe there was a little Eliot Ness left in him, after all.

The bulk of Marilyn's estate went to Lee Strasberg, but the actress had died less than well-off. She would of course generate much income in the future, for the Strasberg family, and a squabble arose with Inez Melson and lawyers descended. Word got out that Marilyn had already set an appointment with a lawyer to remove Lee and Paula from her will, but that didn't matter: the Strasbergs prevailed.

The police had closed its file by year's end, and only a few items about the unusual, suspicious circumstances surrounding MM's passing even made it into Hollywood columns, most prominently Winchell's and Flo Kilgore's.

By most accounts, Marilyn's passing destroyed Dr. Ralph Greenson. "The fire went out," one colleague said. "He never really recovered. He went on, but turned inward after that, and became a bit strange." Unlike certain friends and associates of the actress, Greenson did not capitalize on his famous patient, and refused any interviews on her life and death. The 1963 film *Captain Newman, M.D.,* which garnered an Academy Award nomination for Sinatra's young rival Bobby Darin, depicted Greenson's wartime psychiatric care of battle-traumatized patients. Two textbooks he wrote in the 1960s are highly regarded and still much-used, but for all of this, he is remembered most for having been Marilyn Monroe's final analyst. He died in 1979.

Though she spent her later life in a series of small Santa Monica apartments, Eunice Murray took three European tours in the 1960s. She cowrote a book about Marilyn, and gave numerous interviews (on and off camera), with a story that changed substantially over the years, ultimately admitting Bobby Kennedy's afternoon visit and the post-murder cleanup by his protectors. She died in 1995.

Mrs. Murray's son-in-law, Norman Jefferies, ducked interviewers (the police never bothered with him) until 1993, when, terminally ill and in a wheelchair in a nursing home, he told an interviewer the story he'd shared with me on the Santa Monica pier.

After her sojourn at the Kennedy compound, Pat Newcomb went on an extended European vacation. In 1963 she took a position with the United States Information Agency, headed by Bobby Kennedy's friend George Stevens, Jr. She served as liaison between the Capitol and Hollywood, involved with film festivals internationally and arranging for movie stars to travel abroad and promote America and its film industry. She often socialized with the Kennedy family and was a frequent guest at Hickory Hill. When Bobby ran for New York State Senator, Pat joined his staff. She is now valued as one of Hollywood's most successful and discreet public relations consultants, representing the likes of Barbra Streisand, Robert Redford, and Jane Fonda. She, too, refused most interviews and has turned down repeated lucrative offers to write a book about her time with Marilyn.

Arthur Jacobs became a producer at Twentieth Century–Fox; some have called it his reward from the studio. Among his first projects was *What a Way to Go!* in 1964, with Shirley MacLaine stepping in for Marilyn. He is most famous for producing the original *Dr. Dolittle* and the hit *Planet of the Apes* movies, all of which featured his wife, Natalie. He, too, remained silent about the circumstances of Marilyn's death. He died in 1972.

In 1963, Captain James Hamilton left the

LAPD to become head of security for the National Football League, a high-paying job arranged by Bobby Kennedy. Hamilton died a year later of a brain tumor. Intel's renowned secret files were eventually destroyed.

Chief Parker never got J. Edgar Hoover's job, as the FBI director's own secret files continued to protect *his* job. Parker died in 1966 at a testimonial in his own honor — the Police Administration Building was renamed Parker Center, but everybody still calls it the Glass House. (Upon his death in 1972, Hoover's files were burned by his longtime companion, Associate Director Clyde Tolson).

Upon Parker's passing, Thad Brown finally became chief, but served only briefly. When he passed away in 1972, Brown left behind a Marilyn Monroe file he had secretly assembled, including the impounded phone records and seven hundred pages of suppressed interviews, depositions, photographs, reports, and other pertinent documents. Despite this, two subsequent official inquiries — in 1982 and 1985 — rubber-stamped previous questionable findings.

In 1975 Sam Giancana was shot once in the back of the head and six times in the face in the kitchen of his finished basement at his Oak Park, Illinois, home. He was frying sausage and peppers, and I had an alibi.

That same year, Jimmy Hoffa disappeared.

In 1976, Johnny Rosselli was strangled and shot and partially dismembered before being stuffed into a fifty-five-gallon steel fuel drum, which was found floating in Biscayne Bay.

Frank Sinatra became a Republican.

Joe DiMaggio never remarried. For twenty years, he had half a dozen red roses delivered three times a week to his former wife's crypt at Westwood Cemetery. He died of lung cancer in 1999, and his last words were: "I'll finally get to see Marilyn." I still don't like him.

Dr. Hyman Engelberg, who gave very few interviews about his famous patient, practiced for many decades in Beverly Hills and passed away in December 2005. Rumors that he'd been paid substantial hush money were never substantiated.

Milton "Mickey" Rubin — whose clients included not just Marilyn and Sinatra but Liza Minnelli, the Jackson 5, Elizabeth Taylor, and Lucille Ball — never gave interviews about MM; he died in 1999, protecting his clients to the end.

Until his death in 1998, Sergeant Jack Clemmons was an outspoken voice, much quoted and interviewed, on the subject of Marilyn's murder.

Walter Schaefer, whose ambulance service continues very successfully, has gone public in recent years, confirming that one of his ambulances was indeed dispatched to pick up Marilyn Monroe.

As for Bobby and Jack, I won't insult your intelligence — you surely know the broad outlines of their sad fates. For now, I'll add only that JFK's murder brought me back in touch with both Flo Kilgore and Bobby Kennedy.

After her 1966 divorce from Peter, Pat Kennedy Lawford battled both alcoholism and cancer. She worked with the John F. Kennedy Library and Museum, and the National Center on Addiction, and helped found the National Committee for the Literary Arts. She died in 2006.

Peter Lawford gave numerous interviews about Marilyn over the years, his story changing as if the ravings of a drug-addled mind, which was the case. After Sinatra banished him, Lawford saw his show business career ebb and flow, mostly ebb. He died in 1984, and for a time his ashes were in a crypt fifty feet from Marilyn's. In 1988, however, his ashes were evicted for nonpayment of funeral bills, only to be scattered at sea by his third wife, for a *National Enquirer* photo op.

In 1966, a raid on the home of Bernard Spindel turned up (as Spindel later charged in an affidavit) "tapes and evidence concerning the circumstances surrounding the causes and death of Marilyn Monroe which strongly suggest that the officially reported circumstances of her demise were erroneous." Spindel was a well-known wiretapper, though the A-1 had never used him. But I will wager Roger Pryor had, as Spindel — a known Hoffa crony who died in prison in 1972 — apparently aided him in a non-radio-transmitted, hardwired bugging of Fifth Helena.

An incident involving actress Veronica Hamel seemed to confirm that. When the *Hill Street Blues* TV star bought Marilyn's house, she got rid of the bougainvillea vine Marilyn had planted along the master bedroom wall. Something else had been planted, it turned out, as Hamel's efforts uncovered a nasty tangle of cables extending from roof tiles. She called the phone company to remove the old cables, and was told, "These aren't phone lines, ma'am — they're surveillance lines."

As for me, in the several official inquiries and the many more launched by authors and documentary filmmakers, I routinely declined to be interviewed. Most everything I knew could be had elsewhere, and the things that only *I* knew were still risky to talk about. No statute of limitations on murder, for example.

Anyway, I always told them, I might write my own book someday.

By the way, Fred Rubinski and I finally made some real money off Sherry's, by selling it. The restaurant became the famous rock club Gazzarri's, running from 1963 to 1993. Fred retired in the 1980s and passed away in 1990. My son, Sam, still runs the A-1 Detective Agency, with offices in half a dozen cities. I'm officially a consultant, not that I remember ever being consulted.

Marilyn? Well, I don't have to tell you. She didn't make that many movies, with only a handful that could be called good, and one or two that might be great (for me, *Seven Year Itch* and *Some Like It Hot,* both Billy Wilder). And yet she's the biggest superstar of all, leaving Liz and *Cleopatra* in the dust. The gold standard of female beauty, worldwide, how many years later? But if one thing makes me sad about her luminous, enduring fame, it's the focus on her death. And now here I am adding to it.

Of course, Marilyn gets the last giddy

laugh. Over the years, to make itself look better, the Fox studio had always portrayed her work on *Something's Got to Give* as a drug-addled, unusable embarrassment. Many authors to this day routinely accept that assessment.

But in 1988 master tapes of the lost footage were smuggled out for a group of fans to enjoy. What they saw was a radiant, glowing Marilyn, funny and displaying fine comic timing. Not missing a cue, only rarely flubbing a line, and — between takes — professional and easy to work with. In addition, she seemed sleeker, and more modern, keenly attuned to the 1960s, poised to leave the pinup fifties behind, exhibiting a natural delivery that bore only the faintest hints of her famous dumb-blonde hesitancy.

Eventually the studio realized what they had, and in 1990 a documentary — including an edited version of the existing material, to show what the movie would have been — showcased Marilyn's beauty and her talent, along the way becoming the highest-rated news program in the history of the Fox Broadcasting Network. With Marilyn, their most underpaid star, again making Fox a pot of money.

What it came down to was, the studio had tried to kill her reputation. But the film she shot had told the truth.

You see, the camera had something in common with the rest of us.

It loved her.

I OWE THEM ONE

Despite its extensive basis in history, this is a work of fiction, and liberties have been taken with the facts, though as few as possible — and any blame for historical inaccuracies is my own, mitigated by the limitations of conflicting source material.

Most of the characters in this novel are real and appear under their true names, although all depictions herein must be viewed as fictionalized. Available research on the various individuals ranges from voluminous to scant. A number of the major participants in the mystery surrounding Marilyn Monroe's death have given few interviews, or in the case of some spoken only rarely and then to a highly sympathetic author (e.g., Pat Newcomb to Donald Spoto). Quotes from these real people are mixed with invented dialogue, the latter underpinned by research.

Nathan Heller is, of course, a fictional

creation. A few characters here are composites or are otherwise so heavily fictionalized that I have not used real names. Fred Rubinski, who has appeared in previous Heller memoirs, is based on real-life PI (and former Chicagoan) Barney Ruditsky, who was indeed an owner of Sherry's restaurant. Roger Pryor is based in part on Fred Otash and Bernard Spindel, though neither has been linked to Marilyn's death in the manner depicted here. Heller himself at times fills the historical roles of Robert Maheu and Fred Otash. Flo Kilgore is a composite of journalists Dorothy Kilgallen, Joe Hyams, James Bacon and Florabel Muir, all of whom were involved in covering (or trying to cover) the Monroe death. Hyams is the reporter whose early investigatory article was spiked by his Republican editor.

Fred Otash, incidentally, was a friend of my frequent collaborator, the late Mickey Spillane, who wrote the introduction to Otash's memoir, *Investigation Hollywood!* (1976), a reference I utilized. Though it does cover the so-called Wrong Door Raid, the work does not refer to Marilyn's death; but Otash did write a book on the subject that has never been published. Mickey's wife, Jane, reports that just a few days before Otash's death, he told them of his book exposing Marilyn's murder . . . and that if anything happened to him before it was published, Mickey should look into it. In fact, Mickey did, hiring a private detective in Hollywood, who came back with a report to Mike Hammer's daddy that Otash had died of natural causes.

Often in putting together Heller's memoirs — for example, of the Lindbergh kidnapping (*Stolen Away*, 1991) and the Huey Long assassination (*Blood and Thunder*, 1995) — I have selected subjects surrounded by substantial controversy that have inspired numerous, often agenda-tainted nonfiction works. But certain subjects are particularly contentious — the Roswell incident (*Majic Man*, 1999), the disappearance of Amelia Earhart (*Flying Blind*, 1998) — and during the research stage, I found myself encountering a wealth of material written by zealots with various opposing views. Nothing could have prepared me for this project, however, with its blatantly pro-Kennedy and viciously anti-Kennedy material.

Wading through, trying to drain out the bias and baloney, was a big job. My longtime Heller research associate George Hagenauer helped sort through the material and select what to read (and what not to), and spent several days at my home in Muscatine, Iowa, discussing and exploring the ins and outs of what we are both convinced is the murder of Marilyn Monroe. In addition, countless phone calls and e-mails were exchanged. Because two more Heller novels dealing with the Kennedy brothers are planned, my researcher and I had to determine at least the broad outlines of the prospective novels that this one would affect.

When I began the Heller memoirs in the early 1980s, the late twenties in Chicago seemed quite remote to me. Now, writing about 1962, an era I lived through (I was about the same age as Heller's son, Sam), I am dealing with a period vivid in my memory. Of course, I did jog that memory at times; for example, various cultural attitudes and trends, including fashions for men and women, I culled from *Playboy* magazines intended for my father, snitched from the mailbox because I got home from junior high before he got home from work. I also watched DVDs of *Playboy After Dark,* the '60s and '70s TV show replicating Hefner's mansion parties, at least as much as the medium could allow.

I came to this project with my own seriously pro-Kennedy bias. My first published piece — a high-school award-winner that gave me the confidence to go down the writing road — was composed the evening of November 22, 1963, and titled "Where Were You When . . . When It Happened?" A year later, I played King Arthur in a high-school production of *Camelot,* with JFK as much in mind as Richard Burton. My wife, Barb, and I were college students campaigning for Bobby in 1968, only to have his assassination occur on the final day of our honeymoon in Chicago. Many years later, Jacqueline Kennedy Onassis became my editor on a political thriller — a lovely experience with a wonderful, warm editor — and this personal connection, and the others I mentioned, weighed heavily on me here.

I had to shake off all of that and try to figure out what I thought really might have happened. Like many admirers of Jack and Bobby Kennedy, I have become aware of their frailties, and was even working on a newspaper when the Chappaquiddick tragedy took place, and vividly remember reading every disturbing, disappointing news story coming in over the wire. When I would speak to George Hagenauer of my frustration and conflicted feelings in writing about Jack and Bobby, he reminded me that the

Kennedys we Baby Boomers had all grown up with were a PR glorification. The good they did was exaggerated, and the bad either hidden or downplayed.

The Dark Side of Camelot (1997) by Seymour Hersh was one negative Kennedy book I felt I could trust. Hersh is an outstanding, courageous reporter, and not some right-wing attack dog. Other Kennedy books that proved helpful include *American Journey: The Times of Robert Kennedy* (1970), interviews by Jean Stein, edited by George Plimpton; *The JFK Assassination Debates: Lone Gunman Versus Conspiracy* (2006), Michael L. Kurtz; *A Question of Character: A Life of John F. Kennedy* (1991/ 1997), Thomas C. Reeves; *RFK: A Candid Biography of Robert F. Kennedy* (1998), C. David Heymann; *Perfect Villains, Imperfect Heroes: Robert F. Kennedy's War Against Organized Crime* (1995), Ronald Goldfarb; *Robert Kennedy: His Life* (2000), Evan Thomas; and *Triangle of Death* (2003), Brad O'Leary and L. E. Seymour.

Another factor in sorting through the potential references was the presence of unreliable witnesses. Two in particular stand out in Marilyn's regard: Robert F. Slatzer and Jeanne Carmen. Both knew her, and both undoubtedly held valuable information and insights about the actress. Unfortunately, Slatzer turned Marilyn's death into his own cottage industry, and Carmen used her relationship with MM for sheer self-aggrandizement.

Slatzer indeed discovered pertinent facts and worked diligently (with some success) to have the case reopened. But he also exaggerated his relationship with Marilyn to absurd extremes (including saying he had married her). His claim to have known her in later years, right up to within days of her death, is tough to believe — in 1957, he gave an interview about his supposed affair with Marilyn to the notorious *Confidential* magazine, a betrayal that she would not likely have forgiven.

In her self-published autobiography, *My Wild Wild Life* (with Brandon James, 2006/2007), Carmen spins one unlikely anecdote after another (Jack Benny seeking a threesome?), often reporting all male eyes on her and not on Marilyn. In one documentary, interviewee Carmen appears with a framed photo of a sexy young blonde nearby — herself, not Marilyn.

A surprising number of otherwise reliable books on Marilyn take Slatzer and Carmen at face value. Yes, both Slatzer and Carmen (who lived in the apartment next door to Marilyn, right up to the actress's move to Fifth Helena Drive) did know her and some of what they say is likely true. But how to discern what?

No other subject has presented me with a more wildly differing array of dates for the same event, and contradictory reports for things supposedly witnessed. The variant versions of the notorious Cal-Neva weekend rival those of the Roswell Incident (one Marilyn death theory, by the way, links her to the CIA and a cover-up of aliens at Roswell). I plead guilty to cherry-picking information from certain witnesses — everything I report via Norm Jefferies and Walt Schaefer comes from years-later interviews that also include statements seemingly contradicted by other witnesses; these contradictions I have chosen not to address here.

Of the many Marilyn books that were sources for *Bye Bye, Baby,* four were the mainstays.

Marilyn: The Last Take (1992/1993, updated edition) by Peter Harry Brown and Patte B. Barham is a painstaking look at Marilyn's final months that impressively uncovers the truth of her problems with Fox, and examines the mysterious circumstances of her death with care and diligence.

The Last Days of Marilyn Monroe (1998) by Donald H. Wolfe may be the definitive work on the murder, beginning on the night/morning of Marilyn's death and following the case in all its ramifications up through the two new official inquiries; it then backs up and provides a credible, well-documented look at Marilyn's life.

Victim (2003) by Matthew Smith emphasizes former deputy district attorney John Miner's reconstructed transcript of the tapes of free-associating Marilyn as played to him by Dr. Ralph Greenson.

Extremely valuable was the unusual *The DD Group: An Online Investigation Into the Death of Marilyn Monroe* (2005) by David Marshall. This fascinating, voluminous self-published work charts the research and discussion by a hard-core group of Marilyn enthusiasts in an attempt to create a time line of her final days and to discuss in depth the various suicide/accidental overdose/murder theories with an informed, critical eye. The group includes at least one rabid Kennedy fan, and several murder-mad Marilyn ones, but for the most part (under the calming influence of their leader, Marshall), they explore and discuss with intelligence and insight. Marshall himself is the rare Kennedy supporter willing to examine that family's role and the undeniable evidence of the involvement of Jack and Bobby with Marilyn and her death. Further, Marshall organizes topics and summarizes the treatment of those topics in a large number of Marilyn books, helping to refresh my memory where works I'd read long ago were concerned.

All four of the above are recommended "further reading."

Also helpful were Anthony Summers' groundbreaking *Goddess: The Secret Lives of Marilyn Monroe* (1985); *The Unabridged Marilyn: Her Life from A to Z* (1988) by Randall Riese and Neal Hitchens; and *Cursum Perficio: Marilyn Monroe's Brentwood Hacienda* (2000) by Gary Vitacco-Robles. *The Secret Life of Marilyn Monroe* (2009) by J. Randy Taraborrelli is Kennedy-biased, but otherwise well-researched. The same can be said of Donald Spoto's *Marilyn Monroe: The Biography* (1993). Both were secondary sources for this novel.

Many documentaries have been produced on the life and death of Marilyn Monroe. But the landmark work is the 1996 BBC documentary, *Say Goodbye to the President: Marilyn and the Kennedys,* written and directed by Christopher Olgiati, drawing upon Anthony Summers' research. The DVD of this film was enormously helpful.

For Peter Lawford, I turned chiefly to *Peter Lawford: The Man Who Kept the Secrets* (1991) by James Spada, a surprisingly detailed, massive book. I also read *The Peter Lawford Story: Life with the Kennedys, Monroe, and the Rat Pack* (1988) by Patricia Seaton Lawford with Ted Schwarz.

The major Jimmy Hoffa source here is *Mob Lawyer* (1994) by Frank Ragano and Selwyn Raab. A key mob reference was *All-American Mafioso: The Johnny Rosselli Story* (1991) by Charles Rappleye and Ed Becker. (Some sources spell the name Roselli.)

The most utilized Sinatra sources were *Mr. S: My Life with Frank Sinatra* (2003) by George Jacobs and William Stadiem, and *Sinatra: The Life* (2005) by Anthony Summers and Robbyn Swan.

Information on Chief William H. Parker, James Hamilton, the Intelligence Division in particular, and the LAPD in general came in part from *L.A. Noir* (2009) by John Buntin, and *The Badge* (1958) by *Dragnet*'s Jack Webb.

Other books consulted include *The Anarchist Cookbook* (1971), William Powell;

Coroner (1983), Thomas T. Noguchi, M.D.; *Kilgallen: A Biography of Dorothy Kilgallen* (1979), Lee Israel; *Mislaid in Hollywood* (1973), Joe Hyams; *Mr. Confidential* (2006), Samuel Bernstein; *Mr. Playboy: Hugh Hefner and the American Dream* (2008), Steven Watts; and *Next to Hughes* (1992), Robert Maheu and Richard Hack.

Pitching in with help were my LAPD cop pal (and excellent mystery/suspense writer) Paul Bishop and my frequent collaborator, Matthew Clemens, who was always available to chase down a stray fact, particularly in the forensics area.

My thanks to my friend and agent, Dominick Abel, who has helped me keep Nathan Heller alive; and my editor, James Frenkel, who nudged, encouraged, and believed.

My wife, Barbara Collins, is a Marilyn Monroe buff par excellence. In her twenties, thirties, and forties, she was often stopped by strangers who noted her resemblance to Marilyn, and I imagine this fueled her interest in the actress. (It has not been a hardship to me, over the years, being married to a beautiful blonde.) Barb has assembled — with my help, often at Christmastime — one of the great Monroe collections anywhere: books, magazines, memorabilia, and collectibles. This interest inspired Barb to collaborate with me on *Bombshell* (2004), a fanciful comic espionage thriller that teams Marilyn Monroe and Nikita Khrushchev. The research (mostly by Barb) was solid, and both of us came out of the project with an even greater knowledge of Marilyn and her life and character. I have also written a Nathan Heller novella involving Marilyn, *Kisses of Death,* the lead story in a 2001 collection of the same name.

Because of *Bombshell* and *Kisses of Death,* and due to Barb's interest in Marilyn, I have read many, many books on the actress, and viewed any number of documentaries, which no doubt influenced this novel. I will make no attempt to list them all here, although if you check the back of *Bombshell* for its bibliographic note, you'll find many of them. But I must thank my wife, even more than usual, for being my constant sounding board during the writing of *Bye Bye, Baby,* and for the keen eye and sharp insights she provided as she read this novel chapter-at-a-time during its creation.

ABOUT THE AUTHOR

Max Allan Collins was hailed in 2004 by *Publishers Weekly* as "a new breed of writer." A frequent Mystery Writers of America Edgar nominee in both fiction and nonfiction categories, he has earned an unprecedented fifteen Private Eye Writers of America Shamus nominations, winning for his Nathan Heller novels *True Detective* (1983) and *Stolen Away* (1991), and receiving the PWA life achievement award, the Eye, in 2007.

His graphic novel *Road to Perdition* (1998) is the basis of the Academy Award–winning 2002 film starring Tom Hanks, Paul Newman, and Daniel Craig, directed by Sam Mendes. It was followed by two acclaimed prose sequels, *Road to Purgatory* (2004) and *Road to Paradise* (2005), with a graphic novel sequel, *Return to Perdition,* forthcoming. He has written a number of innovative suspense series, notably Quarry (the first series about a hired killer) and Eliot Ness (four novels about the famous real-life Untouchable's Cleveland years). He is completing a number of "Mike Hammer" novels begun by the late Mickey Spillane, with whom Collins collaborated on many projects; the third of these, *Kiss Her Goodbye,* is a 2011 publication. *You Can't Stop Me,* a serial-killer thriller written with Matthew Clemens, was published in 2010.

His many comics credits include the syndicated strip "Dick Tracy"; his own "Ms. Tree" (the longest-running private eye comic book); "Batman"; and *CSI: Crime Scene Investigation,* based on the hit TV series, for which he has also written video games, jigsaw puzzles, and ten novels that have sold millions of copies worldwide.

Termed "the novelization king" by *Entertainment Weekly,* Collins has written tie-in books that have appeared on the *USA Today* bestseller list nine times and on the *New York Times* list three. His movie novels include *Saving Private Ryan, Air Force One,* and *American Gangster,* the latter winning the Best Novel Scribe Award in 2008 from the International Association of Tie-in Writers.

An independent filmmaker in the Mid-